Mickey Rees was born in 1997 and was raised in her hometown of Phoenix, Arizona, where she spent most of her days writing fictional stories. She had started out small by writing screenplays in her elementary school before exploring her depth and passion as a writer. She was inspired by a user-friendly application—Wattpad, when she was introduced to the application back in 2012. In the start of middle school, Mickey began to get more involved in her community theater. Following onto her early adolescence, she had the opportunity to work with creative individuals with imaginations of their own in the theater class she took part in. There she gained the experience of a lifetime when she put forth her screenplay to the test that helped her grow as a 'young prodigy in the making'. After four years of well-developed hard work, dedication, and strong support from her friends and family, she finally shared some of her very own beautiful stories and brought them to visual life, with *Fallen Faith* being her first publication.

To my dog, Gosha. Thank you for coming into my life at my most vulnerable peak. You were there for me at a time that I needed a companion, when I felt alone. I don't know how much time I have left with you as of now but regardless, I will never forget you. You were the closest thing that I had to a friend growing up and it's going to be difficult for me to accept that you're going to be gone one day. I can see that you're trying your best to be strong around us, your family… you were such a happy dog, Gosha. We know you're getting old and you don't have much long but just know that you are always loved and will always be missed.

Mickey Rees

FALLEN FAITH

AUSTIN MACAULEY PUBLISHERS™

LONDON • CAMBRIDGE • NEW YORK • SHARJAH

ISBN 9781528929189 (Paperback)
ISBN 9781528929196 (Hardback)
ISBN 9781528965774 (ePub e-book)

www.austinmacauley.com

First Published (2019)
Austin Macauley Publishers Ltd
25 Canada Square
Canary Wharf
London
E14 5LQ

Many thanks to all those who helped me with the publication and special thanks to Austin Macauley for giving me the opportunity to make 'Fallen Faith' possible.

Prologue

It all started five months ago, the biggest regret of Jessica Larson's life and little did she know, it was going to haunt her forever...

(Flashback)
Jessica Jane Larson was the go-to for all things; books and being as studious as she was. A party setting was not her adequate environment, but Jessica wanted to do something outside of her comfort zone for once, desperately wanting to rid of her 'good girl' image. Tonight, would be the night of many firsts for Jessica Jane. One being, her first time attending a college party; the first party transitioning into Jessica's senior year of high school. What better way to kick off the new school year during the start of summer? And for a seventeen-year-old gal of 5'2, she would be unknowingly losing her virginity at this party by the end of the night, but it still remains a mystery as to who it would be with. Her friend's car pulled up on her driveway, honking loudly, just as she had applied the final touches of her makeup. She grabbed her wedges, jogging downstairs and stepping outside, barefoot and in a rush.

Her parents had not suspected a thing with her dad having been a few days out of town for a business retreat and her mom having been out with her colleagues that night. She had texted her mom that she would be out with friends and left it at that, she would not expect her mom to wait up—knowing she still had a trustworthy title under her name.

"Come on Jess, let's go!" shouted one of her best guy friends, Jaiden, who happened to be the annoying driver of the night. She slid into the backseat, tucking in her shoes as he backed out of her driveway. "No hi for me?" Jaiden asked with a cheeky smirk forming creases in his face.

"Oh sorry, I was too busy hurrying up for this guy yelling at me," she teased.

"Oh, is that so?" he remarks.

"Yeah, pretty rude guy if you ask me, ugly too!" she jokingly added in, cackling. She knew that the twins resented her when she said that because it offended them both.

"Wow clever, I don't remember the last time I heard that one," Jared frowned, folding his arms down in front of him.

Jaiden and Jared Daniels were her closest friends in the neighborhood where they grew up together. Dark hair, chocolate eyes, the fair olive skin tone of an Italian descendent. They were everyone's favorite twins, what was there not to like? Although Jessica was about to find out otherwise. They were like the two protective brothers she never had, except for the fact that they were a few months younger. But they were taller and much stronger, so she considered them to be her protectors. She had two older sisters, but she could never consider them to be protective, not at all. She resented them for always picking on her when growing up, it was the fucked-up version of a sappy fairytale with her family. And well, Jessica indeed was still waiting on her Prince Charming. See, Jessica never really cared for relationships while being in a girls' academy for most of her life, the only contact she has had with a guy was with her male friends, who lived a few houses down the street. She was almost hidden from the rest of the world, being kept from finding true love. Her academy was torturous, and this night was to relieve her from her life and maybe meet some new friends along the way.

"We're here," Jaiden mentioned after they finally found a parking spot that was about a five-minute walking radius from the manor. She had stepped out as the twins did the same. Jaiden's eyes widened.

"What?" she blushed timidly.

"You look…" He was at a loss for words and Jessica could tell he was uncomfortable. "Beautiful," said Jared.

"Hot, but that too," Jaiden concluded.

"Well, thanks guys, you don't think it's too much?" she worried.

"No, not at all, now let's go inside," Jared directed as he and Jai led her towards the pretentious manor. The music became louder after they appeared closer to the house, and the song 'Rack City' by Tyga, played in the distance.

This was Jessica's first party and although she would have hated to admit, she was intimidated. Only now would the world have known of Jessica Larson and it wasn't until a few months later when she would live to get exactly what she wanted, to be the center of all the attention.

"I'm gonna go get us some drinks. I'll be right back," informed Jaiden before leaving Jess alone with Jared and a bunch of random people. In the meantime, Jared met up with a few of his other acquaintances, introducing them all. As Jessica saw the diversity among the group of people crowding her, she also couldn't help to notice most of them seemed to look older than the twins—college students of course.

10

While Jessica had been sent away to private school, the twins had been enrolled in public school; this was what the families thought would be best for their children.

"Hey, I'm Josh," a tall blond fellow said, gesturing her to a handshake that she kindly obliged to.

"And I'm Zach, but they call me Hobbs," a younger looking guy addressed, "And this is Nick, 'the dick'," he whispered.

"Thanks for the introduction, dish rag!" Nick pestered the young boy. Jessica instantly fell in love with his ocean blue eyes. Snapping her out of her thoughts, Jared soon pointed out that Jaiden came back with their drinks. It was then that she noticed a tall, tan-skinned gentleman conversing with Jaiden in the distance.

"Oh hey, Griffins is here!" the younger looking blond in the group announced as the two came closer towards them.

Jaiden smiled at Jess when handing Jared a plastic red cup, "Sorry, two hands only," he teased, about to chug his cup when all of a sudden, Jessica snatched the cup and began to drink to her heart's desire. With the burning sensation lodged down her throat, she received glances from all directions including one from her very own Jaiden. "Damn, I'll go get you some more. Don't let me hold you back," he chuckled.

"And who is this kinky little firecracker?" the tan gentlemen asked while taking her available hand and softly caressing her palm. *What a sweet talker he was.*

"This is Jess, our new friend," Nick spoke while wrapping his arm around the uncomfortable girl.

"And you are?" she asked trying desperately not to come off rude.

"The name's Zach, but people refer to me as 'Griffins' to not mistake me for Hobbson... but if you're in for a treat, I'll have you address me as Papi by the end of the night," he says.

"Uh, no thanks," she cringed. She had taken another sip from her cup and the strong aroma of alcohol filled her lungs again. In the spur of the moment, she thought, *what the hell, why not?* After all, it was her first party and she needed to loosen up, what is the harm of one drink? So, she finished the remaining pint in her cup and threw it to the floor like she had seen everyone else doing. The entirety of this party was trashed, *such a shame, this was a beautiful house too.*

"Who wants to play spin the bottle?" a bubbly drunken blonde asked when coming up and wrapping her arms around her boyfriend, Josh.

"Hey babe, this is Jessica, she's friends with the twins," he introduced.

"Hi! Oh my God, we are gonna be like the bestest friends ever!" she announced as she embraced her in for a tight hug. "My name's Sienna," she whispered in Jessica's ear before pulling away and giggling again. "Well come on! You all have to play!" She nearly dragged Jessica by her arm to the area she set up for the game. Everyone else shortly followed. "Soooooo, who wants to go first?" she asked while waving an empty soda bottle in the air.

"Wait! This is uneven, there are definitely more guys than girls!" Jaiden addressed.

"Aw, but it's more interesting that way," Jessica playfully insinuated.

"No, Jaiden's right. Wait here and I'll pick up some more chicks," Griffins said while wiggling his eyebrows cockily. He returned with three girls eight minutes later and somehow, they were all poorly dressed and all blonde too. As they gathered into the circle, Jessica felt Jaiden scoot closer to her. The bunch of them were all sitting on the floor.

"So, I guess I will go first," the darker Zach said with one of the blondes on his lap when reclaiming the bottle from Sienna.

"Rules first, before we start!" Sienna declared, which had everyone roll their eyes.

"We know the rules already! You tell us every time!" groaned Nick.

"Well, the new girl doesn't! Besides, I'm changing the rules up this time. Whoever it lands on, has to be dared!"

Yes, Sienna was quite the little daredevil. Griffins spun it and it landed on one of the blondes. He deviously smirked and rubbed his hands together, "Okay Lindsay, I dare you to make out with Lacey for a minute," he grinned.

"Nice one dude!" Hobbs acknowledged when bumping fists with him. Nick soon pulled out his phone to use as a camera to record the dare. In the process of this all, Jessica was trying to keep her head together. She had hoped with this being her first drink, she didn't willingly end up dancing on tables soon.

"Bro send me that, I might need to use that for uh… a science project," the younger blonde intervened as everyone laughed. Jessica rolled her eyes, she couldn't believe the twins were friends with such perverted people. It was Nick's turn next and it landed on Jared.

"Alright, I dare you to lick a spoon of peanut butter… off Jaiden's chest," Nick dared as Jared and Jaiden groaned in disgust.

"Dude, that's sick!" Jared retched.

"Fair, fair, but it could be worse. Would you rather to be licking a spoon from his left nut?" he chuckled.

"I'm sure you'd like that, wouldn't you!" Jaiden retorted at the disturbed boy.

"Are we doing this or not?" Nick threatened as he held up Jared's iPhone. Jared quickly patted all over his body, looking for his phone.

"B-but how d-did you—" he worried.

"You really shouldn't leave your phone unsupervised you know... especially not around me."

"Okay go ahead, you don't even know my password."

"Don't need it, I'm a hacker. So, are you gonna do it or should I just tweet something embarrassing about you that you admitted to doing the last time you attended?"

"Just give him his phone back, you're holding up the party!" Griffins groaned, slumping in his fold-out chair from beside. A stubborn Nick bolted over to the kitchen to grab the peanut butter from the fridge. Jaiden began to take off his shirt and Jessica was quick to avert her eyes. He chuckled, "Don't flatter yourself." She scoffed. She never knew how full of himself he could be until this very moment. Nick returned minutes later with the peanut butter and Jaiden was growing more anxious by the second. Jessica felt more so worried on Jared's behalf, knowing his part was far worse.

"Okay, here's the stuff... go on," Nick directed, holding up the spoon. Jaiden gulped when taking the spoon from Nick's hand before rubbing the spoonful all over his chest. Jared decided to kneel in front of Jaiden now. He tediously began to lick the peanut butter off, using the tip of his tongue. Jaiden whipped his head around the room full of flashing cameras, it had been a painful reminder of another past memory—one involving a golden shower.

"Okay, time!" called Griffins who shot up and managed to retrieve Jared's phone back from Nick's hands.

"Here man," Griffins said throwing Jared his phone.

"You couldn't do that earlier!" Jared shrieked in disgust. Jaiden chuckled and wiped off the excess peanut butter from his chest. He then put his shirt back on as Jared ran to the kitchen sink to rinse his tongue of Jaiden's germs. The game ended on a short note because Nick was being a drunken asshole and ruined the entire game with his immoral requests. He made quite the first impression that night. Jessica knew she wouldn't be friending him on Facebook anytime soon.

"Hey Jess, I want to show you something," Jared said as he lead the tipsy teenager in the direction of the stairs after the game had ended.

Jaiden quickly pulled Jared aside, "Dude, Jess? You really want to bring Jess upstairs after all the opportunities you've had?" Jaiden indistinctly whispered offset. They returned to their friend's aid next to the bottom of the stairs after ending their dry conversation—*God* how Jaiden loved to test Jared. Jared tenaciously grabbed her hand in a hostile manner and guided her up the staircase. She anxiously followed him, and Jaiden was the last wheel on the train, keeping Jess from stumbling down. She almost tripped going up the stairs—the alcohol was finally starting to kick in, *bad timing*. Jaiden ended up in front of her, both the twins leading her down the hallway of this huge abode and beyond this point of her shamed drunken state, she couldn't even tell who was who. One of them took her hand again and guided her inside of a dark room, the other turned on the light. The room was beautiful, lights and colors filled the room and just decorated overall radiantly.

"Wow, this is so amazing!" she exclaimed. Her picture memory was still 50/50 at this point.

"Whose place is this?" she curiously asked.

"It's Joshua's, but every time we would come over, this room would be considered ours. It was a guest room…" She sat on the bed and traced the duvet with her delicate fingers,

"So where are his parents?" she asked unknowing of where the conversation would take off.

"They're always out once a month, twice a week, on business trips, but Josh throws these insanely huge parties every time they're out," Jared answered—at least Jess had thought it was him that answered. Her mind blurred and one of the twins soon exit the room.

****

She woke up in the morning, in a stranger's bed with a massive headache and barely any memory of what happened the previous night. She looked around her surroundings and no one was next to her. She sighed with relief thinking she hadn't done something she was going to regret. Turned out for Jessica, she had spoken too soon when she peeked under the duvet that was covering her body. She was completely naked, no clothes whatsoever. "Oh my god!" she panicked, "D-did I have sex?" It wasn't until that interrogative, self-defying sentence left her mouth, that she realized she was in fact, talking to herself. She didn't even think she would stay overnight. Cautiously, with one more observant look, all of her clothes were scattered on the floor. The worst part was that she remembered Jared and Jaiden were nowhere to be found and they were her ride home. How could they have allowed her to do such a thing with a stranger? They were supposed to look out for her.

She was determined to get an answer, even if it was one she didn't want to hear. What she didn't reckon was that she may have possibly overlooked the entirety of this situation—they were about to be responsible for much more.

(Present Day)

Jessica begins to quiver with tears as she looks at herself through the reflection of her mirror. She is eighteen now and it has been five months since that scandalous night and she still doesn't know whose baby she has been carrying and she is hesitant to find out, because she doesn't want to lose either of her best friends. Ever since she told Jared and Jaiden that she is soon to be expecting, it has been a brutal competition between them.

****

Chapter One

(Flashback—the morning after)

As Jessica patiently sat there, face in hands, she dreadfully tried to recall the events from last night even though nothing came to mind. She heard the door creak open and found herself pulling the duvet even higher up her chest. "Ever heard of knocking?" she asked, watching Griffins roam inside the room with only his boxers on.

"Honey, I practically live here."

"…I take it you were the naughty mistress that I heard moaning all night long?" Jessica let out a staggered gasp.

"Relax, it wasn't with me, but I'll bet you wish it was," he said looking smug. Jessica rolled her eyes at his consistent, insolent behavior, and here she thought Jaiden was conceited after last night's charade.

"Do you happen to know who I did sleep with?" Jess asked with worry filling the surface of her eyes.

"No, but the person who did, probably peaked in high school. I bet you're still tight as hell too. That's what I like about screwing with virgins."

"I can assure you, I'm not a virgin." *Not anymore anyways…*

"Sure you are sweetheart, look at you. Haven't seen you around before, first party I take it? You've even stayed the morning, usually the women grab their shit and dip around midnight, but not the virgins. Pretty little prude like you is probably used to getting everything she wants around here, huh?"

Jessica was rather offended at his words. *He doesn't know me, he doesn't know me at all! How dare he stand there criticizing me!*

"For the record, you should stay away from those Daniels. Bunch of pussies… especially that one, what was his name? Oh Jared, that's right. God, I would hate myself if I was *that* kid!"

"And well, Jaiden's been around. I can tell you he's not what you think he is. Whole tough guy act isn't fooling anyone. Me? I've seen death, I've lived it."

"What's your problem? You don't even know them and just yesterday you were ready to defend them."

"My problem is those twins, they ask for trouble. Trouble follows them. It follows them here. Why I suggest you stay away, it's all a matter of time before it catches up with you."

One thing was for sure, Jessica was not going to sit there and take any more of this young man's crap. She didn't tolerate his behavior and wasn't going to let him insult her friends any longer.

"Thank you for reminding me why I don't come to places like this, get out!" Jessica urged while throwing a pillow at him in an attempt to make him leave the room.

"But before I go, don't forget to make your bed. I know you will... virgin," he taunted. Appalled, she quickly got up with the silk duvet still hugging her body and locked the door. She grabbed her scattered clothing from the floor and quickly changed. Finished, she stepped out of the room and tried to find the bathroom. She then spotted a familiar face in the distance, it was victim number one, Jared Daniels.

She smiled awkwardly when he approached her. He took her hand and kissed her wrist, "Ma 'lady," he smiled. She recoiled her wet hand from his mouth in confusion while he continued to speak. "Last night... was amazing," he whispered in her ear before planting a kiss on the poor girl's neck and softly nipping at the skin. It felt amazing to Jessica but so wrong. Again, she recoiled to pull away from his touch and put her hand up to his mouth to stop him from leaning in again. She couldn't believe Jared was the mysterious man she slept with, she must have been extremely wasted.

"Jared, wait. I'm sorry, I can't do this," she repeated aloud.

She deliberately pushed past him and made her way to the bathroom. Upon entering, she locked the door and took a moment to stand in front of the mirror while enveloping in her thoughts, sulking.

I shouldn't have come to this party at all. I should have just stayed at home and watched Netflix like I intended to do. Damn those boys for being so persuasive. I might as well have just ruined a friendship. My worst fear is to lose either of them and now I've just had to cross the friend zone line. Now Jared's gonna feel for me and I can't feel back because I didn't feel the connection he felt yesterday. I had no intention of coming to this party as a virgin and leaving without it. I wanted my first time to be special. I didn't mind the fact that it was with one of the twins, but I would've hoped it was when I was sober and for a good cause in the future.

She took one last deep breath before closing the door and heading downstairs to find a shirtless Jaiden. *Oh goodie, he was still here.* He was walking around in the kitchen talking to Josh, who had been sitting on the edge of the counter. As soon as he spotted her from afar, he smiled to her and she appeared closer. She couldn't help to notice he had a very visible bruise on his neck, it was a hickey. *The bastard got laid last night, I wonder which one of those bimbos Zach number zero let him have.*

"Hey, Jess, can we talk?" he asked.

"Yeah, sure."

She followed him to a room nearby. They both proceeded to sit on the bed before he began to speak his mind.

She patiently stills for him to speak up as he hesitantly flailed his head, struggling to prevail his subconscious. "Look um, I know you might think that last night was a mistake but uh, if I'm being honest, I enjoyed every moment of it," he sheepishly began to admit.

"What do you mean by last night?" she pondered, second-guessing herself.

"We had... sex," he impulsively reminded. Her eyes bug out of her head immediately as if she had just seen a ghost... no worse, hell in her future. She emerged upstairs, calling out for Jared. She seemed unbothered of who she was waking up in her plea of distress. Alas, she found Jared in a room with Lindsay and the tolerable Zach.

"Jared, please come here?" she sternly waited at the doorway.

"What is going on, Jess?" Jaiden asked as they both follow her to their guest room.

"Sit down," she insisted.

Jaiden and Jared sit down to discuss something with the innocent soul, afraid of what she might have remembered. Jared on the other hand, hoped it was because she wanted to declare her love for him. She paced back and forth in frustration then stopped, facing the twins for an uneasy discussion. In that moment she had wished someone had just given her the proper sex talk; maybe, just maybe, she would've avoided this situation in the first place. If only she had known the dangers of attending a party. She intended to stay pure until after marriage, and that was one of the many beliefs she had promised herself to stay true to in her system of religion. But it was all over and now she's failed the system.

"Okay," she sighed.

"...I wanna know who I slept with last night, and how it happened," she apprehensively asked.

"I did," the two gentlemen deliberately admit simultaneously.

"What! So, like a threesome?" she shrieked.

"No, you didn't! You must have been drunk and thought you did!" Jared incoherently implied.

"I barely drank anything and—" Jaiden started before Jessica interrupted.

"Just shut up and tell me how it happened! … Please!" she miraculously begged on the brink of weeping.

"You mean you really don't remember?" Jaiden asked, and she nodded in agreement.

"What's the last thing you remember?" chimed Jared. She tried to concentrate.

"Uh we were going upstairs and…" she said.

"I took your hand because you almost tumbled down the staircase," Jared continued.

"Oh yeah, you showed me the lights in your room?" she recalled.

"Yeah," the younger twin continued. "We all started talking and you said you needed a couple of minutes alone with Jaiden," he shrugged.

"When Jared left, you locked the door and told me to kiss you," Jaiden continued by saying, "I couldn't resist, and we started getting intimate—"

Jared's mouth hung open within seconds of those words leaving his brother's mouth, *does my brother fancy Jessica too?*

"Should I continue?" Jaiden asked as Jessica swallowed back in guilt, biting down hard on her lower lip when trying to prevent herself from crying. She nodded slowly. "We continued our heated session as you sat in my lap and started taking off my shirt—"

"Should I stop?" he chuckled, noticing her discomfort. "No j-just…continue," she hesitantly responded. "You were about to take off my pants, but I stopped you to make sure you were ready and every time I asked you, you would get angry telling me to, and I quote… uh, 'get inside you already'—so we eventually got to it, sparing you of all the glorious details, but I'll say, you weren't that bad for a first timer though," he anticipated, licking his upper lip. "You told me how you wished it was you who got to lick the peanut butter from off my chest and the highlight of my night was when you in fact, showed me of all the different places you would enjoy licking it off me!" He grinned devilishly after that memory replayed in his mind.

"Oh my god!" she whined, closing her ears. "You idiot! I was obviously intoxicated and not thinking straight, so what gives you the right to take advantage of me!" she cried out in anger.

"You mean to tell me 'you' were the one who took her virginity away, when you knew how much I liked her!" Jared riled, standing up.

19

Appalled, Jessica shot up, "Let's get one thing straight, my virginity is not for discussion! It's not something either of you can take from me! It was mine and I thought you guys were my friends! You guys were supposed to protect me! I trusted you!" she cried into her palms.

She allowed Jaiden to continue with his story after calming down a bit. This time he wouldn't leave out any gory details with how he stripped away her innocence that night. He also continued by saying that he ended up leaving the room during the end of the night, that the guilt was eating him. He didn't know what he had been feeling and he wanted it to go away, to clear his head. Of course, this happened after they were finished, when they had rested, after he 'used' her body. Now it was Jared's turn to unfold his evening well spent with her.

"I was downstairs with the guys all that time, after you had told me to leave you alone with Jaiden. Later on, I saw Jaiden coming out of the room at around two a.m., he took his shirt off and threw it onto the floor. He looked pretty stumped. His arms flew to his head and he kept pacing up and down the hallways, aggravated until he just sat down against the wall and ran his fingers through his hair. I assumed something bad happened between the two of you. I decided to go to you instead to see what happened. I knocked a few times before realizing that the lights were off in the room, so I came in and called out for you, thinking you had been asleep. You thought I was Jaiden, but I corrected you. The room was still dark, but I managed to find the bed without tripping. I wanted to ask you what happened with Jaiden but before I could say anything, you had your tongue down my throat—" Jessica groaned as if she had heard this story for the millionth time, or in her case it was twice. "Pretty much the same thing happened with me as what happened between you and Jai, except it wasn't that intense, so no peanut butter licking involved."

She sighed in relief. "But you did offer me to lick the peanut butter from off 'your' chest," Jared smirked.

"What was your answer?" she timidly asked.

"I told you that I never wanted to think about peanut butter ever again and you laughed." She laughed as he told her that. "Just like that!" he chuckled out again. "I, too, left after we finished but because I was scared we would both live to regret this in the morning and I didn't want you to hate me," he said when dropping his eyes and making indirect eye contact with the floor.

"Well, did you?" she asked seemingly too afraid to ask.

"No, but you obviously did," he shrugged.

She sighed, "If I regret anything from last night, it's because I didn't remember, and you guys aren't to blame for anything... it was my whore-ish alter ego I guess," she giggled. "Hell, I'm just relieved that it wasn't with just any stranger, but please just promise me that this stays just between us... and we take this to our death beds?" she asked.

"Of course," Jaiden said leaning in to kiss her forehead.

"You know we would never do anything to hurt you, Jess," Jared promisingly emphasized when grabbing her wrist and kissing her palm.

"Oh, and please don't ever let me drink again?"

Little did Jessica know was that she wouldn't even be able to drink for the next 9-10 months anyways.

(Present Day)
Consequently, for Jessica Larson, she has been living on her own ever since she confronted her parents of her naughty little mishap. Her entire family disowned her except for one of her older sisters, Mandy. Amanda Anderson, stands the eldest of the three sisters; Beverly and Jessica. Beverly Larson was the second eldest and was soon to be twenty-four. Troubled by her sisters and growing up independent, Amanda remained the closest to Jessica and agreed to help her out whenever she could. When Jess moved out, she found herself a nice little apartment in the city with the help of her brother-in-law, Amanda's husband, Kevin; Kevin was in real estate for the area and a few other locations. He had put in a good word for his in-law because he thought of her as a baby sister.

In order to keep her apartment, this meant Jessica had to get a job and to purchase a car. The twins willingly would drive her wherever she needed to be, but she knew she couldn't rely on them forever. They were mainly the only people who wanted to stay in her life. Her girlfriends at the academy cut her off after word got around campus that she was expecting. Eventually, she thought it would be just a matter of time before the twins would find her needy and leave her as well. After all, that's what they all did, leave. Although, that wasn't the case for her girlfriends in school, or rather *acquaintances* as she identified them. She had been skipping school for the past two weeks because she couldn't handle the glares and whispering from everyone at the school. She couldn't trust anyone and not even some of her female classmates who so happened to be 'close friends' with her. She still didn't know how she plans to graduate now, she just might have to think about summer school or switching to online schooling sometime soon.

Jess assertively walks into her small kitchen, opening the fridge to prepare the ingredients she needs for soup because she was going to be eating for two soon. With her hands being tied to the ingredients she had prepared, she closes the fridge with her back. Her phone vibrates from across the counter. So, she casually drops all her ingredients on the counter to look at her phone, it was a text message from Jared.

*From: **Jare** ♥*
Me and Jai are on the way to chill
*To: **Jare** ♥From: **Jessica***
K

She presses send and throws her phone back on the counter to continue with cooking. She could never stay mad at the twins even though it was practically their fault she was suffering. She's just as much to blame for even entering that god-forsaken party. Minutes go by and she doesn't bother to change out of her pjs, *I'm not going to change just for the twins, we've practically seen each other naked at one point or another.*

She puts on her apron and returns to cooking. Moments later, she hears a knock at the door. "Come in!" she shouts loud enough hoping they would hear her. In enters Jaiden, followed by Jared.

"*Oooooo,* what's cooking?" Jared asks when walking over to the kitchen.

"We've brought you some blankets as you requested and picked up some peanut butter on the way," Jaiden says with a cheeky facial expression as he pulls out the store-bought jar from its bag.

"I am holding a knife, Jaiden," Jessica thoroughly reminds.

"So, what are you making?" Jared asks.

"Veggie soup," Jessica answers.

"For breakfast?" chimes Jaiden, walking up to the counter and setting the jar down.

"Do you hate us this much?" Jared chuckles.

"It's 10:30," she justifies. She drops her knife on the cutting board while wiping her hands on her apron to check the boiling water, switching it to a medium-heat. She then returns to cutting, "And who said it was for you guys?" she says with sarcasm filling every bit of her voice. "If you don't want my cravings then you can make something yourselves."

"Sorry guys," Jessica sighs. She excuses herself on behalf of her mood swings.

"Do you want to sleep? I can take over if you'd like?" Jared asks. What Jessica wants more than anything else in the world, is a twenty-four-hour rest, but she kindly declines his offer. "Well, I don't know about you, but I want some grilled cheese," Jared grins, eyes already glued to the fridge.

"Oh hey, make me some?" Jaiden calls out.

"Sure," Jared replies as he walks over to the fridge.

"Well, I guess that just leaves you and me," Jaiden boasts. Jessica endeavors to avoid him at all costs. *I love him, but he can be annoying at times.* He walks up behind and wraps his bulky arms around her while she continuously cuts onions. He pivots his head onto her shoulders and she can feel his minty breath on her neck. The strong aroma of onions soon makes her eyes swell again and he begins to sway Jessica before speaking out again. "It's okay babe, you don't have to cry... we'll be together soon," he rasps.

She irritably feels his smirk growing.

"Jaiden, let go of me before I kill you," she jokingly warns.

As Jared returns from the fridge, he notices Jaiden hugging Jessica from behind. *She has been spending more time with him than she has with me lately and it's not fair! I'm starting to think she likes him more, even though she made it evidently clear to both of us that she only sees us as friends. What could she possibly like about him though? We may look alike but we are nothing alike.*

He went up behind the counter and dropped the package of cheese slices in front of Jaiden. "Hey dude, can you help me?" he asks in hopes of separating the two for a while.

"How hard is it to make grilled cheese?" Jaiden chuckles. Enraged with his arrogance, Jared grabs the cheese with one hand and drags him by his shirt collar over to the other side of the kitchen with his other hand. He then proceeds to flick him on the head. "Ow! What?" Jaiden screams, scratching his head.

"I thought we both agreed that we wouldn't go after Jess!" Jared whisper-yells.

"Yeah, well things change," Jaiden winks out, patting his naive little brother on the shoulder before leaving him to go try and fondle Jess again. Jared can't just stand around and let Jaiden win again, heat is boiling inside him, erupting like a volcano as much as the soup water beside himself. Before he realizes it, the soup splatters everywhere, and the stove catches fire.

"Uh Jess!" he startles, unsure of what to do. She and Jaiden turn around with their widened eyes. Trying to put out the fire, he lurks in the kitchen for a fire extinguisher but as it turns out, Jaiden already finds it, saving the day once again. *Eye roll.*

Jessica exhales in shock and begins whaling with tears. "Ssshhh, ssshhhh, it's okay," Jaiden coos while embracing her in for another tight hug.

Jared swears under his breath, *unbelievable! He uses any chance, he gets to touch her and throws it in my face!* He tosses the towel he was planning to use to stop the fire, on the counter, feeling every bit of pathetic. "Maybe we should just go out instead?" he suggests, trying to be of any use. Jaiden and Jess pull away, nodding off in agreement.

"Go get changed and get your coat, okay?" Jaiden asks of her before kissing her temple. "Me and Jare will clean this up." She nods and exits the kitchen and Jared stands there crossing his arms, *how petty of him.*

The three head to an outdoor cafe and take their seats, Jared pulls out Jess' chair for her and decides to take the seat directly next to her. Jaiden can't help but shake his head as the two stare down, sharing a menu. *What a joke, he makes it obvious that he likes her, but I play the smart way and play hard to get so it will keep her coming back. Young Jared just doesn't know the tricks. I see the way she looks at him and laughs at his jokes, just thinking about them being together makes me sick, but I know it will never happen so long as I'm in the picture.*

The waiter brings out their drinks followed by their food half an hour later and Jaiden still refuses to believe that Jessica likes Jared more than himself. *The kid's a joke! I love the kid, but he tries so hard to fit in and is so needy. I don't blame him, it's probably the fact that he's never had a girlfriend in his life or because he has only gotten laid once in his entire lifetime that he's trying so hard to keep her.*

They go back to Jess' place and Jared turns on the television while Jaiden crashes on the sofa. Jess puts the takeout in the fridge and heads into her room. "Hey Jess, I'm gonna hop into the shower!" Jaiden calls out moments before she enters her bedroom.

"Okay!" she replies exiting. Minutes pass and Jared takes it upon himself to straighten things out with Jessica and try to make his move. After Jaiden enters the bathroom, Jared quietly creeps up to her door and enters without knocking. She pauses her television to give him her undivided attention. "What's up Jared?" she perches. He takes the opportunity to sit on the edge of her bed and she scoots with her legs to move closer to him. Unclear of what he was hoping to achieve with this, Jessica takes it upon herself to help the shy boy out and grip his thigh reassuringly. He finds himself taking both of her hands in his, confidently now while caressing her fingers with his thumbs. "Yeah Jared?" she tilts her head. Soon, his lips smash onto hers and she doesn't hesitate to shove him away. "Jared!" she shouts in outrage. He earns a hard smack across his face. It was completely inappropriate for him to have done that. But she has no idea that she has been guilty of sending him mixed signals. Scared, Jared quickly stands up after realizing what he has just done. "I'm not interested in being anything more than your friend, please understand!" she overwhelmingly states. She then storms out of the room.

(Flashback)

It was a regular afternoon. Jessica was lying down with the twins on Jared's bed, their faces staring up at the blank ceiling. It was a month after their 'incident', but she was fortunate they all had gotten past it and never brought it up to her attention again. In more technical terms, that had been the second secret they swore to take to their deathbeds.

She was in the middle of them both with her elbows resting at her sides and each of her hands interlocked with her friends'. She was just as surprised to find that they had gotten her into a bed with them for the second time. After about three minutes of pure silence, she began speaking, "I'm bored guys," she whined.

"Me too," Jared admitted.

"I'm gonna go to get some food, you losers want anything?" Jaiden asked, sitting up and removing his hand from the girl's.

"Bring me a soda?" Jared requested.

"Dat ass," Jessica cackled as Jaiden plowed off the bed. He turned to look at the innocent girl with wide eyes causing her to outburst in laughter. "Sorry guys, I've obviously took an unexpected interest to your friends," Jessica said as the two start laughing and Jaiden soon exits the room. "What?" asked Jessica when noticing Jared had been staring at her even after her laughter faded.

"Nothing. You're just so cute saying those words, it's unlike you," he said causing Jess to sit up and punch Jared in his arm. It just caused him to laugh harder, so she crawled to sit on his lower abdomen, trying to pin his arms down. "Oh, what a familiar position," he teased. As soon as she let her guard down for the second it took her to gasp, he flipped her over and started tickling the girl.

"Stop!" the brunette squeaked, trying to fight him off.

"What's going on in here?" a female voice said, causing Jared and Jess to separate from their positions and Jared to finally stop.

In the meantime, Jessica tried to catch her breath.

"Nothing Mom, just fooling around," he stated.

"Jared, play nicely and try keeping it PG in here," she requested when staring directly at the absent-minded girl beside Jared. That woman scared Jessica, she despised Jessica and for an odd reason that Jessica didn't know of.

25

When she left, Jared closed the door quietly before scattering back onto the bed. In swift notions, he got back on top of her in an attempt to tickle her again, but she felt a rush of resentment wash over her and rolled out from under him, sitting on the edge of his bed. Worried, Jared crawled over to her. "Jess, what's wrong?" he strictly concerned.

"It's, it's nothing," she lied. He got up and kneeled in front of her with nothing but sorrow in his eyes.

"It's not nothing. Come on, you can tell me," he assured, grabbing both of her wrists.

Unsure of what to say, Jessica sighed once again, staring at the ground beneath her feet. "It's just that your mom, f-for the longest time… I feel like she hates me, and I don't know what I did wrong," she depressed.

"Hey, don't take it personal, she's like this to all me and Jai's friends, especially girls," he shrugged, joining her back on the bed before proceeding to give her that comforting hug she had been yearning to get all day. Suddenly, she felt this pain at the pit of her stomach and has the urge to vomit. She rushed to the bathroom with the last ounce of energy she has stored away. Luckily, the twins happened to have one beside their room so that she didn't have to cause a scene or run far. She opened the toilet lid up and began to release her fluids. "Hey, is everything all right in here?" Jared asked as he walked in. Seconds later, Jaiden entered as well.

"I got you your soda, but we were all out of ass," he chuckled, unaware of what had been happening with his friend.

She walked out fifteen minutes later, after Jessica had requested the twins to leave her alone to disembowel her gut.

"Are you sure you're alright?" Jaiden asked while she stared down at her hands; she had been a shade lighter than when she had entered fifteen minutes ago.

She nodded enduringly, "It's probably just something bad I ate," she lied. "I uh… I've got to go."

She tried to leave as soon as she could until one of the twins spoke out again, "Wait, hang on, me and Jared will drive you," Jaiden persuaded.

"It's fine, my house is literally five minutes away," she smiled reassuringly, she just needed to get out of there as soon as possible. As soon as Jessica waved her goodbyes to the boys and tried to say goodbye to their mother, she speedily walked to her house which was a couple of houses away from the twins, to prevent herself from passing out on the street. No cars home, *great*. She entered inside and locked the front door before shuffling up the stairs to her designated bathroom. She ended up texting her least favorite sister, Beverly for assistance.

To: **Bev** from: **Jessica**
Hey, can you do me a favor?

Beverly arrived an hour later and entered the bathroom with a brown paper bag. "So why do you think you're pregnant?" Beverly asked, rather annoyed. Jessica snatched the bag from her hands.

"Can you give me some privacy? I'll explain later!" she yelled with her patience wearing thin. Beverly soon clicked her heels out of the room.

Oh no. This was it, moment of truth. Three tests… all positive.

Jessica momentarily stepped out and tried to keep a straight face but couldn't help thinking how her life was going to change forever. *They should just cast me to join the next season of teen mom right now. This is going to kill me.*

She found herself moping into her sister's embrace as she confided in her solemnly. "Promise you won't tell mom or dad?" Jessica worried. She had been beyond flabbergasted that she fretted for what everyone else would think and burdening the twins with this information had completely slipped her mind. She didn't want to tell them; this baby could jeopardize their career.

"How did this happen?" Beverly asked while her younger sister settled down on the bed beside her.

"Well I uh… don't really remember much but I had a drink or two and Jared—"

Beverly wheezed, "You had sex with Jared Daniels?" She nearly fell back on the bed.

"J-Jaiden too," Jessica frighteningly admitted rather sheepish.

"Both!" Beverly exclaimed. "A threesome?" she asked a little more derogative than before. The mood had inclined drastically from the last few minutes. Jessica scattered across the bed to move her hand to cover Beverly's piercing mouth.

"No, separately… look, I don't really remember what happened, just only from what the twins told me. I've trusted that they told me the truth. I just hope they remembered if they used protection or not for my sake," Jessica explained.

Beverly shot up to scold her sister, "Do you think this is funny? What is wrong with you? First off, how in the hell do you even manage to sleep with two guys that look the same, let alone two guys that have been almost like family to us—and by us, I mean you, for years!" she yelled, "That's sick Jessica! Do you even realize that you might lose them both once you tell them or they find out whose baby it is, or did you not think that far ahead? Guys just don't stick around to raise families with the shrew they've impregnated, and for Christ's sake, you're only in high school, Jessica! What in the hell were you thinking getting associated with those boys! Do you have any idea what this will do for our family! Great, there goes my nine months of allowance..." she continued, and the truth really hit her negligent sister as she found herself fighting the urge to drop a tear down her cheek. As much as Jess wanted to shrivel up in a hole and die, she couldn't help but notice how egotistical Beverly sounded in this moment, *is that really all she cared about? Money?*

"You are so irresponsible, and *really*! Jaiden Daniels!" she emphasized, louder than before, "That guy is a douche, a total player! How do you expect that human pogo stick to be a role model to your unborn child if he flaunts his junk around everywhere like a damn car mechanic!" she cried out dramatically. She certainly was quite the drama queen.

"Bev?" Jess worried, awaiting a response, "What's wrong?" she asked again. Beverly inhales deeply and looked up at Jessica, who carefully nodded in approval. Beverly squats back down beside Jessica.

"A few years ago, I was at this bonfire with my friends and we all got wasted, except I wasn't. Our plan was to have a good time and meet some guys. I saw Jaiden with some of his older friends and I knew he was underage," she began and a staggered gasp left Jessica's mouth, unsure of where this was going, but already having a good idea. "He came up to me and we started talking, a-about you actually. It got a little too crowded in our area and we couldn't hear each other so we started walking around until we found this campsite not too far from the party. There, we sat on this log and I remember just clearly staring into his eyes as he was talking, and I couldn't help it. It was the day after me and my boyfriend broke up and my girlfriends brought me here to show me to a good time and make me forget about him. I guess I was just so vulnerable at the time and he happened to be the first one to take my mind off Patrick. Anyways, I-I kissed him and after about a minute, he pulled away and told me he felt he was abandoning someone else—but I didn't care, and I kept going for it until he eventually gave up fighting the urge to resist me. We went into the tent and started to take off our clothes and before I know it, we had sex... he told me it was his first time too—" she admitted.

"Oh my god! How could you! He's my best friend! And he was underage!" Jessica yelled, shooting up. "You say I'm irresponsible, how

DARE you! You know you could've went to jail for sleeping with a minor!" she climaxed melodramatically.

"I know, and I regretted everything the next day!" Beverly protested, pushing her face into her hands. Jessica didn't know how much more of this she could hear, so she stormed out of her room and out of the house.

Jessica contemplated her past history, trying to cope with this disaster her older sister now just admitted to, piling on top of her stress. There, she sat on the sidewalk curb, crying into the insides of her brittle palms. She heard a bike coming closer; it was Hobbs. He noticed her from afar and nodded his head, signaling he would be approaching her. She speedily wiped her running mascara as he hopped off his bike and set it down on her lawn, sitting down next to the emotionally distraught girl. "Hey Jess, what's wrong?" he asked.

"Nothing," she hoarsely answered. "I didn't know you live here?" she asked quickly changing the subject.

"Yeah, my parents just moved in about a week ago," he stated.

"So, how's that science project coming along?" Jessica asked after about a minute of silence.

"Not bad, only took me a good four minutes to finish," he answered as a smile reappeared on the girl's face when covering her ears.

"Gross! So not the image I wanted to have!" she teased. Just then, his phone rang. Leaving him to wrap up his conversation. Hobbs was the one out of the bunch from the group she met at the party, she could tell he was the most loyalist. Everyone else gave her an unimpressionable vibe, *especially Griffins*.

He had been right about one thing though; the trouble had indeed caught up with Jessica.

She stood up after parting ways with Zach and made her way back over to the twins' house, still unsure of what to say or how. They have the right to know, even if she was slightly upset at Jaiden that he would be one to do such a thing and not even tell her. She wasn't surprised that he was capable of doing it, she was more so disappointed that he even didn't even have the decency to tell her about it, that's what hurt the most. More than anything, Jessica expressively aimed hatred towards her sister for being impulsive. Jessica arrived at their house and knocked on their door, thinking about just how the conversation would play out in her head. She waited two minutes before changing her mind and just as she began to retreat in the opposite direction, the front door swung open. "Jared! Jaiden! Jessica's here!" Mr. Daniels shouted. Upon request, she courteously stepped inside and greeted him with a sly smile. "How are you sweetie?" he asked as they waited at the foot of the staircase. The boys shuffle down the stairs interrupting their small-talk.

"Hey Jess!"

"You're back!" Jaiden smiled. Mr. Daniels soon left the room.

"Why did you leave, are you feeling better?" Jared asked.

"Can we all go somewhere private to talk?" the shy girl requested.

They took a drive to the closest park. None of them talked the entire ride and a nervous Jessica fiddled with her hands until she felt a warm hand separating her hand apart from the other, locking one of their hands with hers. She looked over and Jaiden gave her a cheeky reassuring smirk. She hesitantly smiled back until an unflattering image of Jaiden and Beverly having sex, popped in the back of her mind, making her edgy at the thought. She instantly released her grip on his hand just as soon as they arrived. Jared stepped out first, opening the car door for her. They walked around for about five minutes as she used the time effectively to think about what she was going to say. "So, what did you want to talk to us about?"

She took her seat on the bench and they both continue to stand until she speaks up again, "So, when I was throwing up this morning... it wasn't because I had some bad food; well, at least I thought it was until I remembered that I've missed my period for almost two weeks now, which I thought was normal at first," she rambled, hoping there would be a chance that they had caught on before she continued any further to save herself from the embarrassment. Their faces were both still blank with confusion, so she continued, irritated, "... until I remembered that I had sex with the both of you as well," she paused again. Finally, Jaiden's mouth dropped, and Jared slid his fingers through his hair in frustration, signaling they had fully understood what she had been referring to this entire time. "So, I asked my sister to get me a test and as it turns out..."

In the midst of explanation, Jessica broke down, unable to finish her thought. They both sat on each of her sides and Jared coddled the girl to his chest while Jaiden shook his head in disbelief. He turned to face her after being alone in his thoughts for a while, "And you're here to tell us that one of us is the father?" Humbled, Jessica slowly nodded, unwrapping herself from Jared's embrace.

"Except, you don't know which one of us it belongs to, do you?" Jared interrogated.

"No, I must have overlooked the part when you both off-handedly took advantage of me!" she spat in spite before Jaiden interrupted again, "Are you sure, I-I mean there wasn't anyone else y-you...?" he asked hopefully.

"God no, Jai! It comforting to know, you two think so low of me!" she overwhelmingly toppled, wiping her running eyes.

They dropped their heads, "We didn't say that, we're just trying to process everything," Jared sighed, brushing a hand over her shoulder.

"Did you guys even use protection?" she curiously interrogated, a little too loudly. The three got weird glares from a woman and her five-year-old daughter just strolling by.

"Yes!" Jaiden exclaimed quietly as soon as they passed. "I mean if I go to a party, I expect to get laid, so I always bring protection—"

"Enough Jaiden! I get it!" she intolerably groaned. "Jared?" she asked turning to face him with sweat beating down her worrisome eyes.

"I-I-uh-well you might have been my first time, but I always makes sure to bring condoms. Y-you know... just in case," he incoherently vindicated.

"If you guys are going to be immature about this then maybe I should've never told you this at all!" she angrily replied and jolted up.

"Wait Jess!" Jared placed his hand at her shoulder in hopes of her staying, but she shrugged his hand off and speedily continued to walk away, letting the tears fall freely down her face for the last time.

Chapter Two

"Jess!" the two called out in the distance and she started running but she didn't know where she was running to; where to turn, where to hide, where to drown deep in slumber. Returning home would be an option, but she couldn't hide her saucy secret from the rest of her family forever.

(Present Day)

She wakes up at five a.m. to get changed hurriedly to prepare for her day to come. She rushes over to the bathroom to brush her teeth and pee because she knows how demanding her baby is and how it goes when it wants, when it pushes on her bladder. After she washes up, she puts her hair up in a messy bun and steps out of the bathroom to grab a jelly-filled donut from her fridge before heading out the door. She walks to her parking garage to get inside the passenger seat of her sister's car. "You ready?" Mandy smiles.

"Let's do this thing!" Jessica imitates even though she would rather take the day off to relax and rest. They drive to the doctor's and Jessica devours her donut.

"I just can't believe I'm going to be an aunt!" Amanda excitedly announces as Jessica grabs a napkin from the dispenser to wipe her mouth after she has finished eating. Amanda applies a thick coat of lipstick while shifting her eyes between the road and her rear-view mirror before continuing to talk, "I just thought it would be me to be the first to have a child since I'm married you know—" she rambles on.

"Amanda! Keep both hands on the wheel!" Jessica fearfully warns. She finishes her makeup and Jessica rolls her eyes. "So, how's Bev?" Jess asks even though her grudge is clearly still present.

Amanda shrugs, "I don't know anymore, she moved in with Patrick, but that's all I know," she states.

"She's with him again? Is she engaged or something?" Jessica asks, confused.

"No, they're just dating... or maybe friends I don't really remember," Amanda speaks and just as Jessica is about to ask another question, the girls had arrived at their destination and step out. They walk to the reception desk and Mandy signs in for her sister. They continue to take their seats in the waiting room where they continue to talk about their abnormal and complicated lives with Jessica telling her sister about her new job, although she hadn't had a chance to discuss school terms with her sister yet and luckily for Jessica, Amanda didn't remember to ask.

"Ms. Larson, good to see you!" Dr. Reynolds greets. She follows closely to his office, being accompanied by Amanda inside and they start the procedure. "Okay, let's see what you're carrying," he says getting the lubricant gel-like substance ready.

"Mandy, can you grab my phone? It's in the front pocket," Jessica asks pointing at her purse. Amanda hands it to her and continues gazing at the monitor. Jessica begins to dial the twins, reaching Jared's phone first since he was a reliable source.

"Hey, are you guys on the way? I am about to find out," she worries. She had asked both the twins to reserve a part of their day to be there for her in this moment.

"Jaiden can't make it, but I'll be there shortly. Give me ten minutes, okay?" Jessica disappointingly hangs up after ending their brief conversation.

"I am so sorry Doctor, can we put this on hold for about ten minutes?" she asks. He sets the transducer down and shortly exits the room. As Jessica continuously lies down on the patient bed, she lifts her shirt and begins to rub at her stomach. Minutes later, Jared rolls in and she can't help but smile.

"Are we all ready?" Dr. Reynolds asks while entering the door with his clipboard shortly after. The three of them nod, "And you must be the father," the doctor greets while holding out his hand.

"Actually, we don't know yet," Jessica mentions with a light chuckle while Jared proceeds to shake this doctor's hand.

"Oh, how so?" the doctor pries when placing the cold, gel-like substance on his patient.

"Me and my twin brother sort of had a mix-up," Jared explains nervously. Jess reassuringly grabs onto his hand as he then stands closer to her.

"Where's Jai?" Jessica discreetly whispers to him.

"I don't know, but he says he's really bummed he can't make it," Jared mentions.

"Okay, so here is what we've got here," the doctor says directing their attention back over to the monitor. He spends two minutes pointing at the screen and locating the fetus. "Looks like you're having a baby girl… congratulations Ms. Larson!" the doctor emphasizes. Jessica covers her mouth with her hands in awe. A single shed of tear escapes her eyelids and Jared kisses the top of her head, embracing her in for a hug while resting his head slightly above hers.

After her appointment, the three of them head down to the parking garage. "You sure you don't want me to drive you home?" Jared directs when heading towards his car.

"No thank you. I'm just gonna spend the day with my sister," Jessica replies. Jared nods his head and opens his car door just before she speaks out again. "Just don't tell Jaiden, I want to be the one to tell him!" she giddily hops from beside him in the passenger side, contrary to his driver side since their cars had been parked right beside one another. He nods, and she thanks him once again before heading off inside the passenger's seat of her sister's car. After many precious minutes of driving, the sisters get out of the car and enter the nearest coffee shop out in the city.

"What do you want?" Amanda asks, standing up after having thrown off her coat and finding their seats in the back of the cafe.

"Just get me a small hot chocolate please," Jessica shrugs when scrolling through her rose gold iPhone, she was almost too basic for this place. Amanda returns eight minutes later with their orders and what appears to be two blueberry scones. She hands her pregnant sister her requested cocoa and subtly slides over a napkin attached to the bottom of a scone from across the table.

"Eat up!" she insists. The bloated Jessica rolls her eyes and bluntly pushes it away from her sight, too nauseous to be even thinking about forcing any more food down her throat. "You're eating for two and I want my niece to be healthy!"

Jessica laughs at her sister's poor choice of words and accepts her nice gesture after all. Just as Jess finishes like the fat ass she feels like, she makes her way over to the front counter to grab another napkin. Laughter fills the room, coming from the line behind her. Thinking the snide laughter was directed at her, she sighs and prepares to return to her seat, shrugging it off, but she was not prepared for who she would find behind the laughter. There, she finds herself, eyes widened and stricken with fear when she finds Jaiden in his blue letterman jacket at a table with a redhead, sucking face. Her heart breaks a little. Furious, she was on her way over to give him a piece of her mind.

"Jaiden!"

He hears someone familiar snap up at him as he then shuffles away from his scandalous kiss. It was Jess, *crap*. Jessica wore her frown on her face and it was no question why. Jaiden was caught red-handed, literally. "Who's this?" the ginger named Candi asks as Jessica stands there, crossing over her arms.

"I should be asking you the same question," Jessica sneers back. "So, is this why you were so 'busy' huh?" Jessica air-quotes.

"Jess, can we please talk somewhere else in private?" Jaiden requests when noticing they were on the verge of causing a scene.

"Oh, I'm sorry am I embarrassing you? Good. How about when you embarrassed me at my appointment today? You know, the one you 'couldn't' make? Where you left me all by myself, no effort to even call me to explain yourself and you send Jared as your messenger? How do you think it makes me feel finding you in here groping some groupie? You lied to me! The least you could've done was called me up and told me the truth! If you didn't want to be a part of this child's life, you should've just said something! I waited for you, I wanted you to be there for me and you didn't. Thanks for showing me that I can't rely on you to help me when this baby comes!"

"I'm so sorry, I've uh, got to go," Candi interrupts, grabbing her purse and getting up.

"Wait, no!" Jaiden groans, standing up halfway.

"You're pathetic and shallow!" Jess continues and by now they had the whole cafe staring at their table. He continues to stare at Candi while she leaves and before he knows it, Jessica takes Candi's Strawberry Hibiscus and dumps it all over the dimwitted fool before striding away with her last remaining dignity. After Jessica's sister drops her off at home, she storms inside and locks the door, throwing her keys onto the coffee table and kicking her shoes off in the middle of her tidy apartment. She then, goes into her room and locks the knob on the handle before proceeding into her spacious, dark closet where she sits down and begins sobbing into her hands. *I can't believe him, he's hurt me so much and doesn't even realize it. He is not the same Jaiden I knew growing up and I have my sister to blame for that, he would've been less sleazy if she hadn't taken away his innocence. What has gotten into him? I don't know what to do, I'm scared. I just want to escape.*

Her phone has been going off today from notifications, so she decides it was time to check her social media feed. Of course, just what she had thought... *hate.* Ever since the twins' fans found out that Jessica, aka their go-to gal-pal, was somehow pregnant, hate had become the talk of her newsfeed. As she continuously scrolls down her twitter feed, fans of the twins have apparently found out what happened at Starbucks earlier today, and this time they were backlashing messages directly at her; these messages that said these fans were glad that Jaiden had moved on and that this ill-sheltered shrew didn't deserve either the twins, that she had ruined them, and their careers, and that they were better off without her. The more she thinks about it the more she starts to believe it

35

and agree with the comments. At that moment, she wishes everything would stop. It is horrendous enough that the entirety of her primary family disowned her, and the twins were the only ones she was grateful to have stayed in her life, but now that she is re-evaluating, she believes the only reason they chose to stay was because they felt like they owed it to her. She officially feels alone.

It is really no different of a feeling, with their fans having told her awful things from the start, was it jealousy, or was it because they knew deep down she was an awful person? A couple of them even threatened her a few times. But she never thought once to tell the twins because she feared they would back up their fans rather than her and didn't want to risk coming between them. She sobs even harder when overthinking things, not knowing what to do. *It was comforting to know I had no one and I was completely alone in this, supporting myself. Who was I to think I could rely on anyone? It was my mess and I need to clean it up.*

****

(Flashback—after the twins found out)
Jessica had reluctantly found her way back home after walking such a far distance. She entered the front door, slamming the door shut behind on her way up the staircase. Her mother's voice approached her from beneath causing Jessica to divert her attention. "What's going on?" she asked.

Jessica simply replied, "Nothing," before returning up the stairs.

"Did you walk all this way?" she asked again.

Jessica groaned before facing at her attention once again. "I was only at the twins' house," she lied.

"Really? Is that so? Because they called ten minutes ago to make sure you got home safely since you apparently stormed out of the park all the way down in Central." Margret folded her arms and Jessica frowned. "Is there something you want to share with me?" Margret asked and Jessica hesitated to say anything. "No, I just want to be alone!" she burst out unexpectedly, running up into her room and slamming the door closed once again. She could not trust her mother, not now, not ever. Jessica never felt the warmth of her mother's arms and because of that, she eventually learned to self-heal and didn't need her mother anymore, she was stronger alone. As Jessica laid down in bed in attempt to shut her eyes, she failed with these thoughts on her future flooding her every mind. Just as she finally began dozing off into sleep, she heard multiple loud poundings at the foot of her door. She groaned in response. She requested for the noises to leave her alone, hoping it would stop them from banging any further.

"Jess, please let us in!"

"We want to comfort you!" the second annoying voice spoke. "I don't need anyone right now, go away! I want to be alone!" she urged, sliding back under her warm covers.

(Present Day)
She had gotten exactly what she had bargained for.

****

She was sitting on his lap and they started taking their clothes off. She reached for his belt and he pulled away from their lingering kiss that she fought so desperately to stay attached to. He sat back up with her still on his lap. "Jess, are you sure about this?" She didn't reply and instead pushed his chest back down on the bed to continue to smother him. She helped the boy take his pants off followed by his boxers. "Are you sure?" he worriedly asked again. "Jaiden, just get inside me!" she impatiently growled. Jaiden chuckled at this girl's insane sex drive. The aroused boy hopped off the bed to grab his pants from the floor and grabs a condom from one of his front pockets. He tore the wrapper to slide it on his length and returns to the bed. Just as he was about to enter the anxious girl she stops him, "Wait Jaiden, I-it's my first time," she nervously admits. "In that case, it may hurt a little at first, but it will get better after a while, I promise," Jaiden had confidently assured and sealed off with a kiss to her forehead. She nods in permission before he slowly entered her inch by inch, focusing on her face. He could tell she was fighting back tears when he finally entered inside her all the way.

"Jaiden? Jaiden!" someone calls out when snapping their fingers in front of the delusional boy's face, depriving him of his thoughts. "So babe, are you in?" she asks, and he was unsure of what she had asked but he had already nodded off in agreement. "Great!" She claps her hands together excitedly. "My parents are going to be so thrilled to meet you!" she exclaims. Her phone goes off momentarily later, ending their conversation. "Anyways, I'm off. Bye babe!" She grabs her phone from her clutch before waving Jaiden off. *God, Candi is so annoying! How did we even get back together? One thing was for sure though, she was no Jess.* As he stands utterly confused in the semi-crowded hallway of his high school, he grabs his backpack and shuts his locker to walk off in the opposite direction. He spots Jared talking with his friend Lucas across the hall and makes his way over to them. As soon as Lucas notices Jaiden approaching them both, he parts ways, leaving the two brothers to talk amongst themselves. *What was that about?*

Jaiden catches up to Jared in the nick of time, before he too walks away. "Hey bro, I'm gonna ditch, you need a ride?" Jaiden asks when getting his brother's attention. The two have been carpooling to school lately.

"No, I have a meeting after school and then I'm gonna see if Nora can drop me off at Jessica's," Jared mentions.

"Yeah, speaking of which, I might stop by Jessica's later too."

"I don't think that's the best idea, you really hurt her Jai and she's made it evidently clear, she doesn't want to see you," he says, swinging his backpack onto his chest to grab his shades. He puts them on and zips his backpack back up before swinging it back around his back.

"Is this coming from you or her?"

"Stick around long enough and you'll find out for yourself," he chuckles, tapping his older brother on the shoulder.

"Since when are you in student council?" Jaiden brings up, hoping to avoid the subject of Jessica in the hands of his ass-kissing brother.

"There are lots of things you don't know about me, now if you'll excuse me," Jared pardons, beginning to walk away.

"What just happened?" Jaiden mumbles.

Jared turns back around and shouts loud enough for Jaiden to hear over the crowded hallways while walking backwards, "You never really cared to ask!" Jared shrugs before returning to his steps. He is right, Jaiden never cared to pry into Jared's personal life before, so he was not obligated to tell Jaiden anything.

What the fuck is wrong with that kid? He's been very secretive and distant lately. Well damn him, I don't even need him. Since when has he ever been interested in curricular academics, or whatever the fuck you call it. HA! What a pathetic loser.

****

As soon as Jared stepped off the elevator in the apartment complex building, he heads towards Jessica's apartment, to smell something cooking. He enters using the spare key she lent him in case of an emergency. "Hi Jared!" her voice greets from behind the kitchen counter, with her hair tied back in a messy bun, wearing an apron with flour stains around her large waist. Jared throws his jacket on her new sofa. "What's all this for?" he curiously asks, walking around the dining table that is set for about eight people. "I've invited some of our new friends over for dinner," she says with a reassuring smile as she continues cooking. He comes up behind her and she turned around to kiss her friend directly on the lips. "I've missed you so much," she says between breaths when sharing a kiss between their lips. He parts his lips from hers to nervously ask her if she had invited Jaiden. She picks up the knife and continues chopping, her teeth clenched forward a bit when she had begun to speak. "Oh, *him…*"

"Jess, I'm sorry. I shouldn't have asked—"

"I, I need a moment alone," she sighs, dropping the knife down on the cutting board, turning the stove off. She takes her apron off and throws it on the counter before covering her mouth and storming out of the kitchen. She enters her room and slams the door in his face when he follows behind her. *I love how we took our relationship further, but I feel like she has feelings for Jaiden too, and he doesn't deserve her at all.*

It's as if every minute had fallen into place. Just as Jessica finished her final preparations, she heard a knock on the door. It took her a couple of minutes to calm down earlier but luckily, she managed to suck it up and continue working. She loved Jared, Jaiden too. She was emotionally distraught from how Jaiden abandoned her, choosing over someone who has always supported him. Jessica smiles widely upon answering the door to greet her guests. Jared soon joins her at the door from the couch. In enters Josh, followed by Sienna and Hobbs. Finally, in enters Lucas, Jared's closest friend that she would be meeting for the first time. "I hope you don't mind, I've brought my grandma along," Lucas announces, making way for his grandmother to enter.

"No, not at all. The more the merrier!" Jessica boasts widely. His grandmother takes off her coat and notices Jessica's stomach, causing her to roll her eyes at the innocent broad.

"Jesus Lucas, you've really screwed yourself over with this one," Grandmother Rogers implies, turning heads in the room while subtly hanging her coat on the rack. Jessica's mouth strikes wide open before dispersing into an awkward grin.

"Please excuse her, she's a kidder," Lucas apologizes. The air is cleared with laughter. They all gather around the table and Jess returns to the kitchen to grab a few things. She arrives momentarily with a bowl of salad and dressing and sets it in the middle of the table.

"Jared, would you please get Grandma Rogers a chair? They're in the kitchen," she directs as the friends begin to sit down.

She proceeds back to the kitchen with Jared following closely behind, to grab the extra silverware and she makes her way back to the table when suddenly, she's stopped in her tracks. Jared spontaneously spins her around carefully and locks his lips to hers. She doesn't fight back her hormones when she carelessly forgets about the things in her hands while she wraps her hands around his neck. Seconds later, everything slips from her hands. It was a good thing that the plates were plastic, but the cup shattered causing the two startled teenagers in the room to split from one another, fast. "Nice going!" Jessica groans, rolling her eyes to the back of her head and pushing past him. She vigilantly walked around the glass to retrieve the broom from the next room over and during her return, she was surprised to find the kitchen filled with her concerned guests.

"What the hell happened in here?" Josh asks as she begins sweeping. "Just being a klutz!" Jessica falsely smiles, avoiding the topic of how it really broke. Jared groans and exits the kitchen in frustration. Jessica finishes cleaning soon enough, no thanks to anyone but Hobbs and Lucas lending out a hand. She then finally brings out Ms. Rogers' utensils and takes her seat next to a grumpy Jared. Jessica tries to ignore his crude attitude, so that he would not ruin her mood as well even though he had already managed.

Halfway through dinner, of the two ignoring each other and Jared drowning in his own self-pity, Jared stands up and roughly slams his chair into the table before proceeding into Jessica's bedroom, slamming the door behind him. "Jared!" Jessica sighs, getting up from the table, running over to him. She knocks on the door to see if Jared was okay. She pressed an ear to the door until she heard muffled cries. She rattled the door handle a few times until she realized it was open and enters her bedroom quietly creeping up to her friend in comfort. She had a feeling something had been bothering him for a while now. She saw Jared sitting on her bed with his back against the bed frame, knees up and pressed to his face and what appears to look like him crying into his palms. His bloodshot eyes glisten in her direction as soon as she closes the door. He stands up and wipes his eyes in an attempt to leave but she blocks his pathway by placing her hands on his chest. "Jess, I should leave, just please let me go," he insisted.

"Jared, please. You don't have to do this. Just stay here with me and let's talk, okay?"

He sighs before giving in. She takes his hand and leads him to her bed once again. They both take a seat and he takes a deep, elongated breath before speaking up. "It's always about him, he always takes something that I want and he's basically living the life I want. Ever since we were younger, he's always been the noticed one, the respected one and I just try so damn hard to fit in you know?" Unsure of how to react,

Jess begins to pick at the cuticles of her fingernails, waiting for him to continue. "You know how hard it is to put a smile on your face when you're hurting and to just act like it doesn't upset you when everyone forgets all about you? I'm not as cool, or athletic as him or even know how to be as charming as him and no matter how hard I try, I know it's him you'd rather be with," he croaks out while bringing his legs up to his face again. Jessica takes a deep breath after realizing that this must have been what he was so upset about. She pushes his hands away from his face and forces him to look at her.

"Jared, that's not true," she starts to vindicate when cupping his face with one of her hands.

"Bullshit Jessica! That's a lie and you know it!" he strikes, bolting into anger, his wrath meshing with his vulnerability. "You always let him get away with his schemes! I can't even kiss you without you yelling at me and you're 'my' girl!" Jessica wanted to protest but he revolted with, "Don't you even deny it! I've felt your discomfort around me for a long time compared to how I've seen you act around him! I feel so used and betrayed right now. Jokes on me, I'm the rebound!" His jaw tensed and now he had both of his hands locked together with his thumbs rested on his mouth as he paces back and forth in the room. When he turns back in her direction, she brings his hands down in front.

"Jared, enough! This is why I didn't want this to happen! I can't risk losing you over this relationship, Jared! I'll admit, I love you both, but I feel for you both fairly differently now. I was only willing to try us out because I saw potential in you Jared. I saw in you what I never imagined seeing in Jaiden, I want a life with you. Jared, I love you, I only want you!"

He looks away and she turns his head to meet hers once again. "And you are nobody's second choice, I may have had feelings or whatever for Jaiden way back then, but those feelings went away as soon as you came into my life, Jare. I'm not interested in being his friend after all the shit he's put me through and to be honest, I don't think I could ever trust the awful person he is today; but he still is your brother and family comes first so no matter what, you should always be there for each other," she continues. "Even if this baby is his, it won't change anything between us, I promise. And there will always be a special place for Jaiden in my heart but in the end, it's you who will always have it," Jessica explains, caressing her fingers with his before they both begin to lean in.

"Now, where were we?" she asks in a low-whisper, referring to the broken kiss they had earlier. He smiles and attaches his hungry, wet lips to hers while cupping her petite face. As she wraps her arms around his neck once again, she could taste his plump lips on her tongue, his sweet lips that tasted like cherries from the chapstick he's always using to keep his lips moisturized. Their tongues were now fighting for dominance and she suddenly feels a sharp pain in the pit of her stomach, causing her to jerk away. "Oh my gosh!"

"What?" he worries. "The baby… s-she kicked!" she exclaims for the first time. "I felt her!" she exclaimed once again.

"What? H-how?" With her help, he places his hands gently on her stomach and within seconds, he presents his best friend with the same award-winning reaction. "I felt her kick too!" He slides his hands from her stomach to her face and places a kiss at her lips again. "Erm, we should probably get back to our guests now…" Jared reminds her, standing back up.

"Oh, don't worry about them, I've sent them home… I'm all yours now!"

He raises a brow, "You did?"

"One moment," she held up a finger, rushing out tediously to the best of her abilities after struggling a while to thrash out of bed. She walks out and walks back into her bedroom seconds later, shutting the door on her way in, "Okay, 'now' I'm all yours!" she excites, wiggling her eyebrows.

****

The following night, Jaiden was on his way to the restaurant that he was supposedly meeting Candi and her family at. *Should I have brought her flowers? No, never mind. I'm not really into her. Maybe the more of an ass I am, she'll want to leave me.* After he parked his car, he sat there a moment to reflect upon his life choices. *I really miss Jess… why am I wasting my time with someone I could never love?* He takes his phone out and dials Jess. He hopes she answers but sincerely doubts it considering all the stupid things he's done to her. It goes straight to voicemail, just as he thought.

Fuck it, I'm just gonna see where the night takes me.

He takes a step out of his BMW and walks toward the entrance. As soon as he enters, the host asks for his name. "I'm actually here with a family, redhead," he describes, unknowing her last name.

"Ah, Mr. Jaiden?" Jaiden nods. "Right this way," the monsieur directs in his dreadful and pretentious French accent when leading Jaiden towards his designated table. He was spotted and greeted by Candi who walked up, giving him a peck on his cheek with her cherry-red, satin lipstick. She takes her thumb and coats it with saliva in attempt to seduce him, wiping the lip stain off his cheek that she imprinted. He stood in discomfort before she linked her arm with his and led him to their table. "Mom, dad, this is Jaiden, my boy—"

"Friend," he interjected, getting confused glares from all around the table, "Boy… friend," he explains when emphasizing the boy rather than the friend. He introduces himself to her parents, generously giving them a handshake.

"Sorry we are late, I've just arrived from work," a male voice behind Jaiden appears causing Jaiden to pivot around. His mouth instantly drops to the floor. "Beverly?" He muttered under his breath. *What the hell is that bitch doing here?*

"Hey Candace!" the male voice says, greeting Jaiden's date with a hug.

"Ugh, don't call me that, you know how much I hate it," Candi groans.

"Hi, you must be Jaiden? I'm Patrick, Candace's older brother, the one and only," he adds whilst wrapping an arm around Candi. *Candi—ace?* Patrick shakes her date's hand. "This is Beverly, my fiancé," he introduces. *Since when?* Suddenly everything made sense to Jaiden, he stood astounded, eyes widened.

"Jaiden, are you okay? You look like you've just seen a ghost," Candi whispers. He gulps and nods, snapping himself out of his thoughts.

Beverly rolls her eyes, "Yeah, we've met," Beverly clarifies while shaking Jaiden's hand with the tightest, deathly grip.

"Oh, how so?" Patrick asks, shrugging his coat off. "One of my sister's friends," she replied.

"Isn't Mandy a little too old to be fooling around with guys your age?" Patrick jokes out. They soon wrap up their short introductions to greet Patrick's parents, joining them at the table. As they finished their meals, the family begun to take an interest to Jaiden but threw their attention back to Beverly as soon as she and Patrick mentioned their engagement.

"So how long have you two been seeing each other?" Jaiden asks directly to Beverly with a ruthless smile present on his vengeful face.

"We've been together for a little over a year now," Patrick clarifies, reaching for her hand. Beverly uses her other hand to take a sip of her wine in annoyance.

"Did you guys have sex yet, safe I hope?" Jaiden asks followed by a chuckle and Beverly nearly chokes on her wine.

"Not that, that's any of your business, or anyone's… we've decided to wait," Patrick states. "Babe, are you okay?" he asks giving his fiancé a napkin cloth.

"Peachy," she consults, staring down Jaiden from across the table with the dirtiest of looks. She snatches the napkin from Patrick's hands and pats down her dress. "Jaiden, could I talk to you for a moment?" Beverly asks trying to keep her anger down before her food. Jaiden nods and she stands up, roughly slamming her napkin cloth down at her chair before leading her sister's friend out.

"What the hell is wrong with you!" she yelled as they stood in the isolated back part of the restaurant, by a payphone. Jaiden cackles. "This is not funny!" she says through her teeth.

"Then why am I laughing?" he laughs again.

"Because you're an idiot! I swear if you say anything else the rest of the night, I will leak those photos to all social platforms, so don't even test me," she viciously warns.

"Fine," he grits before obediently following her back to the table.

****

(Flashback)
"Tell her right now or I will!" Beverly threatens.

Jessica's mother's face stays neutral from confusion as the young girl's, soaks in tears. "What is going on, sweetie?" she asks, cupping her saddened daughter's face and wiping under her daughter's eyes. Jessica hesitantly shakes her head and looks away. "Please sit down," Jessica directs making indirect eye contact with her mother beyond this point and Margret obliges without question.

"I, I-I-I'm …"

"God dammit, just tell her already!" Beverly yells and Jessica nods slowly, sitting down next to her mother.

"Honey, what's wrong? What's bothering you?" she asks stroking her little girl's hair. Just then, Jessica reaches into her purse from the floor that she has prepared for this moment. She pulls the toilet-paper covered tests and slowly begins to unwrap the toilet paper. Margret's eyes widen as her hands reach out to examine the positive tests. She looks puzzled and the young girl can tell her mother wants to say something, but she is at a loss for words. She excuses herself to look away, feared of her mother and ashamed at herself.

"Exactly! You should be ashamed of yourself, mommy's perfect little angel got knocked up! Can you believe it!" Beverly yells.

"When did this even happen?" her mother's voice raises, foreshadowing her movements from the couch as well.

"At… the party a month ago." Jessica gulps, afraid to go on any further, her mother's eyes dilated.

44

"How could you be so ignorant Jessica? You have disgraced this family, I don't even know who you are anymore!" she spits out.

"Margret, what's going on in here?" her father's voice approaches as he comes toward the girls in the living room. The one person Jessica had feared to face more than her mother, was indeed her father.

"Just you wait until your father hears about this!" Margret warns, and the girl is frightened.

"No, please don't!" she pleads, standing up from the couch.

"Our sweet baby girl got wasted at a party that she went to without our consent, need I remind, had sex and is now pregnant!" Margret explains as Jessica steps away further in fear.

"You WHAT? With WHO!" he bolts. Jessica is too afraid to answer, scared he might harm her friends or even worse, her and her baby. He walks up and yanks her hair. "WHO?" he yells again, and she couldn't look him in the eyes, her tears have dried inside her eyelids and she would rather be caught dead herself than say anything else.

"Jared and Jaiden DANIELS!" Beverly informs, and Jessica crumbled to the floor, crying into her palms after he had released his grip on her hair.

Her mother gasps, "Both?" she worries. "I swear to god, I'm going to kill those boys the next time I see 'em. I never liked them, bunch of smart asses!" her father tenses when clenching his jaw. Just then, the door swings open. Jess was relieved it was only Mandy.

"Hey, what's going on?" her eldest sister Mandy asks, dropping the bags of groceries by the front door.

"Jessica Jane, you pack all of your bags and get out of this house, right now!" her father yells out. "You are no longer welcome in this house anymore! I won't tolerate this type of this disrespectful behavior in my house any longer!"

"Dad, she didn't know any better!" Mandy protests. The anxiety caught up with Jessica and with short uneven breaths, she wipes her tears and nods. Weakness overpowered her. She turns back around so that she may beg him to let her stay,

"I'm so sorry, p-please let me stay," she cried out.

"I can't even look at you. I knew someday you'd disappoint me. Congratulations for living up to your only potential," he said so coldly. Hearing those words broke the girl on the inside.

"But dad—" she cried out again. Seconds later, his hand flies up, and she earns a hard smack across her face, sending her in shock, earning a gasp from Mandy. She rushes over to her sister's aid as Jessica stands there a moment touching over her pained cheek before grabbing her purse and storming out of the house.

45

"Jessica, wait!" Mandy calls out, running out of the house behind her. Jessica exits the front door and unknowingly runs into someone. Mandy follows behind her, unable to catch up and stops after Jess bumps into Jaiden. He can tell she has been crying recently. As soon as she bumps into him, he wraps his bulky arms around her and she looks up.

"Jess, what's wrong?" he had asked as she cries silently stiff on his chest, deepening their hug.

"I, I told my parents... they kicked me out of the house and m-my father..." she hyperventilates, unable to finish.

"Jess, what did he do? Did he hurt you?" he worries, pulling away from their hug, cupping her face in his large hands to examine it. He turns her head slightly after noticing she had a red hand imprint on her cheek. She doesn't say anything and it's enough for the boy to know her father has hurt her, he was pissed. "I promise, as long as I'm here, I won't let him hurt you anymore," he promises, kissing her on the forehead and beginning to walk away with his fists clenched to his sides. He would finally confront this man if no one else was going to. No longer would he stand intimidated by her father, not a chance in hell.

"No Jaiden, don't go in there, please!" she cries out. He had ignored her request and marched right inside. Too enraged to use his manners at a time like this, he bounces inside, nearly kicking the door down.

"What the fuck are you doing here? Get out!" Mr. Larson warns. Jaiden's jaw instantly tenses, and he takes a step closer.

"Jaiden, stop!" Jessica yelled beside the door and Mandy too joins her by the doorway seconds later.

"Get out, slut!" Beverly yells.

"Shut the fuck up!" Jaiden spits. That commentary to Jessica's imprudent sister was long overdue.

"Watch your language you little prick!" Mr. Larson growls as his fist encounters with the boy's uneven jaw when taking the first punch. Jaiden punches back in defense, hard. Alan knees Jaiden in the gut and as he's down, he desperately tries standing up but he's no match against her father.

"Daddy, stop!" Jessica cries, running over. Mrs. Larson tries to cease him now too, defending the almost innocent boy.

Jessica tries to stop his fists as he's now throwing punches at Jaiden while he is still down; Alan wanted to kill the boy. The young man's nose begins to bleed and without warning, Alan pushes Jessica out of the way, throwing her to the cold floor. "Jessica!" Mandy exclaims, running over to her aid again and Margret stops fighting to see if Jessica was okay. In the corners of Jaiden's eyes, he can see Beverly smirking while playing with her phone, not giving a care in the world. After Alan

46

pushes Jessica, it sent Jaiden over the edge. He stood back on his feet with his eye blackened, jaw bloody, as well as his nose, and his stomach internally bleeding, and his rib cage being popped open, or so he thinks. He tightens his grip on his fist and takes one final punch where he knew it would hurt the most, the balls.

Mr. Larson kneels in pain and Jaiden punches him once again square in his face. As soon as he's down, Jaiden painfully limps over to Jessica and attempts the best that he can to pick her up and start carrying her out the door.

Her face was pale, and she was obviously unconscious. It was a good thing she was light, for now. "Yeah, you leave and don't come back here! If I ever see your face back here again, you're dead you little son of a bitch! You hear! Your brother too!" her dad yells as Jaiden steps out the door, ignoring his remark.

"Oh my god, check if she's okay!" Mandy panics after Jaiden sets her down in the backseat of her car, adjusting her buckle and hopping in from the other side. He places a hand on her forehead.

"She's still unconscious," he informs Mandy, who begins driving them to the nearest hospital. He puts his seat belt on and tilts her head onto his broad shoulders. "Jared? Yeah, we are taking Jess to the hospital right now, something went down. I'll tell you later, now can you drive here or not?"

"Okay, I'll see you later then," Jaiden finished, hanging up his call.

"Is he coming?" Amanda asks. "Yeah, a little bit later," he responds.

****

"So, is she gonna be alright? Is the baby still okay?" Jaiden impatiently asks at the hospital.

"In other words, yes. She's just unconscious, the baby's left unharmed and you can take her home once she wakes up again," the doctor informs the two. Jared arrives half an hour later and there is still no sign of Jessica waking up anytime soon.

"She's still not awake?" Jared whispered out.

"Yeah, but you don't have to whisper," Jaiden chuckles, "She's out cold bro, she can't hear you."

"Are those flowers for me?" he sarcastically inferred.

"No, they're for Jessica," Jared smiles out when placing the vase full of red roses by her side. He turns back around, taking a seat by his twin. "What the heck happened to your face, dude?" Jared points out.

"Long story," Jaiden sighs.

"Hey Jaiden, I've got to go to work, do you need a ride back?" Mandy asks while re-entering the room. "Oh, hey Jared," she notices him sitting beside Jaiden, he smiles back slightly.

"Yeah, you might want to go start on that project for Baldwin by the way. I've already finished it this morning and you don't know when she is gonna wake up," Jared reminds.

"Yeah, alright," Jaiden answers Mandy as he stands up to get his jacket. "Stay here, make sure she's okay and then when she wakes up, drop her off at my place," Mandy directs.

"Stay away from Jessica's parents' house," Jaiden warns, Jared nods.

"Are you gonna tell me what actually happened, or should I ask Jessica when she wakes up?" he asks.

"No, don't remind her of anything. Now let's go, I'm running late!" Mandy says still waiting by the door. The two head out.

Chapter Three

(Flashback)

Jaiden was swinging still on the swing while Jess too was swinging, being pushed by Jared on the kiddie desolate playground side of the beach. "So, you're really moving out then, huh?" Jared had asked.

She looks to the sand and slides her sandals to stop the swing, "It's not like I have a choice," she whines, turning around to face him, "My parents threw me out of the house and I really wouldn't want to stay there anyways with my father. I believe my options were to abort and live with them or don't and be on my own in disgrace and be shamed on for the rest of my life," she states and Jaiden cringes at the thought, just tracing over his bruised knuckles. Those really were the worst options he's ever heard. She would continuously be abused at home and she would not survive on her own raising the baby. "Mandy is getting blamed and being put in the middle all the time, having to choose to spend time with me or our parents and it's tough for her, I can't keep putting her through the stress by continuing to stay in her care. It's only a matter of time before I overstay my welcome. She has her own life and plus Kevin is back from his business trip and wants a baby. I don't need to hear them trying for one every night, my ears are still ringing," she continues as she shakes the hair away from her face. "She's the only family member I have right now, and I don't want to lose her by coming between my family."

"How are you even going to afford it, Jess?" Jared asks, grabbing onto Jessica's swing chain.

"Don't worry about it. Mandy's already found me a place that's not too far from hers and she's going to help me pay for the first couple of months' rent, but I'm gonna try to look for a job in the meantime," she states, jumping off the swing with a sigh. She starts walking off further down the beach as the twins scatter behind.

"That seems like a lot of work, why don't you just stay at our house for a little while?" Jared asks, catching up to her from her right side.

Jessica laughs, "Yeah and what? Do you really think your parents will allow a girl one of you idiots impregnated, stay at your house?" she laughs again.

"Come on, you're practically family and technically so is this baby," Jared reminds.

"In which world do you expect your mother to wait on me hand and foot for nine months? She would have me evicted before the first trimester!" Jessica tenses, stopping to get through to the hopeful lad.

"Jai, what's the matter? You've been really quiet," Jess points out, waiting for him to catch up as he walked behind slowly, contemplating with his hands in his short pockets.

"Yeah, sorry just thinking," he exhales, pulling his hand out and focusing on his bruised knuckles, tracing over them as he finally reaches his two friends.

"Please just leave it alone, okay?" she asks of him, resting her hand on his bruised palm, gently rubbing over it. He stares up at her gaze, lost for a moment in her gorgeous unnatural emerald green eyes that reflect off the ripples of the waves. She continues by telling them she couldn't even bear the thought to abort, "I'm one-hundred percent against it, it's murder!"

I messed up and this was the consequence I chose to pay the price for.

"Jess, maybe you should reconsider—" Jared starts to say but not before Jessica intervened.

"I am not going to kill my baby, end of discussion."

"We have our careers to think about too," Jaiden chimes in. Jessica was hoping he would stand up for her and tell his idiotic brother that there is a harm in doing that, but of course he cared more for his ongoing legacy that he was trying to build up and maintain.

"I'm sorry, how self-absorbed of me, Jared, Jaiden! God, you guys don't get it, do you? I'm sorry I even brought it up, I'm sorry I thought out of all people, at least you would be supportive of my decisions and be there for me, telling me I'm doing the right thing. Thank you for proving me that I'm completely alone on this!" She distances herself once again. *No one understands me, everyone is saying I should just give up. I'm not going to, I know this affects them probably more than it could affect me with them being semi-famous and all, but I don't need them. I could raise this baby perfectly fine on my own, just me, myself, and I. No family, no friends.*

What struck her the most was how two people could be so inconsiderate; this wasn't just about them or her anymore, it was about this baby. How can they just allow poor Jessica to kill a fetus, theirs anyway?

(Present Day)

There Jared stood another school day, talking with his boys between class periods. He was making indirect eye contact with his obnoxious brother who happened to be standing across the school hallway from Jared with his even larger group of friends. Hobbs and Lucas persuaded Jared to go over there with them to see what was going on tonight and he follows them over to the group.

"Hey, what's going on?" Hobbs asks the crowd of friends.

"Jared, long time no see…" Jaiden tells him, "I haven't seen you at home all week."

"Yeah, I've been staying over at…"

"Jessica's?"

Jared nods uncomfortably, putting his hands in his tight pants' pockets. "Baby stuff…" he shrugs.

"So, are you guys a thing now?" Jaiden chuckles out nervously, awaiting an answer.

"It's all he ever talks about!" their mutual friend Skylar adds on.

"That's uh… I'm happy for you two, you guys deserve each other," Jaiden lies in spite of his jealousy, unsure of how to react.

"Just like you deserve me!" Candi exclaims, pulling on his cheek muscles as she begins making out with him in front of his group of friends. Aggravated, he slams his locker shut and makes his way out of the school building.

"So, what's going on tonight?" Hobbs asks impatiently again after Candi walks away from the group. "Josh's throwing another party, it's going to be epic! The party of the year! You guys in?" said some blond kid whose face looked a little familiar.

"I'm sorry, who are you?" Lucas asked.

"Name's Alex, I'm new. Just flew in a couple of weeks ago from Alabama to live with my sister," he explains to the group while shaking Lucas' hand.

"Who's your sister, and is she hot?" Skylar asks. His girlfriend, Becca, nudges him in the arm from beside.

"This is Alex, Staci's little bro," Hobbs clarifies. It was a no wonder why he looked vaguely familiar, he looked like Staci… but only if he had a blonde wig and fake breasts. "Griffins told me to keep an eye on him in school," Hobbs explains, wrapping an arm around the kid.

"So, are you guys in?" Alex asks again. The rest of the guys and Becca nod.

"I actually can't, I promised I'd do something with Jessica tonight," the love-sick boy admits.

"Come on chill with us, don't be a wuss and just take a rain-check," Lucas says. It takes a few moments for the young man to think about it before finally giving in, earning a pat on the back from his boys.

In the meantime, Jessica had just got off the phone with Jared, who had told her he had to cancel their plans due to a common cold. *Poor baby, he's sick.* She knew just how to cheer him up, with her special soup. They didn't necessarily have to go out like they had intended—she wouldn't mind taking care of him while he is sick, if it meant spending any time with him at all. After all, they could always just stay in and cuddle. She skips off the couch and makes her way to the kitchen to start preparing.

****

"This is a great party bro!" Jaiden grins, patting Josh on the shoulder.

"We've got a great show coming up! My brother hired us some exotic dancers!" Josh explained over the loud music. Jaiden then, glanced around the room to examine the party from his stance. He saw Candi talking with her small clique in one corner, and in another corner, he saw Lindsay and Lacey making out in only their bikinis, and it was turning him on. He continued to look around the room until he spotted Staci, the third power-puff, sitting on the kitchen counter and making out with some foreign dude, and across from them, he saw Nick playing beer pong with a bunch of chicks, one wrapped around his waist. His eyes make a full 180 around the room, stopping when he finds his brother at the entrance—walking in with his lame group of friends. They walked up to Jaiden, surrounded by his group, before he immediately walked away, leaving Josh, Sienna, Skylar, and Becca amongst themselves.

"Babe, let's go dance!" Sienna whines, tugging on Josh's arm. She drags him out to the living room where the rest of the party was at.

"So, what do you guys want to do?" Jared asks.

"I think I'm gonna go help Lindsay and Lacey over there, anyone wanna come?" Hobbs asks.

"Yeah sure, let's go," Alex agrees, leaving Jared alone with Lucas, Skylar, and Becca. As the rest of them talk amongst themselves now, all the lights completely dim and come back on seconds later, followed by smoky glass and a bunch of half-dressed women appearing all around the party, making their way to the set-up stage in Josh's living room. The rest of the crowd soon follows them to the living room where the dancers began dancing in their cages as the DJ switched up the music.

52

"Didn't take you long to forget me, I see," a tiny voice behind Jared says, causing him to turn around.

"Jared?" she squints, approaching closer. "…Oh my gosh, I'm so sorry—I thought you were Jaiden. I almost forgot he had a twin!" Courtney laughs out. *Yeah, her along with almost everyone else.* Seconds later, the strippers exit their platforms and the music transitions.

"Wanna dance?" she asks.

"Yeah sure."

After all, it's just a dance.

****

"Get out!" Candi demands to the couple that was sucking face on the bed in the room the two had entered. The frightened, under-aged couple nodded and pardoned hurriedly. She lays down on the bed, pulling Jaiden down with her as she sloppily leaves kisses all over his face. She helped him take off his button up shirt and discarded it to the floor, continuing off during their heated session. She removes her blouse and he parts his lips whilst she pulls her blouse over her head causing Jaiden to picture none other than Jessica's beautiful face on her body.

"This is so wrong," he mumbles, leaning forward, sinking into her lips. After she tosses her blouse, she flips them both over while still kissing him and she moves her hands to the clasp of her bra but Jaiden resists, recoiling away.

"Candi, wait stop. I can't do this," he sighs as she cuts him off with her lips once again. He pulls away again, "No please, I mean it," he pleads again, sitting up. She shot up from the bed, sliding her blouse back on.

"I don't even know why I try to waste my time with you, you're such a loser," she scoffed, shutting the door behind her on her way out.

****

Jessica had finished making the soup within an hour maximum and decided against letting Jared know she was coming over. Knowing him, he'd probably tell her to not come near so she wouldn't catch anything either. Now all that was left was to deliver her company. Amanda had lent Jessica her car for the week. Upon arrival, she steps out of her Toyota Prius and walks up to his front door with a container of hot soup in her hands, knocking impatiently yet anxiously.

"Oh, hey Nora," she greets as Jared's older sister opens the door. "Hey Jess," she awkwardly grins. It took Jessica a while to realize Jared was not home after she had peered around the Daniels' driveway and noticed that neither of the twins' car is home. Nora must have noticed because she then told the friend that Jared and Jaiden weren't in fact home.

"They went to a party… I thought you knew?" she asks confused.

"No, but thanks for letting me know… and if you cannot mention I was here?" Jessica requests and Nora nods understandingly. Jessica disappointingly begins to walk back to her car—And during her walk, she begins to skepticize why Jared would lie to her in the first place? She had figured he went to Josh's party since that was the only party she heard that was happening this week. She wondered, *Was he cheating on me?* It was convenient Josh's house wasn't too far of a drive from theirs. She decided she would drive to this 'party' to see for herself what was going on and maybe even give him a piece of her mind for lying to her. A piece for Jaiden last month, a piece for Jared now, she was almost brain dead by now.

Courtney kicks the door open to the guest room impatiently. Her and Jared had stumbled in on a naked Griffins tied up to the bed with his mouth duct taped shut. He yells for their attention and Jared runs to his aid, ripping off the duct tape. "Can you help me out with these ties? A stripper hustled me out my clothes and my wallet," he panicked. With Jared's help, he successfully un-knotted the ties that relieved him from the bed. Zach then picks up his boxers and puts them on about to exit the room while the younger gentleman tries to avert his eyes.

"So… uh," Jared nervously speaks, sitting on the bed.

"Where were we?" Courtney asks, making her way to the bed as she takes a seat next to a nervous Jared. She stares into his soul and he felt himself reeling in, unable to resist those hazel eyes, resting his thumb on her chin as he pulls her face closer. Jessica arrived at the party, entering the door, and there, she recognized some of Jared's friends in the distance.

"Hey Hobbs, hey Rogers, where's Jared?" she asks approaching them. They shake their heads unknowingly, causing the girl to groan. Now she knew he was most definitely hiding out here, because boys will be boys. She makes her way around the first floor, pushing her way past the herd of people in search of Jared with her car keys in hand, wearing a trench coat, uggs, and a beanie. She must look foolish showing up to a party dressed like this, but she didn't care because she did not plan to be at this party, again. She figured the main reason for all her glares tonight was because of her very visible stomach but again, she did not care, she wore her baby proudly on her stomach showing it off every chance she got; she became closer to her baby, no doubt, and adoption was always out of the question.

As she reached the top of the stairs, she found Jaiden wandering the hallways. *So not the twin I was looking for, she thought.*

He jogs up to the pregnant female once he recognizes her from afar. "Jess? What the hell are you doing here?" he asks just as surprised to see her.

"Nice to know I've been missed," she rolled her eyes, pushing past him to try and find Jared.

"Not what I meant," he says following behind the girl again.

"Shouldn't you be with Cassie?" Jessica irritably asks, trying so desperately to get him to leave her presence.

"Candi?" he asks. "About her…"

She had ignored his presence in her hunt for Jared, checking each room in a step ahead of Jaiden who pestered behind. "Why the hell are there so many rooms!" She groans after opening several of them to find either an empty room or invading the privacy of a couple in the process of having sex. "Sorry," she apologetically says before closing that last door in the hallway.

"Hey Jessica!" Griffins greets when making his way toward the girl in only his boxers. "We can't keep meeting like this," he dramatically speaks, and the girl is getting more tensed by the second.

"Have you seen Jared by chance?" she asks annoyed now.

"Yeah, he's with Courtney," he mistakenly slurs with a light chuckle.

"COURTNEY?" Jessica crescendos a little too loudly. *That* drew the line—her 'jealous girlfriend bitch mode' was on, full blast.

"Did you check our guest room?" Jaiden asks. "Yeah, if I knew where it was!"

She follows him around the top of the staircase as he leads the way. "Stand back," he warns after rattling the locked door a few times with no response. She takes a step back and he pushes through the door, breaking it down. In that moment, he was just as surprised as she was that those football games actually paid off. Jessica took one step inside the room, switching on the light and gasps at the sight in front. Jared was in the room, sleeping with a thin cover on his body and some naked brunette sleeping on his chest.

"Jared Jasper Daniels!" an enraged Jessica belts, hoping to wake him. Fear strikes his eyes as soon as he awakes.

"J-Jessica?" he crinkles his eyes in confusion. He stares at his surroundings, pupils dilating the instant he saw a girl wrapped around his body. He gets up, covering himself with a blanket draped around his waist. The people from the party begin crowding around the hallway, peeking through the open door. "I-I can explain," he stutters. Jessica stood there interested to know how he would dig himself out of this one. Flustered, he can't think of a good explanation.

"I can't explain," he sighs. Jessica drops her head.

The brunette yawns, waking up. "Oh shit," Courtney mutters loud enough for the crowded parade of people outside of the door to hear.

"Courtney? You banged my ex-bro!" Jaiden chuckles as Courtney rolls her eyes.

Jared starts to justify the situation, "It's not what—"

She cut him off, "You lied to me for this!" she shrieked, "I trusted you, how could you do this to me!" He sprung out of bed to chase the humiliated girl that had turned around and faced the floor. She had shot her face in his direction after hearing a thud and saw him lying on the floor now. It appeared that he had tripped on his covers. His naked body had been exposed and everyone instantly begun flashing their cameras. He gets back up, and in an attempt to cover his hard parts with one hand, he reaches out to stop her with another but not before she spoke out again. She resentfully stared into the soul of someone she would no longer address to as a boyfriend, "Don't touch me… never again." She let her emotions get the better of her when looking into his guilty, unfaithful eyes. He neglected her and in that moment, as much as she wanted to physically hurt him, she fled without another word, out of the house that is filled with bad memories, once again.

She heard footsteps running up behind, calling out her name and chose to ignore it, proceeding in her path. As soon as Jaiden caught up, he pushed her car door shut with his hand before standing in front of her, blocking the gloomy girl's path. "Move," she demanded, averting eye contact. He denied her request. Agitated, she turned around to walk the distance instead, away from Jaiden. It wasn't long before he ran up behind the stubborn girl again.

"Where are you going?" he asks.

"Home," she said.

He asked, "Please just talk to me?"

"No! Please just leave me alone! I'm done with this, I'm done with you," she indicated, crossing her arms after wiping under her tear-stained eyes.

"In case you couldn't tell—like most people who confuse us both, I'm not Jared," he chuckles, trying to keep up with her fast speed.

"Well, I'm not most people and unlike those people, I don't want anything to do with 'either' of you anymore," she persists. The two ended up walking in the woods near Josh's house. She had hoped to find a shortcut but didn't know which direction she was supposed to travel to get home but she didn't care, she just wanted to leave.

"Wait, what did I do?"

"It's not what you did do, it's what you didn't do, Jaiden."

"I'm not following."

"Keep up Jaiden, this isn't rocket science," she sighed.

"Huh?"

She only took a couple of steps away from him before realizing she had not watched where she was going. She had stumbled on a tree branch in that second and as she prepared to fall to her death, with her life instantaneously flashing before her very eyes, she was saved by a pair of arms, Jaiden's. She gawked at his face in awe as she thought about the turn of events. Maybe she was destined to come here tonight to fall in love with Jaiden. "Y-you saved us," she admirably recites when standing back up straight with his help. He shifts the weight between his heels and toes awkwardly. As a token of her appreciation, she leans in and presses her hand to his cheek, pressing a soft kiss upon it. He turns his head around, transforming the kiss to both of their lips.

She instantly shrieked in repulse when shoving his body off her, "What the hell is wrong with you! You don't just go around kissing your brother's girlfriend!" she scoffed. The moment was ruined.

"Ex-girlfriend..." he reminds. She rolls her eyes, walking away from him until she came across the tree that started it all. "Don't tell me you didn't like it because I know you felt something—" He stopped to stare at this gigantic tree that stood before him. And as much as it killed Jessica to admit inside, she did like the feeling of his lips against hers, or maybe it was just the vulnerability talking. Jaiden was the first to eagerly climb up, helping the pregnant female inside as well.

"This tree house looks so familiar," she says as they both stand inside.

"That's because Jared and I," he starts, and the girl instantly shoots him a death glare for mentioning that god forsaken name. He clears his throat before speaking again, "My brother and I sneaked you out here when we were kids."

"It was your eighth birthday and J' and I were invited to this spoiled rich kid's party... we wanted to hang out with you, but our parents forced us out of the house to socialize and make new friends. We ended up telling that kid about you and he told us of how he wanted to meet you, so we got on our bicycles and we rode over to your house."

"I remember now... I was crying so hard that day because I just wanted to play with my friends and nobody even remembered my birthday," she sniffles.

"We hung out by this tree," he adds. "I remember being so happy that you guys remembered my birthday and I didn't have to spend my birthday alone," she smiles in reminiscence.

"We came up here later, just us two after Jared and Josh left to go play video games," he continues, taking a seat on the wooden flooring as she mirrors him.

"Oh my God, Joshua! How could I forget!" she exclaims. She knew something about him was vaguely familiar. She could never forget a face.

"Yeah, been good friends with that rich kid ever since," he chuckles.

"So... after?" she peers, hoping to see if he remembered. He presses his forehead to hers and she gradually shuts her eyes. He slowly presses his lips to hers before reclining back and opening his eyes as she does the same. She bites her lip and blushes, looking down at the hardwood floor.

"You were my first kiss," he admits when resting his hand over her rested palm from the floor.

She smiled back at him, "You were mine too..." With that, he met her stare with his hungry lips that pressed back on hers and she locked her hands around his neck. She didn't hesitate this time. He trailed his kisses down to her neck and she throws her head back in pleasure.

"So beautiful," he craved, and she giggles, pushing his face away as soon as his sloppy kisses reached her cleavage.

"I'm pregnant," she reminded.

"If you're trying to turn me off, you're going to have to try harder," he teases.

"You're a perv," she giggled, pushing him in the chest playfully. She turns her head after he returned with the blankets and pillows from the back, in hand. He sprawls the blankets out next to her while she scoots herself over to sit on them. She fluffs the pillow behind and laid down as he did the same.

"Jess?" he calls out.

"Mmmmhmm?" she yawned, tiresome.

He starts to talk, only to realize she was fast asleep. He sat up to pull the covers over her body, not caring about the need of warmth for his own body. He then, reached over to turn the overhead lamp off.

Forty-five minutes went by when Jessica had abruptly awoken from her haunting dream. It was almost vivid because for the most part, it was real. She dreamt some different flashbacks of her father striking her in her childhood, a quick flash later and the images scattered to Jared having sex with that brunette whose name she didn't care to remember. Next, the painful memory flashes of Jaiden and Candace at the scene of

58

the cafe, and finally another flash later of Jaiden and Beverly; that does the trick. She awoke completely drenched in her own sweat. She looks around her surroundings, placing a hand to her sweated forehead, breathing rapidly to match her heartbeat. She turned over to find Jaiden still sound asleep, unaffected by her panic, he just rolled over to the other side. That is when Jessica thought long and hard to remember something he too did, that hurt her deeply—What was worse, was knowing that he still had not thought to own up to it after so many years that passed by; *Best friends, yeah right.* She shared everything with them both, that was her mistake—you can never trust anyone in this town, and that was the climax of her whole charade. She slowly and steadily got up when removing the warm covers from her body. Not wanting to wake him, she grabs her coat and carefully climbs down the tree.

It wasn't until he was rattled out of his deep slumber that Jaiden noticed Jessica was no longer beside him. He combed the hair out of his face before sliding into his shoes and too climbing out of the tree in search of Jessica. It was morning now, which meant he had a better chance of finding her from far away in this daytime. In fact, he found her not too far away, walking towards her car in Josh's parking lot, he ran up to her. "Hey, where are you going?" he puffs, out of breath.

"Not in the mood—" she avoids, bitterly crossing over her arms.

"Aw, no kiss goodbye?" he pouts.

"Why don't you ask Beverly," she huffs when continuously walking away.

"Beverly?" He soured his face in confusion.

She narrowed her eyes before continuing to speak her thoughts, "Tell me, do you have a thing for my sister or was it just a one-time thing like you've been doing with all the girls around here?"

"Oh God, what lies has she been feeding you now?"

"It doesn't matter what she said, the point is that you did it and you had the decency to keep something this big from me! I thought we were friends… guess I was wrong," she negligently concludes before walking away. He tries catching up to her once again, successfully stopping her with an arm to her elbow to pull her aside.

"Okay, I don't know what she told you but it's obviously wrong and for the record, I'm the victim in this, not her!" he insisted while she faced him, placing her hands on her hips. "Okay, yes we did have sex, b-but… she tricked me! S-she—" he protested before she cut him off again, "Unbelievable!" she scoffed and shook her head in disbelief. "Do you wanna know what happened or not?" he urged. "I don't know what to believe anymore, Jaiden!"

"It's in your nature, to lie. It must run in the family I guess! Fourteen years Jaiden, fourteen years and you have not opened-up to me about anything! Silly me for trusting you with my life, right? I should have known better. My friendship obviously means nothing to you!"

"Alright you want me to open up? Then have it! After we had sex, *assuming she already told you her side of things, I'll spare you the gruesome details,*" he narrowed his eyes, "She stepped out to get some 'fresh air' when really, she took and hid all my clothes. When it was still dark, I thought it would be the best time to go find my clothes without exposing myself. The noises faded so I thought everyone was asleep or headed home. As soon as I stepped out, the camera and lights began flashing, I was embarrassed! And I 'hated' Beverly and her friends ever since! Ever since, she has always been making me do stuff for her and I couldn't say no because she threatened to expose me with those pictures!"

"A-and I didn't tell you because I didn't want to be reminded again! … Jessica," he sighs, stepping forward, "I don't care anymore, those pictures mean nothing to me, it's all over now! I've been on the other end of the stick and I know what it's like to be humiliated!"

"Enough!" she shouted. "Don't take another step!" she warned. "I'm sorry if I gave you the wrong impression, but I-I-I… I still love Jared, I've moved on… I'm tired of waiting. At a time, I thought I loved you, but I got so tired of waiting for something to happen but Jared—Jared has always been there for me, not you," she harshly admitted, and Jaiden pulls his slick gelled hair back in frustration.

"You can't be serious!" he spat, "You were practically ready to throw yourself at me yesterday!" As soon as the words mistakenly spill from his mouth, her mouth drops, and she shakes her head in disbelief once again, folding her arms and pushing past the boy, as she speedily walks away from him again. "I'm sorry—I didn't mean it like that! … Jess!"

Even though he tried to protest, there was no point because she chose to ignore him when already in her car and backing out of the parking lot, driving off quickly while leaving skid marks on the street.

****

After Jared had returned from the hospital that following morning, he walked straight into his bedroom safely, not running into his parents, shutting the door behind and anemically crawling into his covers with all that remained of his dignity. He whimpers in pain as he sets the block of ice down on his groin given to him by the care of the hospital. The doctor recommended him to ice his genitals to make the swelling disappear since his erection never deflated and now there were pictures everywhere from last night's scandal to prove it. *Why did I have to do what I did? I was only drunk enough to know what I was getting myself into, but I don't remember why.* Maybe it was because of his constant desire to be as cool as his brother that led him into this situation, although he'd hate to admit that to his brother himself. Speaking of his brother, who not to mention, left him all alone in his shamed mess and didn't even come to see if his own blood was okay. *Yeah,* that douche walked through his door just now and didn't even knock upon entering. Jared painfully rolls over to the other side of his bed before his brother had fully entered. "Dude, school is starting in half an hour, get up!" Jaiden reminds.

"Gee, I'm great Jai, thanks for asking. On second thought, I think I WILL go to school with my giant boner," he sarcastically grunts, causing the older brother to let out a cackle.

"That bad, huh?"

"No, 'that bad' would have been when my 'girlfriend' decided to play hide and go seek and found me in bed with some random girl I had no intention of being with last night!"

"Well... if it's any consolation, it's not that big so you don't have to worry about hiding it," Jaiden jokes out. In an attempt to turn around to throw a pillow at him, very feeble, he misses with his very sore arm from football practice a couple of days back.

"Better hurry up, you don't want to be late," Jared grunts when scooting back down under his bed covers.

"Fine whatever, you have fun feeling sorry for yourself," Jaiden shrugs, turning back around to exit.

"Hey Jai?" Jared calls out.

"Yeah?" he asks, turning his attention.

"Did... 'she' say anything?"

"Who?" Jaiden asks.

"Jessica... I-I saw you following her out last night, I thought maybe you spoke?"

"No man, she already left by the time I caught up, sorry," he quickly denies as he then walks out the door. Seconds later, he walks back in.

"By the way, Courtney? My ex? Really bro?" Jai chuckles. In annoyance, Jared throws another pillow at him causing him to laugh his way out the door.

****

As for the erectile dysfunctional teenager, he pulled into his school's parking lot after the tent in his trousers finally disappeared, and scurried into the building, just barely making it to his first period by a long shot. He entered the doorway, making his way over to his seat, earning a few glances and chuckles from all around the room, ignoring them all. "Hey Daniels!" a kid named Robbie whispered from behind. Robbie was a Hispanic kid with dark hair and a decent tan. He always wore these tanks to show off his muscles, he was slightly bigger than Jared, that's for sure. He also slightly intimidated Jared. He knew it sounded crazy, but it wasn't just a movie stereotype, Robbie really 'was' a bully. *Everyone has their bullies and I have mine,* except for Jaiden since he was socially acceptable.

Jared chose to ignore Robbie when reaching into his book bag to get his binder together. "How's your little friend doing?" Robbie taunts followed by laughter from all his equally immature friends. Jared decided against shooting a look in his direction, not giving him the satisfaction. Instead, he shook his head before returning to search in his book bag for a pencil.

"Okay class, please get out your copy of Shakespeare's *Hamlet,*" their English teacher announced. Jared, about to dig into his backpack again to find his copy, is interrupted when his phone starts violently buzzing in his pants' pocket. He checks his notifications under the table, hoping not to get caught. He accidentally accepts a picture message from an unknown number. It was an embarrassing nude picture of himself sent to his phone from last night's party. He automatically figured Robbie had sent it since he heard laughing coming from his direction as soon as he scanned it. He turns his head around to look at him and Robbie puts his thumb and his pointer finger together, leaving a small space in between.

"The itty bitty Jare-Bear went up the water spout," the kid taunted causing Jared to roll his eyes. *God damn Jaiden for getting so intensely shit-faced at that one party that one time and blabbing out that ridiculous childhood nickname given to me by our mother.*

He shifts his head back around at the sound of his teacher's voice, "Jared, is there a reason you don't have your book out yet and following along?" his female teacher asks, gradually lowering her glasses.

"Uh, I uh…" he stuttered profoundly.

"Get your book out and follow along and put your phone away unless you want a detention," she warned. He nodded and flipped his book open, following along as she continues to read aloud to the class. Ten minutes pass and he is unable to concentrate, lack of sleep has his arm rested on his desk with his hand rested on his cheek, about to fall into exhaust.

Just then, he felt his phone buzzing from beyond his pocket again causing him to jolt awake and sit up straight. He decided to check his messages when the teacher walked off in the other direction, off in her thoughts about *Hamlet*. Deep down, he had hoped it was from Jess. He had been wrong when he took a gander under the table; it was from Robbie... again. He accepts the message and the loud sound from the video begins playing. His phone blasted at full volume while he struggled to find a way to shut it off. It was too late; the whole classroom froze to stare at the disturbance he has caused as the teacher did too with her arms now heavily crossed. It was a very shaky video from the party five months ago of when Jared was licking peanut butter off his brother's chest. Jared didn't even realize Robbie had been there considering he's never seen him at these parties before, maybe it was someone else who shared it and Robbie had been the messenger. He finally holds down the power button, shutting off his glitched phone completely. "Jared Daniels, pack up your stuff and make your way to the principal's office," his teacher demanded.

"B-bb-but," he stuttered, looking over at Robbie. "You know how strict our school's policy is about having phones in class," she reminds with a finger pointing out the door. Jared groans, collects his materials back in his backpack, stands up with his backpack swung around his back—roughly pushing in his chair before finally storming right out of the classroom and snatching the slip right from his teacher on his way out. He was a good student. Now with one little slip up, it was going to stand permanently on his academic records and he was hoping to run for student council, *guess that's out of the question now.*

"Oh, hey Jared!" a cheerful voice greets from behind causing the boy to swivel around.

"Oh... hey Courtney," he awkwardly greets.

"Sounds like you're disappointed to see me, maybe I should leave," she frowns, turning around in hopes of him begging her to stay.

"No... no, I j-just," he is unable to come into sorts, but she turns back around again anyways, sliding her book bag strap up.

"So, what are you doing walking here all by your lonesome self? Shouldn't you be in class?" she asks.

"Detention... long story," he says waving his slip.

"What about you?"

"Running errands for the office."

"Oh, that's right, you're a—"

"T.A," they both say in unison.

"So, uh…" he fumbles over his diction, nervously scratching the back of his head.

"Listen, I'm sorry if I've caused you any problems last night, I shouldn't have—"

"No, it was my fault. I should've told you I was in a relationship and stopped myself from doing what we did."

"I understand completely. I hope after all, we could still stay friends… but yesterday was a complete mistake, I don't know why it even happened, it was wrong. I mean, you're Jaiden's brother for one… m-maybe I just thought—"

"That I could replace Jaiden since we look alike?" he interrupted in annoyance.

"What? N-no… I-I mean… I d-don't know, I think I still may have feelings for him, you just reminded me of him last night and maybe that's w-why—"

Yeah, her along with every other girl he's slept with would agree that they still have feelings for my brother. Jared didn't blame him, he was the real ladies' man among the two, the panty dropper as they would call him.

"Yeah, 'friends'…" he quoted. "See you around Court," he pardoned, making his way to the principal's office. *Wow. I feel so used and betrayed right now. I know we barely know each other, but wow I could just imagine the pain Jess is going through, she has it even worse than I do. Stupid, stupid, Jared.*

****

After having arrived home, Jessica had kicked off her shoes in the living room and made her way into her bedroom, swiveling around to push her door shut then trailing back around to throw her coat to the floor. She had spotted a glass cup that glistened on her nightstand from the small amount of sunlight that shone in through her window and made her way over to it. She threw it against her wall with great force, feeling a rush of emotions overpower her judgment to not even realize or feel that the remaining glass pieces, slit the insides of her palms. She goes to grab something else, feeling powerless and useless, hoping to regain energy from the next item. There, she found a picture of herself along with Jared and Jaiden from when they went snowboarding in Vancouver about two years ago with their family. She reminiscences those good times when they were all just friends, no feelings, no relationships, no complications, no lies, no strings attached, and most importantly, no stress. She grows angrier by the second as the bad memories flood to the back of her mind again and with maximum effort, throws it against the wall while screeching at the top of her lungs. The mixture of adrenaline and anxiety caused her to look around the room for more glass items, unable to find any in the room. As she begins to scan through drawers, she comes across one of Jared's white shirts from when he spent the night a few days ago. It gives her such pain just looking at it, so she starts pulling it apart in hopes of ripping it but fails miserably just like at everything else in life. She crumbled to the floor and combusts. Only then does she notice the blood from her hands dripping to her wrists and leaking through the cotton white shirt fabric. She couldn't feel the pain because the only thing that hurt worse was her heart and now that it's broken she knew there was nothing left to feel. She took the shirt and begun crying onto it, lifting her head up once to notice the mascara stains that have drowned the shirt when feeling the mascara running down her cheeks and seeping into her skin.

She shoved her face back in the shirt and could still smell his sweet, fresh scent, whirling in her nostrils. "Why did you do this to me!" she sobs, muttering into the shirt. She tried so hard to just forget everything. She threw the shirt to the floor beside her in her rampage and looks to her wet, red hands. She attempts to extract the small glass pieces from her hands, but it was in way too deep now. She looked back over across from where she had been sitting and the rest of the glass illuminates from the floor. She hesitantly takes one of the closer, larger pieces, assuming it was from the frame and sits there a moment, wondering if she should do what she was about to do. She was alone, she had no other choice. Depression had fully blown over her and without further thought, she could just ignore her problems but that wouldn't help anyone. She would still be alone. Her actions were impulsive, and no one could change her mind beyond this point. *I have no family, an abusive father, no one left to trust and everyone I've ever loved or cared for, was slipping through my fingers, thinner and faster than this blood. Time was inevitable, it was now or never.* She couldn't possibly feel anymore hurt than she felt at this moment, so this should be quick and easy, painless. She let out a deep breath, not wasting another minute. She begins to engrave deep cuts into her skin, letting all the blood drip to the carpet beneath her. She instantly drops the sharp glass after lacerating her wrist, to shriek out in pain, holding onto her wrists. She had been wrong, she regretted it in an instant. She still felt something after all. She panics after her eyes begin to fade in and out. Her eyes then come across her stomach and she felt a dense pressure, endless pain that no one individual could tolerate. She did not even think of what was to come for the future of her child, how could she have been so selfish? Her blood continues gushing out faster and she continues to lay there helplessly, crying out in pain, unable to move or get help. The room begins spinning from the amount of blood lost. She soon heard indistinct poundings at her front door. "Please save us," she faintly requests, her skin as white as snow now. The voice soon comes closer. "Jessica!" a familiar male voice yells. Her mind was blurred, vision was foggy. All she could see was a blurred shadow who now appeared beside her. The shadow lifted her wrists before taking the blood-covered shirt that laid right beside them both to tear it with his teeth, successfully wrapping it tight around her wounds to attempt to stop the gushing. "W-why would you do this?" the voice cries out, cradling her in a hug as she stills violently, trembling in fear. Her mind soon flutters a few times around the room before everything goes blank and she follows a white light into the unconscious world.

They both continue to sit on the floor, with her back leaning against Jaiden, he weeps while he holds her wrists to apply extra pressure to the tied shirt in hopes of preventing the blood to stop gushing and for the skin to start healing. He feels the blood seeping out. Her head falls back on his chest and he noticed that she's now completely unconscious. She was still alive, yes, but he didn't know for how much longer. In panic, he takes his blood-covered hands to reach for his phone and dials the paramedics. He then calls Amanda and she tells him she will meet them at the hospital. When he finishes, he drops his phone on the floor and decides against on letting Jared know. "You're gonna be all right baby, I promise," he coos, cradling her body. *Baby, shit.* He had completely forgotten about the baby, he had hoped she was alright too. Time passes, and the paramedics come in, rolling in a stretcher. "Careful, she's pregnant," he warns as they detach Jessica from his warmth, laying her gently on the stretcher. He stands up and tailgates behind them outside to the ambulance.

"Excuse me sir, you aren't allowed in unless you're family," the woman addresses. "Damn right I am, I knew this woman since we were babies and I am practically the closest thing she has to family right now!" he vindicated, trying to move past her.

"I'm sorry sir—"

Jaiden knew he had to think fast before they rolled off without him. He had to prove himself to Jessica again, he could not let his brother win. He needed to be there for her now. "God dammit! That's... that's my baby in there!" he ordered, even though it wasn't necessarily true. The paramedic sighed, making way for the concerned young man to pass. So, he quickly hops up the van as the paramedics shut the door behind. They have her using a respirator to give her oxygen. He grabs her cold hand leaving a kiss to her cold palm.

After some time in the ambulance, she had opened her eyes weakly, fluttering her eyelids to find Jaiden to her left. "Jess! You're awake!" he exclaimed. From his bloody hands she had realized that it was he who was at her apartment earlier when she was faint, she slightly smiled in acknowledgment and he took her hand in his. She uses her vacant hand to remove the respirator off her face. "J-Jaiden... h-how d-did you g-get inside?" she wondered in confusion after remembering that only Jared had a spare key.

****

Kevin returns from the reception desk with another shrug and Amanda sighs, no word on her sister yet. He takes a seat next to his concerned wife.

"Where are they? She should've been checked in here by now," she stated and seconds later Kevin's phone goes off.

"Hang on, I've got to take this, business," he says excusing himself up to leave and Amanda nods respectfully. Minutes later, the door swings open and in rushed a hospital stroller, some nurses, paramedics, and Jaiden. She immediately rushes over to them in aid of her sister. As Mandy and Jaiden follow behind the nurses, Jaiden is suddenly pulled away by the call of his name followed by an unfriendly shove.

Annoyed, he shouted, "Ouch, what?" he turned around.

"You stole my key!" Jared argues. "J-Jared, w-what are you doing here?" Jaiden chuckles nervously.

"Here to comfort a friend," he replied. "H-how did—"

"I find out? You see, Mandy was generous enough to call and see if I knew what happened since she 'was' my girlfriend!"

"Key word, 'was'. Mandy doesn't know what you did to her! God, if she only knew that you're the reason she's in here in the first place!" Jaiden argues.

"Please, we all know you were the last one with her after the party," Jared accused.

"Yeah, alright. I might have been with her but at least I wasn't as sleazy and STUPID as you to cheat! At least all of my faults happened when we 'weren't' together," Jaiden justifies, crossing over his arms.

"You must be out of your damn mind if you think she will leave me for you after everything 'we've' had!" Jared emphasized.

"What's that supposed to mean, you little shit!" Jaiden snapped, gritting his teeth.

"You know EXACTLY what it means! It's the only reason why she would ever think to look in your direction!" Jared yells, shoving him on the chest. At this point, Jaiden couldn't contain his anger anymore, it's been stored up for a long time and he chose now to take it out on his brother. Jaiden throws the first punch, aiming right at his brother's jaw. Jared swings back but not before Jaiden had blocked his fist with his hand and tackled him to the floor. "C'mon Jaiden!" Jared huffed while being suffocated by his malicious twin. "Show me what you've learned in all those football practices you've missed like the little bitch you are!" Jared aggravated purposely, flipping them both over. He begins swinging on his older brother as Jaiden tries pushing him off.

"Boys! Boys!" the receptionist shouts. She grabs ahold of the phone and calls for security over the intercom. Kevin instantly rushes over and pulls Jared to his feet, restraining him away from the other one as the two security guards rush over and pulled Jaiden away as well. "You're the worst brother, ever!" Jared cries out, trying to pull away from his restrains.

"Yeah well… I wish I never even had a twin!" Jaiden shouts.

"Rot in hell!" Jared fires back and Jaiden rips away from the guards as soon as they let go before beginning to walk off in the opposite direction to find a bathroom, with his bloody and broken nose. On the other side of things, Jared had made his way to Jessica's room after Kevin let go of his hold on the boy. He had finally lucked into finding the room on his own after going in several circles.

"I'm sorry, but you aren't allowed to enter unless you're primary family," says a short female physician just as he stepped inside.

"Then why is HE here?" Jared emphasized when eyeing Jaiden who sat in the visitor chair beside Jessica's aid.

"He's the father." Jared shoots his gaze in Jaiden's direction again and gives him the dirtiest of looks, narrowing his eyes.

"Unbelievable," is all he let out before walking out and letting the door snap closed behind him. *Jaiden 2 – Jared 0.*

****

"Mr. Daniels, Mrs. Anderson," the doctor called out when walking back into the room where Amanda and Jaiden had been nervously waiting for a result of some sort. "She's okay," the doctor announces causing Jaiden to let out a sigh of relief.

"My sister or the baby?" Amanda worriedly asks.

"Your sister… the fetus on the other hand, is being examined…" Amanda's heart skips a beat.

68

"You see, Ms. Larson lost a lot of blood, giving barely any flow through the baby's blood supply. If it wasn't for this young man, tying her wrists tight enough to prevent the blood from spilling out even further and start the healing process, the infant would've had no blood left in its system and you would've lost them both," he finishes. Amanda brings her arms to wrap the savior in for a tight hug. "Thank you so much, you saved my sister's life!" She sobs onto his broad and open shoulders.

"So, what's the problem?" Jaiden asks, causing Mandy to pull away, wiping under her eyes, dwelling further worry.

"We are trying to figure out if the loss of blood could affect the infant's development in any way."

"Meaning?" Mandy asks.

"It's possible, she's at risk for losing the baby soon."

****

Jared, who anxiously sits in the waiting room with Kevin, develops a massive headache thanks to Jaiden. Thirty minutes pass by when he notices Jaiden walking out with his hands slicking his hair back and letting out a deep breath when taking his seat to Jared's right. "Is everything okay?" Jared asks, feeling the most bit of distraught. When he doesn't get a response, he bends down to put his hands in his face, rubbing it out of frustration. He then, courageously stands up and makes his way over to the room for the decisive moment. He enters, and Mandy turns around from staring at a blank hospital bed. Now he was really worried from the way she looked at him with watery, bloodshot eyes. She roams over to him, wrapping her arms around him in support. "W-where's Jessica?" he asks confused. Seconds later, the door swings open and they roll in Jessica on a mobile hospital gurney. "Patient began hemorrhaging during procedure, lost a large amount of blood already," a nurse speaks out.

At this moment, Jared could barely keep up with these fast-paced doctors in this fast-paced environment and all these medical terms. "What procedure? W-where's the baby?" His breath hitches and his voice cracks after noticing she no longer had a pregnancy stomach.

"Clear out," the doctor demands, wearing a white mask as he pushes Mandy and the overwhelmed teenager out the door.

"Will someone just tell me what the FUCK is going on!" he yells in hopes of gaining their attention, seeking answers as some tears start to slip from his eyes. They don't answer and instead, shut the door on the two. Devastated, he turns to face Mandy for some answers.

69

She had apologetically stated that, "They could not stop the internal hemorrhaging that began during her procedure, so they went through the premature labor to remove the baby." She nearly choked out on her words before covering her mouth and the distraught Jared walks up to give her another comforting hug, even though he needed it more for himself.

"Is Jessica gonna be alright?" He was petrified for an answer. She sobs harder on his shoulder.

"I hope so."

****

"Is she okay?" Jaiden had asked when Mandy had approached the other two in the waiting room.

"She lost a lot of blood during and when they had to remove her," she nodded off slyly as Kevin stood up to comfort her. Jaiden had explained Kevin everything after Jared walked away earlier. It has been nearly fourteen hours waiting for answers in the hospital now. It was almost midnight and school was only a couple of hours away for the two of them too. Only for Jared, he didn't care because he wanted to be there for Jess all day if it meant she would be okay. Mandy and Kevin have fallen asleep in the chairs across from the twins and Jaiden had also fell asleep but in one chair away from his brother. On the other hand, Jared couldn't sleep with all this stress and worry, his heart ached in discomfort. He couldn't help but to think that all of this happened because of him.

"Mr. and Mrs. Anderson?" the female doctor calls out causing Mandy and the rest to wake. "She's okay," the doctor assures and the friends and family sigh with relief.

"C-can we see her?" Jared shakily implies. The doctor nods and they all get up to follow the doctor.

"One or two at a time please, family first," she says eyeing the persistent Jared who then slumps back in his seat as Jaiden, *the father and savior of the day,* trails away alongside Mandy. When Jaiden had been the first to enter the room, Jessica had her knees up and crying into them. She was in a hospital gown with a patient wristband draped around her wrist. She shoots her face up in their direction when the door sounds, and Mandy was quick to envelop her in for a hug. Jessica's face was still smeared in black from her previous day's mascara run.

"Amanda, can I please talk with Jaiden for a couple of minutes?" she sniffles, requesting privacy to acknowledge his presence after the two girls had their moment already. Mandy respectfully exits the room and

Jaiden joins her on the bed. She doesn't say anything for a minute until she crawls back over to tighten him into a hug. In his embrace, she begins to weep onto his chest. "I'm s-so sorry," she muffles. She felt vulnerable more than ever. She was crestfallen, bitter over the loss of her unborn and, so she confided in him.

"It's all my fault," she cries again.

"No, it's not your fault," he coos, pulling away and staring into her eyes, but she shoots him down when turning away. He turns her head to meet his gaze once again. "Why did you do it?" he asks when softly grabbing her wrists and rubbing his thumbs along her bandaged cuts.

"I felt like it was the right thing to do... I didn't want to end my life just yet, I guess I just wanted something to physically hurt me, so I wouldn't have to focus on the pain I felt in here," she answered, placing a hand over her heart.

"That's what you do when you feel alone. I do feel alone..." she nods, staring at the door. "My entire life was based on emotional abuse, I was neglected for being the way I was. I feel the same everywhere I go whether it's with you or 'him', or my parents. Jaiden, this experience, i-it fucked me up. It's no excuse to justify what I've done, but I know now I can never be who I was before this accident or else I could do more physical damage to myself than has already happened to me. I don't want any part of my past to haunt me tomorrow and I know it will, I've sinned, and I can't go back from that, that's why I know I can only move forward. God, I've tried so hard to be different, I've changed for you, for my parents. No one wanted to accept me. The moment I got pregnant I lost my self-worth, I've lost my respect. No one could look at me the same and just when I thought I could do this on my own, I gave up because I had failed to realize that I had no one's support but my own. It wasn't enough for me to go on. Everyone put a wall up and I was no longer a priority," she lightly chuckles in disbelief while staring at the ceiling then looking back at Jaiden, drowning in self-pity. "You know what my father told me, he told me I was a mistake, A MISTAKE!" she sobs. "Here I thought you and Jare were the only ones I could trust, but you guys have lied to me and hurt me so many times—" He places his hand on her palms that rested on the hospital bed between them in assurance, but she shrugged his hand away. "I'm sorry but I think it's best if I don't see you for a while... I need some time to self-heal, alone—away from you, Jared, and everybody because I know the minute I walk out these hospital doors and I see you or Jared especially, it's going to kill me. For every time that I have to see your faces, constantly reminded by what once could've been because it's happening right now and as much as I am trying to shake the thought, I can't help but keep remembering the little girl, my daughter, I lost today," she says out of breath, crying into her hands. He tries comforting her again, but she shrugs him away again. "Just go!" she bellows louder with a shaky, out-of-breath voice. He stands up, looking back over at her in hopes of her telling him to stay but she doesn't acknowledge his presence and he proceeds to exit the room.

After Jaiden exits the hospital, without a word when passing by the rest of the visitors, Mandy lets Jared to enter next and he thanks her before heading off inside. "Jess?" he knocks while entering.

"I thought I told you to leave," Jess fired, sobbing into her hands, not noticing it was only Jared this time.

"It's m-me... Jared." She looks up in his direction. "A-are you okay?" He worriedly feared to approach her. Her eyes widened greatly in size.

"You s-stay a-away from m-me!" she panics rapidly while pointing up at him, frozen in place. He takes a step closer, hoping to calm her.

He tried to compromise, "Jess—"

She interjects, "Stay away from me! This is all your fault!" she screamed in great terror.

"Please Jess, I didn't mean to—" he begins to explain while she finds a button near her bedside and presses it repeatedly when recoiling in fear. A bunch of doctors barge in the room seconds later.

"Sir, you need to leave," a male physician says. "Jared, I never wanna see you again! I hate you so much! You did this to me! You've caused this to happen and have caused me so much pain!" she belts out before pulling the hospital pillow from behind her to cry onto.

"What's going on, why is she like this?" Jared disappointedly asks, hurt by her poor choice of words.

"Patients who are severely traumatized by something such as losing a baby, go through mental breakdowns like this, every so often," the doctor informs. "Son, we are gonna have to ask you to leave now," he directs, pushing Jared out the door.

"Why, what are they gonna do to her!" he agitatedly angers on the outside of the door. For once, he wanted a straight answer, he hated being the last one to know things. He punched the wall that was right next to the door upon exiting the room before leaving the hospital, clenching his jaw.

Chapter Four

(Several Weeks Later)

"How is she?" Amanda had asked her husband upon entering the living room where he had been sitting and watching television in his at-home-attire.

"Don't know, she's been in there all day this time," he mentions, focusing his attention on the game that was on, taking a sip of his beer.

"Oh no!" Amanda worried, dropping her keys and phone on the counter before walking over to Jessica's room. There, she saw her sister sitting beside the bay window with one leg up and her other dangling to the floor. Amanda let out a deep breath, "You nearly scared me half to death just now. I thought you did something terrible again."

"I'm not crazy you know? I would never take my own life," Jess nonchalantly stated, still hung on her reflection against this window.

"Yeah, I know, but you're here because Kevin and I want to make sure you're alright with everything else going on."

"Then why am I still here? Can I please go home? 'My' home?" the poor girl emphasized. "We went over this before, your home is being temporarily rented out, so whether you like it or not, you'll be living with us for a few weeks, months even," the eldest sister stated, "And the doctors want me to keep a close eye on you."

"Now go and wash up for dinner," she chimed before closing the door behind and walking out. Jessica had groaned yet again. "Don't forget to take your medicine!" Amanda reminded when walking back into the living room only to get shushed by her husband, who leaned forward in his seat to pay closer attention to the scoreboard on the television screen.

"You know, I don't need a mother!" Jessica barks back. Feeling underappreciated and disappointed, Amanda sighed before returning up the stairs and straight into her bedroom.

****

"Can I come in?" Kevin asks when cautiously entering. Mandy was brushing her hair in the mirror across from their bed. She shot her face up at him with the smallest of sighs escaping her mouth and drops her brush on the counter of their shared dresser. "Jessica and I just ate dinner, you sure you don't want anything?" her husband had asked when coming up behind to wrinkle his arms around her in comfort.

"I'm surprised she even got up and listened... I'm trying really hard to be a good sister," she emphasized when walking over to the bed. "She pushes me away and I know she doesn't need a mother, but I can't help it; it's in my good nature to help her out, I don't know what to do," she furrowed, dropping on the bed with her hands covering her face.

"For what it's worth, I think you're going to be a great mom someday," Kevin acknowledged, plopping down next to her.

"I just don't think I'm ready for the responsibility," she admits, and he sighs profoundly, dropping his head. "Kevin, I'm sorry... In time we will, just not now... Besides, I really don't think now is the best time, given everything Jessica's been through. I'd hate to remind her of what she once could've had."

****

Weeks passed by that Jared hasn't seen or heard from his beloved Jessica. He's even tried calling her many times, but no answer. He needed to see her, he has missed her terribly. His mind replays those words she last said to him and although she might have not meant it, he couldn't help but to think that maybe it was in fact his fault.

"Jared, what's going on in here?" his mother asks when coming into his room with a phone call in hand as Jared then irritably let out a sigh.

"Mom, now's not really a good time."

"You've missed school all week Jared, it's unlike you!"

"...I just got off the phone with your English teacher and she's informed me you've been slacking off!"

"Mom..." his voice lowers.

"You have an F!" she exclaims.

"Here I thought I'd have a son who actually 'is' college material and what's this I hear about you getting a detention? ... Sometimes I do wish you were more like Jaiden but sweetie, not this way!"

He groans and slams his head back down on his pillow, letting his mother continue to babble. Somewhere along with his selective listening, he heard his mother mention Jessica and it sent him over the edge.

"—I told you this Jessica girl was a bad influence! I've had my suspicions on her for a while now and I always knew she wasn't as innocent as she appeared to be! Especially now that she has to look after a child, you don't want to get involved. Believe me honey, I only want what's best for you and she's not it. I'd say part ways as friends now before she starts begging you for child support and sucks you dry of money. Boy, I just feel bad for the poor sap that knocked her up and has to deal with that now, times two, that is if he is willing to stay—" she rambled.

"Christ!" Jared slammed contemptuously, his face redder than ever. "Just give it up with this obsession you have against Jessica already! You don't know her like I've known her my whole life and you don't know what she has to go through every day! She's my best friend and you wanna know what else? I was the random guy she slept with; Okay, it was my fault. I took advantage of her when I shouldn't have but if it's any consolation, she miscarried a few weeks ago and guess that was my fault too, but that girl is my best friend and I think I maybe in love with her and I would spend a million years to try and make it up to her and for her to forgive me if I could and I don't need your permission!" he spat. She stood there astounded by his words, wounded, and defeated. Jared grabbed his car keys from his desk and slammed the door on his way out.

"What's up, dude?" Jaiden asked when going up the stairs as Jared walked down.

"Fuck off!"

He made his way over to Jessica's flat. *I wish I still had the spare key Jessica gave me a while back, but damn Jaiden stole it.* He decided on the old-fashioned way that everyone unmannerly seemed to forget, by knocking. "Hi, may I help you?" a familiar skimpy blonde with green eyes greeted at the door.

"I'm sorry, I was looking for a friend, but I guess I must have the wrong place," he explains when eyeing the room numbers in the building complex around himself.

"Hey, wait a minute… aren't you that naked kid from the internet? … Jared, right?" Jared chuckles timidly. "Hey, it's nothing to be embarrassed about. You should be proud… Between you and I, very impressive," she teases, biting her lip as her eyes scan his body to his lower region.

"Lacey, come here! It's one of Hobbs' friends!" she called from the door. "Hey, I thought I heard someone, how's 'One Direction erection' doing?" the other girl teased when joining her sister by the doorway. Lacey had similar features to her younger sister, but was curvier and had blue eyes, dressed very similarly. Now, he had remembered who they were.

"We were just unpacking a few things, wanna come in?" Lindsay asks.

"No, I couldn't... I actually have somewhere to be soon."

"Oh well, are you sure?"

"You'd be helping us quite a bit; we just rented this place out and we could really use some muscle to help us unload these boxes," Lacey says, eyeing the younger boy up and down, flashing him her flirtatious smile before Lindsay nudges her, rolling her eyes.

"Rent?" he asks, suspicion rising.

"Yeah, someone by the name of 'Anders' or something, let us rent it out for a few weeks," Lacey explains. It all made sense.

"Did the owner already pick up their belongings?"

"Well there wasn't anything here when we arrived so I'm guessing," Lindsay chuckles. "So, what do you say, Jared, help us out?" Lindsay asks while batting her eyelashes up at him.

"Sure, I guess," he shrugs in agreement and the girls giggle, tugging him inside. Meanwhile, Jaiden had been on his way to see Jessica with her sister's permission.

"Thank you for letting me see her," Jaiden says tailgating behind Mandy when entering her estate. Amanda directed him to the guest room where Jessica had been living and parts her way. He had knocked on the door quietly before entering. There she lay asleep, cuddled up under her bed covers. He makes his way to sit on the bed and caresses the hairs out of her face. She whines before fluttering her eyes up at the boy.

"J-Jaiden, what are you doing here?" she asks, sitting up.

"I've missed you," he shrugged in honesty as they joined together for a hug. She pushed her face closer to his chest with her arms around his back before speaking out. "I've missed you too... but—"

"Jessica, I know what I've done, I'm not proud of hurting you or deceiving you. I should've told you the truth and I wish I could make it up to you but just know it took every ounce of my courage to be here today and to be saying this to you now. I didn't realize how stupid and selfish I've been in the past few months. I'm not asking you to forgive me, I'm just asking for you to hold out your faith in me for a little bit longer, okay? Don't forgive me, I haven't deserved it yet, believe in me is all I'm asking. Believe that I am willing to change." She nods her head ambivalently. He then moves closer to press his forehead onto hers before laying a gentle kiss on the top of her head. She lowers his face with her hands and places her fingers at his soft lips, tracing over them. He slowly closes his eyes and she leans in, inviting him to a light kiss.

She pulls away while they both open their eyes. He swoons in kissing her deeper now, lifting her body an inch above the mattress so that she was laying on the bed as he hovered over her now.

"Wait," she pauses with her hand stopping his mouth from attaching to her lips again.

"Too early? I'm sorry," he exhales, about to get off.

"No…" she says touching his arm.

"I, I want to do this… I'm ready again, for real this time."

"Jessica, you sure you're ready this time? Here and now… w-with me? We don't have to if you're still—" she cuts him off, "No." She props herself up with her hands behind her back. "Please, I want this," she assures when touching the side of his face.

"Alright but are you sure you're not drunk?" he chuckles.

"Jaiden," she teases, nudging him on the chest. "If I was drunk, would I be able to do this…?" She stood up to hold her foot up to her ear.

"Impressive…" he grins, licking his upper lip in anticipation. "Alright, alright, you've passed… but let's see if you can bend over and touch your toes," he chuckles cockily. She rolls her eyes and crawls back over, allowing him to spoon her. He goes to kiss her neck causing her to shuffle her body to face his.

"But I don't want to do this here, I want it to be special this time…" she insists, and he nods off. She thought about holding off on sex until marriage but now that she's already experienced it, there's no holding back on anything. As much as the thought of being intimate again terrified her, she knew she had to try again someday. That day might have not been that night, but she knew she needed it to be done soon and get it over with since she failed to remember her first encounter and was still anxious at the thought. Her parents may have failed to lecture her on the dangers of sex in the past, but it wasn't rocket science. She had ill-prepared her first try, but it wasn't on her conscience and she knew better now. Life is meant to learn from your mistakes and she can safely say, she has and will be extra careful next time around.

****

After Jared had finished helping the ladies that following night, he made his way over to Amanda and Kevin's house, hoping Jess would be there so that he could talk with her since they hadn't talked since the night of the party. He rang the doorbell. "Hey Jared, what's up bud!" Kevin greets.

"Nothing much, is Jessica here by chance?" he asks, looking around the house with his eyes in hopes of finding her.

"She actually just left with your brother…"

"Jaiden?" he worried. "How long ago?"

"Um, maybe somewhere around thirty-four minutes ago?" Jared sighed, feeling defeated.

"Oh, well thanks anyways. I better get going." He exits, stepping off the porch.

"See you later man!" Kevin says closing the door. *Wow, I guess it didn't take her long to get over me. One of a kind, I'll say.*

****

"Doesn't really bother me," Jaiden shrugs, "The kid did it to himself," he continues in correspondence to Skylar in their small clatter of friends, the following week.

"Whatever then. Anyways, I've got to go," Skylar nods before parting ways with Jaiden and heading off to class.

"Guess who?" a feminine voice disguises from behind while covering Jaiden's eyes with their hands. He turns around and to his surprise, found it was Jessica.

"Jess, what are you doing here?" he questions, eyeing her up and down to notice that she has a backpack on her back.

"I transferred, silly!" she teases. "Why don't you seem excited to see me?" she pouts.

"No, I am. I—" she cuts him off by unexpectedly grabbing the collar of his shirt to kiss him but retracts away seconds after noticing there had been a friend clearing his throat from behind. "Oh, and who is this?" she asks causing Jaiden to apologetically introduce his friend.

"This is another one of my friends, Wesley. Wesley this is Jessica."

"Oh! So, *you're* the infamous Jessica that I've heard little to nothing about?" he joked when politely shaking her hand.

"Well, aren't you just the smug little son of a bitch?" Jessica bluntly replied, folding her arms.

"Well played, I can see why you like her now," he grinned at Jaiden. Wesley was almost a head shorter than Jaiden, had light brown hair and brown colored eyes. His hair was gelled up like most other guys in the school. He had been wearing a simple purple tee, no designs, and jeans. His skin was creamy and had been clear of tattoos and acne. When Jessica looked closer, she noticed he had a few soft freckles under his eyes. He was certainly a fresh face that Jessica did not remember seeing at the first party she had been introduced to. "Well, it was great meeting you, but I have to get to class, see you later Jaiden and I look forward to acquainting with you in the future," Wesley directs to Jessica before heading off.

"So, your parents are okay with you transferring schools?"

"Jaiden, I'm eighteen and I live on my own. I don't need their permission, they aren't even involved in my life anymore so why should they care now?"

"So, you moved back into your apartment?"

"No," she grumbles. "Mandy has still got me under house arrest. She didn't mind me transferring out though, at least I will be graduating someway. Knowing Mandy, 'education is priority'."

"Have you heard anything from Beverly?" he asked.

"No… why? You're not hiding anything from me 'again', are you?" she crosses her arms. At this moment, all he could comprehend was how cute she looked when she was jealous, the way her nostrils flared up when she scrunched her nose.

"No. I only ask because word on the street is that her and Patrick are getting married."

"Yeesh, at least someone loves her…"

"Come on, don't be like that… she's still your sister, as much as I may despise her," he implied, trying to keep his last meal down.

"Maybe you should take your own advice and talk to Jared since he's your brother…" she quotes.

Meanwhile, Jared roamed the school hallways when on his path to his locker, an annoying mistake and two other annoyances stopped him. "Hey Jared!" the second annoyance named Tanya hollered. They all shared something in common, which was seemingly to have had a crush on the boy, but Jared quickly turned them down repeatedly for the only one he has truly admired, Jessica Jane.

These girls have been nothing but bothersome for the poor Jared ever since he became somewhat of an athlete; he has become a target of infatuation. There was Tanya, the first on the list who was the clingiest to most anyone that knew her. Word around the school was that she was even the fakest one of all and no one needed a mirror to see through that. In fact, just last week she had this complaint to gossip about to Jared who shared home ec with her. She was going on about this song that was driving her to insanity because she heard it everywhere. Then at last week's party that following day, when a guy asked her to dance to that same song, she was quick to change her mind and Jared witnessed everything. Jokes on her, that guy wasn't really interested in her at all. As it turned out, her ex-boyfriend paid some guy twenty bucks to trick her because he overheard her complaining to Jared about that song from someone else and he wanted to prove to his friends how fake she really was and why he had to end their relationship. It was his best bet. You'd be surprised how fast rumors circulate in this school.

Next, there was Sophie who he had to turn down the most of amount of times because in the short amount of time, he's known her to be what most people would think of as 'sullen'. And finally, Courtney Cordova who only recently joined in their posse to complete the insidious trio under Candace Harper's wing. He didn't deny, these girls were attractive, but he preferred the intellectual mind of a woman over their appearance any day. That is what primarily attracted Jared to Jessica. She was embodied into the perfect image for Jared and that is how he looked at her.

"Hey…" Jared smiled awkwardly at the three standing before him. "So, we should all hang out at the movies later on," Courtney implies, linking her arm with his as Tanya does the same, occupying his other vacant arm. He must have missed the part of how they became friends. The absolute worst part was that he was only pretending to be friends with these girls because he had a hard time saying no and also because they wouldn't leave him the hell alone. It was a relief on Jared when Sophie finally found herself a boyfriend. It was one less problem he had to deal with, the only problem was that she still hung out with the girls more. She was dating some new kid on the wrestling team, Ryan. Jared didn't know much about him, he's never even met him. All he's heard about him was that he hung out with Robbie Montoya, his worst nightmare. He was Nick's younger brother, so Jared already could tell he was not going to like him. Nick even started hanging out with Robbie more often. He was too immature to be seen around anyone else. The three girls and Jared stopped in the middle of the hallway and from afar, Jared saw his twin preoccupied by some girl, but he couldn't make out the face, he had assumed it was Candi. "Are we hanging at the mall later or not?" Candi asks the girls, approaching them from the side.

"Eww, what is Jaiden doing here?" she cringed, staring the boy up and down.

"No, this is Jared… Jaiden's twin brother?" Courtney tries clarifying in a tone that makes her sound like she was teaching someone in special ed.

"Candi, your blonde is showing," Tanya adds and Candi giggles.

"Well, I do need to get my hair done, this regrowth is killing me," she babbles on while Jared tried to figure out who Jaiden was talking to in the distance. Once he snaps his head back around, he clearly identifies the face when the girl gives Jaiden a comforting hug, it was Jessica. *What is she doing at our school?* The girls must have noticed him staring because Candi spoke up again. "Wait, wasn't that the chick who was pregnant?"

"How do you know that, Candi?" Jared asked facing her now.

"Jaiden and I were in Starbucks and she spotted us together and she went off on him for not being with her at her sonogram or whatever," she rolls her eyes while beginning to file her nails. *Are you kidding me, he missed that to be with Candi and Jessica still loves him!*

Courtney groans, "He's with her now!" she whines while stomping a foot to the ground.

"Oh honey, you could do so much better than that tool... there's so much more I need to teach you," Candi states and an annoyed Jared, not wanting to waste any more precious time before the next class period started, walks away from their pathetic conversation to make his way over to Jaiden and Jessica on the opposing side of the student lockers.

"Jessica, what are you doing here?" he worriedly asks after Jaiden had whipped his head around.

Jessica rolls her eyes, "Come on Jai, let's go," she says taking his hand and trying to move past him. Jared cuts in between them to try and talk to her but Jaiden swings him around from his shoulder.

"She asked you to leave her alone..."

"She can speak for herself!" Jared gritted through his teeth. He faces her one more time.

"Jessica. D-do you want me to leave?" Jared dubiously asked, caressing her face with his thumb, she stares down to avoid his gaze. "I-I've missed you... I've missed us... Dammit Jess, I love you! Isn't that enough?" he urged in desperation after she stayed quiet.

He heard Jaiden scoff, "How pathetic..."

"Just go Jared!" she demanded, letting a tear fall to the floor. She was still to make indirect eye contact, feared to stare into his eyes, only to feel betrayed again.

He recoiled his hand away, "Y-you don't really mean that though..." He felt a huge lump in his throat.

Resentment washed over the girl after those words left his mouth and she shot her head up, "I wasn't kidding when I told you to leave me the hell alone at the hospital! I meant every word of what I said and what I'm about to tell you now so listen," she confronted. "Jared, you dare so much as to breathe in my direction again and I will run the other way like I see every girl in these hallways do. No not because they're intimated by you but because they wouldn't be caught dead next to you! You're as sleazy as the next guy and I want to expose you for being the disgusting rat that you've proven yourself to be but that would just be an insult to the entirety of the rat species. The sad thing is that I had a more pleasant time playing your girlfriend for a week rather than having you as a friend for all fourteen of my years! I don't just hate you, I 'loathe' you for tearing me apart! You wanted this I didn't, I didn't Jared and you didn't hurt me, you 'broke' me inside!—And guess what? I didn't love you, I fell for you when I was at my most vulnerable, and I believed all the lies you fed me and for what? So 'yes', I'm angry at the fact that you've cheated but even more so I'm disappointed in the fact that you've lied. Best friends don't hurt their friends like that at all and this is why I'm cutting off all ties with you."

Jaiden now steps in front of them after those words staked through Jared's heart and rippled out his soul.

"Leave my girlfriend alone," Jaiden threats.

"G-girlfriend?" Jared asks, mouth trembling.

"Yeah, you've had your chance, thanks for warming her up for me," he winks when throwing his arm around her neck just before walking away together as Jess stares over his shoulder with a gleam of bitter resentment and disappointment directed towards Jared. Just then, the five-minute bell rings and everybody walks to their class as Jared stood there defeated for the last time.

"Aww, what's wrong my wittle Jare-Bear?" Robbie mimics as him and his guy friends come up and surround the depressed boy, cracking their necks and popping their knuckles. Jared knew it couldn't be any worse than this. "So, me and my buds feel truly... deeply," Robbie begins as this kid named Aaron throws him what appears to be duct tape. "Sorry," he says when tugging the roll of tape, "For you, and we were feeling a bit nice today... so, you get to choose your punishment. What will it be, Jerry boy? Will it be the usual beating or..." He snaps his fingers and the Ryan kid restrains Jared's arms against his will. *Yep, if I ever felt doubtful about hating him before, I definitely do now.*

"So, want me to walk you to your classes?" Jaiden asks while taking Jessica's hand and locking it with his on their stroll around the campus.

"No, I actually don't start classes 'til tomorrow, I just thought I'd surprise you today."

"Then what's all this crap in that big ass backpack of yours?" he chuckles.

"Oh, that reminds me," she says throwing her backpack off her shoulders before wrapping it around her chest to unzip her backpack. She reveals a big stuffed teddy bear with his jersey and number on it.

"What's this?" he smiles, surprised.

"Kevin's four-year-old little brother came over two days ago and we all went to take him to Build-A-Bear…"

"He wanted me to make one as well so he wouldn't be alone in the process, so I did, and I automatically thought of you," she continued, "I had mine extra customized as you can see—I requested the employees to include your jersey on the bear after I showed them a picture of you at your last football game."

"Does this bring out my eyes?" he asks, fluttering his eyelashes at her and she giggles. "Hey, I am not this fat!" he defends. "Are my hips really this big though?" he boasted, swaying his hips. They were at the foot of the building now, returning inside the hallway.

"I'm so sorry, the stuffing machine exploded on me!" she cries out in laughter.

"Well, this is an amazing gift," he thanked, kissing her forehead. The warning bell finally sounds soon after.

"You better go or you're gonna be late!"

"How are you getting home?"

"Mandy let me borrow her car again."

"So, I guess I will just see you after school then?"

"Yeah, call me, bye! Hurry!" she exclaims, and he runs up the stairs that they stood in front of, after shoving his bear in his backpack, zipping it halfway.

****

"Someone help!" Jared shouts for what feels like the hundredth time, his voice already strained by now. It seems Robbie and his friends had duct taped him to the toilet seat, leaving him in only his boxers with his hands tied to the bar right beside him. The worst part was that the Aaron guy took a piss on him after being taped and tied down. At this moment in time, Jared didn't know what was worse, being publicly humiliated or losing the girl he loves to his brother. On top of that, after being stripped of all his clothes and dignity, those idiots took his clothes and dunked them into the stall right next to his. They completely flooded the toilet and the water was already now up to his feet. He struggled to put his mouth closer to the rope in order to rip the rope with his teeth but failed, so yelled for help again. The urine had dried up by now and he reeked of the smell. Had he of known this was what he signed up for including to get pissed on, he'd rather have gotten the beating which would have been much quicker although more painful. The stall door soon rattles a few times before finally opening up.

"Oh my god dude, are you okay?" a former classmate named Brennan asks while jumping over to his aid and untying his hands. His jeans wet due to the toilet water puddle he stepped in.

"Thank you!" Jared graciously thanks while attempting to remove the tape off his body.

"Need help?" Jared groans in frustration after many failed attempts.

"Here, let me help," insisted Brennan. "What happened to your clothes? Let me guess, Montoya huh?" Jared nods. "Well for what it's worth, he sucks at being original," Brennan chuckles. "Okay, here we go," he warned.

"One… two… three!"

****

Meanwhile, Jessica and Jaiden had been making out on his living room couch after school. She laid down while he hovered over her. "We should stop…" she worried, sitting up. "Where are your parents at?" she asked.

"I told you, they're on vacation… you have nothing to worry about. Now can we please continue?" he whines, pulling her body back on top of his now. They continued to make out and seconds later, his hands crawl up into her shirt to unclasp her bra, but she swats his hand away before he gets the chance to. "Jess, please," he whines. She sighs and sits back up.

"Jaiden, we are not going to do it here either."

"Why not?" he whines again, also sitting up.

"Your brother and sister could walk in any minute." Before he begins to speak, she cuts him off again, "And let's make one thing clear, I am 'not' like any of those girls you used to bring home, I don't want to be!" she emphasized.

"For the record, I never even brought any of them home… If you must know, I usually plow them at Josh's parties," he chuckled out. "Where are you going?" he asks after noticing she had stood up.

"Come here you big baby," she says taking his hand. He followed her up the stairs into his room while licking his lips in anticipation.

"So why exactly do you smell like urine?" Nora asks when unlocking the front door as Jared then hurriedly steps inside, hoping to avoid further interrogation.

"It just amazes me that how out of everything I tried to explain to you in the car, 'this' is what you're most concerned with. Thanks," he grumbles.

84

"Yeah, you're right… I actually don't really care," she says setting her coat down before making her way into the kitchen. Jared sighs and jogs into his bedroom.

"Almost there!" he heard someone pant from next door followed by a thump and female giggling. He pressed his ear to the wall since he figured it was Jessica and Jaiden frolicking around. He continued to listen hoping to eavesdrop but instead, heard lots of grunting. He automatically recoiled his ear away in disgust. He proceeds to grab some clean clothes from his dresser that he prepared earlier because he wanted to shower regardless, and he knew it was mandatory now. With his stuff in hand, he headed across the hall, slamming the door shut behind himself and enters the bathroom for a shower. He wanted to use the one in his room, but the door was connected to Jaiden's room and he didn't want to hear them anymore. It was a good thing he had spare clothes in his football locker, so that he wouldn't have to leave the school premises in his boxers. He was also lucky to have Brennan help him out and to have relied on his sister to drop him off at home since his brother left without even offering.

"I think your brother is home," Jessica worriedly noticed when sitting up after hearing a door slam.

"I'm exhausted, can we sleep now?" Jaiden asks when standing up from the twister board, helping Jessica up too.

"Only if we cuddle?"

She smirks when hopping into bed and sliding into the covers. He joins her on the bed seconds later. Her small head fits perfectly under his neck, she then begins to trace small circles on his hairless chest. "Jai?"

"Yeah?" he yawns.

"I love you."

He responds by kissing the top of her head and moves his hand to hers. "Jess?"

"Yes, Jaiden?"

"You've really got to get your apartment back…"

"Mmmmhmm, nice try," she says rolling off him.

"What?" he chuckles.

"Sex… we are definitely *not* having sex in my flat either."

"You can't keep teasing me like you do forever…"

"I'll be the judge of that… maybe if you're a good boy, I'll think about it," she teased.

"That's the problem. You see, I am a 'very' good boy, but you have been a 'very' naughty girl," he seduced, climbing on top of her. She giggles in her failed attempt to push him off. "Hey Jess?" he asks again after they had parted ways to try and sleep. She turns her body to direct her attention, meeting him in the center of the bed.

"Did you…?"

"I thought you wanted to sleep, liar."

"Yeah, I just had something on my mind…"

"Hmmmm?" she hums.

"You and Jared… you know… when you were dating…" He breaks his sentences in a very confusing manner as she waits for him to continue, staring blankly in confusion. "Did you and Jared ever *fuck*?"

She shot him a death glare for his foul language. "I mean… h-have sex?" he asks while locking both of his hands on his chest as he stares up at the ceiling.

"Jaiden, I was pregnant when I was with him, remember?" she reminds.

"Oh yeah, I'm sorry."

"No, it's fine."

"I-it's just that, would you have though? …Given you weren't pregnant?"

"Jaiden, you're sounding a little ridiculous right now," she irritably explains, shifting her body back around and melodramatically tugging the blanket closer to her face.

"Would you have?"

She sits up ridiculed, "Jaiden!"

"Just answer the damn question!" he snaps.

"You're unbelievable!" she exclaims, getting up.

"Wait, don't leave! I'm sorry, that came out of nowhere…" She drops her shoulders. "So long as we're on the topic of you having moved on, can you please just answer the question?"

"Congratulations. Way to be such an insensitive piece of shit Jaiden," she mellowed in offense, grabbing her purse from the floor. She exits the bedroom to find a wet Jared wrapped with a towel on his waist and his whistling fades once he approaches closer and spots the distraught girl. He stood closer and they awkwardly stop in the middle of the hallway to exchange glances. Now, she notices visible bruises completely covering his body. She also noticed tape marks from what it looks like and small bruises on his face, from Jaiden she assumed. She quickly snapped out of her empathetic thoughts once her subconscious reminded her of the unpleasant ones.

He scoffs after a minute, "For the record, you shouldn't get too comfortable around Jaiden. He loves using girls, but it's none of my business, so enjoy being used and abused like the unwashed trailer trash you are," he says, touching the bruise on her neck causing her to cringe at his cold touch. She inadvertently slaps his hand away. She looks back into his vicious eyes, completely stunned. His eyes seemed so different, she couldn't recognize him. Something had been off. It was as if he turned off his humanity switch in the last thirty seconds. One thing was for sure, she did not hesitate to fire back, she would not let him wound her. How dare he!

"How DARE you say that and don't EVER touch me again!" she ferociously snaps after smacking him square across the face, pushing past him to run down the steps. Jaiden overhears, swarming out of his room to her rescue. His timing couldn't have been worse since the poor girl had already fled the house in tears. Jared tries pushing past his brother causing Jaiden to back him up against the wall with only an arm.

"Why the FUCK does your mouth smell like liquor?" the older boy yells an inch away from his face.

"Why doesn't yours?" Jared slurs. Jaiden releases his grip on his brother once he had heard the front door slam shut. The flimsy teenager then pushes back with great force, causing Jaiden to fall back against the wall as Jared then enters his bedroom and locks it after himself. Jaiden quickly helps himself back on his feet, jogging his way to the front door in an attempt to comfort his friend. He was disappointed to find Jessica's car screeching as she backed out of their driveway while her tires scratched the concrete when driving off.

****

The rest of the evening passed by when Jessica couldn't sleep because of those hurtful words that replayed in her mind, not to forget when Jaiden snapped at her. Before she knew it, it was now time for her first day of school. She had such hatred for both twins as of now and she had a gut feeling that going to the same school as them was going to be problematic. For the longest time that she has known them, she would have never in a million years have expected this behavior from either of them, let alone never have guessed that Jared would even be capable of forming such treacherous words. That is not even something you would say to friends, not even as a joke. But the more she thought about it, the more she was starting to believe it. Maybe she was only good for letting people use her. Above all, she despised herself for being in the middle all the time. Even though she may be with Jaiden, she doesn't deny what she felt for Jared when they were dating, or maybe it was just pregnancy hormones. *No, it couldn't be though because even after the miscarriage, I kept holding on to those feelings for a period of time until Jaiden came into my life.* Now, she was confused. She believes she finally moved on but there was no way of knowing for sure just yet and after today's turn of events, she would at least try to forget about him. *He does not exist for me anymore.*

She groaned after her alarm went off in the morning, meaning it had officially been time for school. Her official first day in a public school… with the twins, *gulp.* She pulls the covers off her cold body after hitting the snooze button. She got up and walked over to the bathroom to wash up. She then proceeds to wash her teeth and finally heads back into the room to change out of her PJs. "Morning sunshine!" Mandy blooms from the kitchen, hauling the sleep deprived teenager for some breakfast.

"What are you doing up so early?" Jessica yawns, sitting on the counter stool.

"Making your first official school breakfast, silly!" she exclaims when setting her breakfast down in front of her. Amanda's breakfast for Jessica consisted of an omelet, toast, and a side of turkey bacon, with a glass of orange juice.

"Looks great, but I think I will stick to eating healthy after all this extra weight I've gained for nothing," she monotonously explains when grabbing a banana from the fruit display before walking out the front door. She had grabbed her backpack on the way out.

"Need lunch money?" Amanda shouts just as the door behind her sister shut on her way out. Amanda sighs, resting a hand on her face.

"What smells so delicious?" Kevin approaches, opening the fridge while rubbing his eyes.

"Your new breakfast, enjoy." Amanda shrugs before sliding Jessica's untouched breakfast closer to him. He burps after drinking straight from the milk carton. "Excuse me?" she scoffed, snapping her head around at her ill-mannered husband. He stares at her blankly in annoyance before continuing to drink. Amanda rolls her eyes. "Lunch is in the fridge," she irritably announced, smacking her apron on the table. As for Jessica Larson, she managed to get to her first two classes so far without having to see either Jared or Jaiden. She met up with their mutual friend Lucas in history for second hour and now she was on her way to chemistry for her third hour. She confidently walked in the classroom without second-guessing herself, hoping she would see some new faces. As it turned out, she had spoken too soon when she spotted two similar faces sitting on opposite sides of the classroom she had entered. She handed the teacher her schedule and planned to avoid eye contact, hoping they would not see her.

"Jessica?"

Jessica nervously nods in response. "Hello, I'm Mrs. Parker," the teacher says shaking the hand of her newest student. A newly nervous and un-confident Jessica, looks back up at the students as her teacher figures out a place to seat her. Shifting her eyes between Jared and Jaiden nervously, she hoped not to be seated beside them since there had been an empty seat beside them both. Just then, the door opens, "Here you go Mrs. Parker, sorry I'm late," a familiar redhead says passing by after handing in her tardy slip to the teacher then taking her seat in the back of the classroom next to… Jaiden? She drops her book bag beside her chair as Jaiden slumps further in his seat, sheepishly hiding his face behind his textbook. So far it had seemed that he had been the only one to notice Jessica's presence of the two.

"It looks like all the lab partners are taken."

"Oh, never mind. You're in luck! It seems one of our students, Natalie, has moved, and I almost forgot!" Mrs. Parker announces.

"You can be Jared's new lab partner," she says pointing him out as if Jessica hadn't already knew who he was.

How awkward, just my luck.

****

The remaining forty-three minutes of third hour finishes and Jared hasn't spoken one word to his lab partner in the classroom. It felt to Jessica as if they were nothing more than strangers. She wanted so desperately to ask him why he said what he did, but she couldn't bring herself to do it, maybe because she had been too afraid for the answer. She wanted to believe that he didn't think of her as that. Speaking of white trash, she wondered why that 'Spawn of Satan' looking wench, sat next to Jaiden. "Hey Jess, wait up!" Jaiden called out after class had finished. He ran up behind Jess as she walked out the door, with Candi walking in front, nudging the girl on purpose as if on accident.

"Yeah?" she asks eyeing around the room numbers in the crowded main building they were inside, squinting a bit. "Is everything okay… with us?" he quietly asks when looking around as if he didn't want anyone to hear him.

She shrugs, "I guess…" she says continuing off in her trail, not giving him her full attention.

"Alright cool… now what happened yesterday?" he peers, lurking after her from around the corner of the hallway, speedily walking behind and guiding her off to the side after she almost ran into a group of football players. In behalf of her oblivious state with her nose in her schedule, he apologetically waved his buddies goodbye and led her to another direction causing her to finally look up again.

"Nothing," she denies, about to turn the corner in the wrong direction once again.

"Wrong way, it's lunch time," he directed by pulling her aside. He assertively grabs her free hand and guides her to the cafeteria.

"Let me see your schedule," he asks when waiting in line and she unfolds the paper in her pocket before handing it to him.

"We only have chem together, third hour," he says examining her paper.

"Dance? You dance?" he questions, awaiting an answer.

"A little, I've always wanted to experience the class though," she admits as they move closer in the line. As they reach the front of the line now, she allows Jaiden to pay for her meal this one time and they get themselves a table. In the middle of their conversation, Jessica notices Candi surrounded in her group of friends, one of them happened to be the leech who slept with her ex-boyfriend. Soon enough, Candi begins to make her way to their table. She taps Jaiden on the shoulder, waiting to get his attention and Jessica shoots her the dirtiest of looks.

"Jaiden, may I please speak with you for a minute?" she asks as a piece of lettuce from Jessica's salad falls out of her mouth.

"Tell me here," he insisted after noticing Jessica's glare.

He stands up as Candace rolls her eyes and continues speaking, "Party tomorrow night, RSVP?"

In that moment, Jessica felt it was imperative to announce that they were together since Candi obviously didn't get the memo—when in reality, she did get the memo she just chose to ignore it. Jaiden turns around and smiles at the girl like he's about to say something cocky. Jessica then, rolls her eyes and when he turns back around, Candace's narrowed eyes disappear into a fake smile. "Oh, sorry... I must of have gave your invite to someone a little way more... important," Candace implies when handing Jaiden the enveloped invitation.

"Well here, go find it because I just remembered, I'm a loser too," he says, shoving the invitation against Candace's chest, causing her to stumble backwards. He then takes Jessica's hand and pushes her chair in for her as they head off. Outraged, Candace scoffs, clicking her heels away after Jessica had turned around to give her a quick victory wave.

The two had spent the rest of lunch walking around, with Jaiden showing Jessica more around campus. When the bell rings, he walks her to her next class which happened to be calculus. "Well, here you are," he says handing her back her schedule.

"Calculus... how fun," she clearly speaks in sarcasm.

"When do you have it?" she asks.

"I don't. I had to retake an algebra class and I won't have to take calculus."

"Why?"

"I took an online course over summer."

The bell rings and they say their goodbyes before they part ways and she walks inside her classroom. Just what she had hoped would not happen again, Jared was in yet another one of her classes. He didn't notice her, instead he was digging in his backpack. Like before, she handed the teacher her schedule.

Please don't sit me next to Jared.

"You can take a seat next to Mr. Thomas," the male teacher says as he points to this Hispanic kid who was sitting in the front row. Jessica felt relieved, a little too loudly but not loud enough for Jared to hear. "Everyone, welcome Ms. Larson to class!" he publicized like Jessica had hoped he would not do. Jared shot his head up in her direction after realizing that she had been placed in yet another one of his classes.

After the class period ended, she had collected all her items. She then heard her name being called on the way out the door. She turned her attention for a second until she saw who it had been, turning right back around and continuing off on her trail.

"Wait!" Courtney proclaimed, running up to her and grabbing her by the arm.

"What!" Jessica flustered in annoyance. Luckily, she was much taller than the girl so if anything, Courtney should be one to be intimidated by Jessica.

"I'm sorry about the whole 'party thing'—"

"I don't have time for this," Jessica dismissed, beginning to walk away again but the girl runs up in front of Jessica, blocking her path.

"I really didn't know he had a girlfriend, okay!" Courtney confessed.

"So even if he didn't, you think it's okay to just sleep around with someone you barely know!" she shouts in annoyance, dumbfounded at this poor girl's logic. "You would think people would learn from my mistakes, you would think people would be safer! No, it's all just a game to people! Do you think sex is a joke! It destroys lives! It ruined me! So don't come over here to try and apologize because the only person I feel sorry for, is you. I'm sorry you have to be involved, no, I'm sorry you want to be involved. You know, I wish I had listened when people told me that they would only cause me trouble. I didn't because I believed in them, I thought they were different. But I had a reason to believe otherwise. I was wrong to believe anything because no matter how well you think you know someone, they change up on you in the blink of an eye. Before you know it, it's all over the minute you give it up to them.

Whatever you have going on with Jared, good luck to you. I just hope he doesn't hurt you like he hurt me. Was I upset that he cheated? Maybe, but it's nearly not as bad as every hurtful thing he's said to me the other day. It doesn't come close." Seconds later, Jared walks out with his textbooks in hand, wrapping his vacant hand around Courtney, in an attempt to make his ex-girlfriend jealous once he spotted her. "What's wrong?" he asks Courtney causing Jessica to shake her head in distress as he continues pretending she doesn't exist.

"Oh, here. Thought you might want this back by the way," Jessica says, pulling something out of her backpack. She reaches for his hand to dispense the small item before walking off in the opposite direction. He sighs after looking at it, watching his lost love trail-off in the distance.

(Flashback to a month ago)
"This is really nice, thank you," she says when reaching for his hand from across the table. Jared wanted to take Jessica's mind off things, so he drove the two of them to the best pizza parlor in town.

"I know it's kind of late, but I had to save up for a while because I really wanted to get you this, sooooooo…"

"Happy birthday!" she exclaimed when handing him a wrapped little box with a ribbon on top. He unknots the bowtie and tears the wrapper to open the box. "A Rolex, wow this must of cost you a fortune! I can't accept this, you worked really hard for that money and you need it—"

"Jared, shut up and enjoy the gift!" she giggles.

"Well, if you say so," he grins. He admires the watch, never leaving his gaze off it. "Well, I actually have a gift for you too, well actually for little Samantha," he smirks, pulling something out of his coat pocket.

"Jared, I swear if it's a ring, I'm going to kill you," she chuckles causing him to laugh as well.

"No, nothing like that."

"And Samantha?" she questions as he digs into his coat pocket some more before finding it.

"I don't know, just came to me."

"Not bad Daniels, kind of like it," she says, and he hands her the small box.

"I was gonna wait to give it to you in the delivery room, but I feel like I need to give it to you now," he said and she opens the box in awe, covering her mouth. It was a tiny charm bracelet. Some tears started slipping from her eyes as she continued looking at it. "Jess… are you okay?" he worries, reaching for her hand this time. Her tears speak for her before they both lean in from across the table. She set the box down to press her fingers on his cheek before leaning forward to kiss him.

(End of flashback)

He stared at the shiny object in his hands because it meant the world to him to see her face light up when he presented it to her.

****

Jessica had retouched her makeup in the bathroom after she had finally stopped crying. She continued to her next class, a tad late to English. As it turned out, Hobbs was in her English class and they caught up on things. It probably wasn't the brightest idea to befriend all the twins' friends, but she was in no place to make her own friends, the twins owned almost the entire parade of students in school, especially Jaiden. Now it was time for her final class of the day, dance. She was indeed a bit nervous because she didn't know what to expect, considering she's entered the class so late in the school year.

"Welcome, Jessica!" her petite female instructor greets. Boy, was she young. *Did she just graduate high school or something? She had to be at least in her early twenties*, thought Jessica. "Good news! You came in perfect timing! Everyone was just picking their dance groups for a new activity… is there anyone you know that you would like to work with?" Jessica shrugs as she eyes around the scattered dance room. She saw Candi narrowing her eyes at her while some dark polished girl was talking with her in the distance. *Great, Candi's in this class too.*

"She can join us!" a tan skinned girl called out from another group while sitting on the floor with a couple of other girls around her and what seemed to be the only male present in the class. Jessica nods in agreement with a quirky smile and makes her way over to them. She smiles awkwardly while setting her book bag down beside them to join them on the cold floor.

"Now, we've already went over the requirements, so your group can explain them to you … now class, begin!" the teacher announced, clapping her hands together excitedly. This was the one assignment that made up the final grade at the end of the year.

"You're a friend of Jared and Jaiden's, right?" the guy from the group asks and she humbly nods. Jess had hoped they were fans even though she wasn't; it would not be easy to hear people trash talk her friends and try to get along with them afterwards even though she could not stand them herself now.

"How'd you know?" she curiously asked.

"We're good friends with the twins too," he admits, and in the back of her mind, huge relief washed over her.

"They talk about you all the time!" the tan skinned girl agrees.

"You guys are…?" Jess asked, hoping that didn't come out rude.

"I'm Becca and this is Skylar," one girl says, formally shaking the new girl's hand.

"You can call me Sky," he winks playfully before Becca nudges him.

"Sorry, he can be a little too into himself at times," she says flicking him on the head.

"Boy, I know the feeling," Jessica mutters to herself.

"Is someone jealous?" he asks when puckering his lips at this Becca character.

"Very," she whines, pulling his head toward her face as she kisses him.

"So, what are we doing?" Jessica impatiently asks after having to sit through watching her new friends sucking face.

"Each group is performing at the recital at the end of the school year and in our groups, we have to come up with a piece to perform, only each group has a different composition to choreograph and perform. We drew sticks and luckily, got hip-hop," Becca explains.

"It's in our best area of expertise… mine, specifically," Skylar cockily winks.

"What did Candi's group get?" Jessica asks while jealously staring her down.

"I see you've already acquainted with the 'Wicked Witch of Fairview High'. No need for long introductions and we're already off to a good start!" Skylar shrugs with an apathetic sigh.

"I believe they got hip-hop as well. As I recall, there were three hip-hop groups, two contemporary, and two jazzes," Becca chuckles, playfully rolling her eyes at Skylar.

"No surprise there, they're always our big competitors," another girl sighs.

"Okay, we need a group name!" Skylar announces. "I vote 'Team Skylar' for our group name!" he continues.

"No, we need a name that applies to everyone, thank you," Becca sarcastically slurs.

"How about something like, 'Galaxy Quest' then?" he suggests after minutes and minutes of thinking in silence. The group nods in agreement.

"Nice one, Sky!" says another female in their group.

This is going to be so exciting!

****

Chapter Five

Jared had one final look back at his reflection before reaching into his jacket pocket and grabbing the small silver flask, unscrewing the cap before chugging the remaining drop of alcohol, then reaching for his backpack to shove the evidence in his front pocket. He then zips his backpack up before throwing it back over his shoulder. Suddenly, he found himself clutching onto the sink counter to keep his balance as the room began to spin due to the amount of alcohol he already consumed throughout the day. He heard the door rattle, "Just a minute," he insisted, shaking the hair from his face when standing back up straight.

"Oh, hey bud… are you okay? You don't look so good," his friend Lucas noticed when stepping into the bathroom after Jared had opened and unlocked the door.

"Great," Jared had replied with yet another groan, wiping his mouth with the back of his hand. He almost stumbles until Lucas pulls him up by the arm.

"If you want, I could drive you home? After I'm done taking a piss of course," he chuckles.

"No thanks man, I've got practice."

"Alright then," says Lucas walking over to the urinals.

It was after school when Jared made his way to the field after a change of clothes in the locker rooms. Courtney soon jogged over to him in her cheer uniform, leaving the group of cheerleaders she was surrounded by.

"Guess who made captain!" she exclaims, waving her pom-poms in his groggy, washed-out face.

"You cheer?"

"I always have, silly!"

He looks around the field and spots Jaiden huddled with the rest of the team on the field.

"Daniels! Get in here!" the coach shouted in the distance.

"Give me a minute coach!" Jared had shouted back causing the coach to return to his clipboard. He continues to look around whilst Courtney babbles on and in his gander, spotted Jessica on the bleachers with

Becca, Skylar, and Hobbs. He knew they obviously weren't here to support him. Courtney turns to look in the same direction as him after noticing he had lacked on listening.

"So, are we still on?" she asks, enviously staring down Jessica.

"Yeah," he quickly responds, snapping out of his thoughts.

"You haven't told anyone, have you?" he worriedly asked, meeting her gaze once again.

"No, I—"

"Courtney!" Candi calls out, walking over to the two alongside Tanya and Sophie, causing Courtney to divert her attention.

"Let's go, we need you over there!" Tanya indicates on the left of Candi.

"Yeah hang on, give me a second," she insisted causing Candi to roll her eyes, turning away as the girls tailgate behind her. "No, of course not Jare," Courtney answers after turning around again.

"Daniels! I'm not going to ask you again! Get in here!"

"Okay, I've got to go, good luck," Jared bid, putting on his helmet before running onto the field.

"So nice of you to finally show up," Jaiden sarcastically implied out of spite whilst putting in his mouth guard as the players rounded up in their lines.

"I should be telling you that," Jared annoyingly retorts. He stares up at the bleachers for a mid-second to see if Jessica was watching, which she was, but focusing on Jaiden. He faces Jaiden again now, "How long has it been since you've last been to practice, three…four…five months?"

"Relax bro, I had plans… but I'm sorry, you wouldn't know, would you? You see, unlike you, I'm the type of guy people actually 'want' to invite to parties," Jaiden devilishly chuckles, bumping fists with another teammate. "You on the other hand, just tag along as a plus one," he chuckles.

"Tell me something Jaiden, is it still funny knowing that your girlfriend chose me before she resorted to you? And while we're on the subject, how does it feel to be a rebound? To know that you're only the next best thing," he taunted and as soon as those words leave his mouth, they heard a whole bunch of "ooooooos" coming from their teammates. Enraged, Jaiden pulls off his mouth guard, throwing it onto the ground. He was this close to cracking. "Coincidence that she finally chose to date you after I was finished with her?" he continuously provoked. *Oh well look who's the arrogant bastard now.*

Jaiden had enough. He pulled off his helmet, throwing it to the ground and came up to shove him in the chest. "You wanna go?" Jared came back up, shoving him back aggressively in defense. Jaiden punched him, knocking him to the ground like a bowling pin. "I'm tired of your shit, Jared!" Jaiden spat, wrestling him on the field as the team crowds around the two of them. Jared tried kicking Jaiden off and removing himself from under his grip while Jaiden pinned his arms down and continued with giving him hard hits to the face. Meanwhile, Jessica had been discussing with Skylar and Becca about their choreography routine when Hobbs tapped her on the shoulder, pointing over at the field. She couldn't see much from her bleacher elevation with all the players hurdling around the fight that was happening, but she saw two numbers missing on the field and it was enough for her to take a stab and guess that the stars of this fight were none other than her current boyfriend and her ex-boyfriend.

"Oh my god!" Jessica pants, moving past the crowd in the field after a jog down the bleachers. The crowd got massive just seconds before the coach had walked in. "Jaiden, get off him!" Jessica struggles to come between, breaking them apart as they tussled on the ground. Somehow, she knew Jared was no match to Jaiden and wanted to intervene before things got ugly for Jared. That was all anyone could do at the moment, was to try pushing them apart. Especially for Jessica, since she knew how men can get during fights. She did not want to risk ending up back in the hospital like last time. The coach soon pulls Jaiden off.

"Get all your stuff, you're off the team," he says releasing him.

"What? H-how? He fought too!"

"Jared didn't miss nearly as many practices, now leave!" the coach scowls, picking up his helmet and aiming it right at his chest. Frustrated, Jaiden grabbed the back of his head and hounded Jared with bitter resentment. He made one final look at Jessica before throwing his helmet back onto the field and walking away.

"Jaiden!" she yelled, running up behind him. She places a hand at his shoulder hoping to stop him as soon as she catches up, but he shrugged her hand away bitterly. "Jaiden, stop!" she cries out after stopping in her tracks. She was unable to catch up to him anymore, out of breath.

"Leave me the hell alone, would you!" he spat.

"Fine, I guess you want me to just walk away, right? You've got what you wanted and now we're done, aren't we?" her voice cracks. He stops and turns around, red in the face. She then walks up closer to him. "What are you talking about?"

"Jaiden, I've heard rumors in this school. I know what they say about you. I know about you and Beverly—"

"God, this again! Jessica, you don't really believe her?"

"At first, I wasn't sure but everyone else made it so damn convincing that you only use girls. You have a reputation Jaiden. I wouldn't want to stand in your way. So, do it Jaiden. If it means so much to you, just do it already!"

"Do what!" he shouts.

"Leave! Jaiden! Leave! You do it with everyone else…"

"You're different," he sighs, dropping his head.

"Different? Please. How many times have you used that card?"

"Jessica, what do you want from me!"

"I just want to understand why you're pushing me away," she hoarsely said.

"I can't do this anymore!" he hesitantly yells, staring at the ground and then back up at the distraught teenager. "This isn't working out the way I wanted, I thought I could do this but," he says scratching the back of his head.

"Well, what is it that you want Jaiden, 'sex'?" she accused, crossing over her arms.

"You must think I'm only using you for that right?" he says raising his voice.

"That's because that's the only thing on your damn mind!" she yells.

"Jess," he sighs, walking up closer to her until she stops him. "God. Y-you're just like him… aren't you? I put my complete trust in you which was something difficult for me to do considering everything I've had to go through. A-and as soon as I let you in, you give up on me!"

"This isn't about me Jess! This is about your lack of self-control and indecisiveness! I have more self-control than you, believe it or not. God, if you only knew how many girls I've turned down while you and 'Jared' were dating, because that's how much I love 'you'! I'm committed to 'you' and only 'you'!

"When you and Jared were together, I knew I needed to start changing, so you'd want to be with me. O-okay why do you think Candi dumped me? That night you caught Jared cheating, I told her that I didn't want to have sex with her because I couldn't stop thinking about you! Yes, 'she' dumped me and I'm not afraid to admit it because I do love you Jessica, and if I must downgrade my social class because I hang with 'unpopular people' or the 'wrong crowd' then so be it, because you matter more to me than what other people think!"

"Spare me Jaiden, why should I believe you now after all this time?" she cried out again, wiping under her eyes.

"People do change, Jessica. I'm trying so hard to be perfect for you, I wish you could see past that. Hell, Jessica! I don't know what you want me to say! I'm sorry, I'm no Jared, okay!" he frustrates, running his fingers through his hair again.

"What did Jared tell you on that field Jaiden?"

"He told me the truth, I'm goddamn tired of being in second place!"

"Second place? Jaiden, you just don't get it, do you?"

"Jess! Are you coming to practice?" she heard Becca call out in the distance. She turns her attention and holds up a finger to assure them she will be done in a minute. She then turns back around only to find Jaiden has already walked away.

"Hey, we weren't done talking!" she shouts.

"Well, I was," he says walking backwards now, "It's either me… or 'him'," he pointed out behind her before returning in his path.

She turned around while Jared struggled to limp over to her. *What a lovely second day of school.*

"Jared, are you okay?" she asks, walking up and touching his open scar on the right of his forehead.

"Jessica, can we talk?" He grunts in pain while almost stumbling as she quickly catches him. "Jared, you're bleeding!" She helps him while he limps his way, leading them both over to the locker rooms. He sits down on the bench after they had entered. "Water," he pants, pointing to the direction of the water. She hurriedly grabs the small paper-like cup and pours water from the jug in the room. She proceeds to hand it to him and he drinks it all in one gulp.

"Want more?" she giggles, and he nods, no. As much as she wanted him to rot in hell for the terrible things he did or said to her, she still cared for him as a friend. She sighs and takes a seat next to him. "Shame your new 'girlfriend' didn't help," she pettishly implied when scooting away to fold her arms bitterly.

"Courtney?" he chuckles. "Never."

"Then why sleep with her?"

"I honestly don't know why but can we not get into this now, it's in the past and there's clearly no point to care, seeing as you've already moved on to Jaiden." *Now he was being just as petty.*

"Okay if you're going into the name calling again, I don't want to hear it," she warned, getting up.

"Jess wait, I have something to confess," he proclaimed weakly. She inadvertently turned around. "Help me up, please?" In the spur of the moment, she pitied him and decided to help him up as he limps the rest of the way to his locker. He unzips something and makes his way back over to her, reclaiming his seat. He hands her an alcoholic flask and her mouth hung open, she slouched back down on the bench and waited for an explanation from him.

"Drinking Jared? 'Drinking' Jared?" she elevated louder than before, "Really!" she emphasized with distraught. She leaned in to smell his breath. She scoffed, "And of course you'd be intoxicated right now!" It hit her, "You're intoxicated on campus!" she scolded. "Jared, this is so unlike you! Why would you do something so stupid?"

"Better yet," she said setting the flask on the bench, "Tell me once you've detoxed!" she stood up. "I have!" he protested, "It's not that strong, trust me."

"Hmmmm, and how long has this been going on exactly?" she interrogated, crossing her arms. "Couple of days."

"Where did you even get this stuff?" she asks again, snatching the flask from his hands now. "Geez, I feel like I'm being interrogated right now!"

"Jared, this isn't a funny matter, this is serious and a crime, it's one thing to be drunk at a party but in public where other people can notice... where did you get this, Jared?" she continuously interrogated, placing her hands on her hips.

"A friend I recently started socializing with..."

"Back it up, so you mean to tell me you were drunk when you said that awful thing to me the other day?" she asked hopeful, even though it wouldn't completely justify what he said.

"What awful thing?" he asks confused. She shrugged her body forward, "My point exactly."

"Jessica, I'm sorry for whatever fucked up thing I may have said to you whenever, but I wasn't myself!" he tries to protest.

"I want to believe you but even if you were or weren't drunk, it's no excuse!"

"And obviously the drink was stronger than you thought if you didn't remember what you said..." There is an awkward three-minute silence between the two, the tension building up before she joined him back on the bench again. "Besides, why did you ignore me in chem and calculus then, if you being mad at me because I was 'unwashed white trash' wasn't the case?"

"Jess?" He displaces a hand at her thigh, "My god, I'm such an asshole, aren't I?" he says embracing the girl in for a hug, stroking her hair.

"I can't argue with that," she says lightly chuckling. He sighs before speaking out again, "And I only ignored you because you wanted me out of your life forever, remember?"

"They say if you love someone, you let them go... which is exactly what I had to do," he says looking away as sorrow fills both of their young eyes.

"Jared, just answer me this one question… why?"

"Why did you feel the need to cheat or even lie in the first place and why start drinking, why now?"

"I lied to you because I was scared… my friends wanted to hang out and I was afraid to let them down. I lied to you because I knew you would never have let me go to that party."

"Damn right I wouldn't!" she huffs, crossing her arms again.

"I knew how you would've assumed that my friends were more important to me," he sighs, "I still don't know why I slept with Courtney, I was just caught up in the moment, I guess."

"I was drunk yes, but it was a blur, a disaster. I don't like Courtney in that way and we both agree it was only a stupid mistake."

"What would've happened if I never caught you Jare? You probably would have never told me, huh?"

"In time I would have, but if I'm being completely honest, I never thought of it because I knew you would have reacted the same way and I would've lost you anyways…"

"I guess I just wanted to know what it was like being Jaiden for once. And I only started drinking after I started hanging out with this kid; he offered, I tried, and it wasn't so bad. I wanted to stop before it got out of hand, but every time I think of you and Jaiden… I lose it, it eases the stress in my heart."

"Jared, it also turns you into this complete jerk!"

"You have got to stop before this gets worse, please!" she desperately pleas, setting a hand on his lap as he scoots his body forward. She takes the opportunity to lift his shirt, smacking him on the chest as he winces. "Start explaining," she demands.

"You said you were going to ask one question, that was three," he chuckles, still clutching onto his bruised chest in pain.

"If you haven't noticed, I still care for you, you big idiot! So if you want to regain my trust, you have to answer… everything and truthfully."

"Okay, okay," he breathes out shaky. "You're probably not going to believe me though… no one else knows this, but…"

"This guy, his name is Robbie, some people refer to him as 'Montoya'… we go way back, not obviously as long as I've known you, of course. Anyways, we were close friends and he was a good, educated, smart kid. When we were younger, after school when you and Jaiden would ditch me to go hang out all the time, I'd also ditch because I wanted to hang out with my friend, Robbie that no one knew about, that was my mistake because I see now how close you and Jaiden have gotten," he sighs. "In middle school, he got into this gang and would

101

slack off his homework and studies to go meet up with them. Being the good friend that I am, I covered up for his tracks and lied to his mom as he requested. I even started doing his homework for him, barely keeping up with my own... my grades started slipping.

"I didn't even care about my own school work as I was trying to focus on his all the time because he was the only friend I had at the time, school wise. Of course, there was Jaiden, but we wouldn't hang out as much, we'd only hang out together with you. Well, Robbie barely hung out with me ever since that gang he joined, only when I would hand him his finished homework, I'd get a, 'thank you buddy, see you in class', and that was it ever since his new friends. It was like he was embarrassed to be seen with me because of this new image he was trying to build, but enough was enough, I put my foot down; I was really worried about him. I didn't want him to fall into the wrong crowd, so I had to do what I had promised I wouldn't do... go to his mother.

"I told her everything and she thanked me. I knew it would ruin our friendship, but I cared more about his health, if he was taking drugs and, or consuming alcohol. Of course, I broke his trust, but I needed to do the right thing. Who knows, maybe he would one day thank me later for helping his sorry ass in the future? I was wrong, he hated me ever since. His mom started getting violent because she was under a lot of stress since his parents divorced that same year and after she found out that her 'sweetheart of a son' was doing bad things, she kind of lost it, started getting into alcohol. Took these man hormonal pills. Turned into a he-she lesbian. She started beating him and although he didn't tell me, I could tell it was her. Up until freshman year, he had been living across the street from me and I could hear the screams, the cries... He would come to school in bruises because of the stupid shit he pulled with his new friends. Never learned his lesson. Eventually, someone finally snitched on his mother and she went to prison, having to sell the house back to the bank and putting Robbie in foster care since he didn't have any other close relatives. After that, I completely didn't recognize him anymore, he started going to the gym every day. Ever since I broke his trust, he blamed everything on me I guess, and took his anger from home out on me, now I guess he just continues because it makes him popular but as it turned out, my best friend had turned into my bully with just a blink of an eye.

"That day you came to our school and told me to leave you alone, Robbie showed up and duct taped me to the toilet in the boys' bathroom along with his gang and they left me with nothing but my boxers. One of them even took a piss on me, they completely flooded the restroom with my clothes when they dumped it into the toilet. This guy named Brennan showed up, helped me out. He is a smart, straight A student like Robbie used to be. The thing is, Brennan got into a bad crowd as well, he started drinking but only time to time and he manages to get his homework done each day. So, after I changed on campus after having all my clothes taken from me that day, we went around the campus just chilling as he told me of his background. Turns out, we aren't so different… he too was always bullied in many forms throughout his whole life but only recently by Robbie. He offered me a joint, but I declined. I started telling him my story and he said to me when I finished, 'here take this. Trust me, you're gonna need it.' I thought about it, hesitated at first before taking it from his hands just to examine it. He told me, 'Don't take too much', and we were now in the front of the school as his mom honked in the distance and he left before I could give it back."

"But why haven't you told anyone about Robbie?"

"I can't, I'm afraid of him now, he's gotten stronger and I-I—"

"You have to! Tell the principal, your parents, someone! He can't keep hurting you and this, 'this' has got to stop!" she urges, taking the flask from his hands. "Now hurry up and get changed! I'll be in the parking lot," she demands when standing up.

"Aren't you supposed to be hanging out with Jaiden or something?"

"Just hurry up!" she hissed.

She waited in her car for Jared, deciding to check her phone in the meantime. Two missed calls from Becca, *crap*. She proceeded to text her back.

To: Becca
I'm so sorry, I can't make practice… rain check?
From: *Becca* **to:** *Jessica*
Don't sweat it. Yeah, sounds good! We'll talk later .x-B

She continues scrolling through her phone, checking her social media accounts, Twitter specifically. She gets a mention from fans of the twins, tagging her @ name which was a private account, directing her to a status that Jared recently posted, it read:

@jareddaniels: *"It's amazing how no matter how terrible of a person someone is, you are always there for me ♥"*

The tweet was sent five minutes ago so it was obvious he had been indirectly talking about Jessica. She turned her phone off and stares out the rear-view mirror just as Jared swiftly exits the building, barely limping as much as he did about an hour ago. She honks to let him know where she was parked, and he walks closer, opening the passenger door.

When he sat down, she couldn't help but to grin like a bashful idiot. "What?" he smiles out confused, tugging on his seatbelt.

"Oh nothing," she smiled back before backing out of the parking lot.

****

There she was driving, about to make a right turn to his house until he stopped her, "Wait, my parents got home last night, and I don't want them to see me like this."

"Jared, you know I don't have my apartment, right?"

"Yeah," he sighs.

"I guess I forgot."

"Where are you going then?" he asks when noticing as she pulls the car forward.

She takes a deep breath, "You can say one night at Mandy's, if she'll let you but after that, you're going home to tell your parents."

"Of course. I just can't confront them right now, I need to know how to tell them, thank you Jess."

"What did you tell them before?"

"They never saw the bruises on my body, so I told them the ones on my face were from practice or games."

"I will take you to school tomorrow, but we can't let anyone, especially Jai know that you slept over, he's already mad at me," she advises while pulling up on Mandy's driveway. "Okay good, no one's home right now," she noted before stepping out. She unlocked the front door, and they throw off their backpacks by the doorway.

"Do you need anything?" she asks.

"Well, I could use a shower if you don't mind?" he chuckles.

"Hang on a sec," she says walking into her room.

"Here," she directs, stepping out with some clean, fresh clothes. "I found some of your clothes in one of my drawers that I forgot to give you back when I was packing. I re-washed them because I couldn't tell if they were clean or not, you can wear them to school tomorrow if you want," she says handing him the stack of clothes from her arms.

"These aren't mine," he says holding up a pair of boxers.

"I wear briefs."

She snatched the underwear after remembering they were in fact Jaiden's unmentionables, *whoopsie*. "Must be Kevin's then; his laundry is always getting mixed in with mine, damn Mandy!" she lies. "Anyways, the shower is this way, if you'd follow me," she directs, imitating a tour guide. She opens the door and tugs the curtain open while he sets the clean clothes and towels down on the sink counter. She turns on the showerhead and directs him to where everything is at before exiting, closing the door behind. She then enters her room and begins doing her homework on her wooden student desk. By the time he finishes and enters her room, she had already finished her calculus homework and he was freshly clothed.

"Nice room," he says while shaking his damp hair from his face with a towel. The way his bicep flexed as he did it, *wow…* she gulped. "Where can I toss this?" he asks causing her to snap out of her wild thoughts. She quickly stood up from her office chair and held out her hands as he tossed his towel over to her.

When she returned from the laundry room, he sat there on the bed with a small grey packet of pills in his hands.

"What's this?" he asks looking up at her.

"It's my…"

"I know what it is, why do you have it?" he asks again.

"My doctor recommended it since I've been …sexually active again," she admitted, uncomfortably staring down at her feet.

"Oh," was all he managed to get out while his face fell to the floor, saddened. He set it back on her nightstand.

"I'm sorry… you probably didn't need to know all that extra detail," she said walking up and taking the packet, throwing it into a random drawer.

"No, I should've never asked, it's none of my business, but as long as you guys are safe that's all that matters, right?" he lightheartedly mentions. "Mandy or Kevin home yet?" he asks quickly changing the subject.

"Nope. Here, wait hold on," she insisted, exiting the room. "Come here," she directs when returning with a first aid kit.

"What are you doing?" he asks, standing tall before walking over to the girl.

She rolls her eyes, "Come on," she urges, pulling him by the arm. "Sit," she instructs, pushing him down on the couch with her in the living room.

"Ow! Fuck!" he yells.

She giggles in response, "Sorry." She turns his face slightly to hers, examining his wound.

"Do you know what you're doing?" he asks uneasy.

"Of course," she says, beginning to stitch his wound. He stares into her eyes as she focuses on his scar. "I took a medical training program in camp last summer," she explains. He winces in pain before she slapped him on the arm, pulling the needle away, "Would you stop moving?" she hissed.

"I'm sorry, it hurts!"

"Oh, well in that case, please continue. I'll just accidentally poke your eyeball out then," she teased as he promptly arched his back without another breath the entire time. "And there!" she exclaims after finishing her job. He stood up to examine himself in the bathroom.

"Wow, that fast huh?"

He touches his scar again after rejoining her in the living room, "Wow, you're a natural. Thanks!"

"Stop touching my masterpiece!" she laughs out.

"Hey, we're home!" Mandy calls out, entering the house with Kevin.

"Over here!" Jessica directs, and they follow her voice, entering the living room.

"Hey... you're not Jaiden?" Mandy questions, her pitch changing in confusion. She set the groceries on the counter behind them.

"Mandy, Jared got injured so he's going to stay the night... if that's alright with you and Kevin?"

"Of course, are you two?"

"No," they both shot down, simultaneously.

"You know what? I lost track," Amanda jokes out, placing the milk in the refrigerator.

"You're hilarious," Jessica's voice filled with sarcasm. "Come on Jare, let's do our homework," Jessica growls in annoyance, grabbing Jared's hand and leading him to her bedroom. She got all her homework done within an hour and a half, Jared on the other hand, takes longer but they still had managed to finish early.

"Hey, are you going to tonight's party?"

"No, I'm not 'cool' enough to attend, apparently," she bitterly responded, reclining back in her chair.

"It's open invite; Josh's parties are always open invite," he explains, looking up from his phone.

"Do you want to?" she bites down on her lower lip, awaiting an answer.

"It beats staying at home with nothing to do."

"I guess," she shrugged. "Would we go together though?" It was obvious that they would, since she would be his only way of getting there tonight. "Yeah, never mind, bad idea. I can't have any more rumors spreading about me and I certainly don't need Jaiden getting mad." She didn't want to attend with Jared for the fact that Jaiden almost gave her an ultimatum, if she had shown up with Jared, then it would be obvious to Jaiden that she chose Jared over himself. That would not be the case for Jessica. She was determined to prove him that she could be friends with anyone. "But you know, I don't care what he thinks anymore, let him think what he wants! We 'are' going to that party and if he really wants me, he's going to have to deal with 'my' choices!" Jared gives Jessica who was off in her own thoughts, a confused stare.

"Cool? So... what should I wear?" he asks.

"Oh um, here, just swap shirts," she says tossing him another shirt from a drawer that had mostly Jaiden's clothes in it, clean of course. She locked the door to start changing after Jared exited the room. She wondered what to wear while nearly turning her closet upside down. While she continued to toss clothes in pile, a new centerpiece forms, smack down in the center of her bedroom. Just then, she saw the dress she wore in the summer of her first party. She examines it after pulling it off the shelf from the hanger, before shrugging it into the pile as well. As her whole wardrobe is now flopped onto the floor, a dress she came across that she had seemed to forget about, glistens in the distance; the only dress still left hanging in her closet. She picks it up with the hanger; it was a sort of flashy dress, short but not too short, party-type, sparkly (like her character), and perfect.

She effortlessly slides into the dress, it was indeed a perfect fit. She had to be sure to check herself in the mirror before stepping into her small bathroom. There, she applies her makeup, a little darker around her eyes than usual and with an hour left to spare, she grabbed her curling iron to start curling her hair. As soon as she finished, she stepped out, trying to balance in her heels. "Ready to go?" she asks making her way over to Jared, who was currently on the couch playing video games with Kevin.

He turns around and his mouth trembles, "Y-yeah. Wow," he breathes out when standing up, almost losing his balance from getting lost in her beauty.

"Not too bad yourself Daniels," she giggles after examining what he was wearing.

"Is your leg feeling better?" she cautiously reminds.

"Yeah, way."

As they walk over to the front door, they get stopped by Mandy who makes her way over, "Where do you think you're going dressed like that?" she asked crossing her arms.

"Don't see anything wrong with the way I look," Jessica confidently justified, eyeing herself from the heels and up. "Go change Jessica, I'm not going to ask you again."

"I don't need your permission!"

Jessica derogatively grew flustered by each second Amanda had stalled with questions. "Where are you two going this late?"

"A party, can I be excused now?"

"No, I don't want you to go, you know what happened the last time—"

"Which is why I am not planning to drink."

"Ah, I see. Now what about the sex?"

"Oh my God, Amanda! Way to beat around the bush! You're so annoying!" she dramatically groaned, opening the door and quickly walking out.

"Jared, please watch her?" He nods before catching up to Jessica, who was already outside as Amanda closes the door behind the two. She almost trips but he fortunately caught up to her just in time, clutching onto her waist.

He raises a brow, "You sure you can walk in those heels?" She gives him a deadly stare whilst opening the door to her car and gets in without a peep, unlocking it for him to climb inside from the passenger's seat shortly after. As the two arrive in Josh's parking lot, after she had found a parking space, she looked to Jared after he hadn't said a word the entire car ride, "Jare, what's wrong?"

"M-maybe we should go in separately," he worries.

"You don't have to be scared of Jaiden, now let's go," she says stepping out, fixing her dress on the way inside. They walk in through the back and make their way around downstairs to find any of their shared friends.

"Damn, Jessica!" Becca announced, coming towards the two causing Jaiden to shoot his head in her direction.

"Jared, come here!" Jess directs, gesturing for him to come closer. She looks over at Jaiden and his head falls back, finishing the rest of his drink before crumpling the plastic cup to the floor, still never leaving his eyes off her. She knew she was in deep trouble. "So how was practice?" she asked Becca, and Skylar who was right next to her.

"Practice was 'very' good, thanks for not showing up," Skylar slurs with a wink as his lips travel to Becca's neck when hugging her from behind.

She scoffs and pushes him off. "Sorry, he's a little drunk," she apologized.

It wasn't until then that Jessica felt a tap on her bare shoulder causing her to turn around. "What the fuck is this?" Jaiden asked, looking down at her interlocked hands with Jared as his jaw tenses when he looked back up at Jared. "I leave you for four hours and you are already fucking him again!" he says through his teeth, looking raw at Jared now.

"Hey, is that any way to talk to a lady?" Skylar asks.

"Yeah because 'you' know," Becca adds.

108

"Relax, he's just a friend, nothing is going on between us!" Jessica shouted over the loud music.

"I thought I made it clear that it was either me or him!"

"You can't tell me who I can or cannot be friends with!" she sneers, crossing her arms.

"What the hell are you even wearing?"

"You like?" she winks.

"We need to talk," he says tugging her by the arm, dragging her up the stairs. They get inside a vacant room, flickering on the lights. He quickly pulled her inside and locked the door behind them.

"Ow Jaiden! What the hell do you want!"

She was cut off when he smashed his lips to hers just seconds after he turned her around. "Your dress is inappropriate for the occasion. Take it off," he demands between breaths as his lips reach to her neck, she bites her lip and smirks. She then turns around, allowing him to unzip her dress, letting it fall to the floor. She felt him get closer until he backed her up against the wall with his hot breath sizzling onto her skin from behind, and he begins sucking on her neck. "Jump," he whispers seductively into her ear. She obliges, wrapping her legs around his torso as he never breaks contact with her lips. He holds onto her, walking her over to lay her down on the bed. He throws his shirt over his head before she pulled him back down to kiss her.

****

"Good morning," he says in a low rasp, rubbing his eyes open.

"Good mor—"

"Oh shit!" she exclaimed, sitting up.

"What time is it?" she panicked, scanning the room for a clock. There was one on the nightstand that read 6:15 and she sighed in relief. Jaiden rolls on the other side of the bed. "Get up! You're going to be late for school!" she mentioned after a change of clothes. She crawled back over to him, playing with the locks of his hair. He groans, pulling the blanket up higher in annoyance.

"Ugh!" She stood back up on his side, purposely crawling off him. He chuckles in response and hugs her from behind causing her to fall back with him as he lays back down. That was certainly not the response she expected to get after doing that. "You're not getting out so easily," he purrs when flipping the two of them over as he begins tickling the girl. Her fit of laughter quickly faded after she reminisced her déjà vu. "What's the matter?"

109

"Shit! Jared!" She pushed Jaiden off as soon as she remembered Jared. She averted from the bed, "Hurry up and get ready, I'll see you in school!"

"Jared?" he asked after she had already ran out of the room.

On the other hand, Jared was nowhere to be found and neither was anyone else familiar, so that Jess may ask if they had remembered seeing him, probably because they were all on their way to school. She saw one of the last people she wanted to see there, Nick in the distance heading for the door. She decided to go to him to ask if he had seen Jared since he was her only hope. "Hey, Nick!" she called out in desperation.

"Oh hey! Jessica, right?"

"Have you seen Jared by chance?" she straight forwardly asked, not having time for any small talk. "Now remind me again, which twin was that?"

"I don't have time for this," she groaned with an eye roll out the door, past him. Now, *now* she was worried. *Is he in school?* She automatically assumed the worst. *How would he have gotten there? It's a twenty-minute walk and his legs still may be sore. I hope he got there safely at least. Maybe he didn't leave too long ago and if I start driving now, maybe I can find him? Or maybe he got attacked by bears on his way home?* Then there was the worst possibility; that he had met up with Courtney and they left together, *ugh.* She still needed to go home and change out of her dress. She hoped Mandy didn't completely kill her considering she 'was' supposed to be at home last night and Jared 'was' her responsibility; his parents would kill her if they knew Jared stayed over and if they found out something terrible happened to him. She didn't want to be held responsible for that, especially since they thought so low of Jessica already. When she returned home, she noticed Mandy was upstairs, still asleep, and Kevin was already out of the house for work since his car was gone and so were his keys that were once hanging from its designated rack. She was thankful her room was downstairs, so in and out would not be a problem; ironically, she wished someone would have told her the same, to avoid a certain sticky situation during the start of the school year. As she drove up to the campus, she saw a body near the basketball courts, lying on the floor; she curiously drove closer and her heart almost stopped. She sloppily parked on the curb and ran out of her car to help without shutting the ignition off. "Oh my God!" she shrieked, covering her mouth. It was Jared, just as she had suspected. His right eye was completely swollen and black and his lips were puffy and cut a bit. His face was even more busted now than from before Jaiden on the football field. "Who? H-

110

how?" she worried, unable to form sentences. This was definitely not the work of Jaiden since he was with her the entire night.

Chapter Six

"I got jumped by Robbie and his friends on the way to school," he coughs out, sitting up on the verge of noticing himself coughing up blood.

"You didn't drink at the party, did you?" Jessica asks while his head digs into her shoulders.

"No, I've stopped."

"Oh my God!" she gasped, "Your scar ripped!" she noticed gently examining his scar with her touch and he cried out. She quickly brings the boy into the warmth of her arms again when suddenly they are both alarmed by a car door slamming shut in the distance. She whips her head around to find Jaiden walking to them from the parking lot.

"The fuck is going on?" Jaiden angers, making his way toward the two. He pushes Jared's shoulder back standing behind him now in an attempt to remove his brother from the comfort of his girlfriend's arms, but not before she shoves his hand away, "Stop! Can't you see he's hurt!"

"Come on, we need to get you to the hospital, you're bleeding everywhere!" she panics standing up.

"I-I can't move, I-I think I twisted my ankle when trying to outrun them," Jared panted. Jaiden walked over to the other side of Jared to help him on his feet. "Help me take him to the hospital—" Lucas hollers approaching the three of them now.

"Not now, Jared's hurt," Jaiden informs. "Oh shit, is there anything I can do to help?" Lucas insists.

"Grab his legs," Jaiden requests. Lucas nods and they carry him to the parking lot.

"Pop the trunk," Lucas teased after they had approached Jaiden's car.

"We are not all going to fit in this car," Jessica points out.

"I could drive, I borrowed my mom's SUV for the week," Lucas suggests. They continue walking to the opposite side of the parking lot after agreeing with their only and best option at this point. Lucas and Jaiden gently lay Jared down in the backseat as Hobbs, Alex, Skylar, and Becca hop out of their car that they just passed the four in after parking.

"What's going on?" the blond kid named Alex had asked, approaching them from the other side.

"Jared got hurt or whatever, but he should be okay… he just likes to cause a scene," Jaiden chuckles earning himself a hard nudge to the elbow by Jessica.

"It's pretty bad, we're driving him to the hospital," Jessica explained. "I'm going to go wait with him in the car, hurry… please!" she pleads before getting in the back with Jared and closing the door. Skylar and Becca decided to tag along while Hobbs and Alex would stay in school to tell the rest of them what they missed in classes that day since most all of them shared the same teachers. They take their seats, with Lucas driving, Jaiden in the passenger seat since Jessica decided to sit in the back with Jared lying on her lap, and Becca and Skylar in the second row of the van, right up in front of the two. Lucas shifts his eyes between the rear-view mirror and the road.

"Are you okay there Jared?"

Jared groans in response. "Hang in there bud, don't bleed anywhere," he says followed by a chuckle leaving Jaiden's mouth. For Lucas, he made sure Jaiden understood it was no joking matter, "I'm being dead serious… if you bleed anywhere in my mom's new car, it's out on the streets for you," he says directing at Jared from his reflection on his rear-view mirror before proceeding to drive.

"So, what exactly happened to you back there?" Becca asks turning around. Jared responds with yet another groan.

"Jeez Jaiden, you've got quite an arm!" Skylar continues facing Jared and Jessica now, examining Jared some more.

"It wasn't me, I swear!" Jaiden protests lifting his hands.

"He was bullied now back off and let him breathe!" Jessica growled, teeth gritting in defense.

"No further questions," Skylar resigned; both he and Becca turned back around in respect to Jessica's request.

"Bullied?" Jaiden suspiciously wonders.

"God dammit Jaiden! I said no more questions!" she hissed once more. "I'm sorry… I had to tell them," she whispered to Jared, caressing his hairless face while his head rested on her lap. The gang approached the building entrance upon arrival and the three friends: Sky, Lucas, and Jaiden, carried Jared inside. Jessica melancholy stopped herself right at the door and the guys turned to face her from the inside with Becca stopping right behind Jessica.

"Jessica, what's wrong?" Becca asks.

"I uh—" she hesitantly stuttered, "I-I can't do this," she dramatically emphasized, covering her mouth and walking away.

"Jess?" Becca calls out confused. As soon as Jessica walked away, Jaiden let his grip on his younger brother go, letting Skylar take his place.

"Take him inside, Becca go with them. I'll be back," he informs before trying to catch up to Jessica after Becca steps inside.

"Jess where are you going?" Jaiden calls out causing her to turn around.

"I-I don't know where, I just can't be in there... not again," she faintly speaks continuing to walk.

"Hey, wait up! Damn you're fast!" He now ran in front of her.

She sighs and wipes her eyes. She looks up at him with her bloodshot, overworked-out eyes and bites the top of her lip, furrowing her brows. She smiles for a moment, losing herself in his eyes before she covers her mouth again and drops her eyes. He takes the opportunity to wrap his arms around her trembling body as she sobs onto his chest. It was a traumatic experience she could never really let go of. "It's okay, it'll be okay," he coos gently grazing over her hair. She pulls away seconds later and nods. "Who did this to him?" he asks after a few moments of silence.

"I can't say," she sighs sitting down on the curb after calming herself down.

"Well, he's definitely not going to tell me so if I were you, I'd speak up or chances are, if no one's gonna stop that kid that bullied him, Jared will be back here again. So if you really care about his well-being, I suggest—" A worrisome Jessica had interrupted before he even finished his thought, obliging to answer instantly even though she swore she wouldn't say anything. She knew she broke his trust, but she cared more about the well-being of her best friend and former lover.

"His name is Robbie Montoya, Jared only recently told me about him, yesterday actually," she admits, and Jaiden hurriedly ran back inside the hospital cutting her off. Yes, Jaiden had heard all about Robbie Montoya's antics and gimmicks from word on the street. The toughest guy in school, second to Aaron. Never met him once but he knew he had to straighten things out and find the underlying cause of things without needing to know the entire backstory. She whipped her head around when she heard footsteps running, Jaiden had just entered the hospital. He returns five minutes later with Lucas who beeped his car open. Jessica stood up from the curb she was sitting on just before they left.

"Where are you guys going?" she asked stopping in front of them. "Don't worry about it," Jaiden says walking around the girl to open his passenger side door. "Oh my God, please don't tell me you're going to confront this Robbie character?" she groaned, walking over to Jaiden's side. "Someone needs to stay with Jared," she reminds catching Jaiden's attention with a slight touch on the shoulder before he fully sat inside.

He sighs, "Skylar and Becca are in there with him," Jaiden says from inside the car now. Jessica hesitantly spoke out again, "I can't believe I'm letting you guys do this."

She walked over and opened the back door before too hopping inside. "Jess babe, what are you doing?"

"Someone needs to be there to help when you guys get your underwear hanged from a flag pole after getting your sorry asses kicked," she apathetically sighed closing the door and buckling her seat belt.

Lucas chuckles, "Man, quite a girlfriend you got," he says switching his car on reverse as Jaiden shuts the door.

"One of a kind," Jessica grins as Jaiden reciprocated her gesture through the rear-view mirror. They arrive at the school's parking lot.

"There he is. I have him in two of my classes," Lucas confirmed when they saw him playing basketball with his buddies in the courts outside. They finish parking, Jessica took her seat belt off, opening the car door just slightly until she was stopped.

"Jessica wait in the car," Jaiden demands unbuckling his seat belt.

"No." She proceeds to step out.

"I don't want you getting hurt," he says stepping out as well.

"I'll be the boss of my own actions," she assured folding her arms. He backed her up against the car.

"Please…" He presses his forehead to hers and grabs her hands. She tenses and tries resisting those puppy dog eyes. She then, playfully pushes him away before agreeing to get back inside the car. He smirks at her through the window rather cockily before taking off with Lucas. She then smirks back and shakes her head, *God he's so full of himself.* Lucas was last seen locking the door and cracking his knuckles in the distance. She scrolled through her phone waiting for the two of them to come back, constantly shifting her eyes between her phone and the window, although she couldn't see much with all these cars surrounding and the fact that they've parked so far away to remain 'undercover'. It's been twenty minutes and now she had been lying in the back seat, staring up at the enclosed sunroof. She couldn't even get out even if she wanted to because Lucas somehow managed to lock the door from the inside as well.

Thirty minutes and her eyelids become like slowly compressing weights until suddenly, she heard a loud noise, it sounded somewhat like a gunshot and it startled her awake. She jolted up and begun to panic.

She peeked outside and tapped on the window, "Jaiden! Lucas!" She helplessly yelped, trying to get out. She stood up and tried to find an unlock button, or anything. She clicked all the buttons on the driver's side, but still no luck. Then, she tried hitting against all the windows. Crying, she managed to climb around inside the car looking for something sharp. She dug in the backseat until she found a pair of shiny red high heels. She grabbed one and without hesitation slammed it against the window but to her disappointment, the glass didn't crack, not one bit. She apathetically threw it back over her shoulder. Due to her nervous, panicked, and sweaty state, she took off her jacket, tossing it aside. She looked around the passenger seat now to find a big red emergency lock button, and with one press successfully pushes the passenger door open. "It opened!" she exclaimed. *It was a tragedy that she didn't see it sooner, she thought.* She ran over to the basketball court. "Jaiden!" She panted looking for him, in hopes that he was okay. There, she saw him clutching onto his side in pain as his back faces in her direction. She rushed over to his aid and hugged him from behind in relief.

"Oh my God!" Jessica shrieked in terror when she saw what Jaiden was standing in front of. She covered her mouth in disbelief and Jaiden stood there traumatized by the entire thing. He had been hovering over Lucas' deceased body. There, Lucas laid inaudibly shot, bleeding right out of his chest with blood gushing out of his heart. Jessica instinctively crumbled to the floor, sobbing into her palms as the blood rushed through the concrete around her. "Where did they go? Where are the teachers, why isn't anyone helping?" she panicked, taking Lucas' hand as the blood dripped from his hand to hers.

"It's too late Jess," Jaiden sighed, running his hand through his hair. "We have to go…" he continues. "B-but we can't just leave him!"

"The teachers will find him eventually, but those guys took the only evidence we have against them, so if 'we' don't go soon, 'we're' the ones screwed—"

"Not if we call the police."

"Yeah but they can still call us in for questioning."

"Jessica look, I don't want to leave him like this either, but we have to… I have his keys, now come on," he says touching her shoulder. "Jess," he called out while she stood frozen at the sight of Lucas' cold lifeless body, obviously still fazed. She sniffled and wiped under her eyes.

"Yeah… I know, I'm coming," she croaked softly, turning around, and getting up.

"N-no," he coughed. "I need m...my... i-inhaler," he choked out while clutching onto his side again. She quickly grabbed onto him before he too collapsed.

"Where is it at?" she panicked, again.

"I left it in Lucas' car," he breathed heavily with small puffs of air left in his respiratory system. She helped him walk over to the car within five minutes. He threw her the keys and she hurriedly unlocked the car so that he could get in and grab his inhaler from the side-door compartment and puff the air into his chest. She then started the engine and shut the door after they both settled inside.

"You okay?" she asked him before drifting off. He nods reassuringly. "No... about Lucas. Do you want to talk about what happened?" He shakes his head, declining her offer.

"Not now," he states leaning out the window while she attempts to back out.

As soon as they re-pulled up to the hospital, they saw Skylar and Becca helping Jared out of the building with crutches. Jess parked and slammed the door shut to run out and embrace Jared for another comforting hug. He nearly stumbled backwards but she tenaciously clung onto him, locking him in place. Her head nuzzles in the crook of his neck to find warmth and he put his arms around her waist to the best of his disabled abilities when his crutches fall at his sides. Jared could almost cut through the thick tension with his sharp jawline, he knew there was something wrong, he could feel it. "What's going on?" he had dubiously asked. He knew Jaiden would never be okay with Jessica comforting him unless there was something wrong. The crippled boy noticed that they came out of Lucas' car but where was Lucas? He pulled away from her comfort after some time and Skylar bent over to hand Jared his crutches. "Where's Lucas?" Jared asks again looking to a distressed Jessica who impressionably seemed in dismay.

"I'm so sorry man... It's all my fault," Jaiden admitted when walking forward to give his brother a comforting hug as well.

What the hell is going on?

****

(Flashback, moments before Lucas' death)

"Okay so how should we do this?" Jaiden asks Lucas after they reach the courts. "Damn, we're outnumbered; there's three of them," Lucas notices.

"Okay... just follow my lead."

"Hey, which one of you chumps messed with my boy Jared?" Lucas asks cracking his neck. One of them so happened to turn around to chuckle. "It was me!" It didn't take a rocket scientist for the two to figure out that this meaty six-foot teenager was Robbie.

"Hey dipshit, did you come back for more?" Robbie curiously taunted as his friends stop playing basketball to see what he was talking about.

"If I'm not mistaken, I think you're referring to Jared. Believe we haven't had the pleasure of meeting before. I'm Jaiden, his more attractive, less homosexual, twin brother—"

"Jaiden? That's such a gay name! Ha!" Robbie chuckles and Jaiden atrociously rolls his eyes. Lucas then walks up and slaps the ball out of Aaron's hands.

"What the fuck do you think you're doing?" Aaron scolds shoving Lucas against the chest, completely knocking him to the ground. Jaiden immediately helps him back up.

"Guys, come on, you don't want to start any trouble," Robbie warns as Ryan kneels beside him to tie his own shoelaces. "But I'll tell you guys what, since you're desperately looking to, I'll make you a little deal… a little two on two and if we win, you guys get to see what's in store for you and if we lose, which is less likely—"

"You guys have to stop messing with Jared!" Jaiden finishes, in agreement with himself. Robbie nods.

"Ryan be on lookout!" he instructed. Twenty minutes into this match and Jaiden and Lucas successfully play out, winning for Jared's sake, *or so they thought.*

"So, who's ready to apologize?" asks Lucas, folding his arms out in front.

Robbie chuckles, "You thought you guys would actually get away without getting hurt?" He cracks his knuckles before motioning for Ryan to lock the fenced door.

"These guys won't quit, let's make a break for it!" Jaiden whispers discreetly beside Lucas. Without hesitation, Lucas threw Jaiden his car keys indicating they would try and make a break for it.

"Run!" Lucas shouted. They both ran out and tried climbing the fences as their only option out. The gang members consisted of Robbie, Ryan, and Aaron pulled the two boys down before they could escape their wrath, tackling them to the concrete floor while Robbie had begun pounding onto Jaiden and Aaron onto Lucas. With one hard hit to his groin, Jaiden managed to knock Robbie out, escaping from underneath his grip. That always seemed to work for him and most guys. The moment Robbie let his guard down to regain his strength, Jaiden took

118

the opportunity to run over and grab Ryan, restraining his arms behind his back. Aaron soon leaves Lucas on his knees all bruised to help Robbie up. "Yeah, unless you want your innocent little side bitch to suffer I suggest you stop messing with Jared!" Lucas warns standing tall and stylishly hopping over to them. There was no denying, Lucas had a good feeling that they had won after all. Not a second later and a vengeful Aaron threateningly warned the two to let their friend go. His jaw clenched tighter and the longer he waited, he found himself pulling out a handgun from the inside of his leather jacket pocket when stepping closer.

"Aye, we don't mean trouble man," Jaiden forfeits, releasing his grip on Ryan and restraining his hands up in the air while Ryan runs over to Aaron and Robbie across from Lucas and Jaiden. "Let it go man!" Robbie begs trying to get through to his friend, attempting to bring Aaron's arms down to his sides as Aaron shifts the gun between Lucas and Jaiden. Seconds later, the gunshot goes off and Jaiden covered his ears and frightfully squeezes his eyes shut. "What the FUCK!" he heard Robbie scream out in the distance, causing Jaiden to open his eyes after realizing he was still standing. To Jaiden, that could only mean one thing. They all cowardly up and ran away, hopping their side of the fence by the time Jaiden's eyes fully opened. Finally, he turned around to see what the dilemma was and to his surprise, he had guessed correctly. He didn't want to be right, but the gun did go off and if Robbie's friends survived including Jaiden himself, the bullet had to have aimed elsewhere. Jaiden's eyes locked on the dead body below him. His side began cramping from all the adrenaline inside him, and his breathing too increased from stress on the situation. A farewell to Lucas was in his favor, if only he could have saved him. Lucas was wounded like a soldier right in the heart. He had the bravery of no other, he would have jumped in front of a bullet for anyone damn right, but that unfortunately wasn't the case. His life was taken by mistake. "Shit, Lucas," is all Jaiden let out with his now bloodshot eyes, although he couldn't allow a tear to fall. Jaiden rarely cried, compared to Jared that is. If he were to cry, it'd have to affect him deeply. Lucas was his friend, yes, but he was closer to Jared. He wouldn't let this incident get to the best of him. Poor Lucas, he was just helping a friend out. Jaiden couldn't help but think Jared was going to hate him forever now. He already did but not as much as he would now. *It was practically my fault,* or so Jaiden believed. *It should have been me...* but it wasn't, *was I given a second chance at life? Now is the time to redeem my worth on this earth, especially to Jessica. Maybe I'll start with making things right with*

Jared, although it probably wouldn't work considering I have Jessica and he doesn't and the fact that his best and only friend died helping me. (End of flashback)

"Are you okay?" Jessica asks when his eyes find hers.

"Y-yeah," Jaiden responds a little on edge. She takes his right hand that rests on his lap with her left and he brings his left arm around her shoulder while she leans into his chest, sobbing while he strokes her arm reassuringly.

Jared soon takes his seat on Jessica's left when he finishes his eulogy for Lucas. "Those words were lovely Jared. I'm sure Lucas would've appreciated it," Jess acknowledged after shifting her attention over to her somber friend, taking his hand with her now vacant one. He nods and wipes his eyes with the back of his wrist and continues to stay silent in his mourn. It's been a couple of days now since the incident that caused Lucas his life. On a positive note, Jared has fortunately recovered from his small injuries, nothing fatal, but he did use his crutches occasionally for a while. Jared looked around the grassy field the funeral was set up at in the afternoon, which happened to be in the cemetery park. A large amount of their mutual friends were there. There was Jaiden and Jessica, Skylar and Becca, Alex, Hobbs, Josh, Wesley, even people like Courtney, Tanya, Brennan, and Sophie that showed up to pay their respects; although they didn't know him all that well. Like Jaiden, Jared would agree that Lucas was a pretty great guy if you came to know him, he was loud, funny too... one of Jared's closest friends and now he was gone with a blink of an eye. Jared was grateful to have Lucas' mother to ask him of all people to prepare a eulogy, it was the closet way he could reach out to his dear old friend and say goodbye, being that his parents knew that Jared was the closest friend Lucas once had.

The two met at the beginning of freshman year, on the wrestling team. Time came where Jared eventually gave up on that lifelong dream of pursuing a sports career, but Lucas always had ambitions. He had his goals set since the very beginning from when the two met so that he could get into a good college with a high chance of getting accepted with his academic track records all mapped out in front of him. Although he loved getting involved in the community, sports weren't always the plan with Lucas. He often talked about fending off in the military to serve his country like his father once did before him. His interests often traveled between the two—sports and enlisting, but he was more so inclined on protecting the nation than joining some silly Ivy League. With Lucas taking up wrestling back in high school, Jared took an interest in other sports such as football and lacrosse after swearing off wrestling in his last season back in freshman year. "It's not your fault, I'm just relieved it wasn't you," Jessica wept, leaning on Jaiden as they continued to whisper amongst themselves. That really hit Jared; he was devastated that his friend had to go but he was just overall gracious that it wasn't Jaiden. Sure, they argue and beat the hell out of each other sometimes, but he has grown up with him all his life—since they were just tiny embryos in their mother's shared womb, and it'd kill him if he was in that casket instead, he wouldn't be able to survive without him as much as it would kill anyone to admit… he only wished Jaiden thought of his brother in the same way but he never has the slightest sense of care for anyone in that cold heart of his, it's why Jared feels Jaiden always pushes him away. If it was really 'his fault' Lucas is dead, then why isn't he showing at least one sign of remorse on his face? But of course, it wasn't his fault, it was *Aaron's*.

If anything was for certain, it was that Jared Daniels learned a lot about that kid that same year from his newest and alcoholic coping mechanism of a friend, Brennan—and how Aaron Cole is a third-year senior. Luckily, the police got ahold of the school's security camera, releasing the actual footage of Aaron killing his friend, Lucas. Now that everyone was up to speed, Aaron had a trial coming up before they would officially lock him up. Jared had a gut feeling he was going to be found guilty, all the evidence was right in front of their noses. Authorities were already testifying saying that he has been under the influence which is in fact another reason they should have just immediately in-prisoned him and since he is in fact legal to drink now it's still being held accountable because he was intoxicated on campus and his history of drug usage can also be held against him. With all the negative factors in mind, Jared was damn sure justice for his friend's murder would be served on Aaron. Unfortunately, not everyone could pay for his death. After the police took Robbie down to the station and revisited the video footage of him being an accessory to murder, they decided to release Robbie only on bail, due to the fact that they saw him pulling away the gun and deemed it as he was unaware and tried to prevent it from happening. Thus, Robbie was sent home with a warning. Now, Robbie has been avoiding school for the past two weeks. Safe to say, he finally felt guilty on his friend's conscience. Jared saw Lucas' mom weeping on her husband in the distance. He felt for her since Lucas was her only child. Lucas' father was in the military and he died in battle, and from what Lucas told Jared, he was only around the age of nine when he lost him, his father. His mother remained widowed until she met husband number two when she remarried, and Lucas was around fourteen. Lucas was like the last link she had of her previous husband.

121

In the corners of Jared's eyes, he saw Jessica in Jaiden's embrace on his left. "Hey Jared," he heard his name being called. Courtney approached him from his left and he gives her a sly smile. "Do you want to maybe get out of here, so we can talk?" she asks pointing behind her. Jared nodded mournfully. They walked around the memorial park. "So, I guess plan 'break up Jessica and Jaiden' isn't going too well..." she lightheartedly stated.

"I don't really care anymore," he sighs.

"I was going to try and seduce him at the last party but he just kind of disappeared on me."

"He was with Jessica," he sighed again.

"Well... Courtney. I get you love Jaiden or whatever and I love Jessica, but she loves Jaiden now and he, her—And nothing we can do will change that, even if we try, we shouldn't—we can't. It's immoral! We should just leave them be because if anything goes wrong and they find out we had something to do with it, Jess will never forgive me. She's still on edge after everything I did. I don't want to hurt her again—even if she did choose him, it was my fault, I led her straight into his arms, but I've let my hopes of being with her again go, as should you—" He got cut off when Courtney unexpectedly smashed her lips to his, putting her hand on the back of his head to grope him tighter. She pulled away seconds later to stare behind him, causing him to turn around as well, eyes widened. "Jess, h-how long were you standing there?"

"L-long enough," her voice breaks. "I was just going to see if you're okay but looks like you two have some catching up to do. If you'll excuse me."

"Jess!" he shouts grabbing her arm as she begins to walk away. She then turns around again to continue off in her thoughts. "I don't care that you two are together... or not... or frankly moved on, but it upsets me that you'd even consider stooping so low as to breaking Jaiden and I up 'just' so 'you' can have me back!" she growls. "What's your reason huh?" she spat directing her attention at Courtney now, "Looking to sabotage all of my relationships?"

"Hey, what's going on?" Jaiden asks walking up. "We were just leaving!" she publicized, taking Jai's hand before walking away together.

"Courtney, what the hell was that! You knew she was right behind me didn't you!" he growled in frustration. "Jared..." Courtney tried taking his hand.

"Leave me the hell alone!" he scoffed shrugging her hand away. He begins walking to the parking lot.

"Jared, wait!" Courtney shouted running in front of him in hopes of stopping him. "I really didn't know she way there, I kissed you because I…"

"Yeah?"

"I… I l-love you," she nervously admitted, staring down uncomfortably at her hands.

"What about Jaiden?" He cocked an eyebrow. "You're right, I needed to open my eyes. He obviously doesn't want me and why try to hold onto something that was never there? Jessica has moved on, she has Jaiden… why don't you?"

"I'm already second place in Jessica's heart, I don't need to be in another," he berated pushing past her. He dragged his feet over to the parking lot and opened the front door to his car. He then noticed a car that pulled up next to him just as he was about ready to get inside and out comes Robbie, to his surprise. Without realizing, Robbie continuously fixes his suit, patting down his body upon stepping out and unlocks his backdoor to climb over and pull a bouquet of flowers out from the seat. He shuts the door and walks over in Jared's direction after locking his car door. He stopped when he noticed his old-time friend and Jared recoiled a few steps back in fear. "W-what are you doing here?" he gulped.

"Relax, I'm not going to hurt you, you can put your arms down," Robbie chuckled. Jared hesitated, bringing his arms down slowly. "I came to pay my respects… for Lucas."

"Flowers?"

"Are for my mother, I come here every now and then to check on her."

"I thought your mother was in prison," Jared gritted through his teeth.

"She was… until I visited her five years ago she told me she was diagnosed with cancer and she had three months to live… She, she was harsh, but I-I loved her you know?" he wept, covering his eyes.

"So, what now? You kill my best friend, show up here, cry a little and expect everything to be okay?"

"I didn't kill him, I didn't even touch the guy—"

"Your gang friend 'Aaron' did."

"I didn't even know he had a gun," he objected.

"What did you expect gangs to have? Darts? Water balloons…? Why did you even come here for him?"

"Look, I didn't know the guy too well, but I felt terrible. I honest to God didn't know what Aaron's intentions were. I never killed anyone before—"

"Yeah, I'm well aware of your alibi, but it's not convincing enough to me. You're going to have to try harder."

"I don't even know why I need to explain myself to you, I'm sorry for your loss... I'm sorry for turning my back on you... I only did it because I wanted to know what it was like to be popular, don't you remember what it felt like, to be unnoticed? That was me and I was sick of it, I saw the opportunity and I went for it and I didn't care who got hurt in the way, but it truly hit me when I was an accessory to a murder, and I knew this wasn't the life I wanted anymore. I know what I've done in the past, and I'm ashamed. But people do change and that's got to count for something—"

"No. It's too late for apologies or my respect." Jared interjects, getting inside his car and slamming it shut.

"What's up?" Jessica asked Jaiden after stopping at the light. "Nothing, just thinking," Jaiden responds leaning his head on the passenger seat window.

"About?" Just as he opens his mouth to begin to speak, her phone rings in her purse from the back seat.

"Can you?"

"May I what?" he sarcastically corrects. She gave him the most apathetic death glare earning herself a tongued expression back from Jaiden before proceeding to get her phone. He takes his seat belt off and reaches over to grab it from the back seat. She slapped his round plump ass in the meantime and he jumped at the unusual response before sitting back down while Jessica giggles from the driver's seat. It was unnatural for a male to have a butt so rich in thickness and not expect to get that reaction, and she could easily argue that she was merely just observing it.

"It's Mandy," he says handing the immature Jessica her phone.

"Answer it!" she insisted, honking at the oncoming traffic.

"Hello? Yes, this is Jaiden, thank you for calling." Jessica's laughter resurfaced, and she rolled her eyes playfully at his deeply disguised voice when answering the call. "It's for you," he whispers, covering the speaker with his hand.

"Give it," she sighed when taking her phone from his hands. "Hello?"

"So, I have some good news and some bad, which do you want first?" Mandy speaks clearly through the phone.

"Bad," replied Jess, without thought. "Okay well, the 'good' news is Kevin and I were able to get your flat back..." Jessica waited for her sister to continue after she elongated her pause in emphasis. "... The bad news is, you won't receive it unless you come to Mom and Dad's for dinner tonight."

"Amanda..." she gritted. "I guess I'll call Kevin so he can tell the realtors that the flat is still on the market," Amanda said. Jessica felt Jaiden's hand slowly creep on her thigh, wiggling their way up her denim skirt and she instantly slapped his hand away. "Stop it!" she hissed after he tried again. "Wait!" she begged before Amanda completely hung up.

"So, would that be a yes?" Mandy speaks again.

"Why the sudden change of heart?"

"...Why do they want to see me 'now', after all this time?"

"I don't know, but I've got to go. Seven o'clock... and come alone—they still aren't too fond of 'spermy'..."

Jessica's sudden outburst of laughter was too much for Jaiden to handle. "Hey, I heard that!" Jaiden yells through the speaker and Jessica smites his face away.

Hours later passed by when Jessica arrived at her parents' house and her mother now greeted her graciously at the door. She slid her flats off and entered the dining room, following behind her mother. *Great*, Beverly was here with Patrick and an oddly familiar redhead. She went around the table while her mother introduced her to Patrick's parents and grandparents and she greeted Mandy and Kevin, along the way. She attempted to greet her father, but he threw her the cold shoulder, pretending as if she never existed like he had been doing her entire life. *It was really no different.* "And this is Patrick's little sister, Candace," her mother finishes as she introduced her daughter to the last person of the bunch. The redhead got up and revealed her face to the distraught teenager, Jessica. *Oh hell no.*

"What was that sweetie?" her mother had asked after Jessica having realized that she had not thought that in her head like she intended to do.

"Jessica, right?" Candace's snobby upright face perched in the most pretentious manner. Jessica shook her hand gesturing back with the same unrealistic persona. The goal was to pretend they have never met before, obviously. Aside from that one-time lousy introduction at Starbucks, she clearly didn't know anything about Jessica, but that wasn't going to stop Jessica from making any other judgments on her either. Especially since she was dating Jaiden before her; the guy she's been crushing on since time could tell. Candace soon releases her grip on the girl's hand and they take their seats. *Anything else I should know about? Is Courtney here too? Is she a distant cousin? UGGGHHH!*

She slumped down further in her seat. More importantly, the question that irked Jessica was if there was anyone else at this table who hasn't slept with her boyfriend? The only person missing to make things even more confrontational, was no other than the man of the hour himself, Jaiden Daniels. But Jessica would make sure to give him an earful later that night about how her evening went with the ghosts of Jaiden's fornication.

About half an hour into listening about how 'perfect' Beverly's life is and having the life drained out of Jessica, Beverly announces she has big news. "Patrick and I are moving up the wedding!" she exclaimed.

"To when?" Alan asks when pouring himself a glass of scotch.

"Honey, not tonight." Margret places her hand on his palm in discretion, but he coldly swats her hand away. "Excuse me, I um... need to clean up the kitchen," she pardoned, excusing herself from the table.

"Now what the hell were you talking about?" Alan immorally continues to ask Beverly after he set the cup back on the wooden table and scoots himself in. "Well, we want to move it up to next week."

"How do you expect to have everything finished and prepared by then sweetie?" Mrs. Harper asks.

"I'm rich, duh!" Beverly says, and Patrick clears his throat.

"What she means to say is that, with the amount of savings we collected, it shouldn't be hard ordering things, hiring musicians, catering, and such."

Jessica scoffed, "Savings? Yeah right! Beverly has never worked a day in her life! She gets all her money from 'Daddy'," she slumped back, rolling her eyes to the back of her head.

"Jessica shut up and just be happy!" Mandy overwhelmingly speaks through her teeth from across the table; she obviously wasn't buying on to Beverly's bullshit either.

"Well, this was 'truly', a lovely dinner," Jessica says excusing herself, "But I must be elsewhere. Congratulations to the happy couple, goodbye," she retreats standing up.

"Wait! We were just getting to the ideas; won't you stay sister dearest?" Beverly asked when tugging her sister by the arm, before she had a chance to get away. Bev gives her younger sister the gnarliest death glare, but Jessica managed to pull her hand away. "Be my maid of honor?" Beverly insisted.

Jessica scoffed at her sister's lack of sincerity, "Going to be hard to do if I'm not attending, don't you think?" she sneered with the least bit of hospitality for her brattish sister.

"Plea—" But before Beverly had a chance to finish her sentence, Jessica leaned in to whisper in her ear, cutting her off,

"You may have everyone else here fooled, but I know the real you and I still remember what you did—and I will never be okay with that," she disclosed in private before striding over to the front door.

"Jessica!" Her mother ran out of the kitchen to stop her before she left. She grabs her hand, staring sorrowful into the depths of her daughter's emerald green eyes. "Won't you stay? I miss you, come home, you can even have your old room back."

"Hey, here's a crazy thought! Why don't we invite that Jaiden character? He can be one of my groomsmen! I think we really hit it off when we met, he seems like a great kid! What do you say, Candace?"

"Eww, no!" Candi and Beverly say almost simultaneously.

Just then, Jessica shot a glance back to her mother as she waited for a response, "You chose this life," she speaks with bitter vigilance straining her voice, indirectly speaking about her father, "Not me," she coldly vindicated, pulling her hand away and rushing out the door. She decided to walk over to the twins' house straight after to ventilate her anger.

She impatiently banged on the door a few times knowing only the twins were home. "Jeez Jess, chill!" Jaiden irritably groans after opening the door.

"Marriage! This is insane! Why now!" she yelled in frustration when entering the door, following Jaiden past the foyer and into the living room. *"Marriage! This is insane! Why now!"* Jared heard Jessica's voice elevate from the living room. His curiosity led him to travel to where the two were conversing, with his over-filled laundry basket that he would compensate as an excuse to eavesdrop before making any false assumptions.

"Hey Jai! I'm putting in the last load of laundry, got any colors you want to throw in there?" he asked entering the room.

"Did you check the pile underneath my bed?"

Jared nods his head and makes his way into Jaiden's bedroom after his brother dismissed him for some privacy. He didn't even acknowledge Jessica's presence, it had been too soon for that. He found his way to Jaiden's bedroom, turning on the lights before kneeling to reach under his bed, collecting all his dirty clothes, and throwing them in the hamper right beside him. He pushed his hand back a little bit further to make sure he got all the remaining clothes, feeling around the floor until his hand came in contact with something small and dull. He pulled it out and stood up to examine it. On the process of examining it, he nervously covered his mouth. Only one thing came to mind as what could be placed in this small box when he shook it slightly. Nothing rattled but he opened it anyways and he was right. It all clicked to him. That conversation he walked in on a few minutes ago was no ordinary conversation, they were discussing their future together. *Was he going to propose to Jessica? Or did he already?* He heard voices coming in from the hallway outside, so he shuffled off Jaiden's bed and snapped closed the small box, sliding it back under the bed. As soon as the door opened, he shot his body forward, standing upright. "Dude, what's taking so long? Get out!" Jaiden demands as he led Jessica into the room. Jared awkwardly nodded off without making eye contact with either of them. Staring directly at the floor, he grabbed the basket and proceeded to head out the door, closing it behind himself.

"I can't believe you had dinner with Patrick's family and somehow managed to skip the part where Patrick is related to that 'thing'!" Jessica continuously scolds plopping down on his bed now.

"It's in my best interest to not get involved in family affairs," he shrugs joining her.

She shoves him playfully, "Shut up, it's a little too late for that!"

"Oh, and here's the best part, 'you're' going to be one of the groomsmen!"

"What! Says who?"

"I overheard Patrick talking about it when I was about to leave; guess Candi failed to mention that you two aren't together anymore," she shrugged.

"Can't say I blame her, if she told him she was with Robbie now, that would be one distasteful evening," Jaiden chuckled.

"Beverly wants me to be her maid of honor but I refuse to attend," Jessica continued, folding her arms.

"No please, you have to go! I don't want to be stuck alone with Candi, you know me… I-I'm a-a boy!" he pleads.

"—And I don't even know him!" he protested.

"Relax, I'm sure he's changed his mind by now or he was only teasing because he probably already knew Candi is uninterested in you."

Jaiden sighed in relief. That wedding would have been an utter disaster. Jaiden, along with everyone else knew it that Jessica Larson's family was not the most pleasant family to be around. Did they even know how to party? Yeah sure, if you'd consider cocktail parties a party. Suddenly, Jaiden's phone rang; it was from an unknown caller I.D.

"Hello?"

"Oh, 'hey' Patrick!" he said with a fake grin plastered on his face while facing Jessica in emphasis. She had been wrong, and Jaiden made sure to get the message across with his unpleasant reactions. "Good man, how'd you get my number?"

"Of 'course', Beverly has it," he grits. "So, what's up?"

"Well congratulations!—Yeah, sure. I'd love to!" he lies. "Should I rent a tux?"

"Yeah okay, I'll send it. No problem… uh huh," he hangs up.

"Send what?" Jessica asked.

"My tux size. Patrick's delivering it to me… in the mail, how great!" he sarcastically grits through his teeth before standing up to throw his phone on the bed. It ricochets onto the floor and she reaches below to retrieve it. "You're going if I'm going!" he demands.

"What's this?" she asks spotting a box under the bed and pulling it out from underneath. She opens it before Jaiden has the chance to stop her and her mouth drops to the floor. "Oh my—" she covered her mouth.

"Oh, you've found it," he says scratching the back of his head nervously. "It's—it's not what you think it is though," he says reclaiming it from her hands as she sits upright.

"Oh, no? … Not a ring? Why, are you planning to propose to your secret lover?" she chuckles in light.

"No, I mean… it's not an engagement ring. It's more of a promise ring," he says sitting down next to her.

"Jaiden this is so unlike you, it's so romantic and sweet—"

"Yeah, I know I just hope one day we can make this official, but for now, it's just a reminder of my love for you," he says as he hands her the box.

"I-I don't know if I can accept this Jai. I mean a-are you sure?"

"I wasn't sure at first, but when I saw Lucas' life flash before my eyes, I thought about how short life is, I was like why the hell not?" He gets down on both knees, now kneeling in front of the overwhelmed girl. "Will you," he takes her palms, "Jessica Larson, accept this ring?"

"Aww Jai, this is the least self-centered thing you've done for me," she marveled in sarcasm as he chuckled. She opened the box and stared at the sparkly ring.

"Here, let me," he asked but she declined his hand away.

"No, I should do it—otherwise it feels too much like marriage proposal and that's something I'm not ready for." He chuckled allowing her to do so. She pulled the ring out and slid it on her finger.

"So?" he asked impatiently.

"Oh alright," she teased, "I accept." He got up to give her a hug, but she tugged on his shirt instead, pulling his body on hers as they laid on the bed. She caresses his soft brown locks and gazed up at him hovering above her, admiring the precious view of her lover. He grazes her left leg while she cups his face into her petite hands. Soon, they find their lips pressing together.

(The next day)

"Good morning babe," Jaiden rasped into her ear while his arms snaked around her warm and naked body. "I love having you next to me. A guy could get used to this," he exhaled deeply before kissing from the back of her shoulders to her spine. She turned around, fluttering her eyelids awake.

"Good morning," she smiled repositioning to rest her body on top of his with her arms and face pushed up against his chest. "Morning?" she shuffled up with the blanket draped around her chest. "Shit! Did I really spend the night?" she worried getting up in search for her clothes. "Crap, my car is still in my parents' drive way," she noticed when looking out of his bedroom window.

"What's the rush?" he stretched.

"Have you not been listening?" she groaned, "I can't keep doing this with you, especially here. This is the fourth time this has happened," she said sliding back into her jeans.

****

Chapter Seven

"Hold still!" Margret emphasized, trying desperately to zip up Beverly's wedding gown as she squirms around in it. "I don't understand, this is supposed to fit!" Beverly pouts. "Well it's not!" her mother frustrates some more. "No, I don't think you heard me," she gritted facing away from the mirror now, "It's GOING to fit!" she urged. Margret apathetically sighed, "Jess sweetie, can you please run to the bathroom, we need pins?" Jessica nods and quietly exits the room, returning with her mother's sewing kit momentarily later. "Limo's here, you girls ready?" Jaiden asks when entering, without knocking, 'as always'.

"Get out!" Beverly roars. Jessica pushes him out along with herself, closing the door behind on their way out. "What's the hold up with bridezilla?" he asks.

"Her dress, it's too tight," Jessica informs while they reach the bottom of the stairs.

"Are you sure she's not just fat?" he chuckles. "Please, when have you ever known Beverly to be fat?" Jessica responded.

"Anyways, are all the guys ready?"

"Yeah, they're waiting outside."

"So why aren't you with them?"

"I can't stay away from you," he whispered, reeling her in closer.

"Alright, where's my date?" Candi announced seconds later upon stepping out of the room.

"Right here!" Jessica smiled pushing him off her. He blatantly rolled his eyes and made his way over to Candi, sticking out his elbow, waiting for her to link her arm with his after she trailed downstairs. As ready as she will ever be for this unpleasant evening, Jessica walked outside to be greeted with a warm smile of somebody who just also happened to be her escort for today.

"You must be Jessica?" the young man speaks. "I'm Matthew," he enlightens, and she shakes his hand forgetting her introduction.

"Are you a friend of the groom's?" she asks continuously shaking his hand for quite an elongated time without realizing.

Pulling his hand away, "No, we're more like brothers actually," Matthew chuckled.

"And you?"

"Sister of the bride," she nodded off with an awkward grin.

"Well you look gorgeous," he smiles shyly.

"…and taken," Jaiden emphasized when walking up and wrapping his arm around her waistline.

I'm going to kill this kid.

"Yes, this is my—"

"'Boyfriend', Jaiden," he continued shaking this older and taller gentleman's hand. "Sweetie, where's your ring?" Jaiden whispered in no attempt to be inconspicuous.

"I don't think this is an appropriate time to be wearing that sort of thing around; so people don't get the wrong idea," she argued in her softest voice.

"Covering up for the fact you lost it huh? Here, I found it on the kitchen counter earlier."

"Thanks," she apathetically smiled after he handed it back to her. She didn't lose it, she let Jaiden think that. Matt stood there watching as she slid it back on her finger.

"Should I leave you two alone?" he courteously asked. Jaiden and Jessica both had answered simultaneously, only with different responses. Jessica flashes her wickedest glare at Jaiden yet. That look said everything from, *If you don't leave in five seconds, I'm going to kill you,* to, *Stop talking, stop talking now!*

"Look, I'm just trying to have a good time at my best mate's wedding, I didn't mean to intrude. If it makes you feel better, I have no interest in your girlfriend—urrr I mean, fiancé? I respect that, I'm actually in a relationship myself," he explains, and Jessica could feel Jaiden's tension on her shoulder ease.

"Okay, he's good!" Jaiden approved giving Matt an encouraging pat on the shoulder, "You two have a great time at the party, not too much," he winks before walking away. *What the hell?*

"Vince, let's go!" a bridesmaid named Maya says as she walks down the porch steps. A very attractive blond fellow assists her to the vehicle.

"Ready to go?" Matt asked his accomplice of the evening after noticing that the others were already making their way towards the limo. Their elbows connect, and he leads her to the limo with Candace and Jaiden in front of them.

"Ooooo, bubbly!" Jaiden grins, rubbing his hands together. He pulled the bottle from the rotating table in front of them after everyone had settled inside the moving limo.

"Most of us are underage," Jessica reminded whilst Candi rolled her eyes at the buzz-kill who spoke beside her; she snatched the bottle from Jaiden's hands before taking a glass and filling it up. Chugging every sip, she returns the bottle to Jaiden, shoving it back to him.

"Alright who wants? Complementary provided by the bride and groom," he says with a devious smirk, holding up the bottle. They arrived a half hour later—And with Jessica being the closest to the door, she was the first to step out, hiking her dress down while Matt then too stepped out and accompanied her inside. They enter the grand hallway and the other pairs follow behind them.

"There you guys are! You're all half an hour late! You need to get to the altar now!" Mandy informs.

"Now? But the limos just dropped us off, it's going to take another hour for them to pick up the bride," Maya explains.

"Well, then get into your places, we'll just have to stall—we're paying for services by the hour," Mandy hustles. They wait near the door entrance and Amanda, who cued at Kevin, to cue the organ player, began to play while the bridesmaids and groomsmen took their places; Matt and Jessica were the first to enter, followed by Vince and Maya, then finally Jaiden and Candi. The groom was already at his area as intended, standing sturdy in place.

Ten minutes of a lovely organ ballad go by in hopes of stalling the guests when a worrisome Patrick pulled Jaiden aside, "Where's Beverly?" he asked.

"Traffic," was what Jaiden responded with followed by a shrug, when in fact he did not know where she was at all.

"Here!" Beverly panted, fixing her veil from across the altar.

"Start the song!" she directed at the organ player.

(Ten minutes later)
"If anyone has any objections—"

"Yeah, I've got a few!" The crowd gasps as Jared barges into the chapel that was now filled with concerned faces.

"Jessica, you can't do this!" he continued as the bride and groom turned around revealing their angry faces; it had not been the wedding Jared expected to stumble into and objectify to. Jaiden wanted to burst into a fit of laughter, he couldn't control the huge grin on his face caused by his incompetent brother. "Woah, um I'm sorry... I'm an idiot," Jared mumbled, reiterating to himself quite loud.

Beverly looked evidently pissed now, but not as pissed as she was about to get. Jessica held up a finger, "One moment please," she administrated for a pause, drawing attention away from the ceremony as she ran up to the dehydrated boy. From the looks of it, he seemed like he walked forty blocks just to get there, by foot. It was almost straight out of a romance book, except unfortunately for Jared, he was not destined to get his happy ending after all.

God this was not happening. "Jared, what are you doing here like this?" she asked approaching him halfway in the center of the aisle.

"I thought you and Jai were—"

"Oh my God! No Jared!" she frustrated. "How could you have possibly thought—" she started asking but it came out more derogative than she had intended. He held her hand up and it clicked to Jessica how he would have misinterpreted. "No, it's just a ring... It's nothing serious."

"Why, are you considering marrying?"

"Jare, I'm not open for discussion on this right now, especially since you've caused a scene and disturbed the peace of this sanctuary."

"I'm sorry that I wasn't there all those times before. I've let you slip away... and because of that you became closer to Jaiden. I could've been your first kiss, your first time—"

"But you weren't!" she bitterly folded her arms, in evident dismissal; his face dropped as did his heart, he was devastated to say the least. "...and that's the thing, I love Jaiden now. You had me, but you've also lost me. I'm sorry, please try to understand..." She reaches out to grab his arm but before she could, he scoffed it away.

"Can someone get this asshole out of here, so we can continue with the ceremony?" complained Alan, staring at the two from the front seat of the chapel.

"Is everything all right here?" Kevin asked when walking up to them from his seat.

"Yeah, sorry... I was just leaving," Jared informed with a narrow-eyed glare at Jessica before storming out of the building. Jessica sighed and returned to take her position at the altar, nodding to give the priest permission to continue. Jess did not want to end things that way, nor did she want to end things at all. She knew she had to give him the cold shoulder for him to move on so that she too could finally move on and let go of their past. It was better for them both this way.

"As I was saying... If anyone would like to testify, speak now or forever hold your peace—"

"Patrick!" another figure calls out in the distance.

Boy, this was going to be a long night.

Alas, the real showstopper of the evening finally made its grand entrance. The timing couldn't be more perfect as the attention was traveled to the back of the altar once again. "Vivian? Vivian is that you?" Patrick squints stepping forward. "Vivian!" Patrick shouts when running closer to Vivian. They both meet halfway at the altar. "Oh my god, w-what are you doing here?" Patrick asks cupping her saddened face.

"I canceled Paris, I-I traveled here as soon as Aiden—" she pointed out.

"Jaiden," Jaiden corrected with a look so smug that he couldn't help but to flash it in Beverly's direction—and now that he had the advantage of witnessing her reaction to the red-mad he was going for, he knew that justice was served.

"Patrick, what is going on?" Beverly asked.

He held up a finger and turned his attention back to Vivian.

"He told me you were getting married soon and I-I… I messed up, I want you back I never should've left. I still love you Pat," she sobs.

"Really, is this true?" he faintly asked. She keeps her head down and nods too proud to look him in the eyes. He gently elevates her head back up and traces over her cheek with his thumb while their eyes meet now. "I've never stopped loving you," Patrick admits, pressing his lips to hers. To Beverly's additional surprise, the entire crowd began to revolt in appraisal.

"Patrick!" Beverly screamed, being the first to outburst in anger; Patrick didn't respond. Outraged, she walked up to him and patiently tapped him on the shoulder, waiting for him to be done with sucking Vivian's face, to get back to the wedding.

Patrick soon pulled away, "It's over Bev, I never really loved you," he confessed aloud. The words that left his mouth caused Beverly to melodramatically gasp. "I was simply using you for money since your dad is an old filthy rich bastard. Are you kidding yourself? I could never be with someone like you!—this isn't love, this was never love… Do you want to know what love is? 'This' is love!" he stressed before scooping Vivian into his arms for another kiss. Mr. Larson was not amused.

"Piece of shit!" he raged, standing up and separating him from Vivian before punching him square in the face without warning.

"Oh shit!" Jaiden's fit of laughter played itself out when they began fighting. His revenge on Beverly finally paid off. Beverly looked up at the deviously deranged teenager after it was evident that he was behind this and because he seemed to be the only one enjoying it.

"I'm going to KILL YOU!" Beverly screamed chasing after him. The whole wedding goes awry. Candi was now hopping Beverly's father's back as he was pummeling Patrick into the ground with Vivian sobbing, trying to get him to stop. Then there was Beverly, still running up and down the aisles for Jaiden. Time seemed to be frozen for Jessica when she was left standing at the altar to replay between everything from what Jared left her with and from Jaiden and her previous conversation about their future.

"Want to get out of here?" Matt asked. "Yes please!" she agreed, hurriedly following him out the plaza. She needed a good distraction for a while.

Jaiden stopped in his tracks when he saw Jessica leaping out of the building with one of the groomsmen—and in that spare second that it took him to stop, it left Beverly with a window of opportunity for her to plan her attack on Jaiden, by sneaking up on him to tackle him from behind. He grunted in his attempt to turn his body around from the floor and Beverly looked scarier than ever; all her makeup smeared around her face and her ripped frumpy dress splotched with her makeup-like chalk stains. His face was filled with horrid disgust. "You've ruined my wedding!" she cried out. Seconds later she was knocked sideways to the floor.

"No, 'I did' bitch!" Vivian emphasized throwing the remaining pieces of the wooden chair she swung at Beverly aside.

"Thanks," Jaiden puffed out of breath. Vivian then helped the assaulted teenager back up on his feet.

"Hey!" Candi grunted, "A little help over here? 'Please'!" Candi panted in exhaust, still stubbornly clinging on to Mr. Larson's back, presumably trying to gauge his eyes out now. They rushed over for Patrick's aid. Guests and relatives already fled the building in terror including one Mrs. Larson, who disappeared after helping the guests to safely evacuate the disastrous wedding.

"Toss me a chair," Jaiden whispered to Vivian, the chair-whacking expert, as soon as Mr. Larson swung Candi off his back. Jaiden slowly began to approach Mr. Larson who had Patrick in a headlock and who was still facing away from them. Vivian tossed Jaiden the wooden chair as requested, and one swing knocked Alan out cold, releasing Patrick out from under. "Let's run!" panted Patrick who tried to recollect his breath.

"Julio, 32nd Maple Street, drive fast!" Patrick ordered the driver after he, Jaiden, Vivian, and Candace stepped inside the stretch limo that was originally meant to take the happily married couple to their designated hotel after the reception was over. But that wasn't happening anytime soon. "You got it boss!" the driver nodded, getting in and stepping on the gas pedal. Patrick stared out the back window and saw Mr. Larson grabbing onto his neck, running—more so, wobbling, out the door.

"Damn you all!" he screamed after he stopped trying to catch up to them in the middle of the street.

"Phew!" Patrick sighs when wiping off the mixture of sweat and blood that formed at the top of his forehead. "Man, I don't know how I can ever thank you for saving me back there," he chuckled, loosening his tie.

"No need, don't sweat it," Jaiden punned.

"No really—if there's anything I can do. You name it, money? What's your bargain?"

"No, it's fine, really."

"Well, alright?"

"Long story."

"Well, I'd love to hear it, we've got time," Vivian smiles.

"How did you even know about Vivian and me? How'd you contact her and everything?"

"Oh, I have my connections," he devilishly smirked.

****

Jessica averted awake from her sleep. She looked around her surroundings and she was not in her own bed, she was in a hospital bed. She pulled the covers off her body and cautiously stood up. Upon noticing the hospital gown she was wearing, it was slightly bloody. *Where was I?* she thought. She didn't remember how she got there. She heard a cry in the distance, it was a baby's cry. She began to follow the sound. Suddenly, in the distance, she saw a small light shining down on a hospital crib. She approached the sound of the baby and the sound fades as she appeared closer. She finally reached the baby in the room and lifted it up. It stopped crying when she lifted it up as if it were fond of her, like it knew her. She looked at the label that was placed in the crib and the name was blurry. All she could make out was that it said Larson-Daniels. *Was this my baby?* She held it, softly grazing the face. *It was a girl, my baby girl.* She leaves her eyes for a mere second to see if anyone was around and as soon as her eyes return to the baby, it was gone. Suddenly, she was in a different scene, still in the hospital but in a different part, running, searching, "Where's my baby?" she yelled running down the hospital hallways in her bloody gown. She was panting now. It was somewhat dark, only the projector lamps in the hallways were flashing every time she ran across when she would get closer. No one was here, no one could hear her. She found a suspicious hospital room, room '3B'. It was the one she was in when she was here during her miscarriage. Oddly enough, it was the only one that was open, so she entered, flicking on the light. She abruptly felt someone

137

hugging her from behind. To her surprise, as she turned, she found it was Jaiden.

"Ssshhhh baby," he cooed until he lifted her up and set her on the hospital bed, only now it transformed into a regular bed, and she was no longer in a hospital gown, she was in lingerie. The bed and her clothes weren't the only thing that changed though, the whole room did as it became dim after she turned on the light upon entering. The room looked familiar, it was the one in Josh's house where she had made love to the twins. Jaiden left a trail of kisses down her body and it sent her shivers. "I want to love you," he breathed when attaching his lips to hers. "Jaiden," she moaned, unable to resist the sexual tension, she didn't want to fight it. He flipped her over so that she was currently on top of him, he then sat up and continued sucking on her lips. She then felt a cold unexpected breath behind her. She turned her head back around and found Jared with a devilish smirk on his face. "Jared w-what are y-you?"

"Ssshhhh," he cooed as his hands trail up to unzip her lingerie. She felt a pair of hands grab her breasts from in front, it was Jaiden. He laid her down, hovering above. Jaiden began to suck on her neck again with Jared following.

"Ow!" she exclaimed after Jaiden accidentally bit her. He continues biting her violently now. "Ow, stop!" she ordered, successfully pushing him off the bed. Next, Jared then starts sucking harshly as well. "What the hell, stop!" she urged sitting up. With a nonchalant facial expression, he grabbed her arm forcefully and pinned her back down on the bed. She tried removing her arm from his grip, but he was too strong. "L-let go!" she cried out mercilessly. *Why couldn't they hear me?* Next, Jaiden came back up and held her arms up as Jared sucked the life out of her neck again. She tried pushing them both away, but they wouldn't budge. Jared sucks too hard again and she cried out fearfully in pain. "Stop! Why are you guys hurting me!"

She couldn't take it anymore. She felt the blood from her neck rush down and drip to her bare chest. They were like a pack of hungry wolves. It wasn't until Jaiden promptly threw her to the floor when she motionlessly crawled back up, realizing she was thankfully not in that room anymore. She was now in a forest of some sort. It was sunny outside, and she was grateful she could finally see clearly. Large trees surrounded her, and as she looked down at herself, she was completely naked. *Why was I wandering naked in a forest?* Leaves in her hair as she pulled them out, the ones she could see.

"Momma, where are you?" she heard a little voice call out. Again, she began creeping slowly, following the voice as it kept calling out for help. She was again alone, except for the voice that she was drawn to.

138

She approached closer and saw a figure skipping rocks by a lake in the distance. The figure was facing away from her and when Jessica appeared closer, she realized that it was this girl who was calling for help. "Momma, I'm glad you showed up…"

"Where's daddy?" she asked still facing away. Jessica gulped and stepped closer, desperately yearning to stay quiet so that she wouldn't wake anything in this forest and startle this girl. "Why did you leave me? You killed me momma… why did you kill me?" she questioned sitting down and crying into her palms. The little girl looked about six from behind.

"Mommy didn't mean to… I'm so sorry," she solemnly resided when coming closer in hopes of calming her down, eyes filled with sorrow— *still naked of course.* Jessica wanted to see how her daughter looked like, was it possible? She took a step closer, reaching her hand out—about to touch this girl's shoulder when a twig snapped unexpectedly, causing Jessica to divide her attention to Jared and Jaiden walking up to her. "What's your name sweetie?" she asked returning to the girl who had now disappeared. Jared and Jaiden finally caught up to her, but she pushed past them in trying to find the little girl. "Where's my little girl?" she squalled running through the woods. She could hear footsteps coming up behind and in hopes of it being the little girl who has returned, she turned around to find it was just Jared and Jaiden following her again. "I-I lost her," she sobbed, crumpling down on the dirt. She felt a pair of hands wrap a blanket around her as she shivered, feared they will only hurt her again. She was weak, so weak now. Jared helped her to her feet and embraced her in for a hug. She cried even harder in his embrace. "I know, it's okay. We'll find her again, one day…"

"Soon…" the other one spoke.

She regained consciousness and jolted awake. "Jess, ssshhhh it's okay," Jaiden assured sitting up to hug her. She started to sob in his chest while he stroked her hair. As it turned out, she had a double-nightmare, she woke up again and now he wasn't to the right of her, he never even spent the night. It was all just in fact a dream. She was still able to recall every detail of this horrifying dream, but she didn't know what any of it meant. It had been the first night that Jessica had finally settled back into her flat after two wholesome and long weeks of rearranging furniture. She looked to the clock on her nightstand to check the time and she had about three hours of sleep remaining until she had to be up and at 'em for school. The wedding was a few nights ago, on Friday and it was a Monday now. She hadn't talked to Jaiden since that night, Jared as well—but she also knew that her chances of reconciling with Jared fell short since he gave her the cold shoulder at the wedding.

****

She decided she wasn't going to waste any more time trying to fall back asleep; She got up at 2:56 a.m. to be exact and showered, took care of all her hygiene responsibilities, dressed, and had breakfast. And with an hour still left to spare, she decided to watch Teen Wolf on her DVR, a show she was binging on for the past couple of nights, *well that certainly explains what sprung on the night terrors.* She had the biggest crush on Dylan O'Brien, what a heartthrob he was. She made her way to the school and spotted Jaiden talking to his friends in the hallways, so she mindfully walked past him in hopes of getting to her first hour earlier than usual. She also didn't want to speak with him now because she was still torn over casualties. "Where are you going?" he asks catching up to her in the hallways. "Going to class." She continued off in her thoughts, trying to pay little to no attention to him in hopes of getting him off her back.

"We need to talk," he says grabbing her arm and hurling her up against the lockers. She felt his breath hitch when he pressed his forehead to hers and cupped her face. "Why have you been avoiding me baby?" he asks. She inadvertently shoved him away when a teacher walked by and eyed the two. She took his hand and led him to an empty hallway corner. She then, crossed her arms and raised a brow at him.

"Right so, you left without me?"

"I wasn't your responsibility. I came with Matt and you had Candace."

"I don't like *Candace*. Is this what this is about—wait a minute, are you jealous?" he grinned a little too proudly.

"No, I'm not jealous! I was aggravated! You've completely sabotaged my sister's wedding! How could you!" she antagonized.

"Wait, so to recap; you're mad because I ruined your sister's lame ass wedding? — I thought you hated Beverly?"

"I do but… it was her wedding day Jaiden! That's the most crucial day in a woman's life!"

"Relax, I'm sure there will be other weddings for Beverly," he chuckles causing Jessica to roll her eyes. "Think about it this way, I made two people happy, three even… Beverly would've realized it eventually that Patrick never loved her. Why would she waste her time marrying the guy!" he justified standing in front of her. The bell goes off.

140

"Walk me to my class?" she asked. He takes her hand and guides her up the stairs that were beside them.

"So, a bunch of us guys are heading to Josh's lake house later tonight, I'd really like it if you'd come," he mentioned when stopping in front of her classroom.

"Jaiden, it's a school night," she reminds. He glided his hand behind her ear. "That hasn't stopped us before."

"Be ready at six-thirty and wear that sexy, tight, green bikini," he whispered huskily in her ear. "See you in third hour," he says smacking her ass before heading off to class. Now it was time for second hour as the day progressed. Jessica was going to miss having a friend in government, but Lucas is in a better place. The day continued to pass by, slower than usual, probably because she was anxious about going to the lake. She was now in third hour and she had to deal with Jared but not so much since he was planning to ignore her for the rest of his life.

"Let's get to your set up lab stations where you and your lab partner will be mixing chemical substances to form a reaction. You will follow your directions and each of you will produce a different reaction with the different solutes you choose to mix," Mrs. Parker explained before putting on her lab coat. "Put on your lab coats and goggles and begin!" she instructs. Jessica grabs her instructions and makes her way over to the lab table with Jared following behind. Candi and Jaiden were working on the other side of the lab room and in front of Jared and Jessica were Megan and Star, which were the other girls in her dance group.

"How do you—" Jared pesters, staring at the test tubes in confusion. Science was not his best subject, he loved it but math was more his strong suit. As for Jessica, she marveled in both.

"Here, let me," she insisted taking the tubes, beginning to pour the water solution into the hydrochloric acid as said in the instructions. "Well, nothing happened," she noted checking off the first set of instructions. They were now almost halfway done with the class period and they have not said one word to each other since the first set of instructions. She decided to speak up and make small talk after Star glares at her to try and talk to him. *What was this high school? Oh, right.* "So Jared, are you going to the lake house tonight?" started off Star, as a friendly push for Jessica to make conversation.

"Uh… probably not. It's a school night and I don't want to show up alone." Jessica nodded slowly, staring up at him a few times as his eyes never left the beaker he was using.

"Thirty minutes class!" the teacher announced. "Well, that's too bad because Megan really wanted to go, and she doesn't have a date either," Star continued.

"What?" said Jessica and Megan, shooting their attention at her. Jared's eyes went straight to Jessica, her mouth staggers unable to form words before his eyes shift over to Megan.

"I mean yeah, if you'd want to go I don't mind accompanying you. I don't have a date either," Megan replied.

"What a great idea!" Jessica enthusiastically proclaimed with the fakest of grins. She needed him to move on and for him to think that she was okay with it. After all, it was just for one night, *right? Come on, Megan and Jared being a thing? As if! It could never happen, he's too nerdish and she's too… not!*

…And besides, s-she's too good for him. She will never want to be with someone like Jared. Or so Jessica thought.

"Sorry, not really my thing, and Courtney's already asked me," he says wiping the acid from his hands on his lab coat before taking his goggles off and walking away from the station when they finish their experiment. Jessica gives the two girls a death glare and Megan soon shuffles over to him. Jessica would honestly rather have her friend accompany him than Courtney.

"Oh, well I heard Courtney is already going with Brad," she made up, "And I really would hate if I showed up there myself, you know?" she says reassuringly rubbing his arm. He looks behind her, to Jessica's direction and she quickly turned around to continue to clean the lab station as if she weren't paying attention.

"So, what did he say?" Jessica worriedly asked Megan on her return to the table. "You owe me," she groaned, snapping off her goggles before returning to her seat. When school was over, Jessica once again settled inside her flat and found herself heating some leftover spaghetti for lunch. She then rushed into her bedroom to finish her homework before venturing off for a quick change of clothes. As requested by Jaiden, she wore her green bikini which she purchased from Victoria's Secret, under a tank top and a pair of denim cutoffs. Her shoe preference of the night were these new sandal thongs she purchased just last week. And she decided to go with her waterproof mascara and no other makeup since they would be in the lake. *Who even goes in the lake now? The water must be freezing!* The thought didn't occur to her when she went to purchase her bikini last week either. Her reason for purchase was because Jaiden insisted everyone should have a swimsuit prepared with spring break coming up. The more that she thought about it, she realized that this must have been his intention all along, to bring her to this party to get his way—and has nothing to do with spring break. She decided against taking a tote bag since it will be dark outside and for that matter, there will be no use of taking sunscreen or anything else either. She grabbed a towel and soon received a message from Jaiden telling her to meet him in the parking garage of the building in fifteen minutes.

"Hey, you sexy thing you," he ravishes, pressing his lips to hers as soon as she hopped in his car. She put on her seat belt while he examined her some more. "You won't need this," he says throwing her towel to the back seat. "Josh's got extra and I don't want you to lose yours." Jessica couldn't help but examine his attire for the night as well. He was wearing a white beater with lime green swim trunks, the same shade as her bikini that they bought together.

"Why are you wearing sunglasses if the sun just set?"

"It goes with my style," he replied when backing out of her driveway. "Well, you look like a drunk guy at a frat party."

"And you look like the hot girl who's going to sleep with that drunk guy at that frat party," he gawked, slapping her bare thigh in assurance. *Boy, he wasn't wrong.*

****

It was a forty-five-minute drive to Josh's lake house and Jessica had broken the silence after the first fifteen minutes by asking Jaiden what he wanted to do after graduation. "Haven't really thought about it much, but I guess I will continue to pursue my video career with Jared. Maybe do something in the film industry. Perhaps some adult films to start off and work my way up from there," he grinned.

"Jaiden," she groaned, "I'm being serious," she pushed her head forward for emphasis.

"So was I! Go big or go home!" he chuckled.

"Jaiden, let me get this straight; you've had four years of high school to decide and you haven't thought of your future once with graduation right around the corner!"

"Don't stress your pretty little head, it shouldn't worry you."

"Really? You've spent so much time focusing on our future together you didn't even think how your life and what you want to do would affect us?" she frustrated while melodramatically crossing her arms.

"Babe, when the time comes, I'll find something... I'm 'Jaiden fucking Daniels'. Look at me!" He grins, staring up at her for a mid-second, arrogantly. She rolls her eyes at his child's play. "In the meantime, I just want to focus on us," he says rubbing her thighs again.

"And so, making videos and meeting fans, where is that going to get you in life… to what expense exactly? You guys don't even have a talent to showcase. People just admire you because you're all hot, not because they know you," she scoffs, shifting her eyes out the side window.

"Someone sounds a little jealous," Jaiden chuckled.

"Oh please!"

"Sure, I have girls that are all over me 24/7. Girls that are willing to just throw themselves at me. It's a lifestyle."

"What is it that you're getting at here? Because if you don't need me, I can just go," she narrow-mindedly fronts.

"I just admire how jealous you get about this stuff."

"I can well assure you, I'm not jealous. I'm just concerned for the well-being of your future. I can only imagine where you will end up tomorrow, but that's all I care for. Frankly, you can have anyone you want."

"Oh, now I've upset you."

"You didn't upset me, you just frustrated me! I'm trying to have a civilized discussion with you, but you can never be serious!"

"My future is my business, why do you even fuckin' care?"

"No, you're wrong! This isn't just your future we're talking about here, it's my future too! It's our future together! This isn't a career or a lifestyle it's just admiration! I can give you all that, but I guess I'm not enough. I guess your promise and all the bullshit you were feeding me the other day about our future together means nothing to you! So, you go run off and be 'Jaiden-fucking-Daniels, so called ladies' man'. You can have your headlights and all the girls you want but don't drag me into it. I don't want to feel like every other girl, I want to feel like I'm something more if I am, like I deserve to feel. But please don't let me get in the way of whatever you choose to do."

The rest of the thirty minutes was complete silence.

"Jess, don't be like that. Come on. Okay, I don't want any other girl! I want you. Whatever it is, I will do it so long as I get to keep you in my life. You mean more to me than anyone else. I just wanted to let you know that I'm sorry. I love you, I do," he speaks breaking the silence. She turned to face him, and the smallest of smiles reappeared on her face. "Do you think we can please move past this and have ourselves a good night?" he asked meeting her gaze. She grabbed onto his hand and bit her lip, nodding in reassurance. They finally arrived at their destination. "Take your clothes off here," Jai motions when stepping out after they had parked just a little off-side the lake. She too stepped out and pulled her top over her head, throwing it in the back seat along with her shorts. "Damn," he gawked admirably. There was over a hundred people, less than Josh's usual parties, but still loads of people. It was somewhat dark out, but they managed to see the house and the lake which was right across. The lake was huge and there was a swarm of people already in there. People with beer cans, bottles, couples playing chicken. She anxiously began to make her way to the house while Jaiden changes out of his shoes. "Wait up babe!" he jogs catching up with her.

"What's up guys!" Josh greets at the door as Hobbs, Lindsay, and Alex join him by the doorway, all in their swimming attire and some sort of drink in their hands.

"Hey!" Jessica throws her arms in the air as the guys seemingly invite her warmly inside. Jaiden follows behind, bumping fists with his buds on his way inside.

"Hey Daniels! Come shoot some pool with us man!" shouted Wesley on the opposite side of the area from which they had entered—by the pool table along with some other mutual friends of theirs.

"I'm going to go find Megan," Jessica informs awkwardly parting ways from Jaiden, who already ditched her without saying a word.

"Megan DeSanti?" Alex asks standing behind and she nods. "I think I saw her with Jared..."

"Yeah, I know," she lightly chuckled.

"They're by the campfire out back," he directed, drinking his beer. Jess made her way over to the campfire where the rest of the people were located at. She crept over from behind to the two quietly in hopes of them not seeing her as soon as she found them. When she appeared closer and saw them more visibly, she saw the side of Megan's face and the two laughing while Jared roasted a marshmallow. They were in front of the campfire, sitting across from the other couples, so romantic. Jessica would've hated to admit that she was in fact starting to get a tad jealous. But seeing Jared smile again made her smile too. She was honest to God, glad he's moved on. Now that he was happy, Megan should have no problem parting ways, her work here was done. *Whoa back it up*, Megan was now leaning in as Jared leaned in too. That was not part of the plan. *Yep*, they kissed, right in front of Jessica. Megan was only to show him to a good time not kiss him, *yuck*.

It seemed for Jessica, her own feelings for Jared were stronger than she thought. She sighed and returned, heading inside the house. "Oh, hey! There you are!" Jaiden expressed when making his way from across.

"Here I am," she shrugged. He handed her a red plastic cup.

She looked at the cup before he took her free hand and guided her to the lake out front.

"Something on your mind?" he asked taking off his shirt after they stopped in front of the lake.

"Nope," she shrugged, looking up at the lake, taking a sip of her cold beer. "Wow, it's cold," she noticed when seeing her own breath glisten under the bright moon. Jaiden threw his shirt to the floor. "Alright Daniels, if I get drunk and do something I regret for the second time, it's on you," she teased, drinking the remainder of the weird tasting liquid before crumpling the cup to the floor. She stepped out of her sandals and he did the same. They were only hip deep in the pool when he began splashing her. "Stop!" she shrieked, shivering a bit. They continued to push past the other people in the lake, traveling deeper inside. "Oh my god, it's freezing!" she squealed as soon as the water reached her chest. She thought her C cup shriveled to an A cup by now.

They were further away from the crowds of people to a point where nobody could see them. They reached the end of the lake, it was smaller than she had thought, guess that was the point of a private lake house. As soon as they stopped moving, she attacked him in the water by jumping on his back, messing with his hair. "This is payback!" she wickedly laughed, ruining his perfectly slicked back hair.

"Oh, you want to play messy huh?" he says coming closer after she had plopped off. He had been walking closer in hopes of preparing her for the worst of what was yet to come.

"No… I want to play dirty," she grinned. Before he had a chance to do anything, he waited for her to continue. "Alright, let's do this!" she beamed about to undo her bikini.

"Woah, what are you doing?" His eyes enlarged, and she giggled, biting her bottom lip.

"I'm revisiting my inner wild child!" She pulled his face towards hers to sloppily make out. She momentarily retracted away to continue to take off her top bikini.

"You sure?" he asked.

"Mmmhmmm," she softly seduced launching her top into the air as it lands on a bush. "Serious enough for you?" she teased now slowly removing her bottoms in momentum and lunging it as well. She sank deeper inside the water to cover her bare chest. There was no denying that she had always wanted to skinny dip and was now completely turned on like an oven ready to combust into open flames right now. "Come on Jaiden, don't be a baby and join me… besides, no one can see us," she encouraged wrapping her arms around his neck as she made out with him.

"Fuck, alright," he gave in, pulling away to remove his trunks, desperately leaning in to kiss her again.

"Tsk, tsk, tsk," she teased so that he could properly discard of his trunks. After taking it off, he threw it a bit farther than where she had threw her bathing suit.

"Come here," he says before lifting her up and kissing down her neck.

****

Chapter Eight

"That was hot, let's do it again sometime," Jaiden grinned upon climax. "We should probably go grab our—"

"Yeah," she agreed following him around in the water. Jessica climbed out and grabbed her bikini that landed in the bushes while Jaiden searched for where his trunks went.

"Shit, where is it?" he whispered covering his junk after Jessica already finished changing. She shrugged and hopped back into the lake. "Help me find it… please?"

"Nope," she giggled, throwing her head back. They heard rustling in the bushes causing Jaiden to jump back into the lake without his trunks.

"Oh, hey guys!" Sienna exclaimed finding the two. "We're gonna start playing strip poker back in the cabin soon."

"Loser has to streak butt naked, you up for it?" Josh asked when approaching them from beyond the bushes as well.

"Jared, over here!" exclaimed Megan when entering through the passage from behind the bushes too. "Oh, hey Jessica!" she greeted. "Sorry, Jared and I sort of got lost," she giggled with a towel wrapped around her waist, wearing her hair damp, indicating that they've already explored the depths of the lake together. "Jared, where did you go?" she turned around and he walked out holding Jaiden's trunks.

"Jaiden, aren't these yours?" Jared had asked with a towel around his neck and his hair also damp. He holds up Jaiden's trunks as all the friends look now to Jaiden, his face now red from embarrassment. Jaiden looked down at himself and the water surrounding.

"Gee, how did those end up there?" he awkwardly chuckled when Jared threw him his trunks.

"Guess Jaiden started the game without us, right bud?" Josh retorted, stepping forward to kick the water in his face. "Alright so who's in to play?" he asks while Sienna sneaks a sip of her beer.

"You guys go ahead and play, Jessica and I will be there soon," Megan assures. "Don't start without us," she teased, separating her hand from Jared's as he walks off with a reassuring smile.

"C'mon boy!" Josh said helping Jaiden out of the water after he had finished putting on his trunks. They all walk away leaving Jessica alone with the boastful Megan.

"What's up?" Jessica asked after Megan plopped down next to her in the water.

"Okay well, I wanted to talk about 'my' night, but it seems like *you've* had a more interesting night," she joked.

"What are you talking about?"

"Oh, come on, we all heard you and Jaiden back there," she said before getting back up and pulling the bushes apart. As it turned out, the campfire was right behind the two sex-crazed individuals.

Megan entered the water again.

"So… how was it?"

"The same."

"You mean you've… 'before'? I would have never expected that from 'you' Jessica."

"Oh sure, I've been around. That surprises you? Surely you've heard plenty about the girl who got knocked up in high school… you're looking at her," Jessica admits raising her hand shamelessly.

"That was you? Wait, so—why haven't you ever brought it up before… the baby? What did you name it?" she overwhelmingly asked.

"Not something I'm proud of. I don't go around boasting about something that I don't have anymore…"

"You mean…? Wow. Giving up your baby, that's tough. What did the dad not want it?" she chuckled silently to herself.

"No Megan, I didn't give it up. I, uh…"

"Oh, I'm sorry."

"Yeah."

"So, who did you do it with?" she breaks the silence.

"It's more complicated than that…" Jessica continued to admit, "I didn't know whose it was."

"I've only ever slept with two people," she confessed.

"My God you had a threesome!"

"God no, not at the same time!"

"That's not how I heard it," Megan muttered a little too loudly.

"So, you just pretended to not know anything about my pregnancy?"

"I mean I've heard all sorts of rumors in school, but I would have never guessed those rumors were about you."

"So, how was Jared…?"

"I don't remember… Hello, I was drunk! Wow, people suck at gossiping."

"Well, he is irresistible—boy what I wouldn't do to get my hands on him and let him glaze my donut," she says eyeing him after he walked away in the distance.

"What?" It seemed like she wasn't even listening to Jessica at all. Jess rolled her eyes and sat up on the dirt, dipping her legs in the lake.

"What's wrong? You don't still like him, do you?"

"No, it's not that—"

"Great! Because I think we're really hitting it off...! and don't worry, I think he's forgotten about you; isn't that what you wanted?" Megan asked, resting her arms on the dirt by Jessica. "Uh—"

"Okay well! Let's not waste time, let's go play us some strip poker," she winked out, climbing out of the water.

Jessica willingly followed Megan inside the house but not before Becca pulled her aside. "What is going on?" she whispered. Megan didn't even realize that Jessica was no longer behind her anymore.

"What do you mean?"

"I saw Megan with Jared, being all cutesy."

"They're together," Jessica shrugged.

"Just keep a close eye on 'that one'."

"I trust Jared. He's a good guy, he wouldn't do anything to hurt her," Jessica reassured.

"Not him, 'her'." Becca narrowed her eyes at the busty teenager from behind the window frame outside. "I'm getting bad vibes from that bitch, she keeps flirting with Skylar... come on," she said, pulling Jessica back inside.

"Alright, change of plans!" Josh announced as soon as Becca and Jessica step inside. "The majority of us want to play the traditional seven minutes in heaven," Josh states as the crowd cheers.

"Hey Jess, over here!" Jaiden shouts in the crowd, patting down on his lap. Jessica makes her way over. He pulled her down on the floor and hugged her body from behind.

"I'm not playing this, I think you've had enough for one night," she whispered in his ear.

"I could give you more you know?" he huskily whispered back, quite arrogantly. Jessica couldn't contain the creases from appearing on the sides of her mouth at the thought. Everyone else soon joined in the circle, excluding Jai and Jessica, who stayed back. The circle consisted of Sienna and Josh, Jared and Megan, Becca and Skylar, Griffins and Staci, Hobbs and Lindsay, Lacey and Wesley, Robbie and Candi, Ryan and Sophie, Tanya along with a male named Brian, Nick, and some chick he scooped up in the last few minutes, then finally Alex, who was sitting out like Jaiden and Jessica. The only person Jessica was surprised to see missed out on this experience was Courtney; guess Jared had been her last resort after all. The players had soon all dispersed in different spots for a higher chance to land on their partner.

"Daniels, you joining?" asked Hobbs. "Nah, maybe next time," he assured facing Jessica in hopes she would change her mind.

"He's had more than seven minutes in the lake, I think he's good," Nick contradicted causing the circle of players to mock the poor Jaiden in laughter.

"Alright, who wants to be the first to go?" Griffins asked waving the bottle.

"Me!" Tanya shouts beginning the game. She spins the bottle and it lands on Skylar, Becca's plus one. "This is going to be fun!" Tanya beamed.

"Oh, 'hell' no! Try again!" Becca snapped, throwing the cheap plastic bottle back in the middle.

"Aw baby, you're so cute when you're jealous," Sky says nibbling on her ear.

"Wait, I wanna go!" Lindsay shouts, snatching the bottle next. She spins, and it lands on Staci. "Well okay!" she eagerly exclaimed, taking Staci's hand and guiding her up the stairs.

"Fuck, I wanna watch this!" Hobbs anticipated, illegitimately standing up to follow them. They return several minutes later, and Hobbs walks out behind the girls with the widest grin on his face when striding back to his seat wonky.

"Did you just get laid?" Griffins asked after his friend's return.

"Hell yeah!" he broadcasted as the men then hound him like dogs.

"Okay shit, I wanna go next!" Wesley shouts taking the bottle that landed on Tanya after he spun it. He groaned.

"It's okay, have your way with me, I don't bite," she winked. She stood up, taking his hand and guided him up the stairs. Wesley had his head back disappointingly the whole way up.

"Woah," he exclaimed, his eyes bugged out of his head when they return seven minutes later. She bites her lip and he buttons his shirt.

"My turn!" Megan volunteers. She spun the bottle and it landed on Hobbs to Jessica's relief.

"He's already went, choose again!" Lindsay complains.

"Yeah but it wasn't my turn," he protested. Lindsay folded her arms, pestering the boy until he gave up trying.

"Choose again," she repeated. Megan spun it again and it landed on Jared, who sat directly across from her and Jessica felt her heart stop for a brief minute.

"C'mon," she insisted, anxiously biting her lip while trailing off with him up the staircase.

It has been about ten minutes now with no sign of either of them returning soon. Becca gave Jess a death glare from across the circle to go check up on them. Somehow Becca knew Jared's innocence was no match for Megan—she pegged Jared more as a sock stuffer or as someone who relied on tissues to dry more than just their third leg when watching a movie of sentiment—she was not entirely wrong either. "I'm going to go use the bathroom," Jessica informed to Jaiden; when in reality, she would be sneaking up the stairs.

She managed to snake her way up the stairs after losing the two to a herd of people crowding the hallway upstairs. When she found the designated room, she saw Megan hovering above Jared while they continued to make out on the bed. Megan slowly pushed him down on the bed while her hair fell down the side of her face. She kept her hand on his face to steadily kiss him. They were still in their swimsuits which was a good sign. Jessica was indeed starting to despise Megan for acting like a slut. She was worried for Jared coming to the party with Courtney for that reason, but it seemed no different for Jared to be here with Megan either. Jessica didn't know what to feel. She didn't know what hurt more, catching him in bed with a stranger when she was still with him or catching him in bed with a friend that she set him up with when they weren't together, because although she hated to admit, she still had feelings for him. "Oh, hey Jess!" exclaimed Wesley, passing her by while Josh and Jaiden followed behind, joining Jessica in standing beside the door.

"Jess?" Jared sits up gluing his eyes to the door after Megan was about to untie her top bikini.

"Your time is up guys!" Josh reminds.

"What have you been doing all this time?" Wesley chuckled after noticing that they haven't even got past first base. Megan gets up and holds her bikini in place.

She says, "I had fun." She then goes to kiss Jared on the cheek as he never leaves Jessica's eyes. "Maybe we can try this again sometime?" she hinted with confidence. Jared directed his attention back on Megan before agreeing with a sly smile. Jessica pivoted back around as Jaiden waited for her near the staircase.

"C'mon," he said. The defeated Jessica nodded while her eyes fell to the floor and she followed him back down the stairs. The friends all wait patiently for the four to walk back down the stairs and rejoin the circle. Within twenty minutes of exchanging awkward glances back and forth between Jared and Megan, she asks Jaiden to finally take her home. She was no longer in a 'party mood', her intoxication washed away at the sight of Jared being handled by her acquaintance. All Jess wanted to do in that moment, was to crawl in between her blanket with a tub of ice cream and watch her favorite television show, alone. "If you want, I could come inside?" Jaiden offered when pulling up to the parking lot— hinting to perform his favorite task and call it a night. She respectfully declined, kissing him on the forehead before stepping out of the car. Tuesday morning, 5:55 a.m. and Jessica decided to fully wake up. She usually woke at around 5:30 but stayed in a little longer to subdue alone in her thoughts. She spent all of last night watching a romance movie, 'The Notebook', but could not focus on the movie because all she could think about was Jared... and Megan—then Jared and Courtney, and finally Jared and Jessica; although, there was not much to think about for Jared and herself with the other two unflattering images resurfacing her thoughts. All she could remember from their past was the way he would always make her feel special and their relationship wasn't just about sex—or maybe it would've been if she had not been pregnant at the start of their relationship? But, she knew she would not have wanted the relationship to be centered around that, he was... *different. Just be happy for him. He's finally starting to move on and be happy without you, leave him be, keep your distance from his life and all will be fine.* Her subconscious reminded. She knew it sounded like the right thing to do, but she loved him too much to not care and not be involved in his life. Even if they weren't in a relationship, it was okay to love him as a friend. Only, she didn't know what she loved him as.

****

"Hey Jessica!" acknowledged Megan, when Jessica had walked into their shared third hour. Megan of course, was ready to boast about her night with Jared, but Jessica didn't want to hear it.

"Lab day two—get to your stations!" their teacher announced, cutting off all the small conversations in the classroom just before Megan had a chance to continue, to Jessica's advantage. Jessica grabbed her eye goggles and lab coat, tying her hair back before making her way to the station that Jared was already at.

"So that was a fun party last night..." Megan directed to Jared. He smiled humbly.

"Megan DeSanti to attendance!" the teacher called out.

"We should definitely do it again some time," she said making her way around as she touches Jared's shoulder and kisses behind his ear.

He winces at her touch before smiling. Jessica rolled her eyes and continued with her lab while Megan left the classroom.

"Hey Jess, I found this on our lab station yesterday, while I was cleaning up." Jared places her ring inside her palm. She couldn't say she was disappointed when she misplaced it. She was kind of relieved she didn't have to flaunt it around everywhere. Did she make a mistake by accepting it? Was it too sudden and overwhelming? Yes.

"Thanks," she replied cracking a small smile while he proceeded back to work on his lab. Jessica could not stop staring at the shiny ring around her finger halfway through class, it reminded her of her undetermined future with Jaiden. When she glanced over at Jaiden, she saw Candi with her hand on his shoulder, biting her lip and him just smiling back at her and now nodding. Jessica took off her goggles and marched over.

"What's going on here?" she impolitely asked.

"Hey baby—" He attempted to pull his girl down on his lap, but she refused him of the advantage, "Don't 'hey baby' me, I take my eyes off you for one second and you're flirting with this 'hussy'!" she appalled.

"'Hussy'?" Candace scoffed, "Honey, in case you haven't heard, the only 'hussy' people talk about behind these curtains is 'you'," Candace objectifies, wiping her well-manicured fingernails all over Jessica's beau.

"You need to chill girl," Star confronted, pulling the sassy Jessica away. Jessica wasn't going down without a fight. She tried pulling away from Star's restraint to claw Candi's eyeballs out.

"Jessica return back to your station immediately before I write you up!" the teacher warned. Jessica instantly shot the redhead a deathly glare while Candace waved her off.

"So, what the hell happened at the party? I thought Megan 'wasn't interested' in Jared," Star asked, after stopping in the middle of the lab room.

"Yeah well she is and I'm starting to get a second opinion of her."

****

On his way to lunch, Jaiden caught up to Jessica, stopping her in the hallway corridor, "It wasn't what you thought. Candi was just thanking me for stopping the wedding," he stressed.

"So, what now? Was she entitled to suck you off after class?" she berated, crossing her arms.

"No—"

"I saw the way she was looking at you Jaiden and I know how you can get, so don't even start with me! You didn't even back me up in there, what the hell!"

"How I can get?" he emphasized, ill-tempered, "I think you've mistaken me for someone else. 'I'm' not the one who has feelings for two people!" *Oh, he went there.*

"I don't feel like arguing today, so why don't you give me a call once you've whacked one off for the day and maybe get some of that tension out?" she suggested. "Until then... rot in 'hell', Jaiden!" she yelled, dismissing him.

"Okay, but I won't be thinking of you when I do!" he yelled after she had already disappeared further down the hallway; he stood there in confusion after realizing he contradicted himself.

"Hey Jess," Jared greeted in the hallway after Megan walked off, blowing him a kiss.

Jess walked up to him, "So, you and Megan, getting pretty serious huh?" she asked.

"I don't know, she seems nice and all..." he mumbled when turning around to place items in his locker.

"Hey, Jared?"

"Yeah?" he asked unloading his backpack.

"Just be careful?"

"What do you mean?" he asked zipping it up.

"I don't want you to get hurt," she stated causing him to turn around in a confused matter.

"Why should that matter to you? Besides, 'you're' the one who wanted us to go out."

She wished everyone would stop saying that.

"Yeah, I know... but,"

"Hey, it's better this way. I'm out of your life, like you wanted, 'remember'*?*" he reminded shutting his locker.

"No, not like that..."

He turns around again, "I don't know what is going on with your head right now, maybe it's from all the narcotics you've taken since the hospital, but I'm over your mind games—do you think this is a game? This is real life and I'm going to give it to you damn straight. You can't just fucking walk around thinking you own me, like I owe you a favor. I'm not your puppet, I'm no one to you at this point. You don't know what you want. When you were with me, you needed him and when you're with him, you need me, and you can't have both Jessica! I know how hard it must be for you to grasp this considering how stubborn you can get—" That was a low blow, but Jessica felt she deserved that.

"Jared, I—"

"I wasn't done talking and I frankly don't think you understand how 'miserable' I've been just being your friend. I won't ever be okay with what you have with Jaiden, but I also won't let you stand there and use me. I was your friend once and I was okay with that. Now, I don't want anything to do with you because of him and what he's done to you. He's ruined you—"

"No, YOU ruined me Jared. I never wanted to be with him when I was with you!"

"Oh, that's horseshit Jessica!" he spat. "You've wanted him since the get-go, I saw it! You can't handle rejection, he turned you down and you turned to me to baby you around, to be your support system because you knew I would be willing to do 'anything' for you! I was your shoulder to cry on and I allowed you to use me because I didn't know any better! I was in love with you, Jessica! Yes, I'm guilty of doing the same but the only difference is, I owned up to my mistakes and I actually did care about you!"

"Okay yes! I did feel for him, but it meant nothing to me! I was hurt and vulnerable and for a second I believed you would never hurt me because you haven't! When I was with you, I was repressing my feelings for Jaiden, but Jared I fell for you, not him! I got over him! I didn't want to be in a relationship at first, I didn't even know what I wanted. When I realized it was you I wanted, you left me when I needed you the most! You abandoned me, I loved you and I would've done anything for you! I even wanted to give up my life for you when you ended our relationship, while you managed to get by perfectly fine without me!"

"What do you want me to say? Let's not forget you were the one who ended things Jess, not me! You're the one who has blatantly pushed me away! You want me to leave my girlfriend? You want me to run away with you? In case you haven't noticed, I've moved on and so have you, I'm happy now. Does my happiness not matter? We are over Jessica and we have been for a long time—when you made your bed. When you let him touch you in ways I couldn't have. I'm not capable of loving you and I don't think I ever will be.

"...I'll make this decision real easy for you, how about I just go, and you'll never see me again? You can go be with him and I'll be out of your life forever. Don't call me, don't talk to me. I'll find someone who loves me, who believes me, and who trusts me. I'll marry her, I'll be with her, I'll love her and if that girl has to be Megan, then so be it. I'll forget about you if you need me to. For the past two months that I've been with you, that's all I have thought about. It's always been you Jessica, my life. My life has been revolved around you time and time

156

again, Jessica and I 'need' a break from you," he stressed, "Jessica, I'll move on. I'll start my own family that I 'was' destined for this time. I just need you to promise me you'll stay out of my life when that happens because I don't need any complications. I don't want to be tied down to you my whole life. Whatever happened with us in our past, is in our past. Our relationship was a mistake and the way I look at it is we weren't meant to be if we lost Sam. Let's face it, without her there would be nothing there," he shrugged.

How could he think like that?

For the longest time that they have been together, she thought he was the one. At a point, she even believed the girl he was describing had originally been the plan for her. She could see a future with him. That they would be together, forever. He's even promised to love her forever. He understood her, he belonged to her. It hurt to hear that he would throw all of that away. She only pushed him away for so long because she sensed he was different and was afraid to get burned. She constantly worried for the sake of her future, getting close to a guy; if he would only live to end up tearing her apart or damage her like the unhealthy relationship with her parents. She felt threatened by the world, avoiding relationships at all costs. *What if you spend so much time with the right guy that ends up being the wrong guy?* Especially after her father, she feared men. She felt threatened when the only men she had left in her life to trust, let their guard down and took advantage of her—what was to come for her future? She came to the consensus that men cannot be trusted. One thing led to another and soon she believed if she couldn't rely on her friends now to protect her, then how would they let her down tomorrow? She was not ready or equipped to handle that kind of emotional abuse. "How could you say that, Jared? I love you," she croaked.

"Love me? You have a real funny way of showing it," he chuckled, staring down at the shiny materialistic object around her finger. *Did she love Jaiden? Could she love Jaiden? Could Jaiden really love her? Did Jared even love her? Was she just using Jaiden?* "You stomped on my heart and there was no recovering from that. Jessica, you don't love me. You only love the idea of someone, anyone being there for you because you can't accept being on your own! My mother was right. That's what happens when you've been neglected your whole life, you expect too much from me!" That earned him a righteous, sharp slap across the face.

"You know *damn* well I could've raised *my* daughter on my own, how *dare* you! I never asked for any of this!"

"But you couldn't because 'you' couldn't accept betrayal and you hurt yourself the second you felt you were alone!"

"I'm sorry for letting my guard down because I thought you would always be there for me, you made me believe you would stay but you left!"

"No, I never said anything! 'You' wanted to keep the baby, 'not me'. I had no say in it! I had plans for my future that didn't involve 'you'! I had my whole life set out ahead of me until you threw this burden on me in the worst possible time in my life because of your selfish and manipulative ways! After that, I was set to hit rock bottom. And yes, at a time I wanted to stop everything to be with you and this baby, but it's all over now! Those feelings I thought I had are gone, are over! We're over!"

"So why are you telling me this now?"

"I'm just finally giving you what you want. Congratulations Jess, you've got your wish, you've pushed me away. Thank you for opening my eyes and letting me explore my options now. How could I have been so ignorant as to hold onto something that was never there?

"For Christ's sake Jess, look at yourself! You've become this irresponsible train wreck!" She wanted him to be wronged, she wanted to fire back and tell him he was just as guilty for sleeping with her in the first place, but she would just stand there and let him terrorize her further. "Why are you doing these things, Jess! Why are you seeking approval! You want acceptance, but you just don't understand, you're never going to get it."

"Don't even fucking get me started with how much of an unimaginable little priss you've become! Did Daddy finally get his little Janey to crack?" he tormented, merely an inch away from her face now. That, 'that' was the trigger that would wound her for eternity. He didn't need any alcohol to speak his mind this time.

"What have I done to make you become so cruel to me? Haven't I suffered enough?" she whimpered. Jared ignored the girl, meeting up with his better half in the hallway as Jess stood frozen in place with no one to comfort her this time. It felt to her like he was breaking up but far worse, like he was ending their friendship, *he was.* In this moment, Jessica thought being called a whore or even a skank would've hurt just a little less. Everyone left Jessica, any chance they had, regardless of how small the argument. It was a good excuse to cut off all ties with her. Was she that terrible of a person that even her so-thought friend didn't want anything to do with her?

She went to her locker, grabbed her binder, collected her things, and headed home, by foot. She just could not continue with her school day. She should've never even transferred to this school. How was she to get over Jared and act like she didn't know him when he was everywhere?

158

She didn't acknowledge her friends who waved her from behind, they automatically sensed something was up now. "Where are you going?" Becca asked when running up behind her. It really sucked that her friends were friends with the twins. She didn't want to come between them like this, so she decided to keep her distance.

"Home," she croaked, putting on her shades to avoid eye contact.

"Sweetie, what's wrong? Tell me everything! It's Jared, isn't it? Or is it Jaiden?" she worried.

"You can ask them for yourselves,"

"Honey, if you think they open up to me about this stuff, you're wrong. Besides, I got you, you're my girl!" she reassuringly stated. It was enough for Jessica to know that she can trust Becca when it comes to the twins, at least. Jessica stopped a couple of feet away from the exit, turning to glance at Skylar awkwardly.

"Go," Becca excused Skylar.

"But—"

"Goodbye Skylar!" she hissed, scoffing him away. She then linked her elbow with Jessica's and proceeded to exit the building where Jessica had explained everything on the forty-minute walk to her place.

"Okay, so Jaiden is an asshole, what's new? Jared though—I mean 'wow'. They share the same DNA, it's understandable. Still, I would have never imagined those words would leave his mouth. In all honesty, even though I've known the twins longer than I've known you, I think you're much cooler and prettier—you don't need them! Hey, don't get me wrong, I love them too, but those guys are drama, drama I tell you! I think you need something to get your mind off these asswipes," she suggested while Jessica unlocks the door to her flat.

"What did you have in mind?" Jessica chimed, shrugging off her backpack after they stepped inside.

"Damn girl, 'this' is your apartment!" exclaimed Becca, wandering around after Jessica had poured herself a glass of orange juice from the fridge. "I wish my parents loved me this much!" she continued walking up to the counter. Jessica nearly choked on her drink from laughter.

"I'm actually paying for this; well, I mean I was until I got fired from my part time job—my older sister Amanda was helping me pay this off, but now she's the only one paying this off,"

"You have a sister, what's that like?"

"Two actually, and hell," she replied while Becca took a sip from the glass she poured for her.

"You're telling me you're the only child?" Jessica blankly asked, making her way to the couch.

"No, I have four little brothers," Becca sighed, joining her.

"What's that like?"

"For the most part, 'hell'," she laughed.

"So, what were you saying earlier about?"

"About a sleepover?" Becca suggested, facing Jessica while bringing her knees up to her chest. "This weekend, we'll invite all the girls…" Jessica's face lit up at the thought. Growing up with bratty sisters (for the most part), and two male friends, she never had the opportunity. "Not Megan or Courtney or Candi or Tanya or—"

"Got it. Don't worry, we'll just invite Star, Sienna, and maybe even the Brooks," she said pulling out her cell phone. Jessica slowly pushed her friend's hand back down as soon as she started to dial.

"They're still in class," Jessica reminded. "So, what's the deal with Megan?" she asked, throwing her own phone on the coffee table.

"Well, she's definitely changed since we became friends with her. I think we've opened her comfort zone, she's kind of a slut now. I mean she's had to have slept with pretty much the entire football team by now."

"It's a good thing Jaiden's off the team then," Jessica stated, clearly in denial.

"Hmmmm… I don't know," Becca argued, "If we're talking about last season—"

"No, he wouldn't," Jessica declined.

"Anyways… she'll act all sweet at one minute but it's only because she's trying to get on your good side before she sleeps with your boyfriend, so you'll never see it coming," she continued, "In your case, with Jared being your friend and all, she must want him because she knows you still have feelings for him, so she can rip you away from him. It's what she does… she's like a succubus."

"She didn't seem interested in him before—"

"Right, and she gave in a little too easily after you willingly put them together?" Jessica narrows her eyes thinking about it before nodding her head.

"Point proven."

"Has she made a pass on Skylar?"

"You mean besides flirting? I don't think so, but I know it's because she knows I have the power to kick her out of Galaxy Quest."

"With her, she can't keep it in her pants long enough to hold a guy for longer than a week—that's why she'll usually wait until after they've had sex to dispose of them like gloves before moving on to the next. You can just imagine how horny these guys are if she drops them in a week's span… It's basic math, she wants what she can't have—the emotionally undesirable. I guess it all works out for her though, because she doesn't have to get attached and guys aren't bothered by that at all either—they worship her 'because' she's promiscuous. If I were to compare, I'd say she's a less-obscene, female version of Jaiden—only, he's slept with an array of cheerleaders instead of the football team itself," she chuckles causing Jessica to revolt in disgust. "Well, it's true! I only say 'less-obscene' because need I remind, he blew his load in lake 'full' of people!" she chuckled, throwing her head back.

"We were far away!—Well, I thought," Jessica protested before standing up to run over to her bedroom, slamming the door behind her. She hid under her covers as soon as she entered and sobbed on her pillow, lying flat on her stomach. The pillow still had Jaiden's musk on it and she sobbed harder. Becca entered shortly after Jess had entered. She sat on the bed stroking her friend's hair. "I'm losing them both!" Jess whined.

"No, not at all... wow! That is a 'gorgeous' ring!" Becca mentioned, getting sidetracked in its illuminating luster before lifting Jessica's hand to closely examine it.

"Who from?"

"Jaiden."

"Engagement?"

"Promise," she corrected.

"You see, Jaiden loves you!"

"I know," Jess sat up.

"It just doesn't feel right, I still care for Jared—how could he just say that to me!" she cried, getting back under her covers.

"Jared loves you sweetie, it just hurts him to see you with Jaiden."

"...Then there's Jaiden, who I feel is just using me for sex. I mean you said it yourself, that he's slept with the entire cheerleading team, what makes me so damn different from them if he's just sleeping with me too!" she whined.

"For one, he got you a friggin' ring!" Becca exclaimed. "He wouldn't go through the trouble to buying you this ring if he didn't care. He loves you and it goes to show he's willing to make a commitment,"

"Or maybe with this he thinks, I'm his bitch—the one of many he's slept with, that he wants to keep. Gee, how sweet," Jess grumbled.

"Do you love him?"

"Of course—"

"Then don't doubt him. You're with him and he hasn't done anything to screw it up yet because he loves you, and honey, these cheerleaders were his past, you're his future and if you're really meant to be with Jared, time will tell, but not until you give Jaiden a fair chance."

Jess decided she would go back to school the next day. She also decided on talking to Jaiden when he approached her. Maybe she was just over reacting a bit. The first day back in chemistry was awkward for Jessica, having Jared be her partner and all since she had to stop being around him. He managed to ask the teacher to switch lab partners that same day, but she denied him the privilege, so the following day, he decided to overall switch out classes. It hurt Jess, but she had to plaster a smile on her face and pretend she didn't care. It really hurt her seeing Jared and Megan kissing in the hallways between classes just as much. Then, having Megan rub it in her face during seventh hour really was the cherry on top of the icing. *He's happy though and I'm happy... with Jaiden, that's all that matters, right?*

Who is Jared Daniels again?

****

The sleepover was tonight, so Jessica asked Jaiden to help her with grocery shopping. "So?" he asked when walking through the junk food aisle.

"Yeah?" she replied stopping the cart.

"Am I invited to this 'sleepover'?"

"No boys allowed. Clear instructions from Becca," she stated, looking over her shopping list.

"What would you girls be doing at this 'sleepover' exactly?"

"Having loads and loads of lesbian sex," she responded, unenthusiastically.

"Aw, I wish I could come!" he pouted.

"My God, Jaiden, it was a joke! I was kidding!" she groaned.

"I wasn't," he punned when coming forward to slap her ass before she shoved the list over to him. They had arrived back at her flat and Jaiden set the junk food on the kitchen counter while Jessica followed behind to bring in the rest of the groceries. He took them from her hands to set them on the counter. He then took her by surprise when he lifted her by her legs and threw her over his shoulders.

"What are you doing you big idiot?" She giggled while he softly laid her on the couch, hovering above her before she got a chance to get up. He then pushed his lips against hers and her hands trailed up to grasp his hair.

"How long do we have until they get here?" he asked, his lips yet to leave hers while he swiftly held up a sealed wrapper he pulled from his front pocket.

"Hey!" Becca exclaimed entering the door with the rest of the girls, while Jessica inadvertently pushed Jaiden off to shuffle off the couch just before the girls fully entered.

"Not long," he mumbled fixing his hair. "See you later," he said grabbing his phone off the coffee table, giving her a quick peck on the cheek before leaving.

"Why aren't you in your PJs missy?" Star scolded, examining Jessica. They all had been wearing their PJs on their way over there.

"I'll go change. Chips and soda on that table—you girls can set up your stuff over here—napkins, plastic plates, and cups over there and I'll be back," Jess directed, before skipping over to her bedroom. She returns dressed to the occasion minutes later in her new silk pajama romper that she bought at Forever 21 a couple of days ago.

"Woah *mami*, you look 'hot'!" Sienna emphasized in her thickest Latina accent after Jessica had stepped out. Jess smiled back in response and then heard her phone buzz on the kitchen counter, so she made her way over.

It was a text from Jaiden that read:

We'll continue that later (; -Jai

She smirked silently to herself before turning off her phone and setting it aside. She then grabbed the blankets and pillows she prepared for herself and joined the girls on the floor with their floor beds already sprawled out. "So, for the movie, we have Magic Mike and Mean Girls—"

"Sorry I'm late," said Megan when entering the door, without her PJs.

"What, did you invite her!" Jessica whisper-yelled to Becca.

"I didn't no, never!" she protested.

"I'm sorry, she was on to us!" Star sheepishly admitted as they continued to whisper. Jessica slumped down while Megan joined them on the floor.

"Pop the movie and I'll pop the popcorn?" Becca directed to Jessica upon standing up. "Would you like a blanket perhaps?"

"No thanks, I'm not staying—got a hot date to get to tonight," Megan said fixing her lipstick with a touch of her finger in her small hand-held mirror. It has only been thirty minutes of Mean Girls and the night has been a complete disaster thanks to Megan distracting them all with her bright phone light in the complete darkness and her obnoxious giggling while staring at her screen. Just when everyone thought Megan had finally stopped, the door rang. "I'll get it!" Megan exclaimed, sprinting to the door.

"You ready?" a familiar male voice says from beyond the door.

"Come on in," Megan insisted pulling the voice inside as the lights come on.

"Turn off the lights!" Lacey groans.

"Yeah and no boys!" Becca shouts. Pausing the movie, Jessica shifts her attention to the back of the room as Jared is being escorted over to them by Megan.

"Hey Jared!" Lindsay and Lacey greet simultaneously.

"Hey ladies, hey—" His eyes stop when he spots Jessica and he quickly disengages in eye contact in hopes of avoiding her.

"You don't live here anymore?" he directs to the Brooks as they nod in disagreement. "Well, this is awkward," he mumbled to himself loud enough for Jessica to hear him, unintentionally. He looked around and her eyes trail off to where he pauses in his gander. *Damn Jaiden,* who forgot to pick up the condom.

"I'm just going to wait outside babe," Jared announced when glancing back over to Jessica before looking back to Megan upon realization. *'Babe?' Yuck!* That made Jessica's skin crawl.

"Oh, I'm ready, I'll come with!" she perched as they exited, holding hands. There was literally no point of bringing him here; of course Jessica would bet anything it was just to rub it in her face as Megan had been doing since the start of their notorious relationship. As soon as they left, Jessica stood up to lock the door behind them. She then shut off the lights and walked over to pick up the sealed condom from the floor before walking over to the kitchen to discard it while the girls continued to watch the movie after Becca had un-paused it. Jessica had dragged her feet, finding her seat on the floor, and brought her legs up to her chest.

"Okay, stop the movie," Star sighed, hitting the power on the remote as Sienna ran over to hit the lights. "Gather around ladies, we are going to have a deep intervention on boys."

"Can we not? Boys are stupid," Sienna huffed when returning to the floor.

"Anything you'd like to tell us about Josh?" Becca curiously asked while Sienna hesitates.

"Come on, I'll share something embarrassing about Skylar!" she persuaded.

"Alright but, I don't think it will even come close to what I'm about to spill…"

"Josh has a… foot fetish." As soon as those words leave her mouth, all the girls burst into a fit of laughter.

"You serious?" Becca asks. Sienna nods in response, unable to contain her laughter.

"What you got on 'Sky Guy'?" Star asks Becca now.

"Brace yourself for this one ladies, Skylar's voice cracks when he's aroused!" The air is cleared with laughter once again.

"You think that's bad? Josh likes it when we role play in Frozen costumes!"

"Stop, you're making me cry!" Becca shrieks in laughter.

"Enjoy high school boys while you can," Sienna states when taking a sip of her cola.

"Okay, okay, enough about that... serious question time; what was your first time like?" Star asked, breaking the ice.

"Sixth grade, Zach Griffins," Lacey admits.

"You slut!" Lindsay shouted in revelation.

"What can I say, he was quite the expert for a fifth grader."

They all gasped, "Does Staci know?"

"Why would she care... they're not dating, 'hello'!"

"Well... two years ago, Skylar and I were on a family vacation in Maui, we stayed back in the resort to hang out together and it was amazing, we were each other's firsts," Becca smiles as they all awe.

"What about you Jess?" Star asks, slapping Jessica's tender knees.

"Couple of months ago, at one of Josh's parties with Jaiden..." she smiled. She waited to continue whilst staring down at her jittery hands when her smile dropped instantly, "I didn't remember any of it, woke up pregnant one day—and seven months later, here I am with no baby, no job, and what I thought was the only guy I've ever loved, who ended up cutting me out of their life," she finished, indulging in self-pity before breaking down with her head falling into her lap as the girls scoot in to comfort her.

"I'm sorry, I shouldn't have—"

"Boyfriends are here!" Jaiden announces upon unexpectedly entering with the rest of the boyfriends: Josh, Hobbs, and Skylar; each of them holding a six-pack full of beers. Jessica speedily wiped her tears away before they joined the ladies on the floor. "Miss me?" Jaiden asked wrapping his arms around Jess.

"Get out, get out now!" Becca growled.

"No, no... It's okay if they're here," Jess reassured. Jessica knew the girls weren't having as much fun with her being a Debby-downer and all.

"I'm going to need me one of these, thanks babe," Sienna said grabbing a beer from Josh.

"What are you guys even doing here? We did this to get away from you and you're ruining everything!" Star whined.

"Star, get yourself a boyfriend already and shut up," Josh retorted.

165

"Josh, do me a bigger favor and lick my foot!" she embellished throwing a pillow at his face. The room is filled with horrendous laughter, taunting the boy.

"You told them!" Josh pouted, red with discomfort before standing up to exit with Sienna tailgating his rear. *One down and three more to go.*

"Damn! Home girl went from B to G real quick!" exclaimed Hobbs when bumping his fist with Star.

Chapter Nine

Wednesday 2:43 a.m., Jessica woke up in bed, drenched in her own sweat once again, due to the same dream... or rather 'nightmare'. It kept reoccurring throughout the week since Monday. The strangest thing was that this so-called 'reoccurring dream' never finished its strip of film, it was always skipping to the next scene. The only difference this time was that she no longer dreamt about Jaiden afterwards. Jessica thought asking Jaiden to spend the night might help those night terrors to go away. When asked why the sudden invite, Jessica only explained that she was having these nightmares and not what about.

"It happened again," she panted sitting up that night. He startled awake and sat up, giving the girl a comforting hug while stroking her hair like her previous day's dream.

"So, what exactly is this dream about?" he asked after she settled under her covers again.

"I don't want to talk about it," she sighed.

"Good morning, time for school," she heard a soft rasp in her ear.

She glanced over at the clock on her nightstand, "Jaiden," she groaned. "It's 5:27," she whined, rolling over to the side facing away from her street window.

"I know," he said rolling over to spoon her from behind. "I thought we could use a quick shower," he mentioned, kissing behind her ear.

"No," she mumbled while digging her face in her pillow.

"Alright," he said rolling away. He stood up to fix his hair in the mirror. Jessica flipped onto her back to watch him effortlessly get ready for school, biting her bottom lip without realization. He smiled at her through his reflection, watching her watch him. "I'm going to take one if you don't mind, but feel free to join," he implied when pulling his boxers down shamelessly. Jessica pretentiously covered her eyes, staring between the spaces in her fingers. He walked over to bring her hand down so that she may enjoy the free show.

"You don't have to be intimidated by what you see," he cockily smirked. She took the opportunity to throw a pillow at him, just before his lips found hers. Jess rolled her eyes playfully, dismissing her intrusive boyfriend. Most of the school day went great for Jessica. Although, chemistry was boring without a lab partner as it was for a week or so now, but at least she had Jaiden to entertain her the whole class hour with his innuendos. To her advantage, they were in the back row, so no one could see them, except Candi, who was thankfully absent for that class period. Once again, Jessica peeked at the other side of the room to find Jaiden, who had his tongue in between two of his fingers that formed a 'v' shape, flicking his tongue to indicate that he wanted to perform oral later. The next time she looked up in his direction—after desperately trying to avoid him—he had his index finger pushing in and out of a loop he made with his fingers, hidden behind his textbook. She shook her head, disgruntled. With only twenty minutes of the class period left, she tried to catch up with notes. Pretty soon, a new student was introduced to the class, in place of Jared and became Jessica's new lab partner. His name was Chris. The two became friends instantly. He made sure Jessica knew he was not a new student, that he just switched classes—reason being that he didn't like his previous teacher. She had not seen him once in school yet, so she was clearly mistaken.

Chris Mullins was a five-foot-ten Englishman with dirty blonde hair and had sea-green eyes. After he was placed next to her, Jaiden stopped with the racy slurs. In fact, when she looked back over to him, she could feel his jealousy stirring. With halfway until the class period was over, she took her ring off in a flash and placed it in her backpack, hoping her new partner didn't catch that. She didn't want anyone to get the wrong idea and had no time to explain what it meant either. "Lab tomorrow, wear closed-toe shoes!" their teacher instructed just as the bell rang. "Hope you all took great notes because you're going to rely on them for tomorrow's lab!" she stressed on the students' way out the door. *Bummer*, twenty-five percent of notes was not going to do justice for Jessica 'or' her new lab partner tomorrow. Jared wasn't there for calculus today, he must have been absent. When it came time for Jessica to think of it, she remembered that Megan wasn't there for chemistry her previous class period either. She guessed they must have skipped together. *What a great influence she has on his life.*

After what Becca told Jessica, she was surprised they were still together, it's been about two weeks. They must have not consummated their relationship yet. "Okay guys, we need to say something to Megan, she has been missing practice for days now," Becca informs in their dance period.

"Yeah, I don't want to fail because she'd rather play hooky with her new boyfriend," Jessica pettishly muttered, rolling her eyes.

"Is someone jealous?" Skylar teased.

"Shut up and practice elsewhere!" Becca hissed.

"Fine," he muttered under his breath before trailing away.

"We can't just leave her, she'll get a bad grade and fail if we ditch her now," Star mentions.

"She should've thought of that before she started skipping out."

"Let's just practice without her and if she continues, we'll withdraw her."

"Fine."

"Ladies, couldn't help but notice you're a little short, but if you want, you could just forfeit now and join our leading group... after all, we're both doing hip hop," Tanya stated as the rest of her posse follows behind her like minions.

"Couldn't help but notice that your leader isn't here. Did she break a hip while popping and locking on her boyfriend's dick?" Jess backfired, folding her arms.

"No, she's getting plastic surgery for her breasts!" a brunette in their group named Kristen impetuously informed.

"You're an idiot, Candi is going to kill you!" Tanya snapped while Jessica and her group of friends snicker.

"Were her boobs too small? That's what she gets for self-induced vomiting," Star cackled.

"Class period is almost over!" their instructor announced while Tanya rolled her eyes to the back of her head and walked away with the rest of her squad.

"Skylar! Get back over here!" Star shouted from across the room after observing him from the floor, obliviously scrolling through his phone and listening to music through his headphones at full volume.

****

"She did it, I'm going to kill her!" Becca whales in a slump, dragging her feet over to Jessica from across the hallway, hair a mess, mascara dripping.

"Who? What's wrong?" Jessica worriedly asks.

"M-Megan and Skylar k-kissed!" Becca wept on her shoulder while Jessica, unsure of what to do, pats down her back in an awkward attempt at comforting her. "I saw them talking, I assumed it was for the group, but as soon as I walked closer, she planted one right on his lips and he didn't even pull away!" she sobbed unable to form sentences.

"Okay, that's it!" Jessica angered, pulling the emotionally unstable Becca away from her embrace. "If 'you're' not going to kick her out of the group, 'I will'!" Jessica proclaimed, beginning to part ways with her friend.

"Wait, I just saw her enter the girls' bathroom upstairs," Becca stated after running up behind her.

"Okay, let's go—"

"No Jessica, I can't face her... I-I've got to go," she cowardly ran amiss. Jessica couldn't wait 'til Jared heard about this. That his girlfriend was a bigger slut than he thought. She didn't just go after anyone, she went after one of his friends, *disgusting*.

"Hey Jessica!" Megan greeted in the mirror when Jessica entered the restrooms. She was reapplying her lipstick. Jessica crossed her arms.

"Almost running out of that lipstick I see."

"Yeah, who knew Jared was such a great kisser," she winked.

"Cut the crap, I know you made a pass at Skylar."

"Oh my God," she turned around.

"Does Becca know?"

"Who do you think told me?"

"Newsflash, you shouldn't believe everything you hear," she forewarned.

"Nobody had to lie to me, I believe her. It's 'you' I don't trust," Jessica growls, crossing her arms.

"'Oh', so is that what 'this' is? You're upset that I'm with Jared and he chose me."

"This has nothing to do with him!" Jessica gritted, "You better stay away from Skylar, apologize to Becca. And you will tell Jared the truth. You don't deserve him," she scoffed.

"And you think 'you do'?"

"That's right, he told me, everything," Megan says beginning to circle around the agitated Jessica. "He trusts me now and 'only' me. You're nothing but a bench to him now. You're beneath him, always have been, 'always will be',*,*" she said stopping in front of her.

"That's a lie!"

"I believe his exact words were, 'daddy's... little... priss'."

"'Helpless, needy... face it', you don't belong here. You're a nobody, and as long as he's with me, I'll make sure he knows so too."

Jessica fled out of there, revolting down the stairs with her head down. She stormed right past Becca who awaited, hoping that her friend got the message across to leave her boyfriend alone. Jess bolted directly past her and then Jaiden, who awaited her in the hallways too, between periods, like their daily routine. "Jess?" He worried after a gust of wind flew past in his direction. She headed for the door and completely exited the school building. She rushed home and slammed the door with all her might. She promised herself she would not resort to such thing as she paced back and forth in her bathroom now. She broke down just throwing her fists against the wall, silent in her screams. She tugged her hair, shaking violently in her despair. She trusted him, and he betrayed her—*no, he ended me.*

Guess he really was done with Jessica. At what cost did he sell those terrible words about his former friend of long time to his girlfriend of short time? *Is that what he really thinks of me?* She stood defeated in her own battle. She left the door unlocked hoping there would be someone, just anyone to stop her before she did anything reckless. "Hey, I followed you back here," a voice approached when entering the bathroom to find her on the floor. "What are you doing with that?" he asked distressed at the sight he stumbled into.

"Go away, just leave. It's what everyone does best," she vaguely spoke.

"No Jessica, I'm not going to let you do this again! Don't you understand? I love you dammit! Don't do this!"

He bellowed when trying to overtake the razor from her hands, and wound up falling to the floor, to comfort her in another hug. She hyperventilated, just trying to escape; her anxiety became unbearable.

"Just go away!" she sobbed in his forced embrace. He threw the razor in the sink so that it was out of reach while they were still sitting on the floor. "I'm not leaving Jessica, whether you like it or not. I made a promise to you and I'm always going to protect you… no matter what," he wept as she trembled in his arms.

"I-I, I can't do this," she shivered after calming down a bit.

"You're making progress, okay. I got you, I'm right here…"

"I love Jared," she whispered.

Jaiden's hand stopped stroking her back after those words left her unfiltered mouth. She sprang up to vomit right after.

****

"You still love him?" he asked joining her on the couch.

"You have to understand that we had history."

"You and I have history! Still, I would never have said any of those things to you!"

"He didn't mean them… I know it," she denied.

"Do you love me?"

"Well?"

"Yes! Of course I do!"

"…But you love 'him' more?"

"I need to be alone."

"It's a simple question Jessica!"

"I think you need to go…"

"I don't care if I'm not your favorite person right now, I'm staying here to watch you."

"…You'll get over him Jess. You are capable of letting him go. He told you how he felt. It's not fair to you. I won't ever let you down like that—"

"But you have before. That's what scares me,"

"Jess—"

"Please just go Jaiden," she said, swallowing the lump in her throat. He stood up and went to grab his jacket from the couch before hesitantly kissing her on the forehead—and in respect to her request, he exited her apartment.

****

"So here is my place," Jared says.

"Wow, nice! It's so big!" Megan exclaimed, letting go of his hand after they stepped inside. *Safe to say, I never earned that compliment before.*

"So, what do you want to do?"

"Maybe you could give me a little tour of the bedroom?"

"Uh, yeah sure," he says nervously. She takes his hand and he leads her into his room. She shuts the door behind them on their way in.

"So nice… here, let's sit down," she says gently pulling him down on his bed with her.

"What do you want to do?" he asks while she scoots closer to him, pushing her hair back.

"I thought maybe we could talk," she says slowly rubbing his thighs.

"Well, I uh—" he nervously stutters when staring at her hand while she reached higher up his thigh, presumptuously indicating that she wanted more, "You're really special Jared…"

"Woah," his eyes enlarged. He slid her hand back down in an automatic response to her hand reaching his genitalia. She crosses her legs and bit her lip ambiguously.

"You were saying?" she innocently smirked when grazing his cheek.

"So, how's school?" he impulsively asked out of nervousness. She giggled as his quirky innocence, "It's going well, but I currently have other activities on my mind that I want to pursue," she covertly hinted, brushing the hair out of his face. She leans in to kiss him and he didn't hold back this time with Jessica out of his life.

"I thought... maybe I could do you a favor," she says while grazing a hand over his aching bulge. "If you'd let me..." He stared for a mid-second and then nodded quickly in approval. She then stood up to kneel in front of him, getting on all fours. She strokes his thighs, signaling for him to take his jeans off—He swiftly pulled them off and threw them onto the floor. Megan did him the honor of doing the rest, slowly pulling his boxers down to reveal his carefree hard-on. She leaned in forward as her long dark hair fell to her side. He leaned back and prepared for the head of a lifetime.

The night after next:
Jaiden thought a night out would help take Jessica's mind off things for a while. "I'll have the medium-rare steak with a side of rice, easy on the rice... not too mushy," Jaiden ordered, handing the waitress his menu, flashing her a cheeky smile with his pearl-white teeth. Jessica rolled her eyes and hid her face in her menu.

"And for you miss?" the tall blonde asked causing Jessica to shoot her head up, "Yeah just bring me a salad," she murmured, closing her menu and slumping back into her seat in annoyance. "Will there be anything else?" she asked directing to Jaiden.

"'Yes', I would like for my 'boyfriend' to stop flirting with the waitress, so she can get to our orders," Jess smiles with clear sarcasm filling every inch of her voice.

"Huh?" Jaiden asked, clueless about the comment his girlfriend made about his impulsive eyes on the waitress's breasts.

"Pardon? I'm sorry, I'll go get your orders," the waitress excuses herself.

"Jaiden!" Jess urged for his attention, throwing a bread stick at him after he continued to stare off at the waitress who just left their table.

"Oww, baby stop," he chuckled revisiting his attention to his date for the evening.

"If you're not going to pay attention to me then I don't know why I'm wasting my time here—I have an exam in two days to study for," she pardons, excusing herself from the table.

"No, wait please... I'm sorry babe," he apologized, sincerely reaching a hand over hers. She gave in, sitting back down. "See, we can be mature adults and enjoy a meal at a fancy restaurant," he says when taking a sip of his soda from his wine glass with his napkin folded on his shirt collar. She couldn't help but let out a small laugh.

"Yeah, 'adults'," she air-quoted before taking a sip of her water. "So… how's Jared been?" she asked changing the subject after about twenty minutes of picking at her food.

"You're never going to let this go, are you?" he sighed knifing at his steak. She gives him a vicious glare. "Sorry," he said wiping his mouth with the back of his hand.

"I'm just trying to be a good friend!"

"Yeah, but he doesn't want you to be!"

"Anyways, enough about him… He's happy, I'm hap—" she stopped mid-sentence when she saw Jaiden picking at his tooth with his fork. "Well, there's always room for improvement with you," she teased. "I'm just worried about Megan… I don't want her in Galaxy Quest, or chemistry, or in school. I just don't want to have to breathe the same air as her, 'period'."

"To think that bitch actually convinced Jared to switch out classes!" Jessica huffed. "Babe, enough about Jared, please. At this point, it's obvious that I'm the smart twin and he's not," he shrugged so arrogantly.

"Here is your bill, will there be any dessert for you today?" the female waitress asked when approaching the table once again as Jaiden's eyes instantly fell back to her chest.

"Are you kidding me! You know I was finally starting to trust you again, you jerk!" Jessica immediately rose from her seat, parting away from the table. She snapped her head back around after stepping outside and Jaiden wasn't behind her, 'of course'. She hailed a taxi and shuffled in before Jaiden had the chance to run out after her, *if he was even going to.* She took one final look out the window and he still was nowhere to be found, *pathetic.*

"Wait Jessica!" Jaiden groaned, standing up. He threw a hundred on the table to pay off their meals before running after her. He was soon stopped by a familiar face to his right.

"Jaiden? Long time no see bud, how are you?" Patrick grinned as he and Vivian made their way up to him.

"H-hey guys, now's not really a good time," he shrugged, avoiding eye contact while his eyes jitter around the restaurant in search of Jessica.

"Well listen, I can't thank you enough for saving me the night of my wedding. Those marriages are hard to get out of. Please, if you ever have time, give me a call so we can chill. You're a really rad guy!"

"Yeah thanks, I'll look forward to it…" Jaiden replied, keeping his eyes at the exit.

"Well, it was great seeing you again!" Vivian smiled. Jaiden finally directed his attention to them to say goodbye. He nodded them off in agreement, patting Patrick, and hugging Vivian.

"Gotta run!" he anxiously exhaled before running towards the exit. By the time he arrived outside, there was no sign of Jessica. His heart began pounding out of his chest, he was nervous. He walked over to his car and gave her a call a few times, no answer. "Dammit Jessica, you could at least answer so I know you're okay!" he groaned. He soon backed out of his reserved parking space and a car, he so happened to miss, bumped into his BMW. He hurriedly stepped outside to witness the horror. *Fuck!* "Hell man! What's your problem!" the driver bashed, when stepping out, pissed. He steps closer towards the light and Jaiden backed a step away, a little frightened.

"Holy fuck! No way... Daniels?" Robbie realized after stepping closer. Jaiden sighed in relief before looking inside Robbie's car; in the passenger seat was Candi. If he had to guess, he'd probably think they were double dating. "No scratch or dent, thank God!" Robbie said examining both of their cars. Jaiden folds his arms. "Oh, you're the twin," Robbie announced, taking a closer gander. "Jared has the little scar on his chin from the time he fell off the wagon, figuratively speaking, as kids," Robbie chuckled, scratching the underside of his neck.

"Oh, that was 'you'? Everyone assumed I did it to the sap!" Jaiden gritted. "Hey look, I don't mean to cause trouble. I've already apologized to Jared—well, what I thought was an apology. I've paid my respects, been to church couple of times... I'm really sorry about your friend—"

"Don't apologize to me, I'm nobody to you," Jaiden hindered.

"I have apologized to Jared, swear to God, honest. I'm a changed man—" They both startle when they hear a car honk from right beside them, it was Candi. Jaiden waves her off with a cheeky grin before she flipped him off. "I've got to go, have a nice night," Robbie says.

Jaiden then mumbled to himself as he climbed into his car again, "'Nice night'? The fuck?"

****

"Jared buddy, you home?" Jared heard his brother shout from downstairs through his doorway after Jaiden came home. "Shit, the brother's home!" Jared giggles child-like while Megan struggles to get out of his grip.

"Jare, I have to go," Megan informed.

175

"Strawberry lip-gloss, my favorite," he taunted when bringing his hungry lips back to hers. She scoffs him off and fixes her hair as soon as she stood up from his bed.

"Well, go buy your own. I've got to go." She struggled passing through his window, "I'll call you tomorrow," she mentioned before climbing down his tree. Jared closes the window after she hopped down safely. He then shuffled around the room to find and slide into his basketball shorts before sitting on his bed. "What's good bro-ski!" hollers Jaiden while entering. "How was your date?"

"Alright… until she caught me staring at a waitress and then she took off."

Aggravated, Jared shot up to scold him, "You're such an idiot! Are you serious!" he ranted.

"Woah, calm down hard nipples," defended Jaiden, after examining his brother. "It's fine, she's back at her place," he explains. "Anyways, I'm tired. I'm going to hit the shower and then go to sleep. Goodnight," he reported, closing the door behind himself.

****

For Jessica, sitting at home after a terrible night, she somehow came to remember the one-night Jared and she shared when they were dating. It was a very different experience compared to the disastrous date she had just experienced with Jaiden. With Jared, it too was disastrous—but for the most part, she enjoyed her time. She approaches her bedroom mirror with caution and lifts her hair from the side of her forehead… it still had that small scar.

(Flashback, Jessica at 5 months)
"Are you sure you want to do this? A-are you even allowed?" Jared respectfully asked during their walk inside the bowling arena with his careful assistance.

"Jared, sweetie, I'll be fine," she assured when they find their lane.

"Well, you sit here, and I'll go get our shoes, what size?"

"Get me an eight and a half please?" He nodded and jogged away. Jess struggled to reach for the phone in her purse. Jared returned moments later. He took a seat next to her and she threw her phone on the seat beside. He handed Jess her bowling shoes and she struggled to put them on after kicking her opened-toe, sandals off.

Jared chuckled, "Here, allow me," he insisted, kneeling down in front of her and gently sliding her elephant foot inside the shoes. It wasn't a glass slipper, but she could honestly say she sure felt like

Cinderella, minus the extra weight. "I got you Velcro… so you don't slip," he stated when applying the Velcro to the shoes before sitting back up on the chair. "What?" he smirked.

"Oh nothing," she giggled. He set up the game and they soon begin.

"You're up," he says holding out a hand. He assists her up and they walk over to the platform. "Jared, you don't have to help me."

"You think I'm going to risk you getting hurt?" he asked and she sighed before he handed her a five pounder.

"What's this?" she asked.

"The doctor said you aren't allowed to lift more than eight pounds," he reminded.

"Then hand me a number eight and step aside pretty boy." He sighed and handed her the eight-pound bowling ball. With one roll, she successfully landed a strike. She looked over to Jared, who was still near her side, gawking. "Cat got your tongue?" she teased. They finished their first game within fifteen minutes and she surprisingly won the game. "I'm impressed Jess, you usually suck at bowling. What the hell happened?" he teased again. Just as she was about to say something, when returning to her seat, she saw Jaiden in the distance, in the dimly lit arena.

"Jared, why is Jaiden here? Did you tell him we were going to be here?" she questioned when stepping down from the alley.

"No, I—" They soon noticed that Jaiden wasn't alone. In fact, he was talking with some brunette. *What happened to Candi?*

"That looks like his ex, Courtney," Jared mentioned.

"Ex? When was he even dating her?"

"It was only a school fling. You can almost guess why they broke up."

On her way back to the chair, she gripped the seat, about to lose consciousness. Jared, who happened to be right behind her, grabbed onto her hips while she clutched onto her faint forehead. "Are you okay?" he worried.

"Yeah, just a little dehydrated I guess."

"Stay here," he motioned, guiding her to the chair while helping her to stay seated. He speeds over to the concession stand. He returns a couple of minutes later with a plate of nachos and a cold bottle of water. "I'm sorry I took so long, here," he says opening the water for her. She thanked him before taking a sip of the water. "I got you some food," he says handing her the tray of nachos.

"Thanks," she smiled. "So, do you want to continue with the game… 'or'?"

"Why not? Unless you're ready to give up?" she ridiculed standing up.

"Never!" he challenged. After about five games and Jessica winning all of them, they decide to finally head home.

"So how does it feel being around a winner?" she grinned.

"I let you win!" he scoffed. She stuck her tongue at him.

"Besides, I already feel like a winner inside…"

"Oh, and why is that?" she asked.

"Because I've won the prettiest girl in my heart."

She awed, "Jared," she grabbed his free hand that rested in the armrest between them. He looked down for a mere second before smiling up at her. "Oh my God! Jared, the road!" she panicked and instantly released his hand to point up at the car that they almost collided with. He instantly made a sharp swerve after the headlights shone bright in their direction, almost blinding them both. Jessica's head bangs against the side window, but luckily, they both had their seat belts on. As soon as it's over with, Jessica finds herself breathing heavily and lifting the hair from her forehead after feeling a sharp split. She gently brushes over her forehead before looking to her fingers which have blood on them. She further panicked while the small amount of blood dripped down to the side of her face. Jared immediately pulled over to the right side of the road and stopped, turning his emergency blinkers on before his eyes came contact with her forehead again.

"It's okay," he assured, gliding a hand over her head of hair. He embraces her in for a hug and she quivered. The other driver had been at fault for being on the wrong side of the road. Jared drove them to the hospital that was within a three-mile range from their current location, to have the doctors examine Jess and her baby. Fortunately, they were still in good condition. The doctor stitched the side of her head up and her hair thankfully covered that part of her forehead, so no one would notice. They decide to keep this between them and no one else. "Jessica, I'm so sorry," he reiterated while driving her back home, tears filling his worried eyes.

"It's okay, it's not your fault, Jared."

"But it is, I almost killed us all!"

"But you didn't," she reminded while lightly brushing her hand over his shoulder to ease up his tense.

"I just wish I wasn't a fucking screw up!" he bolted with anger, slamming his hands against the wheel while his car honked in response. Her eyes were stricken with fear. She sensed something had been bothering him and she didn't know what.

"Jared? Please relax. It's okay… you didn't do anything wrong. Whatever it is, you're anything but a screw-up."

"You're Jared Daniels and I love you, 'okay'?"

****

Chapter Ten

"Hey Jared!" Jaiden called when lunging towards his brother in the school hallway.

"Yeah?" Jared asked after his brother had caught his attention, stepping between him and his girlfriend who were in the midst of a conversation.

"Excuse me," Jaiden abruptly directed to Megan. "You're excused and he's my boyfriend so speak up or don't speak at all!" she viciously snapped.

"Don't you have a bible study to pertain to? Oh wait, that's right," Jaiden chuckled.

"What I choose to do in my spare time is none of your God damn business, so why don't you troll someone else!"

"'More like who'," Jaiden abruptly retorted.

"Am I missing something?" Jared asked.

"No!" they both shot him down.

"Jaiden, what did you want?"

"Alright well, let's see where should I start? Okay, I saw these two 'really' hot chicks making out in the hallway—"

"I'm out, bye Jare," Megan said kissing him on the cheek before exiting down the hallway.

"You came all this way to tell me you saw two chicks making out?" he questions.

"No, you idiot. I came here to ask you if you've seen Jessica?"

"What makes you think I would have seen her? She's your problem, not mine," he says shaking the hair away from his forehead. Jaiden apathetically exhaled and eyed around the hallway, standing on his tiptoes to get a better view, tilting his head upwards.

"Yes! I found her! Move out of the way dick wheat!" Jaiden exclaimed, shoving his brother away to move past him and run up to Jessica. As for Jessica, she proceeded down the hallway until he spotted her with enlarged eyes like a deer passing through a roadblock and seeing the bright headlights of a car just before it hit. Unlike that paralyzed deer, Jessica was able to maneuver back around and head for the hills up the road. "Wait babe!" he grunted finally reaching her just before she hit the staircase.

"I have to get to class," she said, continuing to speed away.

"Your class is the other way," he reminds.

"I'll re-route," she assured patting his stomach with the back of her hand before jogging up the steps.

"Jessica!" *God damn.* The whole school day, Jaiden had been chasing Jessica around like a leopard, just trying to catch up with her and being on her tail like a predator. 'Besides', it wasn't his fault that the waitress's tits were right at his eye level, at least that's what 'he' would argue.

****

"Jared!—You in here? I'm coming in! You better be decent in there!" Jaiden announced upon entering his room after school. "That's odd," Jaiden thought. He noticed his brother's car was home, only he wasn't. He lurked around his room in hopes of finding anything he can use against him in the future. He quietly shut the door behind him and eyed it a few times before he proceeded to rummage through his drawers. *Nothing*, he sighed with his hand flying up after slamming the last drawer. He came across something suspiciously crumpled up in the trashcan near his desk. He examined it, stepping closer but keeping a peripheral to the door. He picked it up and unfolded it, it was a receipt for what appeared to be... a 'pocket stimulator'*? What the fuck is a pocket stimulator? Ehhuuughh.* Jaiden cringed at the thought. "God this kid doesn't get laid, does he?" he muttered before crumpling the useless paper and discarding it back in the trash. "This kid is cleaner than I thought." He was startled at the sound of a door swinging open.

"The fuck are you doing in my room?" Jared scolds while Jaiden continuously roams around in carelessness.

"I needed your help and where have you been?" he asked folding his arms.

"Out..." Jared responds, sitting on his made bed.

"What do you want?" he asked rather annoyed.

"Someone's balls dropped in the last hour, the fuck is up with you?"

"Nothing, forget about it... Are you going to tell me what you want, or do I need to get Mom to drag you out of here?"

"Mom?" Jaiden chuckles. Jaiden's face instantly dropped when Jared folded his arms, which indicated he meant business. "I need your help, I kind of screwed up with Jessica and now she won't even talk to me,"

"What did you do 'now'?"

181

"Last night—w-when she caught me staring at the waitress…"

"What do you want 'me' to do?"

"Tell me what I should do, you know, to 'get her back'," he air-quoted.

"I don't know…"

"Come on Jared, w-what would you do if you were in my situation?"

"Well, that's easy, I would be able to avoid the situation because I wouldn't even have stared at a waitress to begin with."

"Jared, need I remind you of the night you boned my ex when you were still dating Jessica. You went 'beyond' the situation," Jaiden chuckled.

"I-I don't know really," Jared admitted. Jaiden paced back and forth in front of Jared, with his hands tucked behind his head in frustration. After a minute of thinking, he thanks his brother and makes his way out of Jared's bedroom. "Wait…" Jared dubiously responded.

"Yeah?"

"Well, this is just an idea. With prom coming up and all…"

"Right! I could ask her to prom!—but how would that help?"

"Women like the element of surprise, to be serenaded… if you're lucky enough, she just might agree and dismiss your entire situation."

"What did you have in mind?"

****

"Hey Jess," greeted Skylar through the phone. Jessica cautiously turned down the speaker before Becca returned to the couch. She discreetly replied since she knew Skylar and Becca were not so much on talking terms. She knew if she was somehow found conversing with Skylar, she would be slaughtered by non-other than Becca. "Is Becca there with you by chance?" he asked. Jessica took a glance at Becca, who picked at her ice cream in her messy at-home attire and her worn out makeup.

"No, she uh," Jessica began to say. "If you see her, can you please let her know how sorry I am, and how big of an idiot I am… I really screwed up and it's affecting practices and most importantly our relationship, her and I… us too, we rarely hang out anymore…"

"Yeah sorry, she has custody over me apparently," Jessica teased.

"I've even tried talking to Jared about this but he's just avoiding me."

"Well, that makes two of us," Jess sighed.

"As for the group, I've tried just about everything for Becca to start coming to practices again," he continued.

"Look, I can't talk right now, but we'll talk soon. I'll send her your regards," she said quietly before ending the call.

"Who was that?" Becca asked.

"Kevin," Jessica falsely stated. Becca gave her friend a confused stare while Jessica resumed the movie they were watching to avoid further questions.

"So, are you still not speaking with Jaiden?" she asked after a moment of silence.

"No, but let's not bring up guys right now, please?"

"Agreed."

"Thanks for spending the night, I really could use a friend right now," Becca smiled.

"Just returning the favor," Jess smiled back.

****

The next school day, Jaiden impatiently sat all through third hour staring between his watch and then back up at his teacher, then to Jessica until it hit 11:55 a.m. "Fuck yes," he muttered out seconds before his hand shot up like a cannon.

"Yes Jaiden?" the teacher asked.

"May I be excused? I have to get to the assembly."

"I didn't know you were in any sports?" Mrs. Parker sarcastically interrogated.

"No, well I actually got kicked off the football team a while back ago—" he corrected cocking his eyebrows. *Why did he have to explain himself to her?*

"So, why should I let you leave?"

"Because," he gritted, running out of time and options.

"No," she responded. Jaiden slumped in his seat before returning to his assignment. He tapped his pencil repetitively on the wooden desk. He then stared over at Jessica with his hand rested on his face now. She gave him an uncomfortable glare before returning to her studies. He dropped his pencil smack down on his desk and leaned back in his chair, staring up to rub his chin. *What to do?* Suddenly, a thought emerged. Safe to say, this was one of the only times he has ever thought in this class. He lugged his backpack onto his lap to text from inside it. He sent Hobbs a speedy text to come up with a diversion to get him out of the class period since he remembered that Z TA's for this hour. Z comes to Jai's rescue ten minutes later and tells the teacher that the office called Jaiden down with a fake pass and everything. Hobbs could've gotten in some serious trouble for that. Jaiden then grabbed his backpack and leaped for the door in relief.

"Thanks," he shouts when running towards the gym.

"No problem, don't forget twenty bucks!" Hobbs' shout fades while he travels in the opposite direction and Jaiden continues running. As soon as Jaiden left the classroom, Jessica shot her head at Star who did the same, "Why?" Jessica silently mouthed. Star shrugged her shoulders in response. With only five more minutes of the class period left, a voice came over the intercom telling the students to go straight to the gym for their sports assembly. Mrs. Parker soon dismissed her students and Jessica caught up with Star who was waiting for her by the door.

"That was odd," Star mentioned, following behind the crowd of students in the direction of the gym building.

"So anyways, how are things between you two?"

"I don't want to talk about it. In all honesty, I wish I could just forgive him, a part of me wants to but another part is telling me that he's just going to do it again."

"You have to give him some credit. He's put off so many girls who are just throwing themselves at him, for you."

"God, you sound just like him—"

"Hey, Jessica!" Jessica whips her head around while Chris jogs up. "You left your pencil," he says handing it to her.

"That isn't mine," she chuckled, handing it back.

"Oh well, you caught me. I guess I was just looking for an excuse to come and talk to you again," he blushes, and she couldn't help but bite her lip.

"Christian, if I wasn't mistaken, I think you were flirting with me," she mocked.

"Shut up," he grinned playfully shoving her. He stepped forward and wrapped both of his arms around each of the girls. "We need to stay together," he teased. So together they strode, hurdled in a clump, entering the gym, and then picking a seat on the bleachers. Jessica struggled between choosing to sit with Skylar, Hobbs, Wesley, and Alex—as Skylar offered from afar, or sitting on the opposite side with Becca. It wasn't a difficult choice because Becca was sitting by her lonesome self. Jessica was honestly tired of this, she hated coming between them and having to choose who to spend time with.

"Hey buddy!" Megan greeted to Star as she and Jared pick a seat directly behind Star, Chris, and Jessica. Jessica notably rolled her eyes.

Megan was in school today, but Jess wondered why she skipped third period again. Although, the clever Jess already had an idea why. "Where's Jaiden at?" Star asked Jared and he shrugged. They supposedly carpooled for the first time in forever. Right across from where they were sitting, Jessica saw 'sluts anonymous'. There was Courtney, Candi, Tanya, and Sophie sitting on the opposite bleachers along with Ryan and Robbie all sitting together near Skylar, Hobbs, Wesley, and Alex. The first forty-five minutes pass by very slowly. Jessica felt her back starting to cramp up from shrugging so much and she just wanted the assembly to be over with already. They managed to get through all the sports teams for the winter season by now, identifying all the players in their lineup. Just as Jessica felt herself about to doze-off, she heard Jaiden's voice through the microphone, "Excuse me—everyone, if I may have your attention? My name is Jaiden, Jai, 'J-Money' Daniels," he says as all the girls in the crowd parade him on. Jessica sits up and rolls her eyes, *unbelievable*. "I'm here today in hopes of my girlfriend forgiving me; Jessica, where are you?" he calls out searching for the one and only Jessica in the audience.

"I'll be your girlfriend!" a freshman in the audience shouted with a shirt that read 'Mrs. Jaiden Daniels'. Jessica started to wonder if people knew that he would be promoted in the assembly today and why they would think such thing if he was removed from the team. Indeed, it was unbelievable that he managed to make a name for himself and still be considered a star athlete even after he lost his place in football. Still, Jessica wondered what any of this had to do with her though. Jess hid her face behind her hand, hoping that would be enough for him to not notice her.

"She's right here!" Becca squealed springing out of her seat beside her friend.

"Thanks," Jessica grumbled.

"Hi beautiful," Jaiden said, walking towards her section after the girls in the crowd 'aww'. "Come on out fellas!" he directed as the football players run out and line up, revealing the backs of their shirts, with a different letter that spelled out, "Will you go to the prom with me?" he asked directly facing her now while a bunch of cheerleaders, not including the seniors in the audience, came out with a giant poster that said, 'say yes!' as they waved their pompoms and kicked their legs up in the air. Jessica's eyes shift to the other girls not participating in this to find Courtney mouthing, 'you're welcome' in the distance. Obviously, Courtney could care less, she only did it in respect of Jaiden.

Jaiden cued a random male figure who brought up a bouquet of roses to him, who then held them up to Jess in inquisition for acceptance. Overwhelmed, she hesitantly stepped down. He helped her down the rest of the way and she accepted his prom invitation after he handed her the roses. The band began playing in the background and the confetti blew while the crowds began to cheer. He spun her around and she hugged him in relief. She was conveniently impressed that he took the time to plan all this out, which meant that he cared about her after all. For that, she forgave him. "So, are we good?" he asks setting her down.

"Yes, thank you," she giggled, wiping away the lipstick stain from under his lip. He took a bow and the crowd inconsistently cheered. He gestured for her to bow and she curtsies in the maxi dress she had been wearing. He soon whistles, and a man brings out a horse that neighed when it appeared closer. "Jaiden, you got me a horse!" she exclaimed.

"It's a rental for today, but yes. Climb aboard?" he asked before helping her saddle up. He signaled for Star to throw Jessica's backpack over as he then attached both of their backpacks to the horse. Just before takeoff, the crowd and music instantly stopped, and everyone soon directed their attention to the pesky principle who approached the lovebirds.

"Wait a minute, a horse is not permitted on school grounds!" the principal argued.

"We're taking this horse to go I guess," said Jaiden, hopping up behind his renounced girlfriend.

"You better not exit school grounds or you're in trouble, Daniels!"

"I have approval, you should really talk it up with the dean of admissions—I set this whole thing up myself. And did you know that my father happens to be good friends with the dean of this school? Later gator!" he hollered before motioning for the horse to go by slapping its rear. "Bye my peasants, 'til prom!" The principal stood there defenseless while the crowd begins to cheer once again. The two set out and roam around the school before finding the exit and Jai helps his girl to guide the horse.

"My, my, I didn't know you had it in you."

"What?" he chuckled.

"To be 'this' romantic."

"Well, I had help from a really close friend," he mentions. "Woah, this way," he says wrapping his arms around hers as he guides the horse. She couldn't help but notice how calm and collected he was while he controlled the horse. The way his arms wrapped around hers, it was 'perfect'. "We are totally going to win for prom royalty!" he grinned.

"So how were you so sure I would say yes?" she asked after they reached the traffic light and proceed. A few cars honked at them but there wasn't any sign regulating horse crossing, so they proceeded with confidence.

"Because I'm irresistible," he taunted when bringing his arms around her waist.

"I'm hungry," she complained after her stomach rumbled under his embrace.

"Well, lucky for you, I set up an amazing picnic for us in our special place."

"We have a special place?" she asked.

"'Our' tree house."

"Tree house?" she cocked a brow.

"Yeah, I managed to get ahold of Josh and he let us use it for the day."

"But what about our homework—"

"Ssshhh, no questions and I got the assignments taken care of, just enjoy the peaceful ride," he soothes, hugging her closer

****

As soon as they stepped inside her flat, she threw her legs up on Jaiden's torso as he then carried her over to the sofa, shutting the door behind them. Their lips connecting while he set her down, hovering above her. She helped him take his shirt off and he threw it onto the floor, revealing his six-pack. Her hands slid up and down his chest and his lips travel back to hers. They both get startled as soon as they heard someone clear their throat behind. Jessica quickly shoved him off her and they sat up as soon as she peeked over to the kitchen counter where Becca was standing. "Sorry to interrupt, I didn't know Jaiden was going to be over... I'll just leave," she said, setting her coffee mug down and grabbing her purse from the stool as she was about to head out.

"Please," Jaiden impatiently urged. Jessica nudges him before standing up, fixing her own shirt in the process.

"Wait Becca, don't go," she sighed.

"What?" Jaiden shot up in protest.

"You, get out." Jessica dismissed him, picking up his shirt from the floor. She threw it at him just as she rushed him out the door.

"Sorry," Becca apologized after Jessica closed the door after him.

"No, it was my fault... how did you um, get inside?" Jessica asked trying her best not to seem rude.

"Spare key under the rug outside, good hiding place for most people," she shrugged when setting her book bag down, before sitting on the couch.

"Obviously not good enough," Jessica muttered with an apathetic sigh on her way to the couch too.

"So bestie, what do you wanna watch? Come sit!" Becca insisted.

"I was actually going to go take a nap… tired," Yawned Jessica.

"Oh, well okay," Becca shrugged while Jessica disappeared inside her bedroom. Jessica loved Becca like a sister—like her own sister—hell, more than her own sisters, but she had overstayed her welcome. This had been happening for a week now. So much that she's lost the privacy of her own home and has even missed out on alone time with Jaiden with Becca tagging along and third-wheeling the two all the time. She needed Becca to get back together with Skylar again. Becca even took the extra mile to skip practices just to avoid Skylar—and Megan for that matter. Jess didn't want to see Megan either, but she sucked it up. So poor, bitter-sweet Jessica, being the good citizen that she was, had to spend her days teaching Becca what she learned and memorized from the choreography at practices just so her friend can be prepared for the day of the recital. That was the only day Becca was willing to reunite with the group. Jessica couldn't live on like this forever. She was not going to waste her days comforting her friend for the rest of her life. So, a fed-up Jessica, called Jaiden to devise a plan.

"So, what should I tell 'him'?" Jaiden asked through the speaker while Jessica blow-dried her hair after coming out of the shower.

"Tell him that you've invited him for a guys' night out," she said, turning off the blow dryer. She takes Jaiden off speaker and places the phone to her ear, stepping out of her towel.

"Alright, I'll tell him. When are we doing this?"

"Tonight."

"Good idea—so afterwards, after they've made up and drive home together, we can finish where we left off today," he implied while she had finished changing.

"I've got to go, I hear Becca, bye!"

"Wait!" he pleaded. She allowed him to continue, "What are you wearing?" he grinned.

Dial tone.

"Hey, do you want to do something tonight?" Jessica asked after stepping out of the bathroom, tucking away her phone in the back of her pants' pocket.

"Like what?" Becca asked crossing her legs from the couch while Jessica joined her.

"Well… Star and some of the girls were going out tonight, maybe Lux?"

"Ooooo, that place is amazing, but I don't know if I'm in the mood for going out tonight," she frowned, provoking Jessica to slap her own knees disappointingly.

188

"Oh, come on, it'll be fun! I think we should go…"

"Girls night, away from boys… you need to loosen up, let's go?"

"No Megan?" Becca asked.

"No Megan," Jessica assured.

"Okay, fine!" she exclaimed, shutting off the television. Jessica glanced at her phone after receiving a message notification from Jaiden saying that Skylar was in—she texted him back saying that Becca too was in.

"But I don't have anything to wear," she frowned again.

"Come on!" Jessica assertively pulled her friend up and dragged her into her bedroom. The girls get ready within two hours of actively doing each other's hair and makeup. They drove in Jessica's car rental to the club and waited in the line outside the club. "Reservation for…" Jessica said when checking her phone for the keyword that Jaiden sent her. "Hakunamatatas," she confidently blurted aloud before it hit her.

"'Hakunamatatas'?" Becca cocked a brow.

"Jaiden!" Jess grumbled.

"Jaiden's here!" Becca pouted, folding her arms.

"No, um did I say Jaiden?"

"What was with the ridiculously long name then?"

"Right this way," the usher interrupted after finding their names on the clipboard. The usher allowed them entry as Jessica speedily walked off to avoid Becca's cross-examination.

"Oh my God, I can't believe you! I'm out of here—" Becca argued, turning around as soon as she spotted Skylar next to the bar.

"Becca? You said this was a guys' night," Skylar asked after seeing Becca walk in with Jessica.

Jessica pulled Becca aside, "You are not going anywhere, especially since I am the driver," Jessica stated folding her arms.

"I can Uber," Becca reminded before walking away.

"Becca, wait!" Jessica groaned, running up to her once more.

"Can you at least try, for 'me'?" she pleaded.

"'Let's go out, it'll be fun' they said," Becca sarcastically implied out of mockery.

"You could have at least told me she was going to be here dude!" Skylar directed to Jaiden, fixing his hair.

"Ladies, welcome back!" Jaiden shouted when he saw the two approaching the bar once again.

"'Hakunamatatas'? What the hell is wrong with you!" Jessica angered, slapping Jaiden with her small clutch on her way over causing Jaiden to giggle like a toddler.

"You made me look like an idiot!" Jaiden hysterically clutched onto his side, tears forming at the sides of his eyelids, "I can't believe you actually said that!" he cried. Becca and Skylar's eyes met, and Skylar cleared his throat after Becca haphazardly looked away.

"Y-you look very beautiful today, Rebecca," Skylar said while Becca took her seat on his right, checking her messages, trying her best to avoid him.

"'Don't' call me that."

"Can I get you guys started with any drinks?" asked the bartender.

"Actually, I forgot to grab my purse from my car... Jaiden walk with me," Jess demanded after she shot up.

"Well... this is awkward," Skylar pointed out when noticing that they were left alone at the bar now.

"Are you guys going to order?" the bartender asked. Becca insisted for a few more minutes and the bartender nodded before courteously walking off.

"I miss you..." Skylar admitted, breaking the silence.

"You do?"

"I can't sleep, you're all I think about," he sheepishly admitted.

"Aww Skyyyyy!" she finally gives in, reaching her hand across to find his. But more importantly, it has been about thirty minutes now and Skylar and Becca wondered where their friends trailed off to and what was taking their return so long. "I should probably go check on them," Becca said towering from her seat.

"No, um... I think they're good," he chuckles awkwardly.

"How are you so sure?"

****

"There was a check off my bucket list!" Jess giggled as Jaiden helped her down from the sink counter.

"You think they've made up by now?" he asked while buttoning up his shirt.

"Should be, it has been about half an hour."

"Let's hope..." he says after she had finished sliding back into her outfit.

"Here wait, fix your hair," she noted, tampering with his hair a bit to make it almost as presentable as before.

"Good call on the no bra thing, saved me some time," he winked after they step out of the bathroom.

"Everything okay?" Skylar asked just before bursting into a fit of laughter with Becca joining him in doing so.

190

"Well, it seems like you two have clearly made up," Jaiden points out when pulling out his stool.

"Seems like we're not the only ones," Skylar winked out to Jaiden, nudging him playfully.

"You guys are freaks!" Becca too laughed while Jessica sipped on her drink.

"Don't know what you guys are talking about," Jessica awkwardly grinned.

"Next time you guys want to get freaky, don't tweet about it in public," Skylar teased.

Jessica's eyes widened, "W-what are you talking about?" she worried. Skylar handed her his phone. She read the tweet sent from Jaiden's phone half an hour ago that read, "Never done it in a bathroom before, guess there's a first for everything! (;;;;"

"You tweeted about it!? When did you have the time!"

"Well, I didn't want to go into the specifics, but let's just say it was when you decided to inspect the floor for wood," he chuckled.

"First the pool and now the club? Man, do you know how to keep his balls in check!" Skylar had teased. Above it all, Jess was beyond relieved that Becca and Skylar were on good terms now, even though Becca still refused to show up to practices. Jess had also been aware that Skylar and Jared were still not on friend terms at the moment either. But nothing frustrated Jessica more than having to deal with Megan at every single practice when all she did was text the entire class period. *What was the point of coming at all?* At least when Becca was present, she put in twice the amount of effort. The group didn't want to fail because of Megan so Jess decided to take it upon herself to concoct yet another plan with the crew. The plan that would hopefully cause a drift in Megan and Jared's relationship—for his own good; Megan to leave from Galaxy Quest, and if it all goes as planned, maybe for Jared and Skylar to talk to each other again and most importantly—for Jared to talk to Jess again. "What did you have in mind?" Skylar asked the following day.

"'Well', since Megan won't confess to cheating on Jared and since he is clueless about her bad habits,"

"…We have to make it so that Jared catches her in the act."

"Devious, I like it!" Skylar said, rubbing his hands together in their small circle consisted of Hobbs, Becca, Star, Jaiden, Skylar, and Jess.

"I'm so lost," Star admitted.

"We just need a target," Becca says eyeing around the school hallway. It was seemingly difficult to find just any target—that is, one who had not already slept with Megan. They needed to find the perfect flirt.

"And I think I found the perfect one!" Jess grinned spotting Chris from afar. "Chris! Over here!" Jess conspicuously exclaimed, running up to the boy she would showcase to their circle of friends.

"What's going on?" he asked.

"Mullins," Jaiden grits. Jessica finds her hand slipping off Chris' shoulder.

"Daniels…" he smirked back provocatively.

"We are in need of your assistance," Star explains confidently brushing a hand over his chest.

"Why don't I just do it? I am a pretty great flirt," Jaiden claims, stretching in the midst.

"That is why you 'aren't' doing it," Jessica reassuringly stated, patting his chest. The bunch took the rest of their lunch period to devise the plan and Chris felt hesitant about the plan at first until they reeled him in.

After school, Megan walked to her locker, unlocking it to put her textbooks back inside her book bag. "Well hello there," she heard a masculine voice approach from behind her locker. She shut her locker and was startled at Chris' sudden appearance.

"Aren't you in my chemistry class?" she asked, throwing her book bag over her shoulder.

"The name's Chris," he introduced in his heavy English accent, holding out his hand while her face imminently scrunched in disgust, hesitantly shaking his hand back. She then immediately grabbed ahold of her hand sanitizer from the bottom of her bag and slapped some onto her hand before throwing the bottle back in her bag, clapping her hands together to rid of his germs.

"I don't mean to be rude, but I have no time for small talk," she narrow-mindedly addressed, turning around. Chris immediately looked across to where the gang was hiding behind the wall corners, for assistance. There, he saw Star motion to grab Megan's hand—So then, he ran up to yank the back of Megan's arm just as she was about to tie her hair back. "Oww!" she hissed, "What do you want?"

"My, what beautiful hands you have," he improvised, pushing her hand up in front of his nose to smell her hand until she wrenched her hand away.

"I'm about five seconds away from using my fuckboy repellent on you!" she warned when swatting his hand away, causing him to relinquish in a step back, surrendering his arms up. The spies in the back couldn't hear what was going on but they could tell it wasn't working just yet. They decided it was time to send in Jared.

"Jared? Yeah man, it's Hobbs—I need a ride—Do you think you can drive me home? I'm next to the locker hallway... okay, thanks. See you in a few," Hobbs says in hushed tone before ending the call. Jessica signaled Star who was on the opposite side of the wall with Skylar and Becca to motion for Chris to hurry up since they could see him more clearly from behind their corner. Chris soon received the signal and schemes of a last-minute option.

"I'm sorry, you're right; I shouldn't be doing this—I-It's just that—I have a girlfriend back home and I guess I just miss her that's all. All this stress on me for the end of the soccer season, here I thought I would score with pretty girl like you, but I was wrong. What am I doing? I would never want to cheat on my girlfriend whom I 'love'," he emphasized. "I guess I'll just go sit alone in my sports car and pity over the days I've lost to waste money on my girlfriend, you know with her being 'gone' and 'out of the country'," he sighed, turning around.

"Wait!" she stopped, growing wetter by his athletic charm.

"Yes?" he smirked.

"You play soccer?" she asked, dropping her purse and stepping forward. "I think that is 'very' sexy," she giggled when hiking her skirt up a bit before backing him up against the locker and pressing a hand to his chest. She caresses his face before leaning in to kiss him while his eyes pop open. *Not part of the plan! Abort, abort!* a little voice in his head screams.

They soon heard a male voice call out her name from behind causing her to startle and slap the impeccable soccer player across the face.

"You pig! I have a boyfriend!" she screamed. "Oh Jared!" she cried running to his embrace while Chris stood there astounded, thinking about what he just agreed to when he touched the side of his now inflamed cheek.

"Get off me!" Jared scowled, pushing her off him. Chris sincerely apologized to her distraught boyfriend and Jared sympathetically nodded. "All of my friends were right about you!"

"Jared, I can explain, it was—"

"Give it up!" Jessica cut off, approaching the three of them now along with the other spies of the group following closely behind.

"Ooooo, poor choice of words," Becca whispered from beside.

"You're done Megan!" Skylar continued for her.

"You guys were in on this?" Jared asks when shifting his eyes among his friends then directing his attention to Jessica.

"You guys set me up!" Megan scoffed.

"I guess we did, didn't we?" Jessica says when stepping forward to renounce her importance.

"Hey Jare, I'm sorry—we just wanted you to know the truth about Megan," Skylar admits.

"I see…"

"So, no hard feelings?" Skylar asks and Jared nods. They both step forward and hug it out like men, throwing their differences behind them.

"Well, I guess our time was over anyways. It was fun while it lasted—just wish your performance in bed was better… it's clear to me now why Jessica chose Jaiden, he's definitely more equipped needless to say, but anyways, I'm off!" Megan announced before grabbing her purse and trailing off.

"Ouch! Sorry man," Hobbs says when walking forward and patting Jared on the back.

"Are we okay?" Jessica cautiously asked when taking a step closer.

"Don't speak to me," he warned, and she nodded respectfully, taking a step back before turning her back on her friends to exit the building.

"Sorry, I kind of suck at acting," Chris lightheartedly apologizes when heading out the exit with Star and Jessica.

"No, you were amazing."

"Anyways, my work here is done for the most part. I think I'm going to head home," Jessica says.

"He's just hurting, he'll come around to thank you one day."

Chapter Eleven

The next day after the set-up, Megan had finally decided to call it quits with Galaxy Quest. However, Candi's group, Silver Streetz had no problem with swooning in to take her into their group. "Thanks for the new member," Candi taunted while her larger group of girls passed by Galaxy Quest, chins up, arms crossed and perkier than ever.

"The experience has been… fun," Megan said passing them.

"Yeah well good luck re-learning a new routine!" Becca fired back.

"I just can't believe you're finally back!" Jessica exclaimed nearly jumping in the air at her friends return.

"Ladies… and Skylar, I've noticed you guys are a bit short, which means I'm going to have to ask that you guys join another group," the teacher announced.

"What? No!" Skylar protested.

"I'm sorry, we can't have four people on a team—"

"Says who!" Becca argued, standing tall.

"You can't just separate us! We worked just as hard as Silver Streetz and if it's going to be a crime for being outnumbered, then it should be a crime for being over-numbered too!—Who knows how big the stage is going to be!—One of them could flip into another girl and just like that, brains and guts scattered all over the stage!" Jessica over-exaggerated.

"Shouldn't be a problem considering they don't *have* any!" Becca rebukes.

"Well, you're right—y'all 'don't' know how big the stage is going to be, because I've just found out that we are going to be performing at the Music Valley Festival!" the teacher broadcasted while the students banter in excitement. "And, not only that, but the winners of the competition will receive a full scholarship to the Art Institute of Seattle!" she marveled.

"Are you serious! That's like my friggin' dream!" Becca giggles eagerly hopping up and down boastfully.

"Our school's dance program happened to be selected by the state to be represented and featured in a dance production here at Music Valley with the chance to win a scholarship in a full production done by the students; but, like I said," the teacher faces their group again.

"You can't do this to us!" Star whined. "I'm sorry, you guys just don't meet the criteria."

"But we worked our asses off in these practices!"

"Please—it's too late to start over!" they begged.

"I don't see a problem with that—your ex-teammate Megan did so and it seems like she's adapted quite well," their teacher advised before strutting off.

"What do you guys want to do?" Star asks while Skylar paced back and forth.

"How about we hold auditions—there has got to be 'someone' willing to join our dance team!" Jessica suggested.

"But we can't just take anyone, you heard the teacher—this is a 'dance production', which means they've got to be involved in dance," Skylar complains.

"Not necessarily," Jessica open-mindedly smirked.

"What do you mean?"

"The teacher won't mind but who says anything about the judges finding out?" she grins.

"Okay, when are we going to find the time to withhold auditions?" Becca asks.

"The sooner the better obviously," Star said, enviously staring down Silver Streetz. By the end of the class hour, Jessica was grateful she could return home straight after since it was her last class of the day. She decided to meet up with Jaiden after school at their local gym so that he could train her since he was obviously in far better shape than she was, baby weight and all. She desperately needed to stay in shape before the big recital anyways.

"Okay, now flex and bring your arms up like this," he requested, gently elevating her arms on a weight machine.

"God, this hurts!" she panted in exhaustion.

"It's okay baby you're doing fine," he assured. "So, tell me more about dance. You're actually going to Music Valley?"

"Yeah, that is if we can find another member in time," she grunted in concentration while a bead of sweat drips down her forehead. "Okay, I'm done with this one," she exhales releasing the equipment, struggling to get out. "Jaiden, hello?" she says snapping her fingers. She directs her attention to follow his eyes that led to some woman he was checking out from afar.

"Sorry," he says pulling Jess up after leaving his trance. "I'm done, I'm going to hit the treadmill."

"No you're not, because you're going to do fifty crunches and I'm going to do them with you!" The tiresome girl groans for what feels like the hundredth time that training afternoon. He drags her over to the mat that was placed on the floor. "I hate you," she grumbled when lying down on the floor.

"Here let me help you," he says grabbing her feet while she comes up. "One," he counted. "Two," she continued. "Three," he says attaching his lips to hers as she came up that third time. She smirked and continue his pattern. "Four," she said next presenting a kiss to his lips. "Five," he said reattaching his lips to hers while holding onto her face this time and not letting her go back down with his kiss that lasted longer than the others. During the midst of their heightened kiss, she took the opportunity to bite down on his bottom lip in order for him to stop while she smirked and continued with her sit-ups. "Okay, we're done!" he publicized standing up.

"Nu uh, your turn," she corrected while sitting up. He laid down while Jessica sat in front of him, holding his feet as he did ten in under a minute before shooting up confidently like the antsy show off he was known to be.

"Done, let's go… As your trainer, I think we've worked out enough," he agreed with himself before helping to lift his girlfriend back on her feet. "I'll race you back to your flat," he shouted running out of the building. Jessica's apartment had been a ten-minute walk from the gym, so she willingly took him up on that offer. She ended up defeating him on the run to her apartment. She swung the door open to let out a breath. She was startled at the sound of the door shutting behind, whipping her head to find Jaiden pinning her up against the wall.

"What are you doing?" she giggles as his lips trail down to her wet neck. "You lost the challenge, fifty bucks loser!" she teased.

****

The auditions were the following week and the group had flyers made and posted up on bulletin boards for almost a week now that trials will start today in the small auditorium. Although the group had made very minimal effort to check up on the status of the bulletin in which people would sign up to be auditioned. After school, Skylar, Becca, Star, and Jessica set out to the auditorium where the auditions would be held today. Sitting in one row behind a table in the audience, they awaited the first person to come out after Skylar brought in the audition listing from the bulletin. "Yay we have a full list!" Star exclaimed bouncing in her seat while examining the clipboard with Skylar. "Alright, Jennie

197

Peterson you may come out," Skylar informs in the small microphone after adjusting in his seat.

"Hi," she smiled widely when stepping out onto the stage.

"Hello, thank you for auditioning, whenever you are ready!" Jessica beams. Thirty seconds into the music pass by when Jessica finds herself longing to pin needles into her eyelids because of how rather disturbing this Jennie's audition was.

"Next!" Becca shouts over the music as it finally stops. They go through almost fifteen dreadful auditions before they wait on the next person to walk up. In the meantime, the bored and tiresome Skylar on the far right, tried balancing his pencil on his forehead, Becca who was on his left, had her head down in her arms, Jessica who was looking over the list of applicants and finally Star who was face-palming to Jessica's left.

"Simon, Paula, Randy, care to pay attention?" Jessica asks causing them to sit up and give their full, undivided attention to the next person that walked on stage, respectfully. They all nearly jump back in fear as the female with the dark eyeshadow, white skin and black clothing with piercings covering every inch of her face stands in their presence.

"Is that a guy or a girl?" Star whispers a little rudely.

"You know, I thought it was a girl but I'm not so sure anymore," Becca whispers as they both begin to debate from beside Jessica while she sat tolerably in the middle.

"Enough!" Jessica grumbled growing flustered. "Hi, you may begin whenever you are ready... 'Blossom'?" Jessica cringed looking at the list in disbelief. If anything was for certain about the species, it did not look like someone who should be named anything close to Blossom. As soon as Blossom finished her dreadful audition, Jessica sighed. That was the last audition on the list. "Alright, thank you. We'll let you know when we get the results," Jessica fibbed while the grim reaper exited the door looking glum.

"Hello? I'm sorry, I hope I'm not too late," they heard a voice broadcast offset.

"Nope, I'm sorry we're done with the audi—" Jessica shushed Skylar as the anonymous female stepped on stage, revealing her face. Jessica covered the mic to keep their conversation private, leaning forward. "We're running out of options, she's our only hope," she reminds Skylar. "Proceed," Jessica directed into the microphone.

"Well my name is Jasmine and—"

"Oh nice, like the princess?" Star asked and the girl nods.

"Do you have any background or experiences in dance?" Becca asks.

"I went to a dance camp when I was eight, but I never enrolled in any classes in school because I guess I was a little nervous about going back into dance and when I wanted to join this year, they told me classes were full and that it was too late," she explained.

"Alright, well you may start whenever you are ready," Star informed and Jasmine steps down to hand them her phone.

"Track number eight please?" she requested back on the stage and Skylar nods before running to the back of the auditorium to hand the stage manager her phone.

****

"Okay, well, that was great, we'll let you know after we've reviewed everyone," mentioned Star after the girl had finished auditioning.

"Wait!" Jessica shouts broadly into microphone, covering it as the others turn around and huddle in their mobile chairs.

"She was the best one we saw today, are you kidding? We have to put her in!" Becca says, and Jessica openly nods in agreement.

"What about number five, I think she was something special," Skylar smiles snatching the clipboard from Jessica's hands.

"Oh, please! The only thing that danced were her tits, all over that stage!" Becca scoffed.

"Okay and what about the others?" Star asks.

"Screw the others! You're in!" Jessica exclaimed turning around and shouting directly into the mic.

"Yes, oh my God, thank you so much!" Jasmine cheered, jumping up and down on stage as Becca covers Skylar's eyes when her chest bounces around in her tank.

"I like her already!" Skylar smiles causing Becca to whack him on the head with the clipboard.

"So, we will meet up after school tomorrow in the dance room, so we can begin, let's say three p.m.?" Jessica asks. "We have a lot of work to do and so little time, I take it you've read the advances with this competition we're competing in?" Jasmine nodded. "Alright well, it was very nice meeting you, I am Jessica, this is Star, Becca, and Skylar—" she says going down the line.

"Skylar is my boyfriend," Becca claims pulling on his cheek like an infant.

"Like she couldn't tell!" Star says annoyed.

"Anyways, welcome to Galaxy Quest!" Becca greeted before running up to give her a welcoming hug as the rest of them run up and join warmly in excitement.

"There's my baby girl!" Jaiden announces entering from the back of the auditorium after the group had dispersed. "Let me guess, new member?" he noticed.

Jasmine nodded, "I'm Jas—" Jessica cut the girl off when she stepped down the stage.

"Alright, I'm out. See you guys tomorrow!" Jessica publicized exiting with Jaiden. Her jealous instincts saw no point in acquainting the two.

****

"Jessica, can we talk please?" Jared asked when solemnly approaching Jessica, who stood in the hallway with Jaiden and Star the following school day. She faced Jaiden who granted her permission so long as she agreed to kiss him before they part ways, pointing to his cheek.

"Fine," she agreed, pecking a kiss on his right cheek before he headed off to class with Star.

"I wanted to tell you that I'm sorry," Jared says after she awaited him to continue. "I should've listened to you. You were right about everything, about Megan. I—uh really miss you."

"I guess what I'm trying to say is that… as long as we're both over each other, I think we should still be friends… at least?"

Ouch. Did he really just say that? "Yeah, I couldn't agree more," she answered through her teeth that hid behind a plastered grin.

"So how is chemistry?" he asks as they both begin to walk down the hallways.

"Same old, same old," she lied.

"How is your new lab partner I heard?"

"Chris? He's the one…" she stopped herself from finishing her sentence. It was too soon for Jared to be reminded that his ex was about to cheat on him with Jessica's new lab partner. So, Jessica continued with a different approach instead, "He's great, but I miss having you," she admitted. "But how is your new chemistry class?" she asked avoiding the awkward silence.

"Great. The only good thing that came out of this fictitious relationship was that Megan suggested I should transfer out of our chem class and advance to honors and I actually feel like I belong," he chuckled awkwardly.

"I hardly believe she cared anything about your curriculum Jare, she was just trying to separate you from… never mind," she said dismissing the conversation after he crinkled his eyebrows in concern. The bell rings right after, sparing Jessica of having to explain herself. They say their goodbyes before heading off to their first period.

****

"Aye, see you later, Larson!" Robbie smiles while Jess returns the gesture and heads off to her next period after second period with Robbie ends. After catching up with Robbie in second hour and getting to know him a little more, Jess believed Robbie was rather sweet. She was the type of person to believe that everyone was entitled to a second chance if they were willing to change for the better. And since she didn't know Robbie too well, she thought of this as his first impression to her, and it was comforting to have a new history partner now that Lucas unfortunately couldn't be anymore.

"What do you think you're doing?" Candi asked confronting Jessica in the hallways on their way to lunch.

"What am I doing?" Jessica cocks a brow in confusion.

"Robbie doesn't socialize with people like you, you may have Jaiden downgraded into your social class, but Robbie will never. Consider this a warning, if I see you with him again, Megan won't be the only who ruins Jared and I'll make sure of it," Candi threats before walking away. It was just the cliché Jessica was looking for this school year, *sigh*. "Jaiden!" Candi shouts when approaching the twins in the cafeteria line during lunch.

"What?" Jaiden snaps, turning around. "Tell your little mutt to stop getting in my way," she sneered.

"What are you talking about?" Jared chimes in before Jaiden had a chance to speak.

"Jessica has been all buddy-buddy with Rob lately and it makes me sick. Fix it before I say something else."

"What did you say to her?" Jared asks again.

"Let's just say if you don't fix it, you'll find out soon enough," she huffs, narrowing her eyes as her face is an inch away from his now, her heels making them at eye level. She clicks her heels away pushing her hair behind her face while she walks off sassily in the distance.

"What do you think that was about?" asks Jared.

"Beats me, but boy I would hate to be you right now," Jaiden shrugs as they face forward in the line once again.

"Stay here, I'm going to be right back," Jared directs before exiting the line after spotting Jessica enter the cafeteria from afar.

He joins her at the table, "Jessica, can we talk again?"

201

"What's going on?" she asks setting her water down, traveling a couple of feet away from the table.

"What the hell are you doing talking to Robbie Montoya?" he whispers in anger.

"He's a nice guy, I'm allowed to talk to whomever I want," she defends standing tall.

"This is a serious matter, I'm telling you as a friend right now to stop being friends with him," he demanded.

"What, is this what 'Candi' told you to do?" she asked manifesting her hand out and staring at Candace, who stood in the back of the cafeteria with her posse.

"No. Jared Daniels, former bullied victim, is telling you," he says placing his hands on his hips as she throws her neck back in laughter before he drops his face and narrows his eyes.

"Jared, I don't see what the problem is, he's changed now and he's really sweet, in fact, I've invited him to chill with us at Russo's tonight."

"Who's 'us'?"

"The whole group—you're invited if you want to come, but if you're going to stand there and try to make me change my mind about inviting him, then you can just forget about it," she huffed.

"I don't want you hanging out with him."

"Why must you complicate things!"

"You can't control who I can or can't be friends with," she argued.

"You don't understand—"

"No, YOU don't understand! I tried to warn you about Megan and I just so happened to be right. Don't you think I know what's best for me? Besides, 'you' didn't listen to me so why should I?" she spat. Despite Jessica's belief system, Jared knew he would always loathe the horrible person Robbie became, and will never forget the humiliation he's put him through—throughout high school. He could never possibly forgive Robbie, not in this lifetime anyways.

"I'm just trying to protect you!" he frustrated.

"She doesn't need protection, she's got me," said Jaiden, who walked up with a wrap in his hand. Jess took Jaiden's hand and stormed out after Jaiden had shoved his wrap against Jared's chest. Jared just hoped that for everyone's sake, he wasn't compensating 'that' for sex. Every time Jessica felt closer to Jared, she felt he ruined it somehow. When time came for her to think of it, she remembered Jaiden had pulled that a couple of times on her too. They were more alike than she thought, twins yes, but sometimes although impossible, she felt like they shared the same brain too. At times she often found herself wondering where the stupidity part of their brain came from.

****

After school, Jaiden and Jess drove to Russo's pizza parlor, owned by Skylar's family; meeting with the gang, Skylar and Becca, Hobbs, and Star as well as Jaiden inviting Wesley, Josh, Alex, and of course Jess, who has invited Robbie so there might have been a slight chance that Candi was coming, unless Candi made him refuse to come. Jess, of course, also invited Jasmine since she was the newest addition to the group, and since she was so willing to come, it was led to assume that she didn't have very many friends before. Following on that, Jess had also invited Chris, although Jaiden didn't seem okay with the idea at first. She knew of why Jared might dislike him but Jaiden? She was determined to get to the bottom of why he dislikes Chris so much. Then there was also the smallest of chance that Jared too will show up but will be less likely after the argument they had gotten into earlier today and since he avoids Robbie at all costs. The drama that follows with high school seems to be exact in the movie stereotypes. Jaiden and Jess, although being the planners of the evening, showed up last among the rest of group who were awaiting them in this semi crowded restaurant. There they were, laughing, and what seemed like to be having a good time. Robbie was there as well, surprisingly without Candace. He sat on the opposite end of the table talking to Chris, Wesley, and Josh. Jess slid out of her coat and took her seat next to her clutter of friends while Jaiden made his way around the table to greet his buddies. As the group was oddly enjoying a strange conversation on politics for the past twenty or-so minutes, the door to Russo's swings open and in enters Jared with Jessica's calculus partner, Brennan, also known as the culprit who had been smuggling alcohol within school grounds and sharing it with Jared. For Jared's sake, that boy better of stopped for his own good or he certainly would have gotten an earful from non-other than Jessica Jane. "Aye Jared, you're here! I saved you a spot!" Robbie announced, clearing a seat next to him. Jared inattentively continues in his steps, while he and Brennan picked a spot away from the table that their distant friends sat at and Jessica stares in confusion.

"Hey Jared, care to join us?" Jaiden calls out while Jared continuously ignores them all. Robbie sits back down after Jessica solemnly signals for him to. Jessica excuses herself before standing up and walking over to their table.

"Hello Brennan, Jared um, why are you sitting over here?"

"I'm kind of hanging out with Brennan right now..." Jared antagonized.

"Come on guys, come join, have some laughs," Robbie says approaching their smaller table now too.

"Are you going to hurt us if we don't?" Brennan narrows his eyes.

"Relax, I'm not going to hurt you, those days are over."

"Robbie, come on, let's get back," Jess sighs after the two sitting ducks begin to ignore their presence like before.

"Here, on the house," Robbie insisted, dropping a twenty on their table.

"We don't need your pity money," Jared says swiping it across the table so that it landed on the floor. Robbie sighs and they head back to the table.

"You tried."

Chapter Twelve

"Jessica, what I don't understand is how you could befriend someone who has endlessly tortured me my whole life!"

"…It doesn't just upset me, it hurts me!"

"Jared, look. I'm sorry that this affects you so much, but I just don't see the bad in him. I never did, and I can't judge him based on the person he is to you, accept it or don't, but he's a friend now," she persisted, "And why do I get the feeling that you're making me play favorites all the time? I don't want to have to choose and you're not going to make me," she emphasized, folding her arms.

"Jessica, we need to talk!" Jaiden shouted, approaching her and Jared in the hallways at school. She shrugged her body at his appearance, "Not you too! What do *you* want?"

"I told you not to invite Chris yesterday and yet you've completely disrespected me and invited him anyways!" he dignified.

"Excuse me, we were having a conversation!" Jared argued, annoyed.

"Wait a minute!" the two simultaneously fired at Jared.

"You sure as hell didn't seem bothered by it last night when you had your tongue down my throat in the alley out back!" Jess fired back. That statement alone earned itself an apathetic chuckle followed by an eye roll coming from Megan, who strolled past their conversation. Jessica stared Megan down after she had purposely publicized her appearance in her walk past, before Jess had tugged at her friends' arms to distance themselves away from the public eye.

"Why don't you like him?"

"He's full of himself."

"Like you aren't?" she raises her brows.

"I don't like him, everything is a competition with him!"

"…I don't want you being friends with him and I mean it," he eminently concluded.

"What is it with you two!"

"You're friends with all those cheerleaders and I don't say anything!"

"Yeah, but not by choice," Jared stated.

"What the hell does that mean! Was it a choice that you slept with Courtney?" she angered in defense.

"Not this again," Jared sighed, dropping his face in his hands.

"I'm done talking to you guys," she frustrated, crossing her arms before maneuvering in the opposite direction. "You know, I think I 'will' invite Chris 'and' Robbie over to my flat tonight and NOT YOU!" she squawked, trailing backwards further and further away.

"Yeah well, good luck! Candi will never let you!" yelled Jared.

"Guess I will just have to invite her as well because even though I sincerely despise her, I'm not afraid to give people another chance! But consequently for you, I think I have given you both one too many chances to disappoint me!"

"...see ya!"

"You better not go there!" warned Jaiden.

"Watch me!" she negligently ventured off. "God! I hate when she does this," Jaiden boiled in anger.

"What are we going to do about her?"

"YOU aren't going to do anything; you're going to stay at home and be a good little boy like we all know you to be," Jaiden caveats, tapping his naïve little brother on the cheek.

"I don't want her to be alone with Robbie just as much as you don't want her to be alone with Chris," Jared informed.

"Then I guess we'll just crash the dinner." Jaiden devilishly smirked when pulling out the spare key from his pocket.

****

"This looks lovely, but why the sudden invite?" asked Chris when stepping down to the small circular dining table in Jessica's flat, following behind Robbie, who stood a head shorter than him.

"I know it's a little unorthodox, but you guys are my newest friends and I want to get to know you a little better. Jared and Jaiden kind of have a problem with you guys but I want to prove them wrong," she explains assisting them to the table. Dinner goes by smoothly, and not as awkward as Jessica envisioned. "So, I've noticed that you and Candi have been distant lately, and I don't mean to pry—"

"Oh no, it's okay, we broke up... actually almost two weeks ago. She's kind of cramping my style and I'm not really into girls like her anymore. We're still good friends but that's it," Robbie admits.

"Friends," Jessica muttered with a plastered smile. Jessica had a distinct flashback of when his 'ex-girlfriend' made a big deal about

Robbie and her being friends just the other day. It made sense at the time because Jess thought she was just being a protective girlfriend or whatever, but if they were only friends now, why would she care at all?

"Sorry we're late, Jared was driving," Jaiden says, barging in uninvited as Jared follows behind.

"Hey dudes!" Robbie greeted.

"Come on in, sit down," says Chris, patting down beside him. Jessica stands up to help them to a seat before walking to the kitchen to retrieve some silverware for the unexpected company. Jaiden insisted that Jared sit next to Chris and he sat next to Robbie to avoid problems. "How's it going Jaiden?" Chris asked just as Jessica reappeared, reclaiming her seat after setting the extra silverware on the table beside the twins.

"Good," Jaiden replied, catching his girlfriend off-guard when pulling her onto his lap.

"Wait, you're 'the' Chris? The Chris that hit on Megan?" Jared realized, heightening his voice after taking a good look at him.

"I didn't really hit on her, it was part of the plan, r-remember?" he explained, gulping out of nervousness. He relied on Jess to help him out. Jess on the other hand, was occupied with Jaiden, struggling to get out of his grip.

"Let go!" she hissed, finally able to rip away from him after he loosened his grip in his arms, confused. Distressed, she blew the hair that fell in front of her face before speaking out of turn again,

"What has gotten into you two! Once again, you've managed to ruin my entire night, so thank you!" Jess bellowed before running into her bedroom.

"Jess!" Jared stood. Jaiden too stood up after pushing out his chair, excusing himself from the table to check on her. That left Jared alone at the table with not one but two people he hated.

"So, Jared, we should hang sometime soon. I'd like to catch up with you like those good old days. What do you say, aye bud?" Robbie asked while digging into his food.

"We aren't friends," reprimanded Jared before standing up again and walking over to the couch.

"Babe, why are you so upset? We're just a couple of guys having fun," Jaiden lightheartedly invoked when fully entering Jess' room.

"If it's just 'fun'," she air-quoted, "Then why don't you go over to Chris and apologize for the way you've been acting this entire night!" she cried.

"Not 'that' fun," he jokingly concluded, plopping down next to her.

"You've ruined my whole night! And your disliking of Chris is even more pathetic than why Jared can't stand Robbie! I hardly believe he even knows that you dislike him anyways, for whatever reason that may be."

"Oh, he knows alright—which is why he likes to provoke me by trying to score with my women. He's probably heard all about how I'm the best in school—which would explain why he's attempting to top and replace me with that British charm, *bastard,*" he continued off in his thoughts while staring up into the abyss.

"Would you hear yourself!" she flustered, sitting up and hugging her pillow, "You think just because you're this flirt of the school, you can get with any girl you want!"

"That's because I 'have' gotten with every girl at the school and my record stands," he smirked. She cringed at the utmost disgust.

"Is your record more important than me?"

"No,"

"Really? I find that hard to believe because if I really was a 'priority' then you'd let him be whoever he wants to and not have to worry about losing your place in the school because you don't need everyone's appraisal when you have me."

"That's the problem," he sighed, adjusting himself on the bed. "I'm scared of losing you to him," he admitted when grazing her face, staring into the depths of her eyes.

"You won't. You don't have to be afraid, he's just a friend and so is Robbie."

"Do you honestly think I'd throw all of our years away for some stranger that I have yet to know?" she asked.

"Well."

"No Jaiden, please stop," she sighed, cupping his face. "Are you good now?" she asked when staring into his soul.

"I guess…" he shrugged. He puckered his lips like a fish, signaling that he wanted attention when the weight was lifted. She smirked, pinching his mouth before giving into his request.

"I think this was the first time you opened up to me Jai. I'm proud of you," she said grazing his thigh.

"God, I've been spending way too much time with Jared. I've almost developed a conscience," he chuckled, rubbing over his migraine.

"Now let's go back," she directed, getting up and wiping under her eyes.

"Hey, where's Robbie and Jared?" she asked Chris after the two had stepped out of her bedroom.

"They left, but I'm going to head off too. This has been a splendid meal, thank you for inviting me," he says sliding in his shoes near the door.

"Hey Mullins, sorry," Jaiden speaks just before Chris reached for the door.

"About?"

"You know, with trying to compete with you,"

"…or rather you trying to compete with me."

"There's no competition Jai," Chris chuckled after smugly examining Jaiden from head-to-toe before heading out. Jaw clenched, Jaiden shot his arm in the air after curling his fist into a ball, but not before Jessica restrained his arm back from committing an act of violence on the arrogant lad much like himself, no-less.

(The next morning)

"Jessica?" she heard her sister speak brightly through the phone.

"Yes Amanda, how are you?"

"Good, beautiful, and you?" she courteously replied with such joy in her voice.

"Been better," Jess replied when sitting up and rubbing her eyelids open.

"So listen, if you aren't doing anything tonight, why don't you and your boyfriend of choice stop on by… I have some exciting news!" she exclaimed.

"'Boyfriend of choice'?"

"Sorry, I haven't talked to you in a while so I'm not quite sure which one you've possessed," she sheepishly admitted.

"'Possessed?' You make it sound like a hobby!"

"Well I'm sorry. You switch between so often I was starting to think it was." Jessica dramatically gasped, springing out of bed. "Relax Sis, I get it. So you're a little preoccupied at the moment, I can take a hint. I'm actually kind of jealous. You get two for the price of one! Do I want Jared today, do I want Jaiden today?" Amanda teased with her shoulder holding up her cell to her ear as she slid into her work pants in front of her dresser.

"Stop it! It's not like that at all!"

"Whatever, anyways, which plus one will you be bringing tonight?"

"You'll find out," Jess grits before hanging up.

"Jaiden!" she shouts as he steps outside of her bathroom.

"What?" he asks—walking out half-dressed, brushing his teeth with toothpaste foam all over his mouth.

"Mandy's house tonight, dress nice."

"Well, that's the thing, you think I look good naked—so should I keep the trend alive for this occasion?" he purrs while approaching her.

"Don't be a smart ass," she groans, pushing his un-rinsed face away. The school day goes by faster than usual and now it was time to go home and get ready for Mandy's house, *kill joy*.

"Glad you could make it... ah, no scar on the chin, I declare this Jaiden, and you owe me fifty bucks!" Kevin directs to Amanda after Jaiden and Jess fully step inside their abode. On her way inside, Jess gave Mandy a death glare following behind the men who led them into the dining room. Upon entering the dining room, Jess noticed the place setting and silverware on the table that was set for four people. She realized that her parents weren't going to attend, and this wasn't another intervention, *perfect*.

"Wow, you've really changed it up in here since the last time I've been here," she also noticed when strenuously looking around the house some more. They soon gather around the table to enjoy a lovely home-cooked meal.

****

"So how are Mom and Dad, Beverly?" Jess directed to Amanda in hopes of engaging in small talk well enough to distract Kevin and Jaiden, who sat all through dinner just talking about business and sports.

"Well, Beverly has been avoiding contact with the whole family and—'wow' that is gorgeous! Did he propose?" asked Amanda who changed the subject as soon as she noticed her sister's polished ring flash in her direction when she took a sip of her water.

"Not anything serious," Jess admitted while Jaiden cleared his throat.

"Awe you kids, I remember how Kevin and I were back in the day," she reminisced.

"Amanda, you guys got married a couple of years ago, you make it seem like you guys are so old when you've only met in college."

"Hey! You have your stories and I have mine," she snidely replied.

"Plus, married to you feels like an eternity of happiness already," Kev continued by saying, reaching for her hand from across the table. "So how is the Jarester? I haven't seen him since the wedding I think," Kevin asks.

"Still awkward if that's what you mean," Jaiden chuckles, taking a sip of his water while Jessica purposely steps on his foot underneath; he almost chokes from utter laughter.

"Okay well, we were going to wait until dessert to tell you the good news, but I can't hold it in any longer!" Mandy beams while bringing out some napkins, standing directly behind Kevin's chair now.

"Are you sure you want to do this now?" Kevin asks.

"I'm pregnant!" she exclaims catching them all off-guard. It takes especially long for the news to sink in for Jessica.

"That's… terrific. I'm happy for you guys," she cringed.

"Aw sweetie, are you okay? Because if you are uncomfortable in any way at all—"

"No, no, I'm happy," she reassuringly stated before standing up to give her sister and brother-in-law a congratulatory hug. "Have you told anybody? How many months?" Jess asked after they all were seated once again.

"Three months and nope, not yet; we wanted you to be the first to know, we thought it'd be fair if you knew first."

"Any ideas for the sex of the baby?" Jaiden asks.

"No idea, but we are hoping it's a girl," Kevin responds.

"No, 'he's' hoping for a girl… I want a boy," Mandy informs, graciously clapping her hands together. They talk amongst themselves and Jess finds herself starting to get queasy at the topic. She couldn't believe her eldest sister was pregnant, talk about 'irony'. She was kind of jealous, but she knew she shouldn't be. Amanda was going to have a baby and even though Jess had lost her chance at motherhood, it wouldn't be the last time and she knew it was for the best. Jaiden must have noticed her uncomfortable stare when he took her hand that rested on her thigh and interlocked his hand with hers. She stared up at him to notice that warm and reassuring smile that she needed. "Oh shoot! I almost forgot!" Amanda announced when shooting up. "Come on!" she insisted when guiding her sister and her sister's boyfriend beyond the staircase on the first floor before they had entered the guest room that had once belonged to Jessica. Jess was taken aback once Amanda flipped on the light switch.

"Like it? Took me a month to construct but it was all worth it," Kevin says.

"Perfect baby bedroom for any gender," Amanda continued just before Jess had the opportunity to ask why they have already decorated the bedroom when they didn't know of the sex. Jess felt a few of her own tears ooze from her eyes at the sight. It was all too much for her, too many memories. She could only imagine how she would have set up the perfect nursery for her little girl, who is now dancing with the angels. Amanda gave the two a tour inside the remodeled room, which was beautifully done and well decorated. They had also extended the room for the nursery as well. "So, what do you think? Jess, you're not saying anything!" Amanda excites as she looks around some more before awaiting her sister's reaction.

Jess' eyes glisten like trinkets, "I-it's beautiful," she chokes, locking her hands under her nose.

"I should probably get her home, it's been a long day for both of us," Jaiden says coddling her as they step out.

****

(The following week)

Since the dinner party held at Jessica's apartment last week, she hadn't had contact with Robbie. He hasn't been showing up to classes since then. She had hoped she didn't give him food poisoning. She thought arriving to his residency to check in on him would be the moral thing to do if it had been the case. Then again, she did not want to be caught involved by Candace. Jessica was in sixth period when a voice came over the school intercom. "Attention, students and teachers, this is a lockdown... please hold your students." After almost the whole class hour of hiding under their desks, the students finally were released. It wasn't until her way to seventh period, that she saw an abundance of police surrounding the school when she worried for the sanity of her school.

"Hey, did you hear what happened?" she asked when catching up to her friend Star in the hallways.

"Someone filed a missing person's report for Robbie Montoya. He disappeared I guess," she replied. Yikes. *Food poisoning that bad?*

Oh stop thinking about yourself Jessica, this is not about you!

Seventh hour went by smoothly, but as soon as she stepped outside after her last period and walked towards her car, she spotted Jared talking with some police officers in the distance, so she curiously made her way up to them. "Excuse me officers, what is going on?"

"Are you Jessica Larson?" the larger and hairless police officer asked. She nodded humbly before the man spoke off in code to his partner on the radar that was attached to his shoulder. "It seems that you were the last two to have contact with Mr. Montoya, as his foster care owners have mentioned."

"Yeah, he was at my apartment just last week, although I don't know what happened to him after. I returned from my bedroom and he just disappeared," said Jessica, avoiding the part where Jared was the last person to converse with Robbie to avoid further complications for her close friend. "But he didn't know that my friend Jared was going to be there, so how?" she tried to analyze.

"We're trying to investigate the case, but from what we can tell so far is that it seems as if he's been lying to his family for the past month or so saying that he's reconciled with his former friend and has been hanging out with them, so they wouldn't worry about his whereabouts."

"His foster family told these officers that he was hanging out with me, so I confronted these officers that it wasn't true. We don't talk anymore," Jared denied. The officers dismiss the two and they safely return home, but now it seemed everyone was starting to seriously worry about Robbie's whereabouts until his identity was finally revealed the following afternoon.

"After almost a week of investigation, we have been hit with the unfortunate news that student Robbie Montoya has passed away over the weekend," the principal informed over the intercom while Jess was in calculus with Brennan and Jared. "Earlier today, Mr. Montoya was found in his motel room with a shotgun in his hand and a bullet wound through his head. This is a very sad time and from what we have concluded from his injuries is that he has been deceased for an entire week now. And although we have very minimal information about his death at this time, we will take into account that this is something that should be addressed. Suicide following onto depression, still exists in our world today and everyday one in three people among us is a victim of injustice. As a community, we need to reach a hand out to those seeking help, whether they may or may not ask for it upfront. The students must know that whatever you are going through, that you do not have to fight your demons alone—and for whatever challenge or obstacle it may be, it is important that you stay grounded because help is available everywhere and that is something my team and I need to work better at reinforcing. After contacting the school board, we have decided to release all the students early today, to mourn the loss of our fellow student and grief the death of a beloved classmate in this tragic time."

"I wouldn't call him beloved," a male snickered from the row behind Jessica.

She would not have it, she turned around. "Have you no heart? This student just took his life and you're sitting here making jokes about it?" she scoffed, "You people disgust me!" It wasn't long before Jared stood up to excuse himself out class, a gush of wind escaping the door while the intercom continued talking. Jessica too stood up and followed him out, chasing after him in the hallways.

"Teachers, be prepared to release your students in ten minutes as the police clears out of the parking lot," the principal directed.

Jess finds Jared in a small corner, sitting down, knees up to his chest, covering his eyes. She solemnly makes her way over and sits down next to him. She touches his shoulder and he winces before he shoots his eyes up at her, bloodshot. "No, no, no!" he grieves as she coddled him close

213

to her body in comfort. "It's my fault! It's always my fault!" he wept in somber.

"Jared, it's not your fault."

"You don't know that!" he spat.

"It is my fault! I wanted him to disappear and now he's gone! I s-should have listened to him, I wish I could've been there to stop him!" he screamed, tugging on the roots of his hair. "Everyone around me is leaving! I can't take it anymore! I just want this pain to stop, it should've been me! I wish it was!" he wails, dropping his head into his arms that rested on his knees again when bringing them closer to his chest.

"Hey, stop that! You can't say that!" Jess sobbed out. "You're not the only one that's losing people, okay! I don't want you to think like that, because I've thought like that before a-and it made me lose more than I've bargained for okay!" she bawls.

"Can't anything in my life ever go right! I'm such an idiot, I don't deserve to live with myself! I shouldn't even be here right now! I'm losing everything, and I have to deal with all the pain that follows!" he whimpered into his hands. She detached his hands away from his eyes to force his eyes at hers.

"Look at me," she asked, wiping under his eyes with her thumbs. She could feel his vulnerability, she could see it through his eyes. "It'll be okay, I promise. Please never give up on yourself, get yourself out of this mindset; it's not your fault anything happened, I don't blame you and no one else does... Please just promise me you'll never do anything reckless that you'll live to regret one day because this is only now. It will get better, I promise you Jared. Please, it hurts me to see you so upset like this. I-I couldn't possibly imagine a world without you, okay? It might not seem like a lot right now, but you mean more to me than you credit yourself for. You don't know your worth yet, but you will one day and maybe someday you'll thank me. But you can't do this to yourself, I need you even if we are just friends, okay, because that's enough for me, you're...enough... for ME." She concluded with tears and pulled her hands away from his face to wipe her eyes with the back of her hand. When she shifted her attention back to Jared, she noticed his conspicuous eyes still latched onto hers.

"I need you," Jared trembles with eminent fear in his eyes after a minute of the two gawking at each other. She cracked a small smile in his direction just grazing her hand over his tear-stained cheek. He displaced his own hand back over hers now, slowly pressing his eyes to allow his final tear to shed. He meekly opened his eyes to find her flashing him a comforting smile again. She felt herself pulling closer after they both automatically leaned in. Nearly an inch away from his face, she felt his hot breath right at her lips as he hungrily stared at the plumpness of Her moist lips.

She missed the feeling. She closed her eyes and allowed him to kiss her. She didn't hold back and he took the opportunity to sit up and move faster, both synchronized rapidly in their movements now. She pulled away after a couple of blissful seconds, feeling confused. She felt something she didn't want to believe. "I'm sorry Jared, I've got to go," she pardoned, standing up and running away after realizing what she has just done. It felt so wrong, yet so right to Jessica. The taste of his lips felt amazing; it left her wanting more. It was a feeling she lacked from Jaiden. She thought she finally got over Jared, but everything she felt for him was in fact repressed up until this moment. On her run towards the school bathroom—turning the corner, she ran into someone as the students began to flood the hallways, after being dismissed. She looked up at the tall student she ran into; it was Jaiden, *what were the odds?*

"Hey babe, what's going on?" he asked and she couldn't even look him in the eyes at this point until he went to lift her chin—but she rejected his hand, feeling the utmost guilty and disloyal. He sensed something was wrong but had not suspected anything about her and Jared. It all played out a little too well for Jessica since he had just assumed like everyone else, she too was upset over the loss of a friend.

****

Today was Robbie's funeral—another one of Jared's friends, gone. *Tragic.* Only, he wasn't giving a eulogy this time. There Robbie was, lying in a closed casket due to the amount of damage to his brain. They were burying him right next to his mother. No doubt, there were more students here for Robbie's funeral than Lucas'. Still, Jared could not believe he was gone. It felt like déjà vu all over again. Across from him, he saw Jessica and Jaiden, along with the rest of the group, sitting down in their picket-white chairs. He and Jessica haven't spoken since the day they kissed. The kiss was a mistake, it was a call of desperation and vulnerability. He felt like he had finally seen eye to eye with Jaiden—after so many years of bickering, and if Jess had told him about their kiss now, he knew it would all be over for the sake of their brotherhood. But somehow, he felt that something about that kiss felt very right, it was completely different from when he kissed Megan, better one could argue. He was finally starting to move on with his life and get over Jessica until this happened. He thought all about how she must have felt the same way as he did because she didn't pull away at first either. And although he would hate himself to admit, he did miss

215

the sweet taste of her lips, but overall, he just missed... *her*. He thought of it as best not to approach her, but he also knew they couldn't go on just avoiding each other forever because of this. More than anything, he needed her as a friend—especially in this darkest chapter of his life.

As the field of mourners prepare to farewell their loved one, Jared couldn't help but to allow a couple of tears to drop at the sight of his classmate being lowered into the ground. After all, it was the manly thing to do, *right?* "Jared, I'm so sorry," he heard. He turned his head to find Jessica, who approached him from his right before wrapping her arms around his neck. In the corner of his eyes, he saw Jaiden staring him down in spite while she pressed her soft plush lips to Jared's cheek and he wraps his arms around her waist. He cupped her face in his hands and brought his hungry lips once again to hers. When he held his eyelids together and shot his eyes up, he saw that Jess was still with Jaiden on the opposite side of the field and he sighed in relief. This was a feeling of guilt that was going to consume him. "Hey Jared, over here!" he heard his name being called. He whipped his body around to find Lucas and Robbie smiling at him from the distance, causing him to walk over. "But h-how?" His eyes widened as if he's seen a ghost, or two.

Both ghosts stood before him on the grassy field in white. "I'm sorry to leave you like this, I really was sorry about everything. I needed to prove that to you," Robbie lightheartedly chuckles as his bloodshot eyes don't allow him the advantage.

"And you?" Jared asked Lucas.

"Accidents happen, eh? Heck, it wasn't your fault this happened to me, or yours," Lucas chuckles, in discretion to Robbie. "Sorry, I'm not supposed to swear," he teased after feeling a sting on his wrist.

"I needed this Jared, not just because of you but because I wanted to be with my mother again," Robbie smiles, looking off to his left as she appears in the distance. "Can you believe after all this time? She was battling cancer. She thought if she could toughen up around me, it would make her seem stronger. I forgave her. We've made peace. She's okay now and I'm happy we're both moving on to a better place. I've been liberated to the other side," he says and Jared smiles after she approached and placed a hand over her son's shoulder.

"Damn, it's time," Lucas informed, nudging Robbie as the light shone from above.

"Well, we've got to go," Robbie informed as he held his mother's hand.

"B-but—" Jared struggled to get his last few words out.

"You won't be able to see us, but we are always watching over you. Try to get a good night sleep, alright bud?" Lucas suggested. Jared courteously nods.

"Jared, come visit my motel room, I have a letter that explains everything else you'll need to know," Robbie implied before the sun illuminated brighter than before, blinding poor Jared's eyes while he covered them with his hands. When he went to uncover his eyes as the light was gone—so were they.

"Jared?" he heard Becca call, snapping him out of whatever trance he was in. He couldn't differentiate if what he just witnessed was real or not. Maybe this instance only occurred from the lack of sleep he amounted to in the past two days from all this stress he was under, that had him hallucinating.

"What's going on?" Skylar asks when approaching the mildly paranoid and grieving teenager alongside Becca.

"I think I-I just saw Lucas and Robbie," he choked.

"You poor thing! Come here," Becca insisted while smothering him, obviously thinking he was anything close to delusional.

"I need to get to Robbie's motel," he chanted, pulling away then lunging for his car. Jessica felt a gust of wind pass by, when she turned around, she found it was Jared running away from the scene of this event, with Skylar and Becca following closely behind.

"Jess, Jared has gone crazy! I don't think he should be allowed on the road… he's said something about needing to get to Robbie's motel—" Becca pants out of breath.

"Shit, come on Jaiden!" Jess urged, tugging on Jaiden's arm as they begin to follow Jared in the distance.

"Okay, we'll stay here!" Becca informed, cramping to her side to catch her breath. As for Jaiden and Jessica, they followed Jared's car to the supermarket and then to what appears to be Robbie's motel. He brought the flowers he bought from the supermarket, making his way to the second level of building complex and set them down near Robbie's door before he stepped inside. That is when Jaiden and Jess made their move and sneak up behind him, unbuckling their seat belts. They reach the second level as Jared was on and too step inside the unlocked door. This area looked very dangerous, the yellow police tape was tampered with, even before Jared had entered.

"Jared? What are you doing h—" she stops mid-sentence as soon as she saw him sitting, bawling on the floor with an unfolded note beside him. He didn't acknowledge the two, so she walked up to him, sitting down beside him. She moved his head gently to fall on her shoulder before picking up the letter from the floor to begin reading it as Jared wept onto her shoulder—falling into her covered cleavage for warmth. She read the letter silently to herself while she played with his hair in comfort.

Dear Jared, so you've found the letter? Well, that means I went through with it and it's not because of you though, so please don't blame yourself. I have lived in a world of constant fear and negligence my whole life. I thought if I was the one feared by society, then I could live a happy life, getting whatever I wanted and it worked for a while until I realized that I've pushed away possibly the only people that ever cared for me. In reality, I was just glad to have met a friend like you to show me the ropes. I know what I did was wrong, I took advantage of our friendship and you did not deserve any of it, which is why I completely understood why you wouldn't accept my apology. I'd hate me if I were you too. Jared, I've made a bunch of bad choices in these past couple of years and nothing could ever erase the hurt I've caused you and a bunch of other people, this is the only way I could think of after trying so long to clear things…

I mainly wrote this letter to say thanks. Jared, you're a noble guy, you've got a long way to go. You can make sense of the world which is something I could never do. You've really changed me and made me see my wrong doings—with that kind of power you hold on people, I think you can go very far in life and don't let anyone tell you otherwise. I wouldn't know what a good friend is if I didn't have you, even if our relationship outlived itself, it was a fun run and you've been the most loyal friend I've had growing up. My life may be over now but it's only the beginning for you. Make the rest of your senior year a good one, I'll be graduating in spirit right on that stage with you buddy. Please don't let my family see me like this. I hope you get a chance to read this before they find my body… I hope we meet again one day. I'll be looking forward to reuniting with you on the other side someday. I'll be watching, not to sound like a creep but just make sure you're decent when I decide to check up on you, okay? I wonder if Lucas is here… maybe I'll give him my regards, although if he has been looking over, he'll know that I'm one of the good ones now. I just hope you'd find in your heart to understand it too—why I had to do this. My time is coming soon and I'm scared to pull the trigger but I know I have to do this, it's my own redemption. It's really hard to say goodbye, especially to you… I'm not good at goodbyes so how about we think of this as a hello to a new start and new beginnings? I know you're going to be very successful one day, you're going to have a nice home, maybe somewhere in the city, big family, beautiful wife—that is my wish for you—to be something

I will never get the chance to be. I want you to have all the happiness in the world, you're a good guy Jare and don't you forget it. So here is my final thought, here is to the goodbye for now and the hello that is yet to come, cheers buddy... I hope it's legal to drink in heaven because that is where I'll be,

cheering you on – Robbie Xavier

"Xavier?" Jess asked after finishing the letter.

"His mother's maiden name," Jared sniffled out, rubbing his eyelids in his palms. Jessica requested a moment alone with Jared and Jaiden respectfully nodded when earnestly standing by the doorway.

"I'll wait in the car," he says before he walks out.

"Jared, a-are you okay?" asked Jessica.

"I don't know if I ever will be again, it's all my fault!" he grieved, covering his eyes with his hands.

"Jared, didn't you read the letter? You've got to stop taking the blame on things! It's not your fault!"

"How could you possibly know! You weren't there the last time I spoke with him! Hell, you were with Jaiden!" he spat. Jessica was stricken with worry.

"Jared, w-what are you talking about?" she asked.

(Flashback—Jessica's Dinner Party Last Week)

"So, Jared, we should hang sometime soon. I'd like to catch up with you like those good old days. What do you say, aye bud?" Robbie asks when digging into his food.

"We aren't friends," Jared implied. He dropped his fork and stood up to make his way over to the couch.

"Jared, can we at least try to move past this?"

"No honestly, I don't think I can ever forgive you, I don't even want to..."

"You're an asshole and you've been my whole life."

"Please, Jared. I'm on the line here, what do you want me to do? Anything, you name it," Robbie pleads.

"Fine. You want to know what you can do?" says Jared when staring straight ahead at the blank television screen after kicking his feet up on the coffee table.

"Yeah." Jared stands up vigorously and locks his eyes with Robbie threateningly, "Disappear..."

"Do anything to leave me the hell alone for the rest of my life. I don't need you, or your friendship," he gritted. Robbie gulped in fear,

"Alright, I'll take that into consideration, a-are you sure there isn't anything else?"

"Dammit! You asked what I wanted, so do it!" he immorally spat.

"I'm sorry Jared, I didn't know you hated me so much. Okay, I'll go," he frowns before he exits the door, taking one look back at Jared, who seemed to be doing fine without him.

"Dude, Jared—don't you think that was a bit harsh?" asked Chris when walking over to him from the dining table behind.

"Fuck off," Jared grumbled before storming out of the door.
(End of flashback)

"I'm a terrible person, I should be thrown in hell! He was just trying to make peace and I just shut him out like I do with everyone else and I'm so sorry!" he squalled in misery as she cradled him in her arms. She tried to calm him as he violently shook under her embrace.

"Ssshhhh, you didn't mean it," Jess cooed, grazing his hair as he sobs into her chest harder.

"Hey, are you guys almost do—" Jaiden asks, stopping himself when he saw his overemotional brother being comforted by his girlfriend.

"You go ahead. I'll catch a ride with Jared," Jess assured.

****

Chapter Thirteen

"Beverly? What are you doing here?" Jessica asked after unlocking the door to her apartment. Beverly was the last person Jessica expected to find knocking at her door, that's for sure. "I'm sorry, I-I needed someone to talk to," she says striding into her sister's apartment.

"You know where I live?" Jess inquired.

"Mother gave me your address," Beverly explained, getting comfortable on her sister's sofa.

"So, what's going on?" asked Jessica, joining her.

"I, I just miss Patrick," Beverly wept.

"Bev, not to sound rude, but he dumped you on the day of your wedding and left you at the altar. Not only that, but he said it himself, he's been using you this whole time—why on earth would you be missing that tool?" she asked, awkwardly patting down her sister's back in comfort.

"Could you fetch me a coffee? I can't really think straight without it," Beverly implied, shooting her head up.

"Y-yeah sure," Jess agreed, making her way to her small kitchen. She returned several minutes later with two steaming hot cups of coffee after pouring herself a cup as well.

"I think I'll just get a run to Starbucks later," says Bev after taking a sip, revolting in disgust at the bitter taste before setting her mug down on the coffee table, *bitch*.

"So why have you come 'here'?"

"Well, Jessica."

"For the longest time, you've been the nicest person to me."

That's a lie.

"I have?"

"'Regardless', I need advice."

Jessica raised an eyebrow, but just before Beverly had a chance to explain, a knock on the door was heard. "Hold that thought, I'll get it," Jessica insisted, upstanding the weight on her feet.

"Allow me," Beverly assured, taking her place while Jessica plummeted back down. Beverly opened the door to find one-half of Jessica's *ménage à trois* standing in the flesh at her doorway.

"Hello—" Jaiden started saying until he had realized that he was staring his girlfriend's hellish sister in the face.

"Look what the cat dragged in," Beverly scoffed. "No need for looking squeamish, I'm too emotionally drained to do any damage to your face," Beverly admitted when making her way over to the couch as Jaiden cautiously followed behind. "Besides, I should be thanking you," she says as he took a seat on the opposite couch.

"Excuse me?" Jaiden and Jess both say in unison. "You didn't ruin my wedding. Well, I realize now that your intentions were for a good cause—you were simply just trying to look out for me, to help me realize that Patrick was a fraud and he wasn't right for me."

"I did?" he asked, looking to Jess who stared him down from right beside Beverly hoping he would just go along with it.

"And you obviously did it because you still care for me and I don't blame you for trying to get with this again," she continued.

"What?" Jessica choked out on her bitter coffee.

"I-I mean… yeah," he mumbled after looking back over to Jess, who told him to lie with her obvious facial expressions behind her sister. "I guess I did?" he agreed, even though someone as ignorant as a second grader could even figure out it was clearly an act of revenge.

"I can't believe I ever doubted you. Such a sweet boy, I could just hug you… but I won't because it would take me at least three hours of sanitation to get your stench off my body," she cried out as he then grips his knuckles in his lap. "So, what should I do?" Beverly perched when scooting forward after wiping under her eyes.

"About what?" asked Jess.

"How do I get Patrick back?"

"Patrick never loved you," stated Jaiden.

"Oh Jaiden, that's just the jealousy talking. He's playing hard to get," she assured, sulking in her own pitiless denial.

"He's moving to Paris with Vivian, why in the hell would he spend all that time and money just to play, 'hard to get'?" Jaiden asks.

"Paris?"

"Yeah, they're moving in the summer."

"Babe, could you get me a coffee?" Jaiden asked causing the petulant Jess to narrow her eyes at him. "On a tight schedule, I could really use that coffee, babe," he insisted when pointing at his watch. Just as Jessica was about to head into the kitchen for the second time, his phone rang.

Nothing irritated Jessica more than when Jaiden became Beverly's twin more than his own twin's twin.

"Hold on," Jaiden excused after pulling out his ringing phone from inside his pocket. "I'm just going to take this," he announced before standing up.

"No!" Jessica urged, causing them both to whip their heads in her direction. "Please stay!" she beseeched as soon as Beverly shifted her attention back over to Jaiden. He then answers his call as he stares at Jess profusely in confusion before proceeding to walk away with his private call. She nearly begged Beverly to put off this conversation until Jaiden returned from his phone call which lasted a total of two minutes.

"Yeah, I'll be there soon, bye," he says before joining the girls again, while Jess sets her empty coffee mug down.

"Who was that?" Bev asked, "It was Patrick wasn't it?"

"How did you know?" he asks while a bead of sweat forms in the crevice of his forehead.

"You wouldn't have walked away if it was anyone else, would you?"

"Sorry, I have to go, I'm meeting with him soon," Jaiden says before walking towards the door.

"Well, at least you've became closer," she sobs again.

"Jaiden, wait!" shouted Jess, who hauled towards him in hopes of avoiding Beverly.

"Yeah?"

"Is there a reason you came by?"

"I thought we could catch up on some alone time but clearly you have company, so I'll catch you later." He plants a kiss on the short-tempered girl's cheek before escaping out the door.

"Jessica!" Beverly cries out.

"Coming!" she rolled her eyes while closing the door.

"Why won't this stupid thing work!" Beverly sobbed, down on her knees in front of the television set, smacking the television screen with her hand.

"It could be because the remote is right here," directed Jess, walking over to the couch, and switching on the power.

"Oh, my television is touch screen," Bev stated before crawling over to the couch. "Daddy got me everything automatic so I wouldn't have to worry about breaking a sweat or a nail," she pouted.

"Well, did Daddy ever teach you how not to be lazy?" Jess muttered when making her way over to the kitchen.

"Jessica?"

"Uh-huh?"

"Would it be alright with you, if I spend the night? I'm scared to return to Mom and Dad's house. Patrick sold our apartment today," Beverly shrugged.

"Beverly, you sure? This is a pretty poor environment for someone like you, you might get rampaged by hungry raccoons at night," teased Jessica.

"Oh my God!" shrieked Bev while sitting up on the couch, hugging her knees.

"Relax, I'm kidding." Jess sighed before returning to the kitchen to retrieve her cookbook; she was determined to be productive on this glorious day. Her sister's inevitable incompetence might as well contaminate her so long as she stood in her presence, but she would try to hold out and avoid her as best as she could, for as long as she could. She returned with the thick cookbook moments later, greeting her sister near the dining room, where she curiously approached her while Jess begun to flip through the pages. Beverly, who stood over her sister's shoulder, examining her recipes, smiled down after she came across an exquisite dish, "That looks delicious!" Her mouth watered.

"Too fatty," said Jess who turned around and eyed her sister from the waist up. "But of course, 'you' wouldn't know," her eyes popped out in annoyance before returning to look through her book. Jessica loved to read. She had an array of books lined up on her bookshelf located in her closet in her wee little humble abode—anything from cookbooks to the classics in literature. "Perfect." Jessica bit her lip after finding the page she had been searching to find—so she stood up and made her way back over to the kitchen to prepare.

"Alright, let's do this!" Bev eagerly exclaimed after following behind her sister.

"You mean you want to do something?"

"I love baking, it's one of the very few things Patrick admired about me. Guess it's the only now," Beverly frowned, breaking in a sweat of tears again and Jessica sighs once Beverly sinks in her embrace.

"Okay well,"

"No time to waste," says Jessica after detaching her limbs from the love and care of her sister.

"Do you have an apron? I don't want to get this outfit dirty," Beverly asked.

"Nope. Sorry," Jess lied. What Beverly didn't know wouldn't hurt her since in fact Jess did have an apron to spare. She wanted her sister to learn a valuable lesson in the art of adulthood and snap her out of her delirium reality where she has this idea of a perfect dirt-free world. Then again, Bev was also more than capable of carrying dirt—after all, she had her own on Jaiden for a while.

The two ladies finished the lemon tart within two hours when Jess had carefully pulled it out of the oven. "This looks perfect!" Bev excites. Just as Jess was about to rip a piece of cake with her bare hands, her sister slapped her hand away before she had a chance to sneak a bite. "No eating, Instagram first!" she declared when grabbing her iPhone from the counter to snap a picture. "There!" she says, admirably staring at the image in her high-resolution. "How about a selfie with my sister?" she asked. Jess hadn't felt reluctant to disagree because for the first time in forever, she felt she rather enjoyed a moment with Beverly. Jess was humbled that her sister appeared as another one of them; a normal, hard-working, and compassionate human being.

****

The selfie trend continued later that same following week when Jess had been taking selfies with Star after school, both trying to find good lighting and a good angle when her phone rang. "You have a call from an unknown number," Star pointed out, pausing their selfie.

"Hello?" Jessica answered after reclaiming her phone from Star's hands as they both continue in their walk to the parking lot.

"Hey Jess. It's Griffins."

"How did you get my number?"

"Z gave it to me."

"I'm sorry, 'Zee'?"

"The other Zach,"

"Right."

"Come on, I thought you would be delighted to hear back from me?" he taunts.

"Not really. In fact, I'm seeing someone right now."

"You flatter me, but no. I am calling you in regards to an overdue apology I owe you for how I came off the first night we met."

"Why don't I believe you?" she interrogated, opening the backseat of her car to throw her backpack in while Star did the same from the passenger side.

"All in moderation."

"Yeah, well, why don't you try convincing someone who cares—" she persisted in an attempt to end the call.

"Please just hear me out?"

"I'm listening…"

"We got off on the wrong foot and I'd like to start over."

"Why 'now'?"

"Something tells me you're not the type of girl who anyone would just let go of. There's something special about you Jessica and I'd like to pick your brain."

"Give me one reason I should."

"I know you feel threatened by your peers and I know you would do just about anything to rid of your past."

"You don't know 'what' I want."

"On the contrary my dear, I'm like the human encyclopedia. I've been inside so many women—

"—'s heads, that I know how women think and I know what they want, how they work. Think of me as your get out of jail free card or personal guru and I can solve all of your problems. 'Poof'."

"What's the catch?"

"No catch, like I said—I'm only interested in building a relationship with you, all professional, no strings attached."

"Alright. You have my attention."

"We should meet up, so I can tell you more… Let's say around eight p.m.? I'll pick you up from your place."

"Oh, and don't tell Jaiden… you know to avoid any problems."

"But h-how did you know?" Jess stuttered in confusion.

Dial tone.

Asshole.

"Who was that?" asked Star, after Jess fully sat inside the car.

"A friend,"

"Male, I presume? He sounds pretty hot."

"He's not your type, trust me."

"Whatever you say," she says as they buckle up.

After Jess dropped Star off, she got home and hopped into the shower for a quick change of fresh clothes afterwards. She checked her phone when retrieving it from the outlet near her bedside and saw that she had three missed calls from Jaiden. "Where are you at?" he asked as soon as he picked up her call.

"Well, hello stranger," she teased.

"Isn't it hump day today?" he purrs through the phone.

"Jaiden," Jess groaned. "Not now, I'm busy sorry," she says rushing to answer the door as soon as it sounds.

"What are you doing here? I told you to wait outside," she directed to Griffins.

"Sorry, are you ready?" he asks.

"Who was that?" Jaiden asks through the speaker.

"It's Griffins. I'm busy babe, I'll see you later—"

"Jess, what is he doing over there?"

"He needed my help with something. I'll be home soon, don't wait up for me."

"Jess, kick him out right now and I mean it. Do it now, tell him something came up."

"You're being ridiculous, I'll be back soon."

"This isn't a joke, I don't want you near him and I mean it."

"It wasn't bad enough you've had a problem with me and Chris hanging out and now you're doing the same thing with Zach, I guess some things never change with you."

"FYI, the whole jealousy thing, 'not cute'," she angered.

"Jess, don't you fucking dare—" Jessica rolled her eyes and hung up before tossing her phone on her couch. She would not have Jaiden possess her around any longer during the remainder of her night. The two soon pulled up to a high-end restaurant, different from the one that Jaiden and Jess went to. When the two had finished up with their meals that night—the night filled with the two acquainting and getting to know each other, they return to the car. Just before Zach put on his seat belt, Jess displaced a hand at his shoulder to request his attention.

"Answer me this one question. What's the deal with you and the twins? Is there something I should know about?" Griffins sighs, releasing the shoulder restraint from his hand.

"Not anything that concerns your pretty little head. They just need to learn to stay out of people's business that's all," he says when adjusting his rear-view mirror to the side.

"Hey Zach, are you sure you're going the right way? I think you've missed our exit," she asked during what looks like their car ride home now.

"Exactly."

He deviously smirks, snapping off his seat belt after swerving and breaking sharply to park in the dark baron road they detoured at. "What the fuck, Zach!" Jessica yelled, trying to catch her breath.

"Leaving your phone behind? You make it too easy," he taunted before forcing his tongue so far down her throat, moving at a fast pace. He moved his fingers to lock the doors and windows while she tried pushing him away. His large hand wraps around her petite throat. She squirms under his grip, trying to unlock the door with tears in her eyes as his hands rake up her shirt. She tried to maneuver her hands around to prevent him from touching her while his tongue was still very much lodged down her throat—until finally, she bit on his bottom lip and successfully unlocked the door from her side. She was able to escape while he let his guard down, but not before he grabbed her by her ankle, twisting it while she shrieked in terror. She finally managed to slide out of her heel as it scissor-kicked him in the jaw. He bit down on his lip, "Bitch," he gritted. She ran away terrified while he stepped out of the car and began to chase her. She ran into the woods in hopes of losing him.

"Dammit Jessica, answer your phone!" Jaiden frustrated in anger—slamming on his breaks once he found a car with its headlights on and its doors wide open in the distance. To his curiosity, he stepped out and examined the car. He found a ripped piece of fabric from one of the clothes he recognized from his girlfriend's wardrobe, left on the passenger seat. For Jessica, she had regretted abandoning her phone and not listening to Jaiden. She shrieked in terror once she thought Griffins had caught up to her and found her hiding behind a boulder. Luckily, it was just Jaiden, he covered her mouth after she startled like a car alarm. She dropped in his embrace, shivering in relief. He held her before pulling away to examine her body. Her body that had fresh bruises and her clothes that were ripped down to her thighs—the rips that exposed her chest.

"I'm so sorry," she sobbed in his embrace after he comforted her again.

"I'll talk with you later, where is he?" he gritted after releasing her.

"Well, well, well, if it isn't Jessica's little bitch," Griffins slurred when stepping out from behind a tree upon finding them both. Jess stepped back a couple of feet, frozen in fear as Jaiden stood in front. He held out his arm that Jessica attempted to hide behind while Zach took the last sip of his bottle filled with alcohol before smashing the remaining residue onto the rocks.

"You aren't going to get away with this again. You're going to 'jail', Zach! I've already called the cops," Jaiden threats. "Even if you run, I'll find you and I'll come after you myself."

"It's over," he states, gripping Jessica's hand as soon as police sirens are heard in the distance.

"Jai! Behind you!" Jess warns as soon as Zach picked up a heavy piece of wood—missing when Jaiden dodged his hit. Instead, Zach took the same large splinter and aimed for Jessica's torso this time, "No!" Jaiden shouts. She watched her life flash before her eyes as he plunged it deep into her side. She coughed a puff of blood, leaking from her mouth before she collapsed onto the rocks. Jaiden rushed over to her aid, caressing her face. She was still breathing.

"You're going to be okay, the police are here, s-stay with me!" He chokes on his words while drowning in his tears.

"J-Jaiden," Jess wheezed, trying to get him to look behind as Griffins, who stood behind, waited to attack him with a boulder.

"I'm sorry," Jaiden pleads before he ejected the wood from her side. She jerked in the air from the pain of the sharp object being released from her body. He then used it to plunge it into Griffins to finish him off before he had the chance to make his first move. Griffins toppled out cold, onto a pile of leaves after the wood entered his body. When it was finally over, Jaiden helped his faint girlfriend back to her feet, limping over to the police who barely pulled up to the scene of the crime.

"Hey Jaiden!" Griffins coughed, waving the brick behind the two. Jaiden, who releases his grip on Jess, whips his head around to fend for himself, as she struggles to hold herself against a boulder. Jaiden gets taken out by his swing this time.

"No!" Jess shouts before stepping back as Zach steps closer to her with his weapon.

"Say hi to Jaiden for me," he taunts about to whack her again. It wasn't long before he tripped on a pit that had him toppling over a tree stump with rigid spikes that instantaneously ended his life this time.

"Oh my God!" Jess panics, jumping back in fear after witnessing his insides splatter out of his body. A weak Jessica, climbs over to Jaiden from right beneath her feet, checking his pulse. He was still alive, she sighed in relief. He faintly woke up and they both helped each other over to the police, who had just began to investigate the woods—a few helped to escort them inside the ambulance that arrived on time. At the hospital, Jess seemed to be the only one hospitalized. Jaiden, who only had a minor concussion, visited her room. "You saved my life... again."

"I told you not to go. I knew something like this would happen," he says facing the door, staring out the hallway.

"He's done it before... hasn't he?"

"It was freshman year, my first college party with Jared. I met this girl, who I would end up scoring with by the end of the night. Although, it wasn't just me she was interested in. She had her eyes set on a much older target. Lucky for her, he was interested. I didn't realize that she was interested in him. I only found out when I went looking for her after we—" He dropped his head, still avoiding eye contact.

"There she was, in the room with Griffins. I saw the pained expression on her face, he told me to 'get the fuck out'. I didn't know what to do; her eyes looked as if she begged me for help, but she couldn't find the words because of his grip on her neck. So—I left the room like I was told. I still had my suspicions on him since that night, no doubt. I've also began paying close attention to the strange noises I heard coming from his room every single night that I had attended. The girls that he was with—most of them in high school, never the same again. It's as if they were stripped of their dignity and they never spoke again, at least not in the way they used to. That was enough for me to accuse him of rape because no one else would. I wish I had done something earlier in time, but when I heard that he was with you, I lost it. I knew it was a matter of time before he would strike again, with you and I'm glad I found you in time. God knows If I hadn't—" He soaked up his tears.

"…I can't believe I just let it happen."

"You didn't know what was happening."

"Maybe if I had just confronted him,"

"He would've denied it."

"…Jaiden, it's okay. It's over. You don't have to be afraid anymore. He's gone."

"I'm not afraid dammit!" he shouts, kicking over machine equipment from the distance. "Jared has bullies, I-I have enemies!"

"Jess! Oh my God, are you okay!" panicked Amanda who sprang into the room.

"I'm fine."

"Amanda, do you think I can have a moment alone with Jaiden?" she asked after wrapping up their conversation on a short note while Jaiden continuously stared at the blank wall, with his head against it. Amanda respectfully nods and waits outside of the room. Jaiden drops his head and returns to her bedside. "Are you okay?"

"I will be."

"Good. Because he doesn't have to hurt again and thanks to you he never will," she addressed, grazing his arm in assurance.

****

Sitting alone in his bedroom for what feels like decades with nothing to do besides homework, is how Jared mourns the loss of his friends. It's mainly depression that kept him avoiding human contact. His mom checked on him regularly every now and then. He understood that he was now labeled as the boy who watched three of his friends deprive him of a fair goodbye. It seemed he had served no purpose in life but to watch the people he loved, get taken away from him. So, he came home straight from school and off to his bedroom to continue with his studies and that was all. When he was all alone, it got him thinking:

Lucas has passed—the closest friend he had after Robbie. He was a great soul, kept him company when Jaiden would run off to be with Jessica. Robbie dies about a month later, and he was almost as close as Lucas and he were but of course, he has known Robbie longer. They were close at a point until he made some life threatening choices. Not

230

only that, but he betrayed poor Jared and used him. He took advantage of him and left him like chopped liver in a heartbeat once he found a place in popularity. With time, Jared has learned to trust many people and every time he did, something seemed to betray that trust. His faith in people was weak. In fact, he didn't think he could ever care for someone again after all the pain caused in the outcome of caring at an extent. The one girl Jared has repeatedly loved his whole life, has completely turned her back on him after one stupid incident which he should not be at fault for since he had no memory of how it happened.

When he finally pushed those feelings aside, as soon as Megan came into the picture, she ended up betraying him too—then once again, Jared fell into heartbreak. He was tired of repeating history, he felt so vulnerable that he even kissed Jessica—although, he did enjoy it for the most part to say the least. In all honesty, he would give anything to take back that night and just hold her in his arms again. *God and the worst part*—was that he was finally starting to accept the idea of this creature coming into this world. That he would get to cherish its arrival and love it and maybe even become a family one day with the girl he loved—but all that was over now so he knew he needed to move on. It broke his heart in that delivery room to be the last to know that the baby didn't make it—Jessica and he were over, but he felt as if a part of him died too when he received the news. He wished he could've held Jessica's hand in moral support—to tell her it's going to be okay, if she hadn't sent him packing. It pained him to see her so upset, he just wanted to be there for her, but he couldn't, he wasn't allowed. When he realized it was too late to tell her all of this, he expressed his anger by stating the opposite, he didn't know what came over him that school day. In hopes of trying to forget her, he yelled at her, thinking he was finally at his best and she would only try to destroy that—his 'happiness'. Robbie's words hit him hard, he nearly memorized every single line in the letter by heart while reciting it back to himself every single day—studying his print without blinking. He did believe there is a future for himself, only if it involved Jessica. But if not, it is something he must learn to live without. He knew he would always find someone regardless—but this coming from someone who will never compare to her, the woman who's always going to be in second place for Jared.

****

"Jessica, I know you've been feeling a little under the weather lately, but do you think you can come swing by the parking garage? I have a surprise for you!" Mandy exclaims into the phone.

"You call getting stabbed in the gut as 'feeling under the weather'?" Jessica sarcastically inquired, lifting the covers from her body and getting out of bed.

"Please just come outside!"

"How about you just bring it in here?" Jessica groans when exiting her bedroom.

"That won't fit, silly!"

"Now you get your cute little behind down here and don't make me walk all the way upstairs and drag you out myself, you don't want to mess with a pregnant lady and you should know," Amanda warned just before Jessica heard a chuckle coming from the background.

"What is Jaiden doing with you?"

"You'll see."

"No," she pouted.

"I'm not in the mood to see anyone, I look terrible. Please go away!" she continuously whined.

"Oh my God, Jessica, get over here right now or I swear—"

"Fine," she grumbled. "Just give me a couple of minutes?"

"See you soon!" she grins before ending the call. "What did you guys—" Her eyes widen at the sight as soon as she enters the lot. "You didn't!" Jessica marveled.

"Wanna test it out?" Mandy asks, jingling the keys before displacing it in her sister's hands.

"For me?"

"Uh huh!" Amanda exhilarated.

"Oh my God, thank you!" Jess shrieked, hugging her sister.

"Woah, be careful!" Mandy reminds.

"Hey, don't forget to give me a hug!" Jaiden approached with a smile, "It was my idea to get you a car... I picked it out," he bragged wrapping his arms around her.

"You're so incredible, thank you guys," says Jess when pulling away from her hug with Jaiden.

"So, where do you want to go?" he asks clapping his hands together.

"Hey, do you mind giving me my rental back? And don't worry, we've already registered this bad boy, but I'm gonna let you two go have some fun while I rest up a bit."

"Yeah sure, hold on, I'll get it. Be right back," informs Jess, kissing Jaiden's cheek before beginning to limp back over to her flat like a tortoise.

"Wait a second, I'll grab it for you," Jaiden insisted when speeding past the disabled Jessica and snatching her apartment key on the way.

The hare returned with Amanda's rightful car keys, handing it off to her before she pardoned off to her car in the distance.

"I'll see you two next Thursday for dinner!" Amanda shouted from her car.

"Dinner?" asked Jess just after Amanda backed out of the garage.

"Yeah, we had a little agreement—don't worry about it. Let's take a spin, yeah?" he says slapping the car's rear before hopping in the passenger seat. They drive around the city a bit until Jaiden hatches up an idea.

"Hey, I have an idea?"

"Yeah?"

"Tomorrow is senior ditch day, how about we take a little detour?"

"Who did you have in mind?" she asked when pulling into a drive-thru.

"Us, the gang, and maybe we'll even invite Jared."

"That's it?"

"Yeah—unless you want to bring someone else along?" he chuckles.

"I thought maybe you'd want to invite some of your guy friends—the college ones,"

"Too soon?" she asks dropping her smile.

"No, no, it's alright. I'm just glad to see you smiling again," he admits with a grin.

"We could invite Chris as well."

"No, Jared doesn't like him."

"Yeah, I'm sure 'Jared' has a problem with him," she chuckled.

"The whole 'Megan' thing," he shrugged.

"Hi, welcome to McDonalds! What can I get you?"

"Hi, can I get a Big Mac and for the lady, perhaps a salad?" Jaiden teases causing Jess to punch him in the arm.

"I'm sorry, he loves reciting lines from movies, obviously lacking originality. Anyways, one Big Mac and I'll take a grilled chicken sandwich."

"Would that be all?"

"Yes."

"Alright your total is $10.38 at the next window please."

"Here is your change," the employee says when handing the couple back their change and order.

"Fuck yeah. I'm starving," Jaiden moans reaching in the bag.

"Give me a fry," Jess asks while taking a sip of his cola after backing out of the drive thru.

"Jessica, as your trainer, I don't think you should be eating this kind of stuff."

"Are you calling me fat!" she gasps, coming to a sharp halt on the road.

"No, Jesus! Keep your eyes on the road!"

She pulled over in a resting area and shoved her hand in the brown paper bag to reach for a fry. "Jessica," he chuckled, trying to fight her hand with his.

"Jaiden! I want a fry!" she whined.

"Mmmmm, just like the first time you seduced me—still reaching a hand for that forbidden fruit, aren't we?" he teased while watching her narrow her spiteful eyes at him. "Fine," he says pulling a fry out. He lowers it into her mouth like a crane and just as it reaches the rim of her mouth, he retrieves his hand away. Triggered, Jess tugged his hand back to her reach as he deliberately allowed the fry to fall onto the seat causing her to purposely bite his finger instead. As soon as he let his guard down to apply pressure on his bit finger, she reclaimed the bag to grab a handful of fries before shoving them all into her tainted mouth.

"HAH!" she shouted while all the fries fall from her gaping mouth.

"You're a dork," he says coming to a verdict as they both laugh.

"So how is it that you eat junk food every now and then as you say," she air-quotes, "And still look like that?" she asked after they entered her apartment.

"Like what?" he smirks.

"Like this," she asked lifting his shirt up.

"I work out, you should try it sometime," he suggestively teased and she gasped again. She clung to his back in an attempt to tackle him but fails, falling back down on the floor instead.

"You ass! That is the third time you've insulted me today!" she melodramatically gushed, punching him in the chest while he closed her fists with his hands in her attempt to fight him.

"What are you going to do about it?" he torments while guiding her backwards towards the couch. She takes control by crawling on top of his lap, wrapping her arms around his neck while he places his hands steadily on her hips.

"This…" she softly whispers, pushing her lips past his, he picks her up to lay her on the couch.

"Does my baby girl need her daddy?" he whispers in her ear.

"Please don't," she asks causing him to pull away. She takes a minute to come to herself before she allows him to continue. He flips her over now and gently takes off her shirt before he traces over her stitched abdomen.

"Does it hurt?" he asks, staring up at her while she stares down at his hands.

She nods her head before joining hands with his, "It feels a lot better now that you're here," she confessed, guiding his hand to her chest. "This too," she admits staring into the depths of his eyes.

He sat up and moved his lips behind her ear, "I love you," he whispered. She was taken aback from the words that left his mouth—it wasn't her first time hearing it, but it did feel different. He suddenly stopped and sat up. "What's wrong?" he sighs.

"N-nothing, why'd you stop?" she concerns, sitting up as well.

"You didn't say it."

"Oh yeah, I-I'm sorry, I guess I was just caught up in the moment."

"Well?" he asks after waiting for her to continue.

"I—"

"No, it's alright. I have to be somewhere anyways," he says when checking his phone from his pocket. "I will see you tomorrow I guess," he says purposely dodging her lips to kiss her cheek instead. He throws his shirt back on and quickly fled her apartment without another word.

****

Chapter Fourteen

"Come on, please!" Jessica pleads through the phone. "Jessica, I'm really not in the best condition to be traveling," Jared sighed, running his fingers through his hair while sitting with his back against his bed-frame. "And I am?" scoffed Jessica. "I mean... I'm supposed to be sulking."

"Hey. You weren't the only one that lost him."

"You can't keep beating yourself up over this, he would've wanted you to move on."

"How are you recovering?" he asked breaking the awkward silence after being unsure of what to say next.

"I'm getting there, slowly but surely. Still a little on edge but at least my wound is healing if not me."

"I can't believe he would do that! I wish I had been there."

"Yeah well I'm glad you weren't. We barely made it out alive, Jaiden and I."

"Why don't I hear packing yet?" Jessica worries after the line stayed silent again.

"Because I haven't moved a muscle since you called."

"Well, I didn't know I was such a distraction," she teased.

"For the record, I still haven't changed my mind."

"So, you want to do this the hard way huh?" she grumbled. "I'm coming over, stay put!" she urged. Seven minutes later and she was now standing in front of the Daniels' house, impatiently banging on the door.

"Hey, what are you doing here?" Jaiden asked opening the front door.

"Where is Jared?" she inquired pushing past him.

"In his room... shouldn't you be packing?" he asked following speedily behind her as she marched up the stairs.

"Jared, open this door!" she pounded at his door until she heard shuffling coming from inside the room. She backed away after he unlocked it. He rubbed his eyelids, opening his door just slightly for her to enter.

She strides straight past him, "God, you need some sunlight," she examines, pulling his blinds open. "Okay, now, where were we?" she asked while looking around. "This will do," she says eyeing his backpack by his desk before picking it up.

"What are you doing?" he asked while she dumped out his binder and books onto his neat bed. "No stop!" he begs, rushing over to tug his backpack from her grip. "Jared, you're going!" she demands, snatching it back.

"We can do this the easy way or the hard way, either way, you're going to get your sorry behind out of this room and do something for a change."

"Funny, that's what mother told me this morning," he says with clear sarcasm.

"Do you want to pack or should I?" asks Jess who narrows her eyes.

"Okay, fine fuck. I'll do it," he says rightfully repossessing his backpack again.

"Good choice," she concluded smirking proudly to herself with her hands on her hips. "What?" she asked after he stopped to exchange glances with her.

"Well, I kind of need to change," he mentions. Jess rakes her eyes on his body—he was in a white tank, boxers, and knee-high socks. She apologized after noticing the unshaven five o-clock shadow on his face before shuffling to get out, shamefully. When she exited the room and closed the door on her way out, she met up with a cranky Jaiden who crept up on her in the hallway.

"What's going on?" he asks.

"Just helping Jared pack." After those words left her mouth, Jaiden melodramatically rolled his eyes before heading down the stairs, purposely nudging Jess on his way down. "Excuse me!" she scoffed, running downstairs, following behind until she finds him in the kitchen where he was now raiding his pantry. "Do you have a problem?" she asked, folding her arms out in front.

Jaiden turned around from the opposite side of the counter in his walk, "Me? No, but I think you might."

She throws her hands on her hips, "What?" she asks.

"Don't think I forgot about the other night—"

"Jaiden! You have to understand, 'it' isn't easy for me anymore. I think it's only fair if I take some time to recover after everything if you don't mind!"

"Well I 'do' mind!"

"And it isn't even about that!" he shook his head profusely in denial. "My concern is why all of a sudden you're close with Jared again! More specifically—at around the same time my 'girlfriend' can't even say she loves me anymore!" he emphasized with great fire. "What is going on

Jessica? You're not acting the same. You don't still have feelings for him, do you? 'Because I thought we were past this'," he scolded; although it was more of accusation than an inquiry.

"So did I," she spoke, folding her arms. "Where is all this insecurity coming from, Jaiden?"

"Insecure?" he chuckled, shaking his head in disbelief. He cringed at her poor choice of words, completely thrown off, "You think 'I'm' insecure?" he scoffed apprehensively throwing his head back before continuing with, "Do I look like someone who should be insecure?" his ego manifests.

"You're sure as hell acting like it!" she squinted at ease, leaning forward.

He rubbed a hand over his mouth after dropping his smile, taking a step forward in hopes of scaring the answer out of her, "Answer the question, last time," he warned.

"And if I don't?" she prevailed, stepping closer.

"You best not to fuck with me when I'm angry like this Jessica. Not now, not ever. Do you understand?" he growled stepping closer, "You don't know half of the things I'm capable of doing in this state of mind—"

"Fine. You really want to know?" she heightened her voice of skepticism. He came to a halt, waiting for her to continue. "It's over, Jaiden."

"And I'm not just talking about Jared and me," she sighed, displacing the ring she pulled effortlessly off her finger smack down on the counter.

"Jess—" He dropped his face, refusing to run out after she had fled the house. The heartbroken, confused, and bitter Jessica tagged along for the trip to Disneyland in favor to those of her friends that have not broken her heart. Also, because she couldn't refuse if she wanted to since the friends had already reserved her a room and paid it off in advance. The friends decided to travel in two separate cars: Skylar's jeep and Star's Toyota Camry. Jared, Jaiden, and Jess were all crammed in Skylar's backseat and Hobbs, Jasmine, and Chris were all riding with Star. Unfortunately for Jess, being crammed in the backseat with two people she was hoping to avoid for the rest of the trip, or her life, was not her ideal picnic basket. And for a twelve-hour drive to L.A., it was torturous. The friends agreed that the first exhibition they wanted to explore was Disneyland since neither of the friends have ever experienced it. It was senior ditch day which fell on a Friday, so they had the entire weekend to engage in the comfort of the Golden State. "Dude, can you open the window, it's fucking hot in here man!" requested Jaiden who was fanning himself.

"Yeah man sorry, is it locked?" Skylar asks.

"No dip."

"How long have we been driving?" Becca asks.

"Twenty minutes," Skylar informed while the rest of the passengers groaned. Within an hour, Jessica felt herself drifting off to sleep and in the corners of his eyes, Jaiden saw Jessica slowly fading over to Jared while he awkwardly turned to his brother for assistance. Jared had no idea that the two had broken up in the past hour. Jaiden sighed when grabbing onto Jessica's body, shifting her weight onto his shoulder. She lightly groaned yet still completely unfazed by the motion, while Jaiden then sneaked a kiss on her forehead. When Jared took his eyes off the two, Jaiden sneakily pulled the ring she returned to him from his shirt pocket and placed it gently back over her ring finger. He then took her hand in his and grazed his thumb over her band without her waking up before looking to Jared to await his reaction. Jared, who glued his attention back over to that couple, followed Jaiden's eyes that led him to see his hand playing with Jessica's and his finger that caressed her ring finger.

Fucking loser, he has no chance, Jaiden thought, silently smirking to himself while Jessica hugged his body tighter, submissive by the actions of her unconscious.

"Guys, we're here!" Skylar alarms, waking all his friends up. Jaiden silently woke Jessica up, who noticed she had been sleeping with the enemy, or rather on, on the brink of waking up before she stubbornly recoiled away from his embrace. When she had rubbed a hand over her tired face, Jaiden remembered that he had put the ring back onto her finger and luckily for him, she hadn't even realized it. They enter the hotel lobby after minutes of waiting outside for Star's car to arrive, each of them grabbing onto their own carry on.

"Names please?" the blonde concierge asked, catching Jaiden's eye after they entered the hotel building.

"Yeah sorry, I made the reservation," Skylar informs, carrying Becca's luggage in the doorway while the friends step aside to let him check in for them. He tosses the bag from around his neck aside after making it to the reception desk.

"God damn Becca, ever heard of traveling light?" Jaiden chuckled.

"These are all Skylar's bags," she snidely remarked. The receptionist handed off their room keys to Skylar and the friends prepare to head off to the elevators. Jaiden, being the tail of the group, whips his head back around to the cute clerk, who bit down on her lip, blushing.

"So where am I rooming?" Jessica asks causing the friends to pause and stare.

"Jess uh… I thought you would be rooming with Jaiden?"

"Where on earth did you get that idea?"

She snapped her head to find Jaiden, who awaited her with a satisfactory grin plastered on his already smug face. It was speculated that the friends would determine which room everyone would settle down in upon arrival and it was evidently clear why Jessica would be upset at the situation present. "In case you haven't heard, Jaiden and I are—what is this!" she appalled in a fit of rage upon noticing the pretentious ring back on her finger. "You miserable fluke! How 'dare' you put this back on me when I'm mad at you!" she roared, pulling the ring off her finger with all her might before throwing it down the hallway.

"I'll take that room key now," Jaiden hinted. Skylar struggled to hand him his designated room key while Jess continued to hound the young man. "Alright, you're coming with me," he shrugged, throwing her over his shoulder in an attempt to shut her up.

"Jaiden, put me down right now!"

"Women," he chuckled, pardoning himself on her behalf. "Julio, take our bags!" he condemned Jared. He threw his bag over his shoulder before aiming straight at Jared's chest. Jared struggled to follow behind the two, picking up the ring on his way after Jaiden managed to blindly walk directly past it. The rest of the group disperses to find their assigned rooms. While Jess and Jai set off in one room, Skylar and Becca were in another, Star and Jasmine in one, leaving Chris to a room by himself.

"Ah, here we go—246B," Jaiden smirks, opening the door.

"It smells so nice in here," Jessica marvels after stepping inside with Jaiden following closely behind to switch on the light.

"And we got it all to ourselves," he says stepping closer. His mouth almost drops at the sight he stumbled into. "What the hell?" He scratched his head. "Two beds!" he yelled.

"I don't see a problem," Jess smirks, sprawling out on one of the beds. Jaiden soon bolts out of the room like lightning. He ran out to the hallway, just in time to find Skylar struggling to lug Becca's heavy travel pack across the hallway.

"So, you're the only one that's allowed to get laid on this trip?" He folds his arms, staring the shorter boy down now by at least half a head, blocking his path.

"I think that's something you should take up with Jess," Skylar chuckled, moving past him.

"No, dip shit—I'm talking about the fact that you gave us two fucking beds, what gives!"

"I've gotta go get this luggage to Becca. Talk to customer service," he says proceeding down the hallway—but not long before Jaiden effortlessly backed him up against the wall. In doing so, Skylar prominently drops all his luggage under Jaiden's deadly clasp, leaving the impotent Skylar on his tiptoes.

"If you recall, we were the ones who set this trip up and invited you," Jaiden growled ill-tempered with the back of his arm against the boy's neck.

"Y-yeah and I made the r-reservations," he hoarsely let out, powerless against Jaiden's grip on his vocal cords, turning blue with every second that he was losing air.

"Fuck, you're useless," Jaiden sighed, releasing Skylar from the depths of his clutches before running back down the lobby. He rushes down the lobby to the clerk and rings the bell.

"Yes, may I help y—"

"Oh, hello?" The clerk smiles when recognizing the attractive male standing before her from earlier on, who was evidently younger than her.

"I-I need I-" he choked on his words, getting distracted by her timeless beauty.

"Jaiden?" he heard a voice appear from behind, offsetting the guilty Jaiden when he startled and found Jared standing behind. "Yeah, what's up?"

"What are you doing back here?"

"I…" he concentrates, "Not sure."

"So sorry for the inconvenience sir. I will call up management and tell them to give you a different room," the clerk informs before answering the phone. Once again, the boy was saved.

"What happened?" Jared asked.

"They gave us a room with two beds," Jaiden explained.

"Oh… well they gave me and Hobbs one bed."

"Well I guess that fixes our problem," announced Jaiden with an awkward chuckle. Jaiden grabs the keys and throws him his.

Before Jaiden springs away to save himself from further interrogation, Jared swiftly places a hand on his shoulder, "Is everything okay?"

"…With you and Jessica?"

"Nothing that concerns you anymore, alright?" he says eyeing his little brother down. And with that, he began to speed off.

"Aren't you forgetting something?" Jared asked, causing Jaiden to throw his head back again. Jared walks up and shoves Jaiden's luggage back against his chest, "Carry your own shit, 'fucker'." Jaiden felt a cold wind rush over him. His words hit him like whiplash; He had never heard his brother use such derogative terms before in his life. He was finally starting to see this boy as a threat and not someone who he could just walk all over his entire life like everyone else seemed to be doing. After being exonerated from their dry yet sustainable conversation, he returns to his lonesome female friend who stands outside of their designated room.

"There you are."

"Change of plans, I got us a new room, one bed," he says before anxiously dragging her down into a different hallway—still on the same floor.

"Fine, but you'll be sleeping on the floor," she giggles. After reaching the door, he unlocked it and stepped inside. He dropped the suitcases and pulled her obstinate self, inside with him, shutting on the light, and kicking the door closed. She ran over to the blinds, opening them as a mass of sunshine, beams through their window. They had a clear view of the massive park right from their room. "Woah, this view is beautiful!" Jaiden soon comes up and shuts the window with the blinds before she turns around to furrow her brows at him. He lifts her up by her legs, throwing her over his shoulders to lay her back down on the bed. He throws his shirt on the floor, pinning up her arms against the mattress while bringing his lips to hers.

"I don't want people staring at us for what I'm about to do," he rasped into her ear.

"Take off your dress," he whispers after coming contact with her thick thighs. She couldn't resist his seduction, it was a trap that she had no control over. She had no self-control anymore—too deep into his wordplay, paralyzed under his touch.

****

"Good thing you traded in the room, huh?" Hobbs chuckles, rolling his luggage near his bed, while Jared sets his backpack over his own bed.

"I'm exhausted," he exhaled before belly flopping onto the bed.

"So, what do you want to do?" Zach continuously asks. "Rent some porn, check out some strip clubs, get some bitches perhaps?" he then implied, wiggling his eyebrows.

"Sounds like an intriguing offer, but I think I'm just going to relax," Jared sighs.

"Alright, but I'm taking you somewhere tonight," he insists while Jared adjusts himself down in his bed, directly staring up at the miscellaneous ceiling.

"What are you guys up to?" exclaims Star when entering from a door that both Jared and Hobbs assumed was to the bathroom.

"Shit, where did you guys come from!" antagonized Hobbs, who shuffled out of his sheets while Jasmine came in behind Star.

"What are you guys up to?" asked Star, who beamed onto Jared's bed with all thirty-two of her teeth.

"About to discard our tissues," Hobbs sarcastically implied, switching off the television causing Jasmine to laugh while Star slowly made her way off the bed in disgust.

"Just kidding, that's for later," he winks. "You guys wanna have some fun?"

"You guys called?" asked Chris when hopping into Hobbs and Jared's shared room, shortly after Star had popped the question.

"Jaiden and Jessica weren't responding to our knocks," Becca informed, too entering the room followed by Skylar, who closes the door after himself.

"Alright, what are we playing?" Chris asks, anxiously rubbing his hands together while joining the small circle the friends have made in the room on the floor. "Strip... poker."

"Alright guys, I'm out," Jared announced, shooting up from his seat before walking back over to his bed.

"Come on Jare, live a little!" Skylar persisted, "Don't be so anal!"

"I came on this trip to recover and that's exactly what I'm going to do!" he vindicated before crawling stubbornly under his covers, fully clothed.

"Fine, but you're always welcome to stare," Skylar chuckles. After twenty anxious minutes of tossing and turning, Jared decided to sit up to see how the progress of the game was going to determine when it would be safe to best return to sleep. When he saw his friends wearing their absolute bare minimum while playing the game, he knew it would be over soon enough for him to rest peacefully.

"Have a change of heart? You're more than welcome to join," says Star, who first notices the groggy, sleep deprived teenager in the distance.

"No way are we starting over when I am this close to winning," anticipated Skylar, scooting forward with his nose nuzzled in the cards displayed out in front of him.

"There are no winners in this game Sky. Only losers... which in about five minutes, will be Star, when she reintroduces herself to my co—"

"I never agreed to anything Christian!"

"I can't believe I've agreed to do this," Star grumbled when standing up after losing. She took Chris' hand and guided him in the entrance to her room through the boys' room.

"Hey, I can't help it if you always lose at this game." They returned out of the room ten minutes later with Chris having the smuggest look upheld on his face indicating to his friends that his reward was indeed a pleasant success.

****

Tuesday morning, the gang set out on a drive to Disneyland, which was about eight miles away from the resort they were staying at. When they arrive at the entrance after receiving a wristband, they head off and scatter the park. They came to the agreement not to make it a group thing so while Hobbs, Jasmine, Skylar, and Becca started their adventure on one side of the park, the rest of the group explored another. "Where do you guys want to go first?" asks Chris, staring down at his map.

"California Screaming, who's up?" Jaiden smirks, pointing out to the massive roller coaster ride in front of them.

"No, that's too scary," Jessica whines.

"Would you prefer to ride something a little more exhilarating?" he implied when nibbling on her ear. Jessica repulsed at his impulsive request when she shrugged his body away.

"Let's just go before I change my mind again," she agreed taking his hand.

"Y-you guys have fun… I-I'll just stay back here." Jared gulps, just staring at the height of the roller coaster while it dropped into motion.

"You sure?" Star asks as her and Chris stop to consult him.

"Yeah, I'm not a big fan of roller coasters… or heights for that matter," he admits.

"Aw, well I'm sorry," she says.

"You guys go, I'll be waiting here when you get back," he reassuringly stated, nodding off in approval.

"Phew, you guys walk fast!" Star hyped when she and Chris caught up behind their friends in the line.

"W-where's Jared?" Jessica panicked with her maternal instincts kicking in.

"He stayed back, he didn't want to go," Star informed. Jessica ran her hand through her silky dark hair in frustration.

"Next up!" the employee announced.

"Come on," Jaiden directed, entering the roller coaster—awaiting his girl to join him in the seat beside after locking the safety bar over his head.

"Not now, sorry. I have to go look for Jared!" Jessica apologized before pushing past her friends in search for Jared. She ran out of the line to where the gang was originally standing at before entering the ride. "Jared? Jared!" She shifted her weight onto the tips of her toes to look over the crowd, but it was no luck. Delayed, she placed a hand on her sweated, furrowed brows, rubbing over them in concentration. She turned her body before returning her face only to bump into someone, Jared.

"Oh, thank God!" she hugged him in relief.

"I thought you were going on the ride?" he asked.

"Come on," she insisted, tugging his arm.

"What? No," he recoiled.

"I've already told Star and Chris, I'll be fine here, you go on… p-please I'm very scared of heights; i-it's why I never climbed up Josh's tree with you and Jaiden. Guess I've missed out on a lot, huh?" He nervously chuckled while scratching his forehead.

"I'm just as scared as you are. Roller coasters don't even come close to trees."

"This is my first ride too… but I'm willing to try if you are?"

"I'm not like you Jess, I could never have the courage to face my fears."

"You're just going to have to trust me on this, please?"

"Besides, you kind of owe me one anyways. I waited in that line for so long and I have gone out of my way looking for you," she encouraged. "What do you say?" she asked, extending her hand out for him to grab ahold of before they agreed to return to the line together.

"Jess, where the hell did you go?" they heard a voice call out after they finally reached the front of the line. They direct their attention to Jaiden who snuck in from behind.

"I had to go find Jared, he was lost," she explained.

"He's not a dog and you aren't his mother. He's a grown ass kid that can take care of himself," Jaiden agitatedly answered, standing boldly.

She sighed, "I'm not having this conversation with you again." She redirected her attention just as she was the next in line again. She entered the ride with Jared, abandoning Jaiden, who disappointingly walked off after she had ignored his presence.

"You okay?" asked Jared who scrutinized her devastation as she watched Jaiden subdue his ego in the distance.

"Yeah, I'm fine," she assured.

"You ready?" Jared asked after all the passengers were loaded onto the ride. She gulped before nodding in slow, uneven head movements. He rests his hands on the safety bar as she then placed her hand on top of his after noticing his fingers begin to jitter with anxiety. It was as if all the muscles in his body released tension as soon as her hand intertwined with his—and all his worries flooded away when she gave him that heartfelt smile that left him all warm and tingly inside. The attraction wasn't as dangerous as Jessica thought it would be, thrilling yes, but not as treacherous as her relationship with Jaiden had been composed of. 'Ironically', that statement had not failed in comparison to Jessica's emotional response with Jared compared to Jaiden. That ride was beyond exotic and sensational, that Jared and Jess found themselves coming back to that ride at least three more times before they headed off to locate the rest of their friends. When they failed to realize that neither of them had their phones on them, they decided to scrap that idea and venture off to do their own thing instead… as 'friends'.

"What do you want to do next?" he chimes.

"Ummmm, how about we… ooooo tea cups!" Jess excites when coming across the attraction. They stood in the line filled with joyous little faces, they might as well have been the only two adults in line, but Jess would never deny she was still a child at heart too.

"Here you go ma'am," an employee from behind bearing a box of tiaras says, placing a tiara over her naked head.

"Oh, I'm sorry—I-I don't have any money," she admitted reaching for her head.

"No, it's alright. Today, everyone should feel like a princess. Courtesy of Disneyland productions," the kind gentleman says causing the girl to whip out her best smile in gratuity.

"Excuse me, miss?" a small voice coming from a little girl behind the two directs.

"Yes?"

"Can I get a picture with you?" she shyly asked, holding up a phone.

"I'm sorry," the mother pardoned when running up behind. "She saw the crown and she told me you reminded her of her favorite princess."

"Oh, and who might that be?" Jess smiled, kneeling down in front of the little girl as she hid behind her mom.

"Come on sweetie, these kind folks want to get on the ride and you're holding up the line," the mother says.

"Cinderella!" she giggles.

"That's my favorite princess too! I'd be happy to take a picture with you!" she grinned as her mom took the phone, capturing the picture of the two girls. The girl then ran back to her mother.

"What do we say?" the mother asked too kneeling beside her.

"Thank you!" the little girl twinkled while giving Jess, who crouched down again, a hug. In the midst of her company, Jess couldn't help but run her hand down this girl's full head of dark brown hair, cherishing the girl in her embrace.

"And now you can be a princess too," Jess grins after pulling away to crown the little girl with her tiara while the girl then requests for her ear, "I think your prince is really cute," she giggled. Jess follows her eyes to meet the clumsy Jared, who was shaking the hair away from his face.

"I think so too," Jess sheepishly admitted when curling up to the little bundle of joy before she ran back to her mommy.

"What was that about?" Jared inquired when Jess stood back up at his side.

"Nothing," she smirked, watching the whimsical child teeter off in the distance.

****

"I can't believe you smoked that reporter!" Jared emphasized graciously with his head down on their walk back to their hotel room after being dropped off by an Uber.

"She was following us, I had to do something to get her off my chest and it's not like you would do it—you would never put your hands on a woman and I respect that about you," Jess gleamed.

"Unfortunately, I can't speak the same for a lot of men," she sighed.

"Still, I think we need to get you to a doctor to have that hand checked," he worried, eyeing her swollen hand as she held onto it.

"Please, I can't run to the doctor every time I get injured. You of all people should know at the rate I'm attending, they would have me in a straitjacket just so I wouldn't be a danger to myself anymore," she argued most civilized.

"Before I forget... I think this belongs to you," he says, stopping in front of her hotel room to pull a shiny object out of his pocket. It was her ring that she purposely tried to avoid. It wasn't right that she kept abandoning such a valuable gift, but it felt of no value to her if it wasn't real— *was it real?*

"I have a thief on my hands. Red handed again, aren't we?" she teases, attempting to grab it.

"Here, allow me." He helps by placing it on her finger.

"Not my ideal 'fairytale' moment, but I'll take it... if the shoe fits," she shrugged, feeling every bit of guilty just staring down at her ring.

****

"Come cuddle," says Jaiden, patting down next to him on their huge shared bed. She continuously abides to ignore him and enters the bathroom to change into her PJs.

"Is something wrong?" he asks, entering while she was now brushing her teeth. She spat out the foaming paste and rinsed off her mouth—dabbing a hand towel on her face before exiting the bathroom, tying her hair back in the process. She decided to sleep on the far right, pulling back the blanket covers to get settled inside, facing toward the window and far away from Jaiden. "Hello? Jessica?" he pestered, sitting on what is originally her side of the bed.

"What's your problem?" he asks.

Are you kidding me? The nerve of this kid!

"My problem?" she raised her voice, sitting up now.

"You know what, forget it… goodnight," she dismissed, rolling her eyes—slumping back under the covers.

"I'm tired of this. Why can't we just say what we're feeling? Why is it that I have to guess what you're feeling? Why can't you just say what's inside your damn mind—"

"Because, I'm tired of explaining Jaiden. I talk all the time, but you don't listen—what's the point to talk about anything anymore when you're just going to do it again."

"Do 'what' again?"

"You don't trust me Jaiden—how many times do I have to tell you that you're the only one that I want before you can finally let go of this stupid grudge you have over Jared?" she asked, sitting up again now.

"You always let him come between us."

"He wouldn't have to if you'd just listen to me!"

"I'm listening now—"

"But it's only a matter of time before you hurt me again!"

"I'm sorry," he whispers, leeching onto her neck, but she refused to let him have the advantage, sliding the covers up her face. "Let me make it up to you," he insists, grazing her thigh.

"I can't do this," she exhaled while crawling out of bed. She grabbed her pillow and made her way out the door. "Where are you going?"

"I'm leaving—you're tempted, I'm tempted, and I won't sit here and be taken advantage of. I am 'not' a piece of meat!" And with that, she was out of the room. She didn't know what she was doing or thinking, wandering in the hallways half-dressed. She didn't know where to hide so she decided to go to Jasmine and Star's room. "Come on, answer…

248

please," she knocked impatiently. She knocked a few more times before realizing they must have been out. *Just my luck.*

"Jessica?" she heard the door unravel; it was Jared with his hair a mess in the next room over.

"Oh, hello…" she stood awkwardly.

"Are you okay?" he worried.

"Yeah, no I just um—" she let out a deep breath just before staring up at the hallway ceiling, about to lose her cool. She was emotionally unstable and highly susceptible to vulnerability from the trauma of recent events, piling onto her stress with Jaiden… and Jared.

"Hey, no. Come on," he says leading her inside with his arm wrapped around. He turns on the lights. It seemed he was just about to head off to sleep.

"Where's Hobbs?" she asked.

"Him and the rest of the guys and girls went out, I decided to stay back—but I thought you and Jaiden went as well?" he asks as they both sit down on his bed.

"No, we didn't hear anything," she shrugged while rubbing under her eyes before she stared down at her quivering hands.

"What's wrong?" he asks. "Well… Jaiden and I are not in the best of terms right now," she admits, deciding against lying since that only caused her more underlying stress.

"Oh," he sighs.

"Do you need a place to sleep?"

"How'd you figure?" she lightly chuckled, fidgeting with her hands.

"I was going to go see if I can room with Star and Jasmine for the night, but it seems like they've gone AWOL—"

"You can sleep here for the night."

"No, I couldn't. It would just add onto Jaiden's suspicion besides, Hobbs should be arriving soon."

"There's nothing going on between us—unless, you think there is?" he cocks a brow.

"No. Of course not," she assured, crinkling her face in misdemeanor.

"We have an extra mattress, you can sleep on the bed… no worries," he suggests, putting his arms out before she tosses him her pillow so that he may set it on his bed before taking his pillow and throwing it to the floor.

****

"Just don't make this a habit, okay?" he chuckled, fluffing her pillow at the head of her bed.

249

"What do you mean?"

"Well, you and I both know Jaiden can be a little vain at times."

"That's a little personal—don't you think?"

"Nothing is ever private with twins—as hard as you may try to hide it, evil never fails to rear its ugly head," he chuckled.

"Okay Jared, I think you've been on one too many rides today," she inhibited.

"Hey, I'm still sane. It's you I'm worried about—all I'm saying, is just be careful around Jaiden," he forewarned. Jessica scoffed, dropping the other pillow on the bed.

"I've never needed you to tell me what to do, especially when it comes to Jaiden, I think I can handle myself. I mean, I have gotten to know him on a more personal level compared to you." She folds her arms.

"Ouch."

"I'm sorry, that's not what I meant. I mean—"

"Yeah, I know." He dropped his head.

"You aren't going to drop this, are you? There's always going to be a problem with Jaiden and I being together, isn't there?" she asked, sitting at the foot of the bed.

"Depends. You still don't believe me about the whole Courtney situation, do you?" he asked when looking over his shoulder before bending over to retrieve the covers from off the floor.

"That was different, Jared. You lied to me! That's what upset me," she justified, jumping to her feet.

"No, 'you' don't trust me," he stated, folding his arms, staring her down face to face now. *Déjà vu is what she had walked herself into.*

"No Jared, as a matter of fact, I don't—I wish you could move on!" she groaned.

"God, when are you going to stop denying this!" he frustrated.

"Denying what!" she viciously flared, pushing her face forward.

"This. This tension between us ever since you kissed me, Jessica and I know damn well that you felt exactly what I felt too, because you didn't hesitate to stop either!"

"Now look who's exaggerating," she folds her arms.

"Exaggerating? Jess, you fucking kissed me!"

"No, you're wrong. I love Jaiden, I would never do that to him," she denied. He stepped closer, circulating around the girl in interrogation.

"If you love Jaiden, then why are you here now… with me?" he whispers coldly in her ear.

"I—"

"You kissed me, and you felt something," he says, cupping her round face.

"Please stop—" she helplessly cries, trying to stare at the ground beneath his hands.

"No. I'm not going anywhere until you admit you kissed me," he stubbornly persisted, locking her face in his eyes.

"I didn't," she admits, staring down at the floor again before he drops his release on her face.

"You know what I admire about you, Jessica? You are this crazy, psychotic, 'nutcase' of a woman," he says, pacing around in the room before returning to the girl to back her up against the bedroom wall, "And yet, I can't help but neglect how drawn I am to your absence and how stubborn you are at times like this," he chuckled, staring into her soulful eyes.

"Stop—" she faintly begged, allowing his soft, brittle, and large hands to caress her face.

"What are you afraid of? I'm right here. You want me Jessica, I can feel it. Don't fight this—kiss me," he taunted an inch away from her face now. He dried her tears with his thumbs while his fingers cupped her cheekbones. She tried fighting him off with minimal effort before she resisted and allowed his lips to crash onto hers when he leaned in closer—until finally, she grabbed ahold of his face and kissed him back.

"We can't do this. Not again… it's not right," she distressed, pulling away from what remained of her self-control. "It's not fair to Jaiden," she sobbed after he leaned in again. He dropped his head before nodding out of respect. He then lurked around the room before beginning to speak again, "He's just using you."

"That's the most cliché thing you can tell someone at a time like this!" she fired.

"Ask me the last time he's stayed up all night worrying about your safety. Or the last time he called you just to ask how your day was going or how you were doing?" he emphasized when approaching her again until he stood directly in front of her. That sentence sent Jessica over the edge, sending Jared flying with just the backlash of her hand.

"You don't have a right to tell me that! He's been there for me a lot longer than you have! He didn't give up on me, he never did!" Jared solemnly confided her close to his chest. "Where were you when I was falling, Jared?" She shivered in his embrace, trying to resist again.

"I'm sorry…" he cooed, trying to calm her down but failing with his own tears clouding his better judgment.

"Why am I not surprised? Of 'course', you'd be here right now Jess—this is so 'like' you!" Jaiden proclaimed after swinging the door

251

open, just as Jess finally let Jared comfort her. The two quickly separate from each other.

"He's a friend and you don't get to claim me anymore, we were broken up!" she vindicated when stepping forward fearlessly in hyperventilation.

"If we are 'broken up' then what do you call what we did earlier today?" he gritted, standing by the doorway glum.

"I don't know what you would call it, but I think of it as getting my workout in for the day," she bitterly shrugged, after her emotions washed down.

"You. You are unbelievable, you know!"

"We haven't even been broken up for a day and you've already jumped in a bed with him!"

"Calm down, she was just upset."

"And Mr. Jared has to nose in and save the day once again!"

"Leave him out of this!" Jess snaps, vigorously biting down hard on her teeth like a canine.

"So now you're defending him too?"

"I'm not defending anyone! Just leave him alone, this is about you and me!"

"That's where you're wrong. I 'have' to involve him now because that's what you did by coming here," he confronted, stepping closer.

"Back up," warns Jared, who tries to protect Jessica by placing an arm in front for her to hide behind.

"Don't tell me what to do!" Jaiden growled, pushing forward. The two begin to fight while Jessica tried to stop them.

"This is ridiculous! Please stop!" she implored desperately trying to come between them like a habit.

"Jess, for once, please stay out of this!" Jaiden spat in annoyance. She mournfully leaves, closing the door behind herself without another peep after the two begun to ignore her.

"Jess, come quick! It's the twins!" Becca exasperated when stumbling into her hotel room unannounced after arriving with the rest of the group. She didn't want to see them anymore, she refused to see them until Becca had mentioned the police were involved—unknowing of where the situation was headed herself. The friends storm out in a clutter, only to find both Jared and Jaiden being escorted out of the hotel lobby with handcuffs, to the police station, where they would only be released on a five-hundred-dollar bail each, for disturbance.

The next morning, Jess was there to save the day once again alongside her friends, for lack of transportation and money. The officers unlocked the cell to let the two tired and blue teenagers out of their designated cell. This trip was a complete disaster. They were surprised to find a familiar face greet them on their way out, their one and only savior, Jessica Jane. "Jess, where are you going?" asked Jaiden after noticing she had not even stayed long after release.

"I'm staying out of this." She swarmed away with Becca and Skylar.

"Agree we won't tell Mom or Dad about this?" asked Jared after they walked out of the station. They both shook on it. "Okay, obviously this isn't working out," mentioned Jared after their silent walk back from the hotel to collect their things.

"What isn't?"

"Our rivalry. We need to end this somehow..." Jared sighed. "You're absolutely right. So may the best brother win," Jaiden devilishly grinned.

****

Chapter Fifteen

"Stop calling!" Jaiden growls irritably from across the hallway as he throws his phone in his locker before slamming it shut and walking off. "What was that all about?" Becca asks as her and Skylar stand near Jessica's locker.

"Who knows anymore?" she carelessly shrugged. The bell rings and the friends part ways to head to class.

"Hey Jessica, wait up!" Hobbs calls out, running up from behind. "Hey… what's up?"

"I never really got the chance to apologize on my friend's behalf."

"What are you talking about?" she asked when turning the corner.

"Griffins… Jaiden told me what happened."

"So much for that trust factor and anyways, you don't need to apologize, he got exactly what he deserved."

"I want to go off the record by saying that I take full responsibility for giving him your number, but had I known for what extent—"

"I believe you," she interjected. Hobbs nearly drops his body forward in relief.

"Good. Otherwise I would have had to dedicate my entire life in trying to persuade you that I'm good."

"Yeah? Well, get in line."

****

During his seventh hour dance period, Skylar had started to gossip about the rumors regarding a fellow classmate, Alexander Underwood. Star's mouth hung open upon hearing the news. "He's moved back to Alabama," Skylar says.

"Why?" Becca asks.

"Something about Staci and Griffins. Z told me since they had already broken up—before he brutally had to die, she packed up and moved to her family back in Alabama, taking Alex since he's still a minority to live on his own," he explained.

"He was under Staci's supervision here," he continued. Jess was no scientist, but she was pretty sure Staci and Griffins' relationship was anything but hearts and giggles, it was exclusive, and anyone could tell they were primarily using each other for sex. It was no longer foreign to Jessica why he had the sudden urge to reunite with the brunette, he was obviously desperate to unload himself after his broad had left him in the sheets, so to speak.

"In a week, ladies and gentlemen, we will be officially practicing on the Music Valley stage!" the teacher publicized.

"You will be required to provide your own transportation for this class hour. We will be meeting there every day in the school week until the day of the show. Although, it is only required you stay the class hour, it is up to you whether or not you want to stay to continue practicing or until they ask us to leave, or you can just go home after the hour is over with… the school board is being lenient about us going off campus to continue with our competition. It is after all, a big opportunity for our school to be advertised," the teacher announced before breaking off the groups.

"Okay guys, let's practice the flip one more time and then do you guys want to run it from the top?" Jess asked, reclaiming her position. "Hit the music!" Jess directed to Jasmine, who obediently skipped over to the boom box, hitting the play button before dispersing into formation. After the group had finished practice, they returned home for the remainder of the day. Jessica combusted beyond exhaustion; she had endless amounts of homework to attain to and not enough sleep. Finals were just around the corner—a couple of weeks away, and she was not mentally prepared for any of it. After some thought to her future, she realized that if she didn't win that one-hundred-thousand-dollar scholarship to the Art Institute of Seattle, she was set for failure since she would not know what she wanted to take up as a plan B career. It's times like this, where her life was at gunpoint. She needed to focus on keeping up with her grades. It took her this long to learn that boys were only a distraction that kept her from reaching her goal and she just didn't want to have to deal with the drama that follows. The only problem with that was, so long as she tried to ignore it, it just kept on finding ways to sabotage her life. Something a wise boy once told her was that a greater force of evil never prevails to rear its ugly head when it comes to privacy. Jessica had the opportunity to finish her assignments in most of her classes today so that she may get home and relax, curl up in the sleep she has deserved and missed out on. She woke up in the middle of the night at around 8:45 p.m., checking her alarm clock after having a very lucid and sensational dream. In the dream she had been having, she was getting an early checkup at her gynecologist. Only, it was no ordinary dream, Jared was her doctor and it started getting very intimate. She woke up before she had dreamt something she was going to later feel guilty of. When she remembered it was only a dream and no one could possibly get inside her mind, she plopped her head back under her thick covers and slowly shut her eyes. The dream continued, and it was a figment of bliss; it was wrong, yes, but it was like some sort of fantasy come to life, only inside her deepest thoughts. She erotically felt herself moaning his name in the process of her deep sleep. Her guilty unconscious had tried stopping it a few times, but her words were silenced when the boy purposely chose to ignore her, riling up the girl's sexual frustration.

10:13 p.m., the girl had awakened to a loud ringing in her ear. At first, she thought it was her school alarm, warning her it was time to wake up, but to her disappointment, it happened to be her phone buzzing with a nuance of bright light on her nightstand. So, she stubbornly reached over and picks it up, checking the caller I.D. before accepting the call as she rubbed under her eyes and struggled to sit up. It surprised her for this certain someone to be calling her this late of night, so it had to be an emergency, at least that is what she sadistically hoped for. "Hello?" she crankily answered.

"Hey Sis, sorry to be calling you so late but Kevin had to take a red eye last minute and I need someone to take care of me while he's away," Mandy informed.

"Couldn't you have just called, I don't know, 'Mom'?" Jess groaned.

"I didn't want to bother her."

"So you decided to bother me instead, huh?"

"I helped take care of you when you were pregnant, don't forget!" Mandy boasts. That was a deal breaker.

"I'll be right over," muttered Jess before hanging up. Jess contemplated getting out of the cozy comfort of her warm bed; it took her so long to get in such comfort and now she was taken from its ambiance. When she finally managed to slip past her bedroom door, she reclined to grab her car keys from her coffee table and walked out in her fuzzy slippers and phone in one hand, and pillow and keys in another.

****

"Why didn't you bring you stuff?" Mandy asked upon Jess stumbling inside her home, half-asleep.

"How long do you expect me to stay with you?"

256

"Let's see, Kevin should be back in a week so… a week," Amanda nods.

"Where am I sleeping?"

"Oh um, the couch should be comfortable," she implied.

"You're kidding me, right?"

"Sorry, the future baby is renting out your guest room permanently," she chuckled while making her way to the cabinet. "Here," she says returning with some blankets in hand, handing them to her bitter younger sister.

"Thanks," Jess mumbled, rolling her eyes before making her way to the couch.

"Here, let me help you with that," Amanda insisted, walking over to help her with the blanket.

"Hey Mandy?"

"Yeah?"

"So, Kevin goes on these business trips often, huh?"

"Uh huh," she says, focusing on scattering the blankets neatly.

"Don't you get a little suspicious?"

"Why would I be?" she pauses, staring at her sister to await an answer.

"Well I don't know, but he's been very quiet and distant these days… are you sure everything is okay between you two?"

"Sweetie, I'm pregnant… everything is more than okay with us," she chuckles reassuringly before continuing to prepare the pull-out mattress from the sofa. "Done," she announced, touching her sister's shoulder to make her way around and exit the room.

"Goodnight."

Jess watched as her sister headed up the stairs with the small stair light to guide her, before she drifted off into her own deep slumber. She was revived by a flash of light in her face, minutes later.

"What the hell?" Jessica frustrated, sitting up, rubbing over her baggy eyelids.

"Jessica, I'm scared," Amanda feared, squatting down next to her sister.

"Come again?"

"Were you implying that Kevin might be having an affair?" she worried.

"All I am saying is you should keep him on a shorter leash if he has been hiding things from you."

"That's the thing, I don't know."

"What do you mean, do you guys ever talk about… anything?"

"He keeps quiet about his business, no pun intended."

257

"So, what do you think I should do?"

"Amanda, it is nearly twelve o'clock in the morning, I have school in a couple of hours, and I haven't been getting much sleep lately,"

"Well, neither have I, hello!" Amanda exclaims, waving a hand in front of her unborn child.

"Where is he at? Did he tell you?"

"He said he was going to Vegas—"

"Vegas! You've 'got' to be kidding me, who does business in Vegas?"

"He's a real estate agent…"

"I know but you don't buy homes in Vegas, you go to Vegas to gamble, to drink, have a good time, get 'hitched' even!"

"Okay, I'm going to try not to panic," Amanda says hyperventilating.

"Don't jump to conclusions—we don't know all the facts yet, breathe sweetie," Jess claims.

"You're right… you've got to help me!" she panicked.

"What do you expect me to do—jump on the next flight to Vegas so I can spy on him for you?"

"No, don't be silly," she says. Jess let out an exaggerated sigh of relief. "… we must go together so I can witness it for myself!" she grins, standing tall before walking away.

Jess sinks herself lower inside her blanket, "Should've kept my mouth shut," she muttered. Ten minutes of complete silence and Jess managed to fall asleep again. It wasn't until early sunrise when she was startled awake by the tireless Mandy again at around 4:25am, *so much for sleeping.*

"Jessica, get up, we're going to Vegas!" she beamed while heading into the kitchen.

"Amanda, are you insane! You're pregnant first off, and second off—are you just insane?" she convicted, shooting up behind her.

"You're the one with the brilliant idea!" she gloated.

"I was being sarcastic!"

"Well, sometimes it actually pays off," she says filing through her kitchen cabinets.

"I have school in a few hours!"

"Oh, don't worry your cute little head off, I called in sick for you."

"You did WHAT?"

"No Amanda, I'm already way behind—"

"It's just one day, relax… now go home, change, and be back here at exactly 6:30. Our flight is at nine something a.m."

"Oh shoot," she sighs, stopping in her tracks. "We need a ride… do you think one of your little boyfriends can give us a ride to the airport?"

"No, forget it."

"Fine, I'll just call them up myself," she says before reaching for her phone on the counter.

"Amanda, don't you dare!" Jess warns when taking a step closer as Amanda moves her hand closer to the phone. When Jess finally reached her, Amanda picked up her phone and began sprinting around the counter while Jess tried getting her to stop.

"Who should I call?" Amanda teased while scrolling through her phone.

"Mandy, come on, stop... you should know, I'm not speaking with them right now," she sighs while Amanda drops the phone.

****

"Hey listen, thanks for taking us to the airport. I know it was kind of a stretch last minute," Jess sincerely informed the driver during their drive.

"Yeah, no problem—don't sweat it. I love helping out my uncle in his taxi service. It's kind of my job," Matt chuckles, adjusting his mirror.

"Yeah, I remember you mentioning that at the wedding, I must have forgotten," Jess smiled.

"So how have you been?" he asks. "Alright, and you? How has college been?"

"Great, trying to obtain my masters for dentistry."

"Oh, how lovely... it's a no wonder why you have such nice teeth," Jess flirted.

"You have a really lovely smile too," Mandy agrees from beside in the backseat.

"Thanks," he said flashing both girls a smile through the rear-view mirror.

"So where are you ladies traveling might I ask?"

"Vegas. Where my sister has apparently forgotten her trust in her husband, so she's going over there to see if she can get it back," Jess informed, earning herself a nudge from Amanda.

"How has Patrick been?" Mandy asks, avoiding the subject.

"He's great, better than ever... he has what he's been missing for a long time now, no offense to your sister."

"Oh, none taken," Mandy encouraged.

****

259

After a long, four-hour flight to Nevada, they had successfully arrived and checked into their hotel room. "You do know where he is at, right?"

"No..." Amanda sheepishly admitted, pulling her teeth forward at her best attempt to smile.

"Mandy, would it be an okay time to kill you right now?" hissed Jessica.

"Relax... I can just text him."

"And you think he will tell you where he's at?"

"Well, I don't see why not—it's not like he will ever expect me to be here... even though I am, *wink wink.*"

"Or... how about you call one of your friends to make it less obvious and find out where they are located at, so you can just follow him from there," Jess concocts slowly and feasibly. "Or, we could just do it your way, I guess." She shrugged, reaching for her phone in her two thousand-dollar Prada bag.

"Okay, my friend Sarah just texted me. They are staying at the Caesar's Palace," she reads after about five minutes of relaxing on the sofa in their hotel room.

"What is that?"

"We are about to find out," she infers, grabbing her purse on her way out of the room with Jess following behind.

"Mandy, we don't have a car—do we have to go now? I'm jet-lagged," Jessica whined.

"Well luckily, a little ol' me ordered us a chauffeur for the day," she interpreted when stepping into the elevator.

"Woah." Jessica's eyes widen at the sight of Las Vegas; so beautiful, even in the daytime; it was truly gorgeous. They passed by around the city in search for Caesar's Palace, their final destination. The place was so rich in detail. It looked like paradise.

"I'm surprised Kevin can afford a luxury like this," Jessica marveled, lurking up behind Mandy who entered the hotel.

"Yes, may I help you ladies?" the male concierge asks at the front desk.

"Pardon, I was wondering if you had known what room a Mr. Anderson was staying at?" Mandy asked, approaching the desk.

"My apologies, we aren't allowed to give that type of personal information, but I'm sorry, who are you?"

"I'm his... err... wife?"

"You don't seem convinced..." He stared in confusion.

"No, she really is!" Jess insisted. When she found he wasn't buying into it, she raised her extra meter to full blast.

"Please, it's an emergency! She needs a heart transplant!" she over-exaggeratedly exclaimed.

"What?"

"He's the only possible blood match, our last hope!"

"She doesn't look like she is in critical condition—"

"That's because she is staying strong," Jess croaked, solemnly looking over to her sister. On the other hand, Amanda stayed civilized, looking back over to Jess like she had gone ballistic.

"Alright, I'll call up Mr. Anderson to confirm that—" he begins to say while picking up his phone before Jessica pushed his hand down.

"That won't be necessary, please… she's pregnant and she could lose the baby."

"Well, I do love babies and if that is the case, who am I to stand in the way? I don't want to be the cause of you to have lost it. I know how terrible losing babies go."

"Oh, do you now?" Jess scolds, crossing over her arms.

"Jessica, now is not the time for a schizophrenic episode," Mandy whispers, causing Jessica to snap out of her trance of Jaiden's head on this innocent gentleman's body.

"I'm sorry… just please tell us?"

He nods and scans his computer, "Room 215-D."

"Wow, you should be an actress," Amanda acknowledged on their voyage to the room. After they had approached the door, Mandy intrusively knocked, awaiting an answer.

"Amanda, what the hell are you doing!" Jess whispered, stepping out of the doorway just before the door unraveled. They had not even discussed a proper full-proof plan, while she was determined to impulsively demand an answer.

"Mandy? W-wha—what the hell are you doing here?" Kevin worried as she pushed the door wide open and stepped inside. Jessica spitefully came out from hiding and follows behind.

"Hello Kevin."

"Where is she?" Mandy asks looking around.

"Where is who?" Kevin asks.

"The girl you're cheating on me with," she snidely remarks, crossing her arms.

"Amanda, you flew all this way because you thought I was cheating on you?"

"Am I right?"

"No, I am not cheating on you," he calmly says.

"Then look me in the eyes and say it," she demands. He sighs as he takes a seat on his bed, resting his face in his hands.

"Oh my God, I knew it," she says before anxiously pacing back and forth.

"Amanda," he stands back up, grabbing her hands.

"I am 'not' cheating on you, okay?" he verified, staring into her soulful eyes, it had all seemed familiar.

"I love you more than anything and I can't believe you would think that," he says.

"Then why are you here? Why are you keeping things from me?"

"I am not keeping things from you, where would you get such a crazy idea?" he asks as Amanda shoots her head in her sister's guilty direction.

"I-I should probably get going—"

"No, you stay," Amanda warned. Jessica nodded and obediently stayed, sitting down on the bed.

"If we are being honest though, I'm not here because of business... well, I thought I was, but that's not it at all. Here, come sit down," he requested, guiding her on the couch.

"It's my new boss, she has this keen infatuation with me... she tried to seduce me last night."

"Oh my God!" Mandy retched, facing away.

"I turned her down and so she threatened that I will lose my job if I didn't comply... so, I chose to lose my job last night."

"But I swear, I didn't know her intentions. She would always send me off to these high-end locations when I left on business trips and they were the real deals. I don't know why I thought this time would be different too—especially in a place like Vegas, but it was just a scam," he shrugged. "But I would never cheat on you Mandy... I love you," he stated while caressing her face.

"Awwww," gushed Jessica as they then startle and disposition in her presence.

"Hey, don't look at me, I would've waited outside but you've caused me to eavesdrop," she manifests.

"I'm sorry Mandy, I really wanted to provide for this family, but I don't know if I can anymore—since we are a one-income-family now, we are going to have to come up with a new method to pay for our home in order to keep our baby. Without this job, we're looking at years of debt," Kevin says.

****

"What are we going to do?" Mandy cries on their fifteen-hour car ride home, the next morning.

"Guys, I'm really sorry about your whole financial crisis, if you want, I could get a job and help you—"

"No thank you Jessica," Kevin assures. "What if I moved out?"

"Jessica, now you know we couldn't possibly ask you to do that," Mandy reminds.

"Or I could sell my car?"

"Jessica, sweetie, you're too generous, but that was a gift from us to you and you deserve it. Rest-assured, we will find a way to pay off our home in no time," she self-assured. It was nice to see her finding the silver lining of things even if her lining was black as coal. "I could always work double time," she optimized.

"Yes, but for how long Mandy? You still have a maternity leave to think about when this baby comes!"

"I get you want to help the situation, but you're not helping, please. We will figure it out."

"Mandy, in the eyes of God, you deserve a family. You deserve the opportunity to have and to hold your child in the sanity of your own home! Let me help you!" Jessica insisted.

****

"Daddy, please! It's a temporary loan!" Mandy whined when following her father around the counter as he looks through his mail in his best effort to avoid her.

"Hell to the no," her father dismissed, while Jess sat patiently on the couch with their mother, dreading the day to go by faster in her slight discomfort. It was no surprise that their father came close to living the life as a stinking multi-millionaire, but he also spent money like the cheapest bastard alive. Jess was content that she never had to implore for money. Since Jessica was the last child, and the third girl—that meant she was the least spoiled and thinking back to it now, she was fortunate to not have been spoiled rotten like the two bratty sisters she has come to know. Beverly was certainly the most inhibited of the two because she was always 'daddy's favorite' since Mandy was by default, mommy's favorite. In technical terms, one could argue that Jessica was the unloved child and was the mistake, as previously admitted. You would also think the baby of the family would require the most attention but as it turns out, it was not the case at all for the Larson family. Aside from her sisters, Jess grew up independent and earned money from the hard labor she put in. She was independent in most instances but recently she had depended on a lot of people and in the end, it went to show that she could not rely on anyone but herself.

"Mr. Larson," Kevin says jogging up to him.

"Yes son?"

"Forgive me if I'm stepping out of place here, but please don't do this to her, to us… we are just asking for some money, I promise we will pay you back. I just don't want to disappoint your daughter, I love her, please… don't do this to us."

"Oh Alan, give these kids a break for crying out loud!" Margret howled from the couch.

"Margret, you stay out of this… this doesn't concern you."

"This damn well concerns me! If you think for one second that I want my grandchildren growing up in an unsafe environment, then you are clearly mistaken—and you are 'not' going to keep them from me!" she implemented while walking over. *She certainly felt otherwise when Jessica was pregnant.*

"Where do expect me to pull all that money you're asking me for? Out of my ass?" Alan angers, slamming the mail on the counter before making his way up the stairs.

"I thought you could just cut the allowance you were planning to give Beverly this week."

"Allowance? I never got an allowance, unfair," Jess grumbled, crossing her arms.

"How much do you pay her?" Kevin asks, walking near the staircase.

"I don't know, somewhere between ten-thousand," says Alan.

"Christ!" Kevin says rolling his eyes. Jessica's college tuition was going to be fixed on her own income, depending if she received the scholarship or not. If not, then she would apply for a job soon to pay off her loans—but nothing bothered her more than to know how much of her sister's money was being taken for granted.

"You better watch your mouth, boy!" Kevin's father in-law flared when spitting his murky drool on the wooden floor. *Disgusting.*

"Sorry sir."

"Alan, I think we should really think about this… Beverly could afford skipping at least one allowance, these kids need it—"

"Forget it Margret, I said no! You don't need kids anyways, bunch of money sucking machines!" he bitterly stated before storming away into his room and shutting the door behind him.

"I'm sorry guys," Margret excuses on his behalf just before she returns to the kitchen and Mandy begins weeping into Kevin's chest.

"Maybe it isn't over yet," Jess schemes when walking over to the two from the couch.

"What are you talking about?" Amanda sniffles.

"We could just ask Beverly?"

"What makes you think she will say yes?" Kevin asks.

"Hello, are we overlooking that she's the only blonde in this family?"

"She might be the only blonde in the family, but she would never sacrifice her allowance," Mandy cries.

"We are having that baby and we are going to live in that house, I promise," Kevin cooed, kissing her on the forehead. Jessica couldn't help but give a small sympathetic smile when a flash of Jared's kind words, that always gave the girl hope when she was pregnant, replayed in her mind. At the end of it all, it was just being with him that got her through the day. It's as if she forgot what breathing felt like when she was with him. All of her worries flooded away, just staring into the depths of his faultless eyes. All the hate and all the negativity outweighed in her life when she was under his clutch, and she honestly never felt safer. And she has too, been so far away from home, that she didn't even begin to understand where her home was, until she was in his arms.

"You want me to do 'what'?" Beverly asks, completely appalled at such request.

"Bev, I never ask you for anything, even now, it's not for me—it's for Amanda, and she needs this more than anything, okay? I just don't want her to end up like me, or you for that matter—the feeling of loving something so much and finding out you can't have it, hurts... Amanda is so full of life and I can't imagine her not being happy for once in her life, you know?" Jessica explained.

"Again... you want me to do 'what'?" her voice heightened. "Beverly... how did you feel when you lost Patrick, or maybe just anyone you cared deeply about?"

"Well... I felt disappointed," she shrugged.

"Okay, and if Mandy doesn't have the money, just think about your feelings, she will feel the same way. It's not a good feeling, is it? She needs this more than we do. She's been wanting this ever since we were kids. She's waited her whole moment for this, being a mom. Please don't be the one to take it away from her, you're our only hope Bev, you're a good person, we know you are... we are counting on you to do the right thing."

Beverly hesitates before nodding. She slyly nods with the smallest, sympathetic smile, concluding their arrangement.

****

265

Chapter Sixteen

Being in school these past couple of weeks ever since Robbie committed, Jared could not concentrate at all... so much stress in his mind and so many worries that he just wanted the pain to vanish. He needed something, anything to allow him to peacefully sleep through the night for a clear state of mind. "Hey Jared," a male voice says from behind on his journey to his next class; it was Brennan. Jared took that as a sign for help. The only way he remembered, helped him to get through even the toughest of days was from the help of his hands. He remembered Jessica addressed him not to, he promised her he wouldn't. But, desperate times call for desperate measures.

"Brennan, I've been meaning to talk to you... are you busy after school today?"

"Well, just the same old with the group," he says nudging his friend in the arm. "But I can clear my schedule, what's up?"

"Actually no, if you don't mind, I kind of want to join in again?"

"Really?" he smirked.

"Yeah."

"Alright cool, so just meet us at Cody's house like last time," he says before parting ways.

After school, Jared took a drive to a fellow by the name of Cody's house. He stepped inside just as soon as Brennan located him from across the house and made his way over. The house was filled with a bunch of nerdish guys, much like Jared, but most of them freshman that wanted to be 'different'. "Hey, you made it!" Brennan exclaims, handing the boy a plastic cup. It was just then that Jared took a gander of the smell before his face turned sour.

"Gross, what is this dude?"

"Very strong drink, I forget the name... you're gonna like it, trust me. Cheers," he says bumping drinks with his. Jared cautiously waited for his friend to take a sip before he took his first.

"Bleehhh," Jared retched. He then drank the remainder of the alcohol before crushing the cup against his head and flailing his arms up in the air.

"Woah, slow down man!" Brennan cackled, while guiding Jared through the crowd. He hands the anxious Jared a shot glass from the counter and gets one for himself too. "Bottoms up," says Brennan, bumping glasses with his friend before digesting the rest. "Okay alright, we got a new game going here... sort of like Russian Roulette," he announced when walking around the kitchen counter where a pyramid of mini shot glasses were filled with different color liquids. "You wanna make sure you get a good tasting drink, otherwise you've got drunk for no reason," he chuckles.

"But how will you know what you're drinking?"

"That's the point!" he laughs.

"Wouldn't it just be easier to play beer pong?" Jared jokes.

"That's for later, my friend," Brennan teased.

"Are you down?"

"Sure," Jared shrugged.

"Alright, ready set..."

"Go!" Jared shouted next while they both reach for a shot glass from the array of glasses dispensed in front of them. "Oh, that's disgusting!" Jared squinted, coughing from the burning sensation left in his throat after setting the shot glass back down.

"Here, try this one," instructs Brennan when handing him off another shot.

"And you try this one," Jared directs, picking a random one as well. On the count of three, they chug down their second shot, third of the night for Jared to be exact.

"Mmmmm, slightly better," Jared nods when licking the cherry aftertaste from his lips. The two go at it for an hour, emptying all one-hundred of the small glasses, each consuming fifty and at this point, Jared barely felt his head. His eyes were droopy, and his head was dizzy. When they decided to take a break, Jared had followed Brennan to the couch to sober up a bit. He checked his watch to the best of his abilities and it was already half-past seven and had yet to start his homework.

"How do you do it Brennan?"

"D-do what?" he chuckles.

"Make time for everything..."

"I don't," he slurs.

"What do you mean?"

"I'm failing my classes man!" he laughs harder than usual and Jared couldn't help but to laugh along with him.

"You are?"

"Y-yeah man."

"So am I!" he emphasized louder than before.

But that was a bit of an overstatement, he was only failing one of his classes and not all of them. "Dude... I gotta get home."

"Give me a second," Brennan pardons before standing tall on the couch. "Hear ye, hear ye, everybody! Is any... one here, 'not' drunk enough, to take my good friend Jared home safely!" he slurred. Everyone paid attention, but no one raised their hand. "How far is your house?" he whispered from above.

"About a ten-minute drive."

"Alright. I'll drive you," he hopped down. He drove Jared safely to his place, being his only option because Jared didn't want to risk his family finding him like this. On their way, they almost crash into a car, but survive. Jared was still loopy and that whole experience just made the two laugh their socks off. "Okay, off you go Jare, but don't you worry, I won't charge you for bus fare," he says while Jared steps out. Jared signaled Brennan to roll down his windows just before he drove off.

"Are you sure you can drive on your own?"

"Nope," he says as he parks, stepping out.

"I'm going to stay at a relative's house."

"Aren't you worried they are going to see you like this?"

"They're used to it; how do you think I started?" he asked wiggling his brows.

"Holy shit!" Jared laughs out, tripping over the stairs on his way up after having entered the manor. He conspicuously enters his room at around eight p.m. when Jaiden had overheard. "I'm tired," he admits to himself before belly flopping onto his bed but failing and bouncing off the floor instead.

"Damn!" Jaiden winces before springing to his aid while Jared laughs harder.

"Did that not hurt?" he asks when helping his younger brother to his feet, noticing something had been off.

"Stop tickling me Jai!" he continuously laughs.

"Jared... are you drunk?" Jaiden's eyes widen in concern when Jared doesn't deny, he just continues off in his laughter instead.

"Hey, mirrors aren't supposed to talk!" Jared slurs giddily.

"Here, let's get you up," Jaiden says, carrying him to his bed. He finds his troublesome brother snoring within seconds after having thrown him on the bed. "Well, you are 'definitely' going to feel 'that' in the morning." He dusted his hands off after exiting his brother's room and closed the door behind. It wasn't long 'til he saw his parents curiously approach him in the hallways.

"What's going on in there boys?" his father asks while Linda flicks on the light switch in the hallway.

"Mom, can I speak with you... alone?"

"Sure," she says following Jaiden down the stairs after Pete entered his own room again.

"Mom, Jared has a problem and I'm kind of worried about him."

"What do you mean?"

"Drinking."

"He's drunk!" she yelled standing up.

"Yes, but don't do anything now. Personally, I would hold it off 'til morning, when he is back to himself, trust me."

"How long has this been going on?"

"For a while now..."

"Jaiden, I'm disappointed in you... you knew about this and didn't tell us, so we can give him the help he needs?" In the process of all this, Jaiden couldn't quite understand why he was the one held accountable for Jared's actions. "He's not an addict... at least I don't think."

"Alright, get a good night's sleep... I will discuss this with your father—"

"No Mom, please don't tell Dad!" he groaned.

"I can't keep this from him, it concerns us both," she advises, placing a kiss goodnight on his forehead before returning up the stairs.

****

"Jared Jasper Daniels, you get your sorry ass out of this bed!" Linda's voice roared, coming through Jared's door in the morning. He jolted out of his sheets to prepare himself for death busting down his door. He could not recall what happened yesterday, but he knew he got hammered with Brennan. Both of his parents standing bold in front of him now, with his massive headache, numb legs, and back ache, standing in the way of his concentration.

"What the hell is wrong with you kid!" Pete shouts. He heard Jaiden chuckling in the background after he had entered his doorway as well, hiding far behind his parents.

God damn that kid, he snitched didn't he?

"You get your ass out of this bed, right now!" Linda demands, pulling on his ear while he winced in pain just trying to get up. His father attempts to snatch his belt from his pants while the boy stood frozen in fear. That escalated out of proportion.

"Oh no, please not the belt," he trembled.

"Maybe I should talk to him alone," says Linda, unaware of Pete's actions.

"Linda, you can't just be easy on him, you've got to teach him a lesson! This is wrong!"

"Honey, he is a teenager, you can't just spank an eighteen-year-old!"

"Like hell I can!" he grits when taking a step forward with his belt folded in his hands, ready to whip him like cream.

"Oh shit!" Jaiden smirks, clapping his hands together.

"Pete, stop it!" their mother yells.

"Fine, I'll be in the garage," he mutters.

"What the hell were you thinking!" Linda shouts as soon as he leaves.

"I'm sorry, I-I,"

"This is so perfect!" Jaiden smirks.

"Jaiden, get the hell out!" Jared roared.

"Hey, watch your language! He was trying to be a good brother!"

"Good brother?" he narrowed his eyes. "How is making light of this, being a 'good brother'?" he air-quoted, folding his arms under his pits.

"If you don't remember, I was the one to help drag you into bed last night after you stumbled in here all willy-nilly and kissed your floorboard goodnight!"

"Yes, and he told me everything. I can't believe you drank! You're underage—what in the world were you thinking!"

"Yeah Jared?" Jaiden mimics as he crosses his arms.

"Would you get the hell out!" Linda frustrates, grabbing her slipper and pointing it at him while he skedaddles, shutting the door behind him on his way out. "So, tell me Jared," she crosses her arms. "...This was Jessica's doing, wasn't it? God, I can't stand that girl! She always has been a bad influence on the both of you!" she dragged on.

"I'm sorry I did what I felt I had to do, but it was NOT her fault! She is not a bad influence and you have to stop seeing her that way and blaming her for everything! Ever wonder how she feels? Always being blamed on for everything—well, that's sometimes how I feel. I'm sorry my friend died, and it was my fault—when my friend Lucas died, it was because of me too! If I had kept my 'mouth' shut in the first place, none of them would be where they are today, they would still be here!" he combusts, crying into his hands.

"Jared, I didn't know you felt this way... I'm sorry," she says smothering him in her arms. "But what you did was wrong. There are other ways to cope with this Jared! You don't have to resort to this behavior."

"Are you kidding me?" Jaiden whispers after having heard everything through the door. Yeah, sure—if Jaiden gets in trouble for doing something on accident, he was acquitted to get the belt and poor Jared does something like knowing what he was getting himself into and it's always love and cuddles with him. Nice to know who the favorite child is around here.

"What's going on?" Nora asked.

"Jared is getting in trouble."

"What did he do?"

"He drank, a lot."

"Tell me how it goes," she asked before parting off in her room.

"Not well…" he mumbled. He continued to eavesdrop from outside the door until he heard the two stop talking, which meant they were about to step out of the room. He then sprinted back to his room as if he weren't listening.

"What would you like Mommy to make you?" Linda asked, grabbing Jared's hand while Jaiden causally steps back out of his room only to find them descend back downstairs.

"Some bacon would help," he sniffled.

"Oh my God, you've 'got' to be serious!"

This guy gets treated like royalty here. Unfair.

"Can I get some bacon?" asked Jaiden from above the staircase.

"Jaiden, shut the hell up and go inside your room. I'm not done talking with you… and neither is your father," his mother forewarned. Jaiden frightfully gulped after a flash of his last talk with his father, involving a belt, backlashed in his mind.

"Oh, and by the way Jared, you're grounded," he heard his mother offset, causing Jaiden to smirk in satisfaction. He then returned inside his room and safely climbed down the window to get to his car and sneak away to Jessica's apartment.

"Hello?" she greets; her smile drops.

"Hello honey, have you missed me?" he teased while entering her apartment.

"I see you've been avoiding my calls, again—"

"I'm just doing what you want. You wanted me to stay out of your life and so your wish is my command," she said, folding her hands together and bobbing her head forward.

"I didn't mean it like that…"

"Yeah, that seems to be the excuse with you these days."

"You try running up and down a hotel room worried about your girlfriend's whereabouts and finding her being fondled up by your brother!" he frustrated, staring her down.

271

"I didn't realize you had been so worried. I'm sorry," she sighed, propping herself on the couch.

"Where do we go from here?" he asked sitting by her. "I still love you Jess, I do, and I care about you a lot."

"And I, you."

"I don't want one little argument to stand in the way of us being together, but I can't help but to also think that there's something else, someone else, standing in our way," he said staring down at his hands that play with hers.

"There's not."

"In order for this to work, I need you to confirm that you've never had any feelings for him up until this point."

"Okay. I don't love him and there's nothing going on between us," she said reflecting in his eyes.

"Okay," he says, grazing her hair in relief. "It smells nice in here, what are you making?" he asked while weaseling his way around her kitchen.

"Bacon… and it's all mine!" she called, running over to slap the bacon out of his hands.

"Too bad you don't need it," he shrugged, selfishly recoiling the plate away from her before shoving the bacon bits into his unholy mouth.

"Hey, not fair! Give me it back!" she hissed before hopping on his back, only causing him to trip and knock the plate over. "My bacon!" she shrieked. "…Looks like neither of us can have it now," she snickered, raising her nose in the air.

"You can't, but I can," he says, reaching to dust the bacon off a bit before continuing to put it in his chopper.

"What do you even want? I'm mad at you if you haven't noticed," she says, crossing her arms and periodically checking her nails in such manner.

"You're mad? I'm mad!" he clenched, joining her near the couch.

"You can't be mad, you have 'no' reason to be!" she agitatedly growled.

"I have every damn right to be mad, you know what you did!" He narrowed his eyes, bringing his face closer to hers now so that their lips were nearly an inch away from contact.

"Oh yeah?" she aroused with her hands on her hips, stepping closer now. "And what are you going to do about it?" she proposed while seductively biting her lip.

****

272

"I'm still mad at you," she says, re-clasping her bra while Jaiden continuously zipped up his jeans.

"Uh…huh."

"So, is 'this' what you came here for?" she asked rather annoyed at his presence.

"No, I came here to talk about Jared actually." She was taken aback at the topic of interest. "You said I should start being more concerned about him, so I am. I have noticed he has been consuming alcohol—"

"AGAIN?" she fixated.

****

"Hey you! Brennan!" Jaiden snarled from across the school hallway. He was alone, this was a perfect opportunity for Jaiden to confront him.

"Stay away from Jared, he's a good kid!" Jaiden compulsively threatened after slamming Brennan up against his locker.

"I-uh, it was his choice, I swear," he apprehensively pleads, struggling to be released.

"I don't care—you better stop interacting with him if you want to live a longer life, do we have an agreement?"

"Yes," he cowardly nodded.

"Good." Jaiden finally released Brennan after coming to an agreement on Jaiden's notion. It wasn't long before Brennan ran away, pushing straight past a very ticked off Jared, who marched closer.

"What the hell, Jaiden!" Jared raged.

"You should be thanking me," Jaiden smirked, cracking his knuckles.

"For what, you just scared my friend away!"

"He isn't a friend—a 'friend' is someone who motivates you to do the 'right' things," Jaiden cleared up, shoving him in the chest.

"Oh, 'really' now? Well, do you consider yourself a 'good friend'?" Jared asks while dusting off his shirt.

"Yes, I would say I am," Jaiden arrogantly nodded while arching his back and pointing his chin.

"Really, because a 'good friend', or in this case, 'brother', wouldn't scare away my friends, let alone snitch on his own 'brother'," he bitterly responded while pushing back hard enough so that Jaiden's body slammed back against the lockers.

"I did it to protect you!" he grunted, standing back up.

"It's a little too late to play big brother and besides, you only did it to get me in trouble!"

273

"If I wanted to get you in trouble, don't you think I would tell someone… I don't know, a little more important to you?" he chuckled.

"Jared!" Jessica yells from across the hallways, causing Jaiden to apathetically sigh and shake his head at the worst timing possible.

"Jessica," gritted Jaiden, on behalf of her unwelcome visit.

"Are you freaking kidding me!" Jared shifted his attention to let her scold him some more.

"You told me you would stop—no, you promised me!"

"Are you serious, you told 'her'?" he asks facing Jaiden now.

"I'm sorry," Jared says when taking her hand in hopes of calming her.

"No, you don't get to apologize anymore," she says melodramatically, folding in despair before racing away.

"Okay, 'now' you've crossed the line!" Jared angered before dropping his backpack.

"Oh, I've crossed the line? What the hell was that about?" Jaiden tensed, dropping his backpack too before backing Jared up against the locker again. Jared, who fell down before his brother, locked his jaw while staring his brother down who lifted his shirt over his head before picking up where he left off—joining his brother on the floor to finish him off. They began to tussle, Jaiden trying effortlessly to swing at Jared. The hallway floods with students recording the two with their phones, as the twins were now the center of this student formed circle.

"I hate you… so much," Jared grunted, rolling on top of Jaiden, repeatedly punching him square in the face until Jaiden took charge and flipped them back over. Jaiden desperately tried strangling Jared while the younger boy struggled for air supply, pushing both his arms up to grasp Jaiden's neck to choke him back, both lacking coloration on their skin at this point. Meanwhile, Jaiden took his free hand to force Jared's most dominant hand down.

"Tap out little bitch," Jaiden hissed.

"N-never." Jared breathes unsteadily, turning blue.

"I should just kill you right now. Prison doesn't look too bad after all," Jaiden clenched when slamming his brother's head back against the concrete.

"You never had the balls to, you pussy," Jared taunted, licking the blood droplet from the cut on his bottom lip.

"Boys! Boys! Break it up!" a teacher implored as her and the school's security speeded over, pulling the two apart—first lifting Jaiden from off his knees.

"Son, put your shirt back on," the principal demanded, walking over to lift Jaiden's shirt from off the floor before tossing it back to him.

After Jaiden had put his shirt back on, the school's security held the boys' arms behind their backs and led them into the principal's office where the principal then called up their parents. They waited for them to arrive before they began to say furthermore.

"Your sons have caused yet another disruption in our learning environment, the first two were warnings but this time they could've killed each other. I ran over as soon as I heard... the two were nearly blue in the face from loss of oxygen, they were strangling each other, I will not stand for this adolescence!" the principal angers.

"You don't have to stand," Jaiden silently retorted earning himself a nudge from his brother.

"I'm sorry sir, we don't know what has gotten into them but—" their father apologized before Linda interrupted, "Principal Abrams, I can assure you these boys are well-behaved. Now this Jessica character, I'm not so sure about. I can guarantee you they only act up in her presence—which is 'exactly' why we have chosen to keep you boys in 'separate' schools in the first place," their mother rambled.

"You can send me to a foreign exchange school for the hell I care and that still wouldn't keep us apart! The only person you 'should' have me separated from is with that dickhead over there!" Jared spat.

"Son, sit down please," the principal requested.

"Son of a bitch!" Jared sighed, dropping down.

"Jared!" Linda exclaimed.

"Sorry, sorry, sorry," he flinched.

"I won't have this tolerated at my school, you two are hereby suspended for two weeks!"

"Two weeks!" Jared protested, shooting up.

"Jared, 'sit' down!" Pete angered.

"Sweet, no homework!" Jaiden grinned, rubbing his hands together. Linda felt the need to slap her impulsive boy upside the head for that unnecessary commentary.

****

"Way to go Jared!" Jaiden grumbled during their walk out to the parking lot.

"Shut up, it was your fault."

"No, it was yours! If you recall, you started shoving 'me'! You were basically asking for a fight!"

"Maybe if you didn't threaten my friend, I wouldn't have to you prick!" Jared fired back.

"Boys, get in the car and stop fighting!" their mother demanded, walking behind the two.

"We have our cars mom," Jaiden reminded.

"Give them, both of you," says Pete stepping in front of them now.

"But dad—"

"Now!" Jared and Jaiden both stared each other down in spite with resent flaring in their eyes before reaching into their pants' pocket to disarm themselves. Linda opened the back seat of her Honda Pilot for Jared and Jaiden to enter, Jared sitting in the back seat while Jaiden sat in the middle row, far apart from each other.

"You guys nearly killed each other, what is with you!" their mother cried out.

"Yeah, well, he's still breathing, isn't he?" Jaiden muttered under his breath before looking back at Jared with spiteful eyes. The family arrived home in dead silence for the rest of the car ride, only hearing the sound of their mother's sobs the rest of the way.

"I'm disappointed in you boys," their father says on their walk up to the garage door.

"Wait—give me your phones."

"Dad, come on," Jaiden pouts.

"'Don't' make me ask you again, now give them!" he threatens, sticking his hand far out. He was determined to not let his sons through the garage until they abided by what he insisted. "Here, but can I just—"

"'Get' your sorry ass in there!" Pete ill-temperedly yelled as the two then rush to apprehensively enter the door. The last time the two of them were this deep into trouble, was when they were about eight years of age; when they were penalized for egging their neighbor's car and house. Their punishment was they had to scrape all the eggs off everything they vandalized, *good times.*

"What the hell are you smiling about?" Jared asks.

"Shut up!" Jaiden barks.

****

For Jessica Jane, she continued with her day just thinking about how Jared could do such a thing after he promised the girl he would stop. What was even worse was that she continued to sleep with Jaiden with the guilt of kissing Jared still haunting her. She would try to avoid him the rest of the day, but it seemed far too easy since he was not on campus anymore. It was Skylar, who pointed out that he saw him leave the campus earlier, with Jaiden. She tried calling Jaiden first to see if everything was alright but no answer. When she noticed the twins' cars were still on campus, even after hours, she decidedly went over to the twins' house from which she knocked on the door that was soon answered by their mother. "Oh, hello Mrs. Daniels."

"What do you want?" the bitter woman asked, folding her arms. Jessica could feel Linda's eyes judging her wardrobe selection from the waist up.

"Are Jaiden and or Jared here by chance?"

"Yes, but they're in trouble," she says viciously, staring her neighbor's kid down; that was all Linda would ever see her as her neighbor's annoying daughter that brain washed and ruined her sons.

"Oh… okay," she frowned.

"Okay, now run along," expelled Linda.

Jaiden was the first to see Jessica pulling onto their driveway from his bedroom window. He wanted to go down and see what she came for, but the twins were forced to stay in their rooms for the remainder of the next two weeks. It wasn't until then, that Jaiden realized he had a window and a gigantic tree he could escape from, that's all he really needed to survive these upcoming two weeks. He made his way to his door to shut and lock it as soundless as possible. He then tiptoed to his window, slowly rolling it up before he climbed down the tree. When he reached the bottom, he jumped off to find Jessica trudging to her car unbothered. That is when he made his move and swooned in on her, startling her. She shrieked just before he covered her piercing mouth. She then drove them both to her apartment where Jaiden claimed he would explain everything, as he did.

"Jaiden, I have to tell you something that has been bothering me for a while now. I was waiting for the right time to come out and tell you, I just couldn't bring myself to it," she says when shifting uncomfortably off his lap while he patiently waited for her to continue. "So, a couple of weeks ago, when Robbie had passed—it was in calculus when Jared and I had received the awful news—right before they released all the students. He stormed out of the classroom so upset, so I followed him, and he was so hurt—I felt like I owed it to him or something. I was just caught up in the moment, I-I wasn't thinking, and I kissed him, Jaiden. I'm not proud of it, I have never felt guiltier, I'm so sorry. I didn't mean for it to happen," she finishes under one breath. Jaiden stayed silent until she grazed a hand over his thigh to await his reaction but not before he rejected her hand away.

"You've been lying to me all this time?" he asked while staring straight ahead. "It wasn't lying, I was scared to tell you—"

"Even when you had the opportunity to tell me upfront when we crossed paths in the hallway that day?"

"I didn't know how to tell you, I-I'm sorry; it was a lot for me to take in," she protested while letting her tears fall freely to the floor.

"I, I can't even look at you right now," he scoffed, throwing her legs off his thighs, "All those times we were together, you had the decency to look me in the eyes like nothing happened!"

"I—"

"I can't believe this!" he climaxed, standing up as she revolted to protest.

"Please, don't leave! Jaiden... haven't I suffered enough?" she wept, squeezing her eyelids shut in hopes that it would be manipulative enough for him to stay.

"No. No you haven't," he tensed while curling his fist into a ball and with that, he slammed the door on his way out.

"Jaiden!" (*slam!*) Jaiden felt devastated to know that no matter how hard he tried to be in her life, she pushed him away. It seemed customary in the love triangle that formed between the three. Jessica knew she was not going to win if she kept this charade up, not with Jared and surely not with Jaiden, they were no fools and they would not tolerate her games either. They could not stand being played this way, it was not a healthy relationship for anyone. Maybe everyone was right and that they would all be better off as strangers...

(Flashback)

"And here we are," says Jaiden, helping Jess up inside the tree house after they spent two hours strolling through the park and having a picnic.

"Just like old times," he reminiscences.

They sat in three minutes of silence before either of them spoke out again. "Not as fun as it used to be," Jaiden admits when shrugging forward while his legs dangle outside of the tree. "Yep..."

"Remember the last time we were up here?"

"Yes, ugh don't remind me," she groaned. "That's got to be the worst way to break up with someone, and to have your whole body exposed on the internet like that!"

"He deserved it! No one plays Jessica Larson and gets away with it!" she fended proudly. They spent the remainder of the hour in the tree house making out until they heard a neigh come from below. "You should probably return that horse," Jess chuckled.

"Oh shit, what time is it?" he asked checking the time on his cell phone.

"After school hours," she replied.

"Crap! Come on, let's go!" he urged when rushing them both back out of the tree house. He climbed on top of the horse and lent out his hand to assist Jess up behind. "Sorry, but I have to be in front now, you work better from behind," he teased.

"It wouldn't be the first time I've heard that," she smirked. When they arrived back on campus, the owner of the horse charged extra for taking longer than expected.

"...and I didn't know you can get a ticket for going over horse speed limit, I mean what was that all about?"

He chuckled when grabbing his car keys out of his pockets. "I want to thank you," she says grabbing both of his hands after stopping in front of his car. "This was possibly the best day I could ask for," she admired, cupping his square face in her hands before lowering his head to kiss his nose.

"Who knew you could be so romantic?"

(End of flashback)

Jessica spent her entire day bawling, when contemplating over her sanity about the relationship with her two childhood friends, it was a daily norm. *Why is my life so confusing? Why can't I just figure my life out already? One minute I am head over heels for Jaiden and the next, I'm lip-locking and complicating my feelings for Jared. What is wrong with me? Why can't one of the twins just show up at my doorstep so that it'll be enough for me to know who is really worth my time and commitment?* After having thought that, there was a knock at the door. She vitally rubbed her eyelids behind the door before answering it; it was...

Chapter Seventeen

"Jared, w-what are you doing here? What happened?"

Jessica gave him space to enter her flat upon noticing that he was not in the best condition to stand. "I'm guessing you told Jaiden about us... he wasn't too thrilled," he explains while sitting himself down on the couch.

"I'm so sorry Jare. I couldn't hide it from him, it didn't feel right," she confessed. "... I tried telling him that it was an accident."

"Was it?" he interrogates. "Because, I don't think it was—it felt right to me..." he admits.

"Jared, I can't believe you walked all the way over here like this!" she exclaimed before instantly standing up to retrieve water for him, ice-cold.

"Thanks," he says before drinking the full glass.

"Would you like some more?"

"No thanks, I'm good," he assured when setting the cup back down while swishing the remaining water around in his mouth before swallowing it.

"Do you need a place to stay?"

"No, I'm going to go," he inferred before wobbling over to the door. He almost falls but she conveniently ran over to assist him in time. "You think you can drive me home?" he self-consciously invoked with the lightest of chuckles.

"Of course—but we need to talk first," she directed before guiding him back over to the couch. They both repossess their seats before she proceeded to speak her mind this time. "Jared..." she sighed, running her hands through her hair.

"Look, I know what you're going to say, I did something I shouldn't have..."

"Not only, but you made a promise that you would quit."

"I know, I'm sorry... it's hard to quit old habits, it's hard to quit you too."

"I don't need you to be sorry Jared, I need you to stop, you say sorry but how do I know you're not going to do this again?"

"You trust me."

The following school day, Jess decided to miss her first few classes to confront Jaiden about yesterday's scandal, but she refused to knock on the front door, so she decided to climb his tree instead. He helped her inside before continuing where he left off in his weight lifting. "We need to talk."

"Kinda busy…"

"We need to talk NOW!" she demanded when marching forward.

"Okay. What?"

"Did you harm Jared?"

He chuckled. "Well I'm not going to deny it," he says while continuously working out his biceps.

"Jaiden!"

"The lil' dipshit has been ruining my life since day one and you expect me to just stand in the sidelines while I watch him take everything I've ever cared about, away from me?"

"You self-righteous, pompous 'swine'! I don't understand how you could physically hurt someone who you should be closer than ever with! He's your twin for crying out loud!"

"Well, excuse me for trying to claim what's mine!" he flares when scratching his nose.

"I am no object Jaiden, you can't just claim me. And besides… what if I don't want to be claimed?" she inferred while lifting her nose high in the air. He drops his weight and Jess retracted back in fear, startling at the sound. He spits on the hardwood floor in his attempt to step closer to her.

"This isn't a discussion, you want one? Here it is, you're mine and that is that. You chose me when you accepted my proposal, it's a done deal. No taksies backsies," he says grabbing her arm forcefully.

She was triggered, "What, this ol' thing? I'd hardly call it a proposal and more like your way of tying me down. A dog tag would've been less obvious!"

"Yeah? I'll buy one to match those pretty little earrings—" he taunted, flicking her earring before she slapped his hand away. "If this is the kind of respect I get for trying to be a part your life then you could just leave right now!"

"Gladly—but we're not done here! I—"

He takes her by surprise when his hand clasps her neck, bringing his lips to hers when she desperately tried to resist from his clutch. He then guided her hand down his chest and to his lower abdominal. His face was flushed and his body was wet from sweating, it turned her on to see his bare flesh flaunting before her. He stepped closer and pushed his head forward before raking his lips to hers—about to touch but not yet, his heavy breath right above her tortured soul. She was about to give in to his death trap before he walked away, lifting his weight to continue with his work out. "Jaiden, what's wrong?" she worried, taking a step closer but he didn't allow her the advantage to get close to him as he backtracked away. "Don't fucking come near me, I'm still pissed at you," he snarled, flaring his nostrils.

"Wh—"

"You don't know h-how fucking tempted I am to rip all your clothes off your body. I fucking want you so bad, but I can't because it hurts to know that I'm not the only one you're thinking of when you're with me!" he outbursts.

"Please leave."

"I want you to know—"

"Just go!" he grits, turning around, redder than before. "Please, I can't control myself when I'm with you, especially when I'm this angry, I don't know what I'm capable of." He climatically paused while resting his head on his fist from beside the wall.

"You won't hurt me…" she assured, stepping forward.

"Don't be so sure." He violently slammed his door on the way out causing his bedroom walls to clatter, only it wasn't only his walls that were shaken up in the moment. Deep down, she knew he was not genuinely capable of hurting anyone not even her, not physically anyways. She climbed out of his bedroom window and entered her car, heading back for the high school. She tried getting through the school day without breaking down in the middle of class but failed and ended up having to excuse herself to use the restroom in almost all the rest of her classes. She couldn't contain herself until seventh hour—so she had up and decided to skip to head home for the remainder of the day. Of course, she received concerning calls and voicemail messages from all her friends, wondering where she was and why she cut class. She was at her deepest condolences to her dance group for missing so many practices. She had expected them to sympathize with her personal reasons still, she had no excuse for being out of focus for everything lately. She prayed she could make it through the rest of her senior year on time and get back on track. What she desired mostly, was to be back to simpler times when there were no relationships and she could talk to the twins about anything without either of them getting hurt, but that was not the case. Jessica felt like she was coming between them, like she had ruined their relationship with each other and their parents by being their subject of affection. She didn't ask to be that person, she hated being in the middle as much as she hated being the last child; she felt at fault for everything.

****

"Don't think about making this a habit just for the makeup sex!" Jessica underlined, throwing a shirt over then pulling her hair out of the neck hole.

"Alright well, I've got to go," Jaiden announced while walking out of the girl's bedroom after a quick change of clothes.

"Excuse me?" she snapped causing him to turn around.

"I'm kind of grounded," he grumbled.

"And I don't like your tone of voice!" He stayed silent while she strides over to him to dispute their differences.

"So, you're just going to go?"

"Yeah... did you expect seconds?"

"No... I just thought we'd cuddle," she sheepishly admits while wrapping her arms around his neck, but not before he put his hand out in front, to back her away.

"I think we're finished here," he states while putting on his shoes.

She frowns, "So, you got what you wanted and that's it?"

"Don't be so ignorant."

"What did you just say?"

"I wasn't the only one who got what they wanted..."

She nearly yelled at the top of her lungs now, "Fucking goodbye, Jaiden!" she angered while opening the door and sending him packing on his way.

"Wait, Jessica?" he pleads while sticking his foot between the door.

"Yeah?" she asked, innocently tucking a piece of hair behind her ear, batting her eyelashes in hopes that he would change his mind.

"Can you grab my ray-bans?" he asked. Her smile dropped.

"You mean this?" she walked over to the couch and picked it up. He held out his hand and she purposely missed to chuck them at the wall behind.

"What the hell! Those are expensive!"

"Go fuck yourself!" she fired back when slamming the door on his misshapen face.

****

"I don't fucking believe this! I don't need to be here!" Jaiden disputed while flaming up from his seat.

"Jaiden, please sit down," requested the therapist.

"NO, I'm leaving!" Jaiden announced just before swinging the door open.

"Jaiden, sit your ass down!" Linda directed from the opposite side of the door now.

"You got it ma'am!" he obediently complied on his return to his seat while staring at the ground beneath him on his way back.

"Sorry Dr. Henry, please continue… and remember boys, I pay by the hour," Linda addressed, closing the door behind herself.

"So, Jared, why don't we start out with you? Tell me, what causes you to have such anger towards your brother?"

"Well, it's mainly the stupid things he does…" Jared begins by explaining while scraping the bottom of his shoe that was dispositioned on his lap.

"I may be stupid but at least I'm not ugly," the older brother grumbles, placing his hand on his cheek. Jared resentfully looked over to his malicious brother for disrupting him and clenched his jaw before taking a deep breath and continuing with, "For the record, WE LOOK THE FUCKING SAME!" he emphasized.

"If you'd continue," Dr. Henry responded while examining his clipboard.

"I try to be a good brother, with every good intention and every-time Jaiden may think he tries, it's only to get me in trouble. And he 'always' feels the need to compete with me—"

"You're the one who repeatedly admitted to wishing you were me…" Jaiden apathetically sighed.

"Ssshhh, Jaiden, it is not your turn to speak yet—"

"Fuck! I don't give 'two' fucks!" he snarled, shooting up with his veins evidently popping out of his neck. "Every time this happens! Every time! Jared has to come first at everything! ALWAYS! Just because he's the youngest he gets this 'special treatment'! We're only ten goddamn minutes apart! Well, no more! Now it's 'my' turn to speak! Jared, I fucking hate you! You're a waste of DNA," he resentfully spat.

Jared arose, "I don't fuckin' like you either! You fucking stole my girlfriend!" he charged.

"I didn't steal 'anyone' from you! Jessica jumped at the opportunity to be with me after you fucking left her to screw the president of our fan club!"

"It's not like I did that on purpose you mentally challenged idiot!"

"This is good boys… really focus on that negative energy," the therapist says, shutting his eyes to focus on their thoughts.

"Why do you think she even went for you anyways? 'Exactly!' She wouldn't have if she were still with me!"

"What can I say? She couldn't resist the way I make her feel… when I fuck her." Jaiden evilly triggered the boy.

"Don't fucking talk about her like that!" warned Jared, pushing against his brother's chest.

"I can talk about her like that all I want! You're just jealous that you will never be half the man I am! It's a pretty big shoe to fill and let's face it, your dick will never compare to size—" he taunted.

"That tears it!" Jared growled just seconds before tackling Jaiden onto the carpet.

"I'm sensing some sort of pattern here. I can see where this problem evolved from now," the therapist inferred while petting his grey beard as the twins continued to brawl.

"Why do you have to do this to me! You knew how much I liked her!" Jared grunts, flipping them both over.

"No… I didn't!" Jaiden objected while he struggled to shift his weight back on his brother.

"I saw her first!" Jared choked out.

"I fucked her first, so what!"

(Flashback to 4-year-old Jessica)
"Beverly, don't let go!" Jessica screamed.

"Too late!" she snickered.

"Good job Jessie, you're doing it!" Amanda cheered.

"I am doing it!" Jessica joyously agreed when picking up her speed and pedaling through the neighborhood. "Owwww! Stop it!" she heard in the distance. Jessica decided to pedal over to the saddened boy that was on the sidewalk down the block, sitting on the curb and crying his eyes out in front of his house. She unclipped the child safety lock on her helmet after parking her vehicle. "Are you okay?"

"No," he pouts. "My idiot brother pushed me down the stairs."

"Siblings are mean!"

"I got two… how many do you got?"

"Two."

"Me too!"

"Looks like you got a boo boo," she noticed.

"It hurts!" he lisps while lifting his knees up to his distressed eyes.

"Jessica! Sweetie, there you are!" her mother pants after jogging down the street with Jessica's big sister, Amanda. They detach her away from the little boy, "What did we say about talking to strangers?"

"Come on, let's go," she says dragging her arm as Mandy grabs ahold of her bike.

"But—" Jess worried turning around, "He needs help mommy!"

Jaiden remembered being at the grocery store when he saw Jess for the first time the next week, with her mother. She was so excited to see him, only he had no idea who she was. She ran up and hugged him, asking if he was okay after what happened with his brother.

"Sure," was all he said, confused.

Only, he didn't care that he had no clue who she was, he was a boy and even at that early in age, he was an absolute chick magnet and she was a total babe to him. "Jaiden, is this your girlfriend?" his elder sister Nora snickered from beside him in line.

"My name is Jessica," was what a four-year-old Jessica had responded with, introducing herself to her new friends when shaking Jaiden's hand. Little did Jessica know was that it was in fact Jaiden's twin that she ran into before.

(End of flashback)

"She thought I, was 'you'?"

A present-day Jared sighed when trying desperately to recall the events. What Jared failed to remember was that he did not see her again until she finally realized there was two of them and 'til this very day, she never found out that it was Jared who was that kid she first met on the sidewalk.

...talk about irony.

****

"Hello?" Jessica answered, not recognizing the caller I.D.

"Yes, is this Jessica?"

"Yep, that's me. May I ask who's calling?"

"Hi, yes—I'm sorry, this is Barbara. I'm close friends with your mother, Margret... she told me you were in desperate need of a job and I was wondering if you'd be available to babysit this Saturday night?"

"Sure, I'd be happy to... I love kids!" she excitedly exclaimed.

"That's great! I have no one to watch them. You see, my family and I are attending a barbeque and they have school the next day, I'd take them along, but because of that—"

"Say no more, you've got yourself a deal!"

"Fantastic! How much do you charge? We'll pay any amount."

"How about ten dollars an hour, to start?"

"You got it! Thank you so much, you're a lifesaver! I'll forward the address to this number."

"Sounds great!"

****

Saturday night, Jess showered, changed, grabbed her backpack, and headed for her car. She took a drive to the Smith household where she was greeted by Barbara and Richard on their way out. "Thank you so much! We're in a hurry but everything else you'll need is in the house!" Barbara explained while stepping down her porch steps. Well, that would certainly explain the wordy email Jess got a half hour ago with precise instructions to follow.

"Well, alright?" Jess cocked a brow before stepping inside their house.

"Hello? Kasey? Kyle?" The kids attack her from behind and hug at her feet after sneaking up on her. They were two blonde children about six years of age.

"Hi kids, I'm Jessica and I will be your babysitter for the night," she informed, struggling to walk towards the living room with the kids at her legs. This was Jessica's first baby-sitting service and she didn't want to screw it up.

"Intruder!" the little boy by the name of Kyle shouted.

"No, your parents were in a rush to a party and they've asked me to come and take care of you," she grunted.

"I'm gonna call the cops!" the little girl warned when getting up and running towards the kitchen while Jessica detached the boy from her leg to run after her.

"Please don't!" she begged, creeping up to Kasey in the massive kitchen as the girl stood on a chair, dialing some number on their house phone.

"Please put that down," she calmly warned.

"No!" giggled Kasey when hopping down and running off with the phone. These kids were going to drive Jess to insanity soon, she felt it. It took Jessica approximately fifteen minutes to finally reach this little girl and snatch the phone away from her. She then put her ear against the phone and heard nothing but the dial tone coming from the other end, sighing in relief before opening up a random cabinet and hiding it far from the kids' reach. She let out a couple of heavy breaths when reaching for her forehead while beads of sweat formed at her hairline.

****

It was half past nine p.m. now and the bratty kids that Jessica had to put up with for the night, were refusing to go to sleep, they have put Jessica beyond exhaust. Their parents have left Jess a note with precise instructions to follow including giving them their allergy medication, which they refused to take along with their dinner that they barely touched. They have even sprayed her in silly string and tripped the poor girl a few times. Not only that, but they also topped her off with a couple of water balloons in their prank wars. She was completely drenched in water now although she wouldn't bet her life on the substance being water. She was in desperate need of help… she whipped out her phone from her back pocket, texting the first person that she could rely on to help in this situation. She then maneuvered over to fetch the doorbell after about fifteen minutes of waiting for help. "Alright, where are these lil' munchkins?" asks Jared while stepping inside the massive house after Jessica lent him some space in the doorway to enter. She chose Jared to help her knowing Jaiden would only be a distraction.

"I am so glad you're here! These kids are killing me!" she tiredly whined before squeezing the ends of her hair to get the excess 'water' out.

"It was not easy to persuade my parents to let me go out, but I'll let you in on a little secret… I'm their favorite," he playfully winked. "But what happened to you?" he asked when following her to the living room.

"It's been a long night, I just want to get home and sleep—they are tiring me out and what's worse is that they are refusing to go to sleep!"

"Ooooo, Jessica's got a boyfriend!" Kyle teased when running into the living room.

"Hey kid, scram!" Jared hissed, putting a foot forward as Kyle hid behind Kasey, intimidated by the taller man now.

****

"We did it!" Jess exclaimed after releasing a puff of air when looking back at the kids who have passed out in their bedrooms. It was 11:02 at night, and after so many failed attempts at getting those darned kids to sleep, they finally passed out from a sugar rush that Jared and Jess were forced to have put on them. The two teenage sitters then went to the kitchen and began to rid the place clean of junk food, disposing of the evidence. Jess had bent over to clean the soda spill that those children left amuck and nearly tripped on it before Jared swiftly caught her, causing her to break even in hysterical laughter. "God, we would make

288

terrible parents!" Jared chuckled with his shirt covered in chocolate syrup from the junk food incident that he took part in just before the kids finally settled in the hay.

"Look at this!" Jess exclaimed, brushing over her wash-clothed jeans that were splotched with ice pop stains. They finished cleaning up at around 12:00 and collapsed on the couch to watch television until the parents returned. Jessica woke up to a flicker of light, rubbing her eyelids open and shifting her legs that were curled up at her sides onto the floor before sitting tall. She finds herself looking the kids' parents dead in the eye, surrounded by this awkward predicament. She then looked to her right and found Jared yawning while stretching up, much like a feline when taking his time to notice his surroundings.

"Oh shit, hello," Jared awkwardly greets, quickly standing up after Jess had already stood up and slapped his shoulders awake to direct his attention to the rightful concerned parents of Kasey and Kyle. Jess, who fixes her hair, innocently waits as the mother throws her keys on the rack beside her and approaches the two in the living room as the father sets his coat down and does the same.

"I'm so sorry, this isn't what it looks like, Jare—uh, I mean, he was just helping out..." The parents stayed silent and the father ran upstairs to check in on the kids—returning minutes later as the mother stays put to examine the guilty teens standing before her some more.

"Well, the kids are safely asleep," noted the father.

"And... this wasn't the best scene to walk into but at least you guys weren't doing anything inappropriate," the mother concluded when folding her arms.

"And you've cleaned up?" the father noticed when walking around.

"Yes, and we have checked everything off the list," says Jessica, nodding off with her hands behind her back. The mother reaches into her purse to retrieve her wallet. She handed both Jess and Jared a three-hundred-dollar tip.

"A-are you serious?" Jess questioned, carefully lusting over it.

"You guys have earned it... really."

"I don't know how you managed to stay here and put the kids to sleep but well done, I mean thank you!" the father praised.

"Those kids are a nightmare!" chuckled Richard while wiping his glasses on his sweater. "Every babysitter we've had has either ran off on us or refused to do services for us ever again, mostly both," he continued.

"Well, it was not easy, but we managed," Jared says, scratching the back of his head.

"Yes, we can tell," the parents cackled at their social experiment, examining over their hired babysitters.

"Well, thank you for having us. We should get going," Jess excused before taking herself and Jared out of the house upon remembering that they had left the kids in mess when they forced them into a sugar rush. Although in Jessica's defense, she wouldn't say 'forced' since the kids enjoyed it and marveled at the idea. The only problem with that, was that the children passed out on Jared and Jess who had to drag them into bed with their chocolate infested clothes. Somehow the parents overlooked how the two succeeded in putting their children to sleep and Jess and Jared fled out of the house before they remembered to ask. The kids would most likely end up telling their parents whenever they woke anyways, but the two accurately didn't want to be there when that monstrosity happens, so they rushed out.

"That was interesting," Jared laughs out when stopping in the middle of the garage parkway with Jess.

"Yep, never doing this again, that's for sure… but we do make a great team."

"I guess I better get going…" he says clapping his hands together.

"Yeah… thank you so much, I couldn't have possibly done this without you," she admitted.

"No problem," he says walking towards his car.

"Wait… Jared?"

"Yeah?" he turned around in the middle of the roadway, ten feet away now as she ran up to him, "This time, I mean it," she stated after pulling away from the kiss they just shared.

No regrets.

****

When Jared arrived back home it was one a.m.

He contemplated in silence how all he wanted in that moment was more, on his car ride home. In that moment, he just wanted to lift her up and kiss her all over, proclaiming his love for her once and for all, but not until he got Jaiden off his back.

"Hey, where were you at?" Jaiden asks standing by his doorway.

"I uh, had to help a friend," Jared says while scratching his chin.

"And Mom and Dad just let you drive and have your phone back?"

"No, I took my phone without their consent and yes, they let me drive this one night."

"Why are you covered with shit?" he chuckles.

"It's not shit, it's chocolate syrup, dumbass."

"Okay, so why are you covered with 'chocolate syrup'?" he air-quotes.

"I don't fucking have time to play twenty questions, I need to take a shower," he announced, excusing himself out of his room.

"You were with Jessica?" Jaiden asked when following him out.

"Maybe I was," he says entering his bathroom. "She asked me to help her babysit," he continued by saying, sliding the glass shower door open to turn on the water.

"Wait… why would she ask 'you' to help, why didn't she just ask 'me'?"

"I don't know…" says Jared. "Maybe it has something to do with the fact that you were never around to help her when she was pregnant or maybe because you're irresponsible," he shrugged, pulling out a towel from the shelf in his bathroom closet from behind his brother, setting it on the rack beside the shower.

"Huh," Jaiden sighs before exiting the room.

Jared takes a fifteen-minute long shower before hopping out of the bathroom and making his way to his esteemed room, closing the door behind himself. It seemed Jared was at a loss of privacy with Jaiden invading his room every ten or so minutes, to bother him with his intrusive interrogation; he heard a chuckle causing him to startle under his covers when Jaiden interrupted him momentarily later again.

"For fucks sake Jaiden! Don't you knock!" Jared panicked, covering his lower half with his blanket, freeing his hand from under the premises of his trousers and tossing his phone aside after locking his phone screen to cut off the sound. "Cold shower not enough?" Jaiden shamed before stepping out of the room to give Jared the few minutes he requested to change. Meanwhile, Jared threw on some basketball shorts before answering the door.

"So I was wondering, since you haven't given up your keys to Mom or Dad—" Jaiden continued off in thought after Jared re-opened his door.

"No Jaiden," Jared cut-off, growing annoyed.

"You don't even know what I was going to ask!" he protests.

"You can't drive my car to go see Jessica."

"Alright… so can 'you' drive me to see Jessica?"

"No—"

"…It's nearly two in the morning, she needs rest and so do you."

But that wasn't the exact reason Jared didn't want Jaiden to go over there. He knew exactly what would happen if Jaiden showed up, *vulnerability at its finest.* She was just starting to accept Jared back into her life and in comes Jaiden, sweeping her off her feet with his charm, it

291

wouldn't be long before she forgets about Jared again and he would not have it. *He doesn't deserve her,* he thought. *Jaiden is a player, he uses every girl he has ever dated for sex and only sex. He's the type who can't control himself, especially around girls who flash their bare minimum at him. The most partial of skin, arouses him. If only Jessica knew how many fan girls Jaiden has fooled around with in his time before she became a priority in his life. Girls just don't understand his nature, they continue to do this to themselves. When tour comes around, their relationship is destined for failure,* thought Jared.

"Come on man, help a brother out!"

"Jaiden, I'm fucking exhausted..."

Jaiden cackled when taking a step closer, before placing a tight death grip around Jared's neck, it was his signature. "Are you exhausted now?" he threatened when curling his hand tighter around his brother's neck. Jared instantly tugged Jaiden's arm down, twisting it at his sides with an even tighter death sentence, "Are you?" he taunted back.

"I'm impressed kid, 'been working out?" Jaiden disgruntled in pain.

"Gotta keep up to fight you off big boy," Jared implied before releasing his grip on Jaiden who lets out a breath. "Now why don't you do yourself a favor and get the fuck out of my room," he whispered in his ear from behind when clasping the back of his neck now. Jaiden nods and stands back on his feet just as Jared pushes him out the door, locking it after him. Jaiden feared the day his brother would fight him off, he didn't know that day would be so soon, let alone happen. He considered himself more powerful than Jared—after all, he has been working out a lot longer than he has.

****

Chapter Eighteen

Sunday today, was the day Jessica Jane decided to step out into the real world to tackle a 'real' job, and not one involving ditzy kids. She had been employed before, of course, if by a couple of weeks count for something. During the winter, she had been working in retail until she was laid off for lack of business and the store having closed. Only recently, has she applied to many different locations in the past week and the only place she knew of that was hiring was at a local Starbucks that she went in to interview for in the early morning. The manager decided to train Jessica as a barista right away since the location was short of employees for the busy day ahead. Today, she had to spend her working hours watching Tammy handle orders. Tammy was an olive toned girl who was in her early twenties and had beautiful beach blonde hair.

"You ready to try an order?" she asked, chewing her mint scented gum while she lids a coffee order before writing the person's name down with a sharpie. Jess nodded humbly.

"Alright, who's next?" asks Tammy after swiftly serving the last order off to the person and making bank. Jessica stood at the front register to serve the next person in line now.

"Yes, can I get my regular order? Make it a venti and make it fast—I have an appointment to get to," the next customer directed when turning around after ending her call.

"Mrs. Daniels?" Jess stood frozen at the woman's appearance after she took her shades off, revealing her face.

"Jessica… what a tedious surprise," she says so under-amused.

"Linda is our regular," Tammy approached with. If Jessica had known 'that', she would have never filled out the application form. "This is our newest employee, Jessica—and you are her first client. You will need to rank our services at the end by filling out a small survey," Tammy cheerfully clarified when handing Linda a small form.

Oh god, this was not happening! This woman hates me and would do anything to rid me from ever crossing her again. And that is exactly how Jessica explained that to Tammy on the other side of the cash register.

"You watched me make a million of these today, you'll do great!" she says patting her assertively on the shoulder before exiting through the employee door in the back.

"Alright..." Jess tensed when grabbing Linda's credit card before sliding it in the machine.

After Linda paid, Jess grabbed a paper cup to begin brewing the fresh pot of coffee. When she looked over at Mrs. Daniels, she noticed her eyeing around the counter, probably looking for something she can hold against the girl for later. As the coffee brewed, Jess struggled to remember where Tammy kept the rest of the 'special' coffee mixture. She found it in the distance on the back counter; there, it laid on the table. She sprinkled some of that into the cup just as the coffee finished. She then poured the hot liquid in with the mix and mixed it with the special wooden mixing utensil. As soon as she finished, Tammy walked out to examine her.

"Excuse me, may I please get a pencil?" insisted Linda when approaching the ready counter. Tammy grabs the pen from behind her ear to hand it to the woman. Jess then handed Linda her paid hot-n-ready coffee from the counter. The faulty cup came apart in the woman's hand and Linda shrieked in terror as the hot liquid came crashing down on her blouse, imprinting her skin.

"Oh my gosh! I'm so sorry!" Jessica apologetically panicked.

"You forgot the cardboard!" Tammy yelled.

"I-I'm so sorry..." she sympathized. Tammy rushed over to grab some napkins. A bitter Linda, snatched the napkins from Tammy's hand after she handed them over. Linda dabbed the napkins all over her stained white blouse.

"Excuse me, may I please get a coffee over here!" the next woman in line shouted causing Tammy to give her newest employee a small shove in the direction of the register.

"We will get you a fresh coffee, on us," Tammy assured when removing the old cup from Linda's hands.

"Don't bother, I'm late for a meeting," she huffed, storming out of the place.

Jess was on cleaning duty for the remainder of her shift after Tammy took over. "Don't worry, accidents happen. You'll get it next time, I have faith in you," she said when closing up shop.

"You mean... there will be a next time?" Jess asked while releasing her hair at her sides.

****

294

It wasn't until the next week, that Jess became familiar with the routine and began moving along with the pace of business. It was also that second week, when Jaiden had surprised her at work for the first time. She also happened to remember that 'this' was the place Jaiden had come to escape when he missed her sonogram appointment to be with his beloved Candi, aww... *asshole*. "Look at you, looking so ravishing behind the counter," he flourishes during her break hours while she tried to finish cleaning the counter free of coffee spills.

"At least I'm working. We can't all thrive on the internet for our success like you," she bitterly responded. She was having the worst day today.

"Okay, that was a cheap shot," he says walking up to the counter.

"Don't you have school to catch up on or something?"

"Was in the neighborhood, thought I'd swing by and check this place out. Although, I could use some assistance now that I'm here. I've been working up an appetite all day and all I have left to offer is my self-service," he flattered.

"Charming."

"Jessica, you are free to go," her manager says, walking out from the back.

"But I never asked—"

"Your husband here, requested you to take the day off and I think you've earned it!"

****

"My 'husband', is a big idiot!" she grumbled while stepping into his car.

"Relax, now you can spend the day with me," he grinned, grazing a hand over her thigh before she rejected it away.

"I can't believe you lied to my manager and told her I was 'married'! Are you insane!"

"Insane, but smart. You think she'd let you take the day off if I were a stranger? Think again," he deviously smirked.

"Yeah and now she's going to think of me as a liar because last I checked on my résumé, I was single and sure of it!"

"Oooo baby, that's cold," he says wrinkling his face.

"Fucking, don't touch me!" she snapped, removing his arm from around her neck.

"Grouchy... is someone on that time of the month again?"

"Are you kidding me right now? Stop the car!" she demanded.

"No, we're on the highway, I can't just stop,"

"I'm not going to ask you again Jaiden, stop this damn car!" He slams down on the breaks, stopping on the right side of the road. Jessica then, unlocks the passenger side door and steps out before slamming the car door. He parked his car, setting his emergency brake on and ran out after her.

"Wait up!" he insists when grabbing her arm.

"Where the hell are you going! You can't get home from here!" he ridiculed.

"You can't keep controlling me! Is this how it's going to be like from now on? If we're married in ten years, is this how it's going to be?"

"Woah, back it up. I never said I wanted to marry you—"

"Unbelievable," she scoffed, turning away. He ran up, clutching to her wrist again.

"No, I didn't mean it like that. Why are you so worried about the future?" he asked.

"I need money Jaiden, I need to pay for my rent, tuition. I'm independent again, I can't rely on my sister and brother in-law to pay for me every step of the way! I'm in debt."

"I got you, don't worry about it—"

"I 'am' going to worry about it! I don't need your money! I 'need' to try and finish things on my own and without you ordering me around! I don't need you to think you're going to weasel your way into my life and sabotage 'my' work schedule! This is 'my' job, 'my' responsibility, and 'my' earnings! You can't just take that away from me!" she hyperventilated with the wind from the cars passing by them and blowing her hair behind her face.

"I'm sorry, it was just a one-time thing, I promise," he convinced when grabbing her hand.

"Please get back in the car and I'll drive you back to work if you want?"

"No… just please take me home."

****

"Jessica! Over here!" the interviewer requests while Jessica walked across the red carpet with both twins occupying her arms. The flashes of camera everywhere almost blinding her, but luckily, she had the support from both the twins to keep her balanced in her heels. "Here today with people bigger than the Kardashian's—the story of the love triangle that gave people hope. Joined with Jessica Larson and the Daniels; so Jessica, tell us… how did it feel to have finally legalized polygamy in the United States?"

"The question hath not how I felt, but really lies in the hands of other people with the same struggles that I have experienced—and to know that I made a difference, a peace in the world is blissful."

"How has the relationship with your children and their fathers been? There must be some sort of confusion?"

"You know, there are kids out there in the world with divorced parents, who struggle with two fathers, two mothers even, there is really no difference except for the fact that I'm still in love with both of these two men and it's not wrong at all. We all support each other..." Jess finished her statement before walking down the red carpet. When she backed out of the interview, her very pregnant lump on her stomach became the focus of the camera lens in her mind before a flash caused her to jolt awake; terrified and panicked. She sat up with a novel across her face, the one she had been reading herself to sleep, it was the Shakespearean classic, *Hamlet.* She could somewhat see the correlation of her night terror to the book she dozed off to, but with her own twist on things playing out in her mind. Greed, could have been the hidden atrocity that resurfaced in her nightmare. Her hand flew up to clutch at her forehead, she was drenched in sweat once again, puffing her chest inwards and outwards very rapidly. This whole 'love triangle' was becoming an issue that she needed to rid of, immediately. She once again, checked her stomach to be sure it was only a dream and the only bump she thankfully had was from lack of exercise.

She was forced to wake up at around two a.m. because of that nightmare—not being able to fall back asleep. It wasn't until three in the morning that she had drifted back off into REM sleep after curling up to a soothing playlist given to her by her sister.

The next realm she had dreamed herself into was of Jaiden and Jared jousting over her affection. It was a very medieval period and she looked like a renaissance explosion in the horrible poofy and flamboyant dress with the pointed pink veil she had been wearing. She was graciously redeemed back to life before either of the twins got extremely hurt in this particular dream. Still, she wasn't sure who was who underneath all that iron armor, but she had a pretty vague idea that Jared was the one who was about to lose—he was just not that physically cut out compared to Jaiden. So, she finally decided to wake up at four a.m. after ending that glorious nightmare. She spent the rest of her morning tiding up her apartment before she had to ride off for school again.

****

After school, Jaiden had requested that Jess help him catch up on notes and classwork… at least she had hoped that was why he wanted to come over. *Eye roll.*

"Damn you."

"Forgive me for being so irresistibly sexy," he smirked when helping her down from the wooden table.

"So, did you still want to study?" she asked while sliding into her jeans.

"Nope," he says throwing a shirt over. "I actually have to be somewhere soon."

"Jaiden," she narrowed her eyes.

"No regrets, right?" he chuckles, and that word instantaneously sent shivers down her spine—the kind of shivers that made her think back to the night when she scandalously kissed Jared, on purpose. "I'll see you later," he says while buttoning up his plaid shirt and kissing behind her ear before he headed off. The decent most thing that came out of that distraction was that Jessica had finished all her homework prior to helping him study, so she was done for the day. When she went into her kitchen to retrieve the Windex from underneath the sink to begin wiping the sweat glands from off the sin-filled table, she noticed Jaiden's phone on one of the chairs that he was sitting on earlier.

Hmmmmmm, she thought. He was getting shadier and it would help to know why he has been so distant lately. "Should I?"

Maybe just a peek, she thought to herself before gliding a hand over the back of his neon blue iPhone case. She turned it on after five minutes of consulting with herself. Just her luck; as it turned out, Jaiden—like most other people, had a password—which led Jessica to assume that he had some unresolved trust issues with her. She tried a couple of different and random combinations, having to wait nearly five minutes before trying again. "Could it be my birthday?" she asked while typing the six-digit passcode, *incorrect.*

"Could it be … 'his' birthday?"

She laughed at her own ridiculous suggestion, but just to be sure he wasn't as conceited as she thought, she tried anyways—hoping to be wronged. Only a complete self-centered moron, would put a six-digit lock of his birthday; and she stood corrected, *he WAS a moron.* She scrolled through his messages after successfully unlocking it, nothing new. She then scrolled through his call history and it surprised her to find a repeated number throughout his call history that she didn't recognize because it had no caller I.D. Although she was tempted to find out who had been calling, she was also squeamish to know… it could change everything between them, this collect call. Something didn't add up about his behavior lately and she was about to get an answer. She spent fifteen precious minutes pacing throughout her flat, contemplating with her fingers in her mouth, phone in other hand, trying to figure out who this person Jaiden had been calling was, assuming the worst. *What if he has been cheating on me?* She takes in a deep breath before dialing the number, putting the phone to her ear after muting the call. The caller picks up within seconds, "I'm so glad to hear back from you," the female voice says through the speaker as Jessica's end of the line stayed silent. "Hello? Jaiden?"

Jessica abruptly ended the call and stumbled backwards, brushing a hand over her lip. Her feet almost gave out as soon as she recognized the voice and she instantly dropped the phone onto the floor. Seconds later, her own phone went off.

"H-hello?" she hoarsely answered without even looking at the caller I.D.

"Jessica? Hey babe, I left my phone at your place, you mind if I come over and pick it up?"

****

"Hey thanks, you're a lifesaver," he says walking inside after she had opened her apartment door.

"Courtney! Fucking Courtney! I knew it!" she cried out when shoving his phone directly in his hands before storming out.

"Wait a minute, what's going on?" he asks, stopping her with his hand around her wrist.

"You got caught is what happened! Now get away from me and I mean it!" she yelled, pointing a finger without making eye contact.

"You went through my phone?"

"Obviously you were hiding something from me if you didn't want me to look at it! Now just go, I don't want to see you ever again!"

"Baby, she needed me for a history project. I would never cheat on you and you know that."

"Like you 'actually' do homework, you showed me your definition of 'studying' right here on this table!" she melodramatically manifested.

"I swear on my brother's life, I did 'not' cheat on you!" he says beginning to cradle her.

"Don't swear on his life, swear on your life! His life is more valuable than yours!"

"If his life is more 'valuable' than mine, then why did he cheat!"

"You did too, you just didn't get caught in the act," she huffed.

"Jessica, god dammit! You kissed Jared!"

299

"Yeah and it was just a friendly kiss! It meant nothing to me!"

the first time...

"You slept with her! There's a difference!"

"Jessica, I didn't cheat on you... but I will confess something else that I need to get off my chest—this is going to be hard to tell you but," he shakily respired before taking her by the hand to guide her over to the couch. "Jared and I aren't going to be here for the rest of the school year."

"W-what do you mean?"

He sighed, dropping his face in his hands, "We got offered a three-month tour... we signed a contract and everything today."

"Well, you certainly didn't waste any time to think about this," she bitterly incriminated.

"You have to understand, this is really important for Jared and me— we can get classes in the summer and graduate then, but this is a once in a lifetime opportunity—"

"How much longer do you have?"

"We leave in four days."

"W-what about graduation... prom? Jaiden, I have never been to prom or any school dance you know that. You know how much that means to me now—" she whines.

"I know, I can't figure this out right now but in time we will..." And with that, he was off.

She tried not to let it mess with her head too much and tried to see the positive side of things, even though it killed her inside. How could he just walk away like that? She only had four days to try to make what was left of her senior year memorable with the twins, but it was challenging for her to do when she was still uncertain of her feelings for both. This meant she had four days to think about who mattered most to her and hoped that would be enough of a confession to make them stay, as selfish as that sounded. Not only was that a challenge, but with the twins suspended for all this time, she had even less time to make up for lost time.

****

The twins were finally back at school after being liberated from their two-week probation—this was Jessica's last week with them and 'twas not fair. The following day at school, while Jessica was on her way to the restroom, she saw Jaiden and Courtney talking in the distance, adding onto her suspicion—so, she curiously walked up to listen in. "What's going on?" she asked when walking closer.

"Nothing. We were just done here," he rudely excused, hinting at Courtney.

"We are 'not' done here!"

"You promised me!" she melodramatically crossed over her arms.

"I didn't promise 'shit', Courtney! You need to take your little obsessive ass back to a psychiatric!" he snarled.

"Care to elaborate on what the 'hell' is going on?" Jessica pried.

"Jaiden here—"

"I'm warning you…"

"Fine! 'You' tell her!" Courtney spat, shoving him against the chest before walking off.

"You told me you weren't going to keep secrets from me anymore… tell me now or I swear on your grave I will approach Courtney myself!" said Jess through her teeth.

"Fuck… alright! Fine, I'll fess up."

"So that night—a-at the party, fuck, come here," he says dragging her by the arm to a hallway corner, where they were now alone.

"What party, what night?"

"Please just know how sorry I am and that I never meant to hurt you—"

"Jai, you're scaring me…"

Word vomit.

"I never cheated on you… but neither did Jared."

"What are you talking about?"

"T-the night of the party, w-when you saw Jared and Courtney… I might have slipped him a mic—"

"What kind of 'mic'?"

****

"You gave him a rapist pill!" Jessica angered after gasping out.

"Hey! Lower your voice, no one raped anyone!" he urged when attempting to cover her mouth. "I will let go as long as you promise you won't leave until you fully hear me out, okay?" She nodded under her will. He released his hand from her mouth once he made sure they were still alone and sighed before continuing. "I was so mad at myself that I let Jared steal you away from me," he rambled, staring at the ground beneath them, avoiding eye contact. "I thought I was doing Courtney and myself a favor—she told me how much she admired Jared and I came up with this plan in hopes of winning you back. It was a win-win and that's why you saw her number in my phone. She has been calling me since. I would have tried changing my number, but I didn't want to have to explain this to you…"

"So you would've kept this from me?"

"I—"

She began to turn away, but he stops her again. "I'm not finished… Her plan backfired, and she never got him, regardless if you two had broken up—but she's been giving me an earful about this and how somehow I owe her money now—" She was horrified.

"How could you let Courtney rape my boyfriend!—Your brother!"

He chuckled at ease, "I'm your boyfriend…" he assured when grabbing her hand before she rejected it coldly away.

"…No, you 'were' my boyfriend…"

"But you couldn't just leave well enough alone, could you!"

"…No, you're fucking sick!"

****

At lunchtime, she ran up and down the hallways and cafeteria to find Jared and explain the situation. "I'm so sorry, you were right. You were right about everything!" she emphasized with great distress. She repeatedly apologized to him after a shortcoming explanation while still muffled in his chest. She did not know a person could be capable of such evil as to drug his own brother and sabotage thy brother's relationship. Jared stayed quiet while she recited everything back from what Jaiden told her, before he left to go consult Jaiden himself. He found Jaiden, standing in the hallways, surrounded by fellow classmates; there, he tapped him on the shoulder to get his attention. As soon as Jaiden turned around, Jared swung at him, busting his nose and sending him straight against the herd of people. It took all his might and anger to kick him down, but he finally did it. His resentment paid off and in that moment, Jared didn't think of the consequences when he threw his fist. He knew that if he were to get caught fighting on the school grounds again, he would be at a disadvantage for prom and even worse, to graduate. It's not like he would be able to attend either now. But still, no one stood in the way of him and his love and he would make sure of it.

Jaiden got the message loud and clearly. Jaiden lies there wiping his mouth full of blood as Jared exits the school. Jessica tried searching for him again, but he had already left.

****

302

Jared hadn't been answering Jessica's calls and had been avoiding school more often. It was not easy to take in, his brother deliberately tried to ruin his life for his own twisted amusement. They were off to tour tomorrow morning and Jared has refused to see her, or daylight to process alone in his thoughts. He wasn't alone and not for a long time though, he had to see his brother for the next three months. Ignoring him wouldn't be a possibility as much as he wanted to do for the rest of his life. "If it was any consolation, Jessica told me you were planning to do the exact same thing to break us up," said Jaiden when entering Jared's room.

"So I guess we are twins after all," he smirked.

"But I couldn't go through with it because I cared more about Jessica's feelings aside from my own. I knew how fragile she was and how much it would break her inside, but you couldn't do that for her, 'could you'?"

"Hey, you're the one who slept with Courtney, you didn't have to," Jaiden insinuated.

"You drugged me, you bastard! Your own fucking twin brother, you sadistic 'fuck'!"

"...How was I supposed to know what the hell I was doing, I was under the influence! God, you see what you've caused!" he revolted. "You even made me believe that it was my intention to sleep with her! I didn't fucking want to, I never would have if I wasn't drugged! Why don't you understand, 'I love Jessica!' God, you've practically ruined the best thing that has ever happened to me! WHY CAN'T YOU JUST LET ME BE HAPPY!" Jared roared when throwing his clothes into his luggage.

"You're not the only one who loves her okay."

"You don't love her! You think you love her because she's the only one who was willing to put up with your crap but enough is enough! She is a good woman and she has been through a lot! She doesn't deserve your shit either!"

"Jaiden... I need her. You don't understand her like I do, okay. Nobody gets me like she does! I watched her lose my daughter and I let her push me away for so long because I didn't want her to hate me for doing it to her..."

"Y-your daughter?" Jaiden's eyes widen. Jared unfolds his hand to stare at the hospital wristband that was left behind.

"Yes Jaiden, my daughter... 'our' daughter. I looked Jess in the eyes and I lied to her because I was ashamed of myself and what I had done to her. When I finally realized that she was everything I ever wanted, it was too late and I only caused her to be miserable again. I couldn't do that to her again… but dammit I 'never' stopped loving her! Please, just get out."

"Jared, I-I don't know what to say—"

"It's too late to say anything…"

"I-I'm sorry—" Jaiden came to sympathize, but it was too late for his pity.

"Don't worry I'll smile… if it makes 'you' happy, but just know, she's the only person who has ever sincerely made me happy and you took that away from me! I hope that's something you God damn live with knowing for the rest of your life!" Jared spat before exiting his room with his luggage.

****

For the rest of the day, Jared salvaged without speaking one word to the one he was forced to call his brother. Jared knew he could never forgive his brother for ruining the best thing that has ever happened to him. Eighteen years he had been dealing with him—eighteen years too many. Jared knew he would need to confront Jessica about this soon. *How do you even go about and try to be what once was after all of this?* He longed for the idea that they would still remain the same, but he thought she would never want to return to the way things used to be before Jaiden meddled into their affairs. He entered inside the travel bus that waited for the brothers in front of their house, hoping for one final goodbye from Jessica as he blankly stared out his window, prepared to leave. Part of him wanted to be the one to knock at her door and say goodbye, but then he would be prompted to explain his own dirty confessional and he was just not ready yet. During the ride to their first stop in Montana, he could not stop thinking about what could've been between Jess and himself if Jaiden and Courtney hadn't sabotaged their relationship. Holding on is easy but letting go was the difficult part and for Jared, being with Megan, he never lost hope in what once was between Jess and himself. He only thought long term with Jess and Megan was just a good distraction for a while. He wanted to be the one that held Jessica when she was upset, the one she yelled at when he forgot to do the dishes, the one in her life. He wanted to be the one at the end of the aisle to smile up at her in the moment he realizes his life has ended but began a double. He wanted to share everything with her, spend every waking moment with her, to be the one going to the store and buying her medicine when she gets sick in the night. To be the one to squeeze her hand when she gives birth to his child, and to grow old together, sitting by the fireplace. He had so many plans for them in the short amount of time they begun to get serious, but only because he had already fell in love with her as a child. Lately, he had been feeling weak because she had been lacking in his life.

All he needed was Jessica—without her, he was nothing. Without her, he felt there was no point to living or breathing. She was the only one who has never once failed to disappoint him or give up on him. He would've been long gone if it wasn't for her—if it wasn't for his endless hope and holding onto the hope of reuniting with her again someday. He hath learned the value that if two people were meant to be, no matter how far they become, they will find a way back to each other; that was what Jared Jasper's definition of soul mate was. He has kindled the hope for Jessica over an open flame, no matter how much she thought she loved Jaiden. But unlike Jaiden, Jared remained imperceptible and watched their love drift apart. He still believed that they didn't belong and with time, faith had always found a way to bring Jessica into his life—and this travesty just furthers his theory that Jess and Jaiden weren't right for each other. Jaiden needed to remember that you can't built happiness at someone else's expense.

****

Chapter Nineteen

"Jessica, this is not how I wanted to tell you this, but here it is… and I don't want this to influence the way you feel about me and I wish I could tell you this in person… It was I who got you pregnant, but not intentionally, I swear. I noticed the tear and thought nothing of it at first until you brought up the fact that you might be pregnant. Jessica, I still love you, I'll admit I was a coward. Above all, I was afraid you would hate me for doing such a thing to you, and now I'm even more afraid you'll never want to speak to me again for telling you now. You have every right to be upset with me, I still haven't forgiven myself. You can tell me how not being able to face you in person was a new low, even for me and how it was spineless. There is nothing more I want than to see you right now, I should've told you this sooner and I'm sorry, it was selfish of me to have kept this from you and it's okay to hate me, I hate me too. I never wanted to lose you. –Jared."

Send.

Jessica received the voicemail the next morning at 8:55 a.m. She reiterated the recording back a few times to grasp the idea of what he was saying. He was right about how she felt but didn't know how to respond quite yet. He lied to her, Jaiden lied to her too. She was in the epitome of disaster. With the help of her sisters and mother, she came to a consensus, a settlement, and agreement. They were all gathered around her dining room table in the process. She still loved 'him' and there was no turning back from her decision now. "First off Jessica, I'm extremely sorry on how I've reacted when you first told me you were pregnant. I was your age when I had Amanda, I was terrified, and I married into a relationship I didn't want to begin with. I was at this college party when I met your father, Alan. He was ten years older, we were both drunk and I didn't even know him. Our parents forced us into matrimony and by the time I wanted a break, it was too late. I found myself pregnant every year or so, I had a lot of miscarriages too. Your father…" Margret paused for effect to stare down at her hands. "H-he didn't want me to get pregnant anymore… he wasn't too thrilled when he found out. I was lucky for a time when I went out of town to visit my parents out in

Maine—and for long periods of time, so that when I returned, it was too late to get an abortion and less likely to get a miscarriage, I was lucky to have kept you two, three darlings…"

"Mom… Dad has been hurting you. Why do you do this to yourself?" Mandy asks when trying her best to stay composed.

"It's so hard to let go after you've created so many memories, how do you even start over, you know?" she admitted, and it hit Jessica. "Sweetie, I was just scared for you. I didn't want you to fall into my same mistakes and resort to someone just because they were the father of your child."

"Mom," Jess fronted. "We had a past and I care for them both deeply, but not because it's my obligation, but because for the longest time, they have supported me and my irrational decisions; they accepted me and believed in me. Believe me, I never wanted to hurt them this way, it's not fair that I have to come to this and it's not fair that I have to lead anyone on. I don't know what I feel, and I want to make the right decision. I need them both, but I've been selfish for far too long now to know I can't have both. That is why I must end things with Jaiden… until I know for sure what I want. It's not fair if I keep stringing him along with all these feelings for Jared messing with my head.

"Until then, I'm at a crossroad. They both have had their share of faults, where do I even go from here?"

This was the first time in years that Margret Larson had opened up to her children and the first time in four years, she had given her daughter a hug out of sincerity. 'Twas also a first for Jessica having felt closer to her sisters. And finally, the first time any of the sisters seen Beverly shed a tear without a selfish cause. For the first time in forever, Jessica felt she could talk to her mother about anything now that she had finally let her in. As it turned out, they weren't so different.

****

That night, Jessica transitioned into bed with her recurring dream that she thought she had resolved. Only, as strange as it sounded, it took a different turn of events.

Jessica averted awake from her sleep. She looked around her surroundings and she was not in her own bed, she was in a hospital bed. She pulled the covers off her body and cautiously stood up. Upon noticing the hospital gown she was wearing, it was slightly bloody, "Where was I?" she thought. She didn't remember how she got there. She heard a cry in the distance, it was a baby's cry. She began to follow the sound. Suddenly, in the distance, she saw a small light shining down on a hospital crib. She approached the sound of the baby and it began to fade when she appeared closer. She finally reached the baby in the room and lifted it up. It stopped crying when she lifted it as if it were fond of her, like it knew her. She looked at the label that was placed in the crib and the name was blurry. All she could make out was that it said 'Larson-Daniels'. She held it, softly grazing the face. She left her eyes for a mere second to see if anyone was around and as soon as her eyes return to the baby, it was gone. Suddenly, she was in a different scene, still in the hospital but in a different part, running, searching. "Where's my baby?" she yelled, running down the hospital hallways in her gore-filled gown. She was panting now. It was somewhat dark and only the lights of the projector lamps in the hallways were flashing every time she ran across. No one was here, no one could hear her. She found a suspicious hospital room, room '3B'. It was the one she was in when she miscarried. Oddly enough, it was the only one that was open, so she entered, flicking on the light. She abruptly felt someone hugging her from behind. To her surprise, as she turned, she found it was Jaiden, "Ssshhhh baby," he cooed until he lifted her up and set her on the hospital bed, only now it transformed into a regular bed, and she was no longer in a hospital gown, she was in lingerie. The bed and her clothes weren't the only thing that changed though, the whole room did as it became dim after she turned on the light upon entering. The room looked familiar, it was the one in Josh's house where she had made love to the twins. Jaiden left a trail of kisses down her body and it sent her shivers, "I want to love you," he breathed, attaching his lips to hers. "Jaiden," she moaned, unable to resist the sexual tension, she didn't want to fight it. He flipped her over so that she was currently on top of him, he sat up and continued sucking on her lips. She then felt a cold unexpected breath behind her. She turned her head back around and found Jared with a devilish smirk on his face. "Jared, w-what are y-you?"

"Ssshhhh," he cooed as his hands trail up to unzip her lingerie. She felt a pair of hands grab her breasts from in front, it was Jaiden. He laid her down, hovering above. Jaiden began to suck on her neck again with Jared following. "Ow!" she exclaimed after Jaiden accidentally bit her. He continues biting her violently now. "Ow stop!" she ordered, successfully pushing him off the bed. Next, Jared then starts sucking harshly as well. "What the hell, stop!" she urged, sitting up. With a nonchalant facial expression, he grabbed her arm forcefully and pinned her back down on the bed. She tried removing her arm from his grip, but he was too strong. "L-let go!" she cried out mercilessly. Next, Jaiden *came back up and held her arms up as Jared sucked the life out of her neck again. She tried pushing them both away, but they wouldn't budge. Jared sucks too hard again and she cried out helplessly in pain. "Stop! Why are you guys hurting me!" She couldn't take it anymore. She felt the blood from her neck rush down and drip to her bare chest. They were like a pack of hungry wolves. It wasn't until Jaiden promptly threw her to the floor when she motionlessly crawled back up, realizing she was thankfully not in that room anymore. She was now in a forest of some sort. It was sunny outside, and she was grateful she could finally see clearly. Large trees surrounded her, and as she looked down at herself, she was completely naked. Leaves in her hair as she pulled them out, the ones she could see.*

"Momma, where are you?" she heard a little voice call out. Again, she began creeping slowly, following the voice as it kept calling out for help. She was again alone, except for the voice that she was drawn to. She approached closer and saw a figure skipping rocks by a lake in the distance. The figure was facing away from her and when Jessica appeared closer, she realized that it was this girl who was calling for help. "Momma, I'm glad you showed up…"

"Where's Daddy?" she asked still facing away. Jessica gulped and stepped closer, desperately yearning to stay quiet so that she wouldn't wake anything in this forest and startle this girl. "Why did you leave me? You killed me Momma… why did you kill me?" she questioned, sitting down and crying into her palms. The little girl looked about six from behind.

"Mommy didn't mean to… I'm so sorry," she solemnly resided, coming closer in hopes of calming her down, eyes filled with sorrow— still naked, of course. Jessica wanted to see how her daughter looked like, was it possible? She took a step closer, reaching her hand out— about to touch this girl's shoulder when a twig snapped unexpectedly causing Jessica to divide her attention to Jared and Jaiden both walking up to her. "What's your name sweetie?" she asked, returning to the girl who had now disappeared. Jared and Jaiden finally caught up to her, but she pushed past them in trying to find the little girl, "Where's my little girl?" she squalled running through the woods.

"Momma?"

The little girl approached Jessica again, she could see her face clearly now. "She looks beautiful… just like her mom."

She whipped her face in the other direction, it was Jared. It was Jared all along, she smiled. He wrapped a blanket around her. "What's your name beautiful?" he asked the girl when holding out his hands. Now

Jessica was back at the hospital, in her blood-stained gown, by the incubator with her rightful daughter in it. The name was visible now.

"Samantha Larson Daniels," she melted joyously, lifting her up and holding her in her arms now that she was able to. She then felt a pair of arms wrap behind, "She's so precious," Jared cooed, reaching for her tiny hand.

That's when Jessica Jane woke up and knew… Jared Daniels was the one.

****

(A couple of days later)

It was him and it all made sense. She loved him, he was the one and couldn't wait to tell him. The great thing would be that he was arriving today, so she could reclaim him in person. She didn't care that he kept this secret from her anymore, it was in the past and let bygones be bygones because she would not let it stand in the way of her relationship with him, she would not hold it against him. She was beyond overwhelmed that she didn't want to wait anymore. She thought it would be better to surprise him at his place so long as she made it past his parents. She made her way over to his parents' house in her car. When she stepped out of the car, she noticed Mr. Daniels solemnly exiting the house followed by the twins' sister and Mrs. Daniels. "Did Jared arrive by chance?" she asks upon approaching the family.

Nora sat in the car as Mr. and Mrs. Daniels exchange glances before one of them finally decided to speak up, "Jess sweetie, why don't you head home?" Mr. Daniels suggests with a sigh as the girl's smile fades. Pete was usually delighted to see her over and never dismissed her off in such manner.

"Is something the matter?"

"We have just received news, it appears that Jared and Jaiden have been involved in an incident…"

Her heart sank.

"Oh no. Are they going to be okay?" she worried. "Their bus collided with a larger truck, doctors are having a hard time telling, we are on our way to the hospital, but it's—"

"None of your concern," Mrs. Daniels excused before opening up the car side door for herself.

"No please," Jess intrusively pleads, grabbing her arm as Linda stares her down with great vengeance. Jessica scrunched her face.

"Not 'my' concern?"

"I understand that you're a mother and it's your job to protect your cubs, but what I've had to experience is far more painful than you could ever imagine and when I thought I couldn't go on with life, it was your sons that picked me up. I've known these two for far too long to let go of our past and I care for them almost just as much as you do. I'm ashamed of what I did, yes, but I do not regret that it happened, if anything, it has shaped me into the willful person I am today. And frankly, I don't think I would have gotten the courage to tell my best friend that I love him today, if it weren't for what happened that night. I'm sorry I tried to cut ends with you, all I've ever wanted was for you to like me, but even before my past, it seems as if you still looked down on me. Now please stand aside and tell me what hospital they're in so I can finally tell Jared that I love him, and you can accept it or don't, because not even 'you' can stop us from being together." Linda sighed causing Jessica to drop her grip. Jessica was not expecting that response, she assumed she would have gotten back-handed from the women after so many years of holding her anger back.

"I'll admit, I wasn't thrilled when you ran into my sons' life, but after hearing how much you care about them, really sets my mind in perspective. I guess I was sort of jealous of you. I had the best of friends back in grade school, we grew up together and they were brothers too, but my parents were always strict about the type of friends I made. Compared to most girls who befriended other girls, I was a bit of a tomboy, I just wanted to hang with my guy friends and preferred them over Barbie dolls. They eventually moved away, and I never got to see them again. Getting twin boys was like getting a second chance at life. Now I realize that because I've missed my friends, you were this reminder of the girl that I wish I got the chance to be but never could be. I was just holding onto that fear of my boys growing up too fast and getting into girls with a blink of an eye that I guess I never really gave you a chance."

That sounded like someone Jessica once knew, *herself.*

Jessica assertively grabbed Linda's hand and smiled. "I love both of your sons, I would never want to hurt them… not as much as they've hurt me anyways, but that's in the past and I value our friendship above all." Linda's eyes swell with water as does the girl's.

"Thank you, I'm sorry for underestimating you. I'm so glad they have someone as kind as you who has deeply impacted their lives for the better. That kind of influence is better than any other girl I can think of."

Jessica was relieved that she finally got through to the twins' mother. "Did I hear you say that you love Jared?"

Jess nodded humbly, slightly blushing. "Well, he loves you, and you have my blessing," Linda implied, grabbing Jessica's hand back reassuringly. She tucked away a strand of Jessica's hair behind her ear before leaning in to hug her. With Linda's blessing, Jessica hops a ride with the Daniels family. They shortly arrived at the hospital where the paramedics made her wait in the waiting area since she was not primary family.

"Hey Jess!" Jaiden approaches. Jessica jolts up and clings to his body.

"Thank God you're okay!" she whispered in his chest.

"Just a couple of head stitches, nothing bad…"

"What about…?"

She had been afraid to ask. It was as if everything was wrong in the universe, the world was out to get her, and tried to separate her from her true love.

"He's in ICU. It's looking bad… he hasn't woken up yet," he begins to explain. He explained what happened on the road just before the accident and why Jared suffered a greater trauma. Jessica's mouth gaped wide open as did her eyes. She would have ended this conversation on a short note to see him immediately if it hadn't been for the visiting restriction. "But… is everything okay between, you know… us?"

"No, it's not! I still can't believe, all this time!" she shrieked, hitting him with her heavy purse.

"Ow!" Jaiden yelped, trying to separate her hands until she stops to dig into her purse.

"Jaiden, I love you but what you did was unforgivable, and you've hurt me so many times… I don't think I'm meant for this…" she stated when grabbing his hand from his side to unfold his palm. She displaced the shiny object in his hand.

"Why?" he asked when looking at the ring she had planted back in his hands.

"I'm in love with Jared, I always have been… these past couple of weeks, I'll admit, I have been a little unfaithful. I kissed Jared more than that one time and it wasn't because I felt bad for him, I love him and it's not fair to you…"

"He's not innocent Jessica, we both aren't."

"I know, but I'm no saint either."

"Jess?" Nora called out. Jess let out a deep staggered breath before directing her attention to their older sister.

"Yeah?" Nora somberly nods, indicating it had been time for her to visit. She turned to Jaiden, who had let a tear fall down his face as his eyes never leave the ring placed in his palm.

"I wish it never happened, I'm sorry…" he whispers.

"I know."

****

Jessica followed Jaiden into the room where Jared had been resting at. She set her purse down next to his bedside after having approached him. "Jared, wake up…" she mellowed when hugging his chest. She then brushed her lips over his plump, blue, swollen lips. "I love you, I want to be with you," she wept. The family stepped out to give the two some privacy. She grabbed his rested hand from his side before pressing a kiss to his cold, stitched knuckles. His whole body was covered in heavy machinery, all connected to a monitor. His arms were wrapped with an IV. She watched his heart beat on the monitor, he was alive, but for how much longer in his critical condition? She waited a couple of a seconds before sitting up to wipe the beads of tears from her upper lip when she heard his irregular heart beat pump faster on the screen. When she looked up, his eyes blinked open.

"Jared!" she exclaimed, hugging him in relief.

"How's my head?" he groans.

"You survived a concussion, I should be asking you that…" she giggled in light.

"Well listen, can I get some water?"

"Of course, I'll go get you some…" she said caressing his head with her brittle fingertips before standing up. She returned with his water momentarily later as he sat up.

"Jared, there's something I've been meaning to ask you—" she said, sitting down by his bedside again.

"Okay?"

"Did you mean what you said when you told me you still loved me?" Jared sat his water down beside with her help, she also adjusted his pillow, so he could sit up comfortably.

"Um… I think we're just getting to know each other here, I wouldn't feel very comfortable, besides, I don't think that's very much appropriate since I am your patient…"

"Patient?" Her face scrunched in confusion.

"Jared, it's me, Jessica," she stated when caressing the right side of his numbed face with her hand.

"Okay? But I don't see how that's going to help…"

"Can we come in?" Mr. Daniels asked once the family re-entered.

"Hey, when did you all get here?" Jared tiredly spoke in surprise.

"What's going on? Why is he acting strange around me?" Jessica asked.

"Jared has always acted strange around you, it's nothing new," Jaiden shrugged.

"I'm sorry, have we met before?" Jared asked.

"That's what I'm talking about…"

"He doesn't even remember who I am…"

****

"It appears he's going to have amnesia for a while," the doctor says when reading his CAT scan on the monitor. The doctor had also spent time to explain that according to Jared's brain wave, he has no recollection of what he thought of during the time of the accident. This meant that whatever he had been thinking of when it all happened, all erased from his short-term memory stimulus.

It was horrible enough Jessica lost time with him because he chose to forget she existed and now he failed to remember her entire existence altogether when unintentionally wiping her from his hard-drive. Jessica found herself trailing off out of the hospital in tears once again after hearing the news that her best friend had forgotten her. She couldn't bear to stay in the room for another minute while the doctor informed the family with more news that would only further disappoint her.

****

Jaiden had told Jessica that they canceled their tour at least until after Jared regained his memory again. They were going to finish the school year together after all but not in the way Jessica had hoped. *How could he not remember me? We had so much history together. He was thinking of me before the crash? How is it even possible for him to forget me after so long of being in his life? All I need is to refresh his memory, right? That always seems to work in the movies.* The week had washed over and before she knew it, it was already the first day of the fourth quarter. The twins were only gone for spring break which didn't affect their GPA just yet. There were now only a couple of weeks left before graduation.

"Oh good, you're here!" exclaimed Jess, finding Jared, who stood beside his locker.

"Yeah, those pain killers do wonders on my body! Glad to be walking again after being immobilized at home all week," he chuckled.

"So, you remember me yet?" she teased.

"Of course!" Her mouth widened in astonishment at the short-lived miracle until he spoke out again, "You're that pretty nurse from the hospital," he grinned causing her to face palm.

"Jared, I thought we discussed about what happens when we talk to strangers?" Courtney addressed, walking up and linking her arm with his.

"'Strangers'?" scoffed Jessica when popping a hip at her.

"Sorry miss, my girlfriend's right... um, see you around?" he implemented in confusion before Courtney led him away—down the opposite hallway after closing his locker.

"'Girlfriend'?"

Her heart throbbed at the word. *Does Jared honestly not remember the terrible thing Courtney did with Jaiden to break Jared and I up? Then, she tried using him to get back with Jaiden, and now she's with Jared again! She needs to make up her mind—No, better yet, I'll make up her mind... with my fist.* Jessica tightly gripped her fists at her sides as her eyes never snake off Jared and Courtney when they walk down the hallway, holding hands. "Hey Jess! Whoa, you look angry!"

Jessica snarled her lip at Jaiden, not saying a word before shoving him against the lockers. She then brought her fist up to her eye level and made her way over to Courtney to clobber her face off. "Whoa! Bad idea!" he warned when rushing over. "I hate her too but—"

"Stay away from me Jaiden!" she declared over the hallway of students. "She's ruining everything for me!" she sobbed. Jessica collapses to the frigid hallway floor, just weeping into her hands while receiving weird glances from students as they passed by. "Jess, Jared has amnesia. His memory—"

"Yeah. I know what it means!" she huffed. He helped her back to her feet after she had vented her anger to him.

"Courtney most likely wants Jared simply to get back at me," Jaiden stated.

"Or to piss me off because she 'hates' me!" Jess revolted.

"So, to prove how sorry I am... I'm going to give her what she wants, because I'd rather have you back as a friend and lose you as lover than to lose you at all," he says kissing her forehead before trailing off.

"Wait," she takes his hands and looks soulfully into his eyes.

"Thank you for understanding. Your support means a lot..."

"So, you're 'not' mad?"

"Of course I am!" she aggravated.

"...but," she paused. "You did love me and it's understandable to do stupid things for someone you love, even if it means you have to fight to

315

win them back… which is why I need you to stay here, I'll be right back."

She ran away, trying to find Jared before school started in seven minutes. She stumbled in on the two in a corner, open mouth kissing with their tongues down each other's throats. Jessica's body shook violently in disgust, *yuck*. He has certainly never kissed anyone like 'that' before. She tapped Courtney on the shoulder before punching Courtney in the mouth when she got her attention. Jessica's aim was off that time but at least Courtney got the point. "That's for my best friend," she grunted. "This is for my boyfriend," she gritted with another punch when knocking Courtney to the floor like a bowling pin. "And this… this is simply from me," she smirked when tugging Jared by his shirt collar to lure him in for a kiss. When Jess retracted away after a minute, Jared looked more satisfied than ever. Jessica almost didn't pull away, enjoying herself too much.

"So…?"

"'Nope', nothing," he shrugged.

"I'm sorry you feel that way."

"I'm sorry you forgot everything we've been through… Most of all, I'm sorry that I've waited so long to finally realize that you've been the only one for me, but I guess it's too late now," she shrugged. "I believe this is yours… you probably don't remember this, but I do. I don't care what you choose to do with it but if there's even the slightest chance of your memory coming back, then you'd keep it long enough to reminisce its importance," she sighed when pulling the bracelet out of her overalls and placing it in his hands. She dropped her head to the floor and turned around, freely releasing the droplets of rain from her eyes once more. The whole hallway of students have their eyes locked on the ensemble of them and Jaiden came out from hiding behind the wall to embrace his friend in for a hug.

"I'm sorry," he says but she declined his presence and comfort.

"Jessica, wait!" Jared shouted.

"Jessica? But—"

"Jessica Jane Larson, born on October 6th—star sign Libra," he continued walking forward as Jessica stood frozen. "Favorite color is yellow—like the sun, likes adorable little kittens, favorite animal is a pinecone and you don't like peanut butter," he says looking up.

"Neither do I," he chuckled, meeting her halfway.

"You remembered?" Her eyes bulk with sweat.

"How could I forget?"

"When you left, the doctor said it was possible that with one valued possession, his memory could be restored in a flash..." Jaiden remembered.

"Guess I'm cured then?" Jared flashed her his teeth, walking up as he whips the bracelet out in front.

"Jared Daniels, you silly boy. You scared me half to death," she sniffled while beads of tears streamed down her cheeks like waterworks. He took her hand that rested on her mouth to kiss her knuckles. She then raked her thumbs over his cheeks, admirably cupping his large face in her small hands while he held her arms. "So, I guess it's my turn?

"Jared Jasper Daniels, born on December 11th—twin. Favorite color is red, likes Ferraris—your dream car. You don't like Jaiden, but you make an effort," she giggled when looking back at Jaiden before back at him. "Your favorite topping on pizza is pineapple and your favorite animal is a cactus, although I disagree to pinecones." She smiled after he pushed his forehead on hers. The universe was in order again.

"You forgot one thing... I'm in love with my best friend," he grinned. Jessica bit her lip in anticipation, waiting for him to kiss her. He smashed his lips to hers and it was the perfect fairytale—the one that gave you false hope on reality.

"So, what does this make us babe?" Jaiden asked, swinging his arm around Courtney's neck.

"Screw off!" she exclaimed, stepping on his foot before stomping away. Jaiden attached his hand to his foot in pain. But he was overall happy to finally get her off his back after so many months, hurrah!

Jared lifted Jess up during the continuation of their kiss and the whole hallway banters in excitement.

****

Thursday night was a stroll through the park after grabbing two coffees to go when clocking out of Jessica's shift for her and Jared's coffee date. "How is it that, I, Jessica Larson, landed the sweetest, most smartest, and sexiest guy of the entire school?"

"The three Ss, wow—smart and sweet, I guess, but sexy? I don't think I've ever been considered 'that' before," he chuckled when nervously scratching the back of his head with his free hand.

"Well, believe it because you are and so much more than that."

"So, what happened?" he asked with his foggy breath glistening in mid-spring as they continued their walk hand in hand, rightfully as boyfriend and girlfriend.

"You tell me."

"Well, I remember I was talking to Jaiden about you, before I knew it, my life flashed before my eyes…"

"It's remarkable how I suffered amnesia and he only managed to get stitches—his big head must have caught on as a self air bag," he chuckled.

"Your turn," he asserted when holding her coffee for her as she sat down on the cold concrete park bench, as did he. "I wanted to believe I was over you and I needed to be sure. It's just a different feeling altogether—being with him compared to you. I can go days without having contact with Jaiden and not worry so much about him… but you, I would absolutely drive myself to insanity for being far from you for far too long. I should've trusted you, I knew you were innocent. I wanted to believe you…"

"You had every right to be upset with me Jess. I would have automatically assumed the worst if the roles had been reversed.

"And I'm sorry… about everything. I didn't mean to hurt you in the way I have. I said some awful and nasty things that I wish I could take back. It was all untrue. I only said them because I was grieving over the loss of my friends and then losing what I thought was the single best thing in my life. I only wanted it to work out with Megan because I grew tired of waiting for you. I guess what I'm trying to say here is that my actions resulting from the drinking to what I have said to you in the past, was my way of trying to mourn my feelings for you—and what better way to do that then denying you've ever had feelings for someone you really cared about?"

"I know the feeling, I've lived it. You don't have to apologize, I know you didn't mean it and about my baby—our baby, I can learn to move past it. We're both guilty—and my entire relationship with Jaiden was my way of getting over you too. I'd be lying to myself if I said I didn't enjoy it for a while because he did help me to forget you even if just for a little bit and I needed it."

"I understand, you needed time…"

"I'm just blessed we got through all of it and that we're here now. I've never felt more alive now that I get to finally be with you again and back to my normal self too, so that we can finally start over the right way." She takes a deep breath after pausing in her thoughts.

"Why are you upset? Was it something I said?"

"No, I just hate that I've waited so long to realize that I still loved you and because of that I…I almost lost you."

"You didn't lose me. I'm not leaving for a long time I promise," he cooed. "No Jared, you were right, I am stubborn and if I hadn't waited so long to tell you, none of that would've happened in the first place."

****

"So now that you've regained your memory... is it back on the road?"

"That's part of what I've been wanting to tell you... I am quitting, resigning from fame you could say—Jess, all I've ever wanted was to be with you," he says caressing her face. He lifts her beanie to kiss the top of her head before she wraps her arms around him.

"I love you Jared," she faintly murmured onto his chest. "But what about Jaiden, your fans... won't you be disappointing them?"

"I'm hoping they would look past it and morally respect my decisions. I need to grow. I couldn't possibly stretch this out forever. Guess Jaiden will just have to find another twin," he shrugs. "In the meantime, I was wondering—and I am apologizing in advance for this unflattering invite, but would you care to escort me to my senior promenade?

"And I completely understand if you're still going to go with Jaiden," he continued. She took the opportunity to shush him by pressing her lips onto his cheek before transforming the kiss to both their mouths like two magnets when pulling towards each other.

"Yes," she nodded, biting down at her bottom lip before leaning in to greet lips again.

"I guess I should be apologizing that this wasn't as extravagant a proposal as Jaiden's," he shrugged.

"Jared!" she gasped after connecting the dots.

"What?" he asked when retracting away from their hug.

She pokes at his chest, "You are the sweetest brother ever, you know?"

"Ouch, my nipple," he teased, rubbing over his chest.

"You planned that whole arrangement for Jaiden, didn't you?"

"I don't know what you're talking about," he says, clearing his throat before looking guiltlessly away in the other direction.

"The horse and the dozen roses had Jared written all over it! Come to think of it, Jaiden never bought me flowers and I only mentioned my favorite flowers on a date with you one time..." It also did help to know that Jaiden mentioned he had help from a 'friend'—well, more like brother in this case.

"That's because I've waited my whole life to make the perfect prom proposal for you. You've always talked about your dream prom and the fact that you couldn't have one because of being in a private school."

"I remember those talks! But there was only one thing missing from all that..."

319

"What's that?" he asks.

"…My knight in shining armor was you."

She brought her lips back over to his before he spoke out again, "How are you going to break the news to Jaiden?"

"I don't think finding another date is a problem for Jai," she chuckled.

****

They stumbled into her apartment, getting deeper in physical contact with each minute that passed. Jared sat Jess on top of him on the armrest of the sofa in her living room. He then fondled her breast through her shirt fabric, looking up into her eyes as if she were supposed to give him permission to unclasp her bra. She moaned in response as his lips traveled to her neck and she grasped his dark locks between her fingers. "Wait, wait Jessica," he panted in low heavy breaths after she ripped open his buttoned-up shirt, revealing his very well-toned chest. "I want this to be perfect—I know we have done this before, but not in the right state of mind and I want it to be really special when we do," he whispers in her ear while locking his left hand with her right. She nods in response and he helped her to stand back up.

"I do love you, I just don't want to rush things this time," he says, kissing her cheek in reassurance.

"Thank you. Thank you for respecting me as a woman," Jessica sincerely recognized while playing with his hand.

"I should get going…" he says buttoning up his shirt.

"Stay the night?" she requested.

****

"I love you," she whispered while running her hands through his hair as he hugged her body below hers on the bed.

"And I love you," he replied kissing her clothed stomach as she giggled.

"Jared, why are you kissing me there? You know I'm not pregnant, I'm just fat," she frowned while propping herself up.

"I've waited forever to hold you like this again."

"Jared," she groaned, burying her face in the depths of his hair. "Mmmmm, fruity," she teased, admiring the smell of his shampoo, feeling the tenderness of his hair with her hands. She missed this feeling and his scent. "Your hair is so soft, I'm jealous," she admitted, biting on the ends of his dark brown hair gently.

320

"'It's so fluffy!'" she rasped while curling his hair with her finger now.

"What are you doing you weirdo?" He scooted up closer to meet her face now.

"You're the weirdo, weirdo," she mocked, staring into his eyes before he leaned in. Their legs intertwined and he hovered over her, holding onto her face while he closed his eyes and prepared to kiss her again.

****

Jessica wanted to wake up bright and early to make Jared breakfast but as it turned out, he had already beaten her to the punch. "Morning babe," he greeted with a cheeky smile. Jessica yawned and stepped out of her bedroom with his long, oversized t-shirt that he was no longer wearing when she saw him cooking this morning. "Hope you're hungry," he says when carrying the hot pan over to the plate he had prepared at the table. She followed him to the kitchen island. "Eggs Benedict with a side of veggies and bacon, voila!" he says when removing the lid from the dish.

"You're going to make me fat, aren't you?" she teased. Never in Jessica's life, has a guy took the time to prepare her a meal. It showed her how much Jared really cared and she was infatuated, deep. The flashbacks of Jaiden were enough for her to appreciate Jared in this moment because all Jaiden could amount to, was a bowl of cereal, and there were even times he's forgotten the milk called for in the recipe.

****

Chapter Twenty

So now the prom, dance recital, and graduation were all one to two weeks away and Jessica was growing more anxious by the hour. It was during her second hour when Jessica was sent to the principal's office only to be escorted out by Mandy and her brother in-law, Kevin, who urgently pulled her out of class. They drove home in utter silence, everyone refusing to speak. They drove right past their own house and straight to Jessica's parents' house. The driveway was filled with police sirens, squad cars, and even officers. Jessica sprinted up to her mother, who was talking with Beverly and... *Jaiden?*

"What's going on? What is happening?" she asked, shifting her eyes between the three of them, awaiting a response. Jaiden pointed out to the front door, where her father had been handcuffed and led into the back of a police car. "Your father finally got what was coming to him."

When Jaiden looked back at the cruel man being evicted from his house and executed into the vehicle, he remembered the only time he has ever had anything close to a normal conversation with the man that happened a few months back.

(Flashback)
It was a sunny day outside when Alan Warner stepped out on his front porch. But what he was not pleased to find, was his daughter's male friend peeing on his varnished tree outside. "Hope you don't mind Mr. Larson," Jaiden said after retracting his head back around. "Your lawn looked a little dry... While I'm here, why don't you tell Jessica I've stopped by? I'm sure she would be delighted to see this view again considering it's not the first time she's seen it," he insinuated while continuously watering the man's plants with his leakage. "Oh, the times she's begged me to show it to her! What can I say... she's 'tight' like that," he provocatively implied. It was his way of showing her father his gratuity for abusing his daughter and abandoning her in the care of her prudent sister.
(End of flashback)

The weary Margret wept onto Jaiden's broad and masculine shoulders, he was much stronger than the woman, as were most men she came contact with. Including the notorious Alan Warner, *former stockbroker and wife beater.* "Ma'am, I'm going to need you to come with me," another officer directs. Margret compliantly nods before proceeding to follow them to the courthouse. Jessica's eyes widen as her mother walked past, the left side of her face was completely busted. Her left eye was swollen shut and she had visible fist markings imprinted on the side of her neck. Jessica reluctantly pulled Jaiden aside, now standing under an oak tree while Beverly joined her mother in the police car.

"What happened!"

"I was taking a stroll in the neighborhood when I heard your mother scream and I panicked. I called the cops and next thing I knew, I was here, standing outside as your mother started explaining how he harassed her, degraded her, defiled her, and beat her—pretty soon the cops got ahold of you all as requested. She was telling me that she was asking for a divorce which as a result, left him infuriated. He didn't want her to leave him." Jessica's hand flew directly to her mouth as she watched her mother drive away with Beverly. Mandy and Kevin too left, following behind in a separate car after warning Jessica that they would too be leaving.

"Where are they going?" she asked.

"Court."

"Your father is having a hearing today… after that, it's the court's decision whether they want to keep him in jail or not but—"

"He needs to be in jail!" Jessica protests.

"He has some pretty good lawyers, so I don't know," Jaiden shrugged, scratching the back of his head.

"What the hell are you talking about! He 'is' going to jail and I'm making sure of it, let's go!" she urged, dragging him to his house to retrieve his car.

****

On that particular day, Alan Warner pleaded guilty from previous attempted murder cases to three of his victims in his past. He was also charged for assault, sexual harassment, and other unbelievable charges that sentenced him for a total division of twenty years. Jessica was sent to the stand to plea the case in helping her mother settle this dispute after having sworn an oath to tell the whole truth. Then, she told the jurors how he pushed her around, after all these years in the household where she grew up. She has heard the screams, the cries, witnessed the bruises on her sisters' backs. They swore all these years not to tell, shrugging it off as if it were just an accident they got from tripping on their way to school or riding a bicycle, but it was no accident, and this was all news to Margret. She thought she had been the only victim for so long. Well, not anymore, it all unfolded right in front of her very eyes. Margret Larson won the case after all this commotion and the court made sure to make the divorce final right then and there. The family ended up suing him for all his worth which estimated to about 1.2 million and all his property was going to be returned to the bank minus the manor, which Margret successfully got to keep since after all, it was rightfully under her name. Margret waited for this day to happen for a long time, so she thought ahead and changed the title of her cars and insurance under her name too. This meant Mandy and Kevin were safe from having to give up their dream house. Alan was no father to these girls and solitary confinement should serve him justice for mistreating his family.

****

Jessica decided to move back in with her mom for a while to help her settle down and catch her up on the drama in her life. Now, it was time for school. The dance group consisted of Jessica, Skylar, Becca, Star, and Jasmine took extra drastic measures to make sure they got all the choreography down before the big night in a couple of days. They were all just thankful for the opportunity to perform on one of the biggest stages in America, regardless if they win or not. "So, I heard you and Jared are back together," said Megan, strutting over in her practice outfit which consisted of a black sports bra, grey sweats, and a grey hoodie.

"Not that it concerns you, but yes," she smirked proudly.

"Well congratulations, I mean someone has to date that loser." Megan shrugged apathetically when playing with her polished nails before walking off.

"Just like someone has to put up with America's biggest slut," Jessica muttered a little too loudly.

"Excuse me?" Megan scoffed, whipping her head back around. *I'm not going to stoop to her level, just walk away Jessica. Keep your cool.*

"Did the gaping hole in your vagina drain all of the water from your ears? You heard me!" she confidently strides. "Why don't you save some of that water for the rest of the thirsty hoes in your group!" she strikes again just before Becca came up to cover her piercing mouth when she noticed they were drawing attention to themselves.

"Megan, get over here!" yells Candi, from all the way across the stage. Megan rolls her eyes and leaves.

"I was on a roll with these, why did you stop me?" Jess whined.

"We need to practice, you can save those commentaries for later when we win."

****

Monday morning was the start of senior testing day. Wednesday is the recital, Friday is prom and Sunday is graduation. Monday morning was also the first morning that Jared gave his new girlfriend a piggy back ride to her testing class, deeming their first official high school appearance as boyfriend and girlfriend. "Good-luck, you'll do great," he says when setting her down.

"Thanks quarterback," she winks.

"Which reminds me, I have to go return my uniform since the season is over now," he shrugs.

"Interesting how the game was never brought up to my attention…"

"I uh, I got cut from the team. I've skipped out on so many classes when I was with Megan that it affected my GPA for a while, so they dropped me from the team."

"What about student council?"

"Oh, right. Well, I withdrew from that race a while ago, when I was with you actually. Not because of you—I had too many things to own up to… at the time anyways," he says balancing his weight on his feet.

"Jared, I'm so sorry. I had no idea."

"No, don't be. It was a hobby anyways, not a career," he shrugged, scratching the back of his head.

"I know but I was your girlfriend, I feel like even as a friend, it should have been in my best interest to ask about your life, especially since I knew how much you've wanted it. I've just been so caught up in myself lately, I guess I forgot to ask—" He cut her off with his lips.

"Don't worry about it," he states. Before he headed off to class, he abruptly took her hand to turn her around, transitioning it into a dip before lowering his face to give her a quick smooch. She giggled at his romantic gesture before he helped her back up. She then skipped inside after moments of standing in the company of a sappy, love-struck Jared, who didn't want to leave her. Jessica soon found her seat next to Star who happened to have the same testing room as her.

"That's not Jaiden," Star pointed out in confusion after Jared had left and Jaiden entered the room. Jess smiled silently to herself when watching Jared sprint off like he was in a marathon, to his next class in the distance after the minute bell went off.

"Did I miss something?"

Jessica didn't blame her friend for having the attention span of a squirrel and dozing off on Friday's conversation between her and Megan in dance class.

"Please get out a pencil and you may use one scratch piece of paper," the teacher instructed.

"The heart got what it wanted…" was how Jessica chose to limit her words to her friend when the instructor came by, handing the students their individual exams.

****

'Twas from five days to one day until the recital now. The friends have had their costumes ready so that they may practice dress rehearsals before the show tomorrow. It wasn't until this moment in time when the friends were informed that this was going to be on live television. Jessica consumed with nerves just thinking about the friends and family that were going to be in that audience in support of her tomorrow. Alas, today was the day—the biggest day of Jessica's future to come. College administrators were going to be there to present the award of a one-hundred-thousand-dollar scholarship on the biggest platform in America to the winning group of tonight. Jessica was very proud of her group, she knew that no matter what happened after tonight, at least they've tried and got the experience of a lifetime.

The groups arrived at Music Valley at around four p.m. after having spent the remainder of the class period at school due to the stage crew setting up for tonight. After a last-minute change of events, provided by false information, it was said that only two groups would represent the school on the Music Valley stage and the only way it would be fair, would be to include the two best groups in the class, Silver Streetz and Galaxy Quest. It was unfortunate that the other groups came a long way only to give up their position but if anyone should be represented it should be the two most worthy groups in the class as decided by the teacher during a mini re-audition in the class period. The guys and girls would have separate dressing rooms, so it was going to be difficult for the rest of the group to meet up with Skylar. Meanwhile, Becca, Jasmine, Star, and Jessica got their hair, makeup, and costumes ready just in time before the televised event. Jess peeked out the curtains just before the show started to find a diverse group of people sitting in the audience. She saw her family, friends, and her beau, staged left in the audience. Jared waved to her and she generously waved back. He brought his family along. She could see Jaiden obnoxiously texting someone the whole time she was looking over the audience. Jared must have read her mind because he too noticed and elbowed the disrespectful lad in hopes of getting him to pay attention to their friends. Jared was proud of her and wanted everyone to know it and see for themselves, how bestowed his girlfriend was. In the row before Jared's family, there her primary family sat, including: Her mother, two sisters, brother in-law, Kevin's parents and a few of her distant relatives that flew in to be here with her on her special night. They were also staying the weekend to attend her upcoming graduation as well. In the row behind Jared, Jaiden, Nora, Linda, and Pete, she also found a couple of mutual friends and classmates such as Hobbs, Chris, Sienna, and Josh. She blew Jared a kiss before closing the curtain for the final curtain call.

The announcer told the group to wait backstage until they introduced their act. "What's going on?" asked Jessica when walking over to the group who was carrying a green Skylar over.

"He's feeling a bit of stage fright," Star explains.

"You guys are up in fifteen!" a backstage crew worker reminds after the group helped Skylar to a chair.

"Here," Jasmine says, setting a trash bin next to him.

"Skylar, how are you feeling?" Jess worriedly asked after he had stopped vomiting seven minutes ago.

"Actually… I'm feeling be—" He puts up a finger before he lifts the bin to vomit again and they all groan.

"Oh my God, we aren't going to make it," Becca panicked before pacing back and forth.

"Becca, stop being a jinx and go figure out a way to calm your boyfriend down," Star directs. Becca jolted off to her boyfriend's aid seconds later.

"Five minutes," the woman directs when running back over just as the show continued.

"Ladies and gentlemen, without further ado, I now present to you Fairview High's very own… Galaxy Quest!" the director announces, and the friends jitter backstage.

"Alright, let's do this!" Skylar says, standing up as the makeup crew runs back over to clean him up and darken his pale skin a bit.

"Are you feeling better?"

"I feel refreshed!" he excites, clapping his hands together. The friends scatter on stage and prepare into their formations just before the lights drop, waiting for the backstage crew to re-open the curtains and cue the spotlight before they begin their piece. As soon as the lights drop, and the friends finish their dance, with limited exit time, they ran backstage and hug it out, *mission accomplished.* They were able to get through the seven-minute routine without Skylar spilling his fluids on stage… what a mess that would've been!

"We did it!" Star exclaimed out of breath.

"And now please put your hands together for another sensational group also from Fairview High… Silver Streetz!"

Galaxy Quest watched as Candi and her posse passed by, all of them with their chins pointed in the air and purposely nudging their rivals on their way to the stage. "Watch and learn," mocked Tanya, being the last to enter the stage. As soon as they finished, Jessica's group gave them a celebratory clap, out of pity. The rest of the groups wait an hour more for all the crews to finish before the director makes the big announcement where they would call all the contestants back on stage. Of course, they wait until commercial break to get to the results, but at this point it was down to Galaxy Quest, Silver Streetz, and some group representing a Michigan school who address themselves as, 'ES3'.

****

"It has come to our attention that Galaxy Quest has snuck in a member who is not part of their school dance elective, which is an automatic disqualification," the announcer informed. The friends stomp in disappointment.

"I'm sorry guys," Jasmine apologizes.

"The winner, as presented by Music Valley, by default, is…"

"Silver Streetz!"

The friends look to the audience to find that most people rose in protest including Jared, who had a giant fan poster that read, 'I love you Jess' … *how sweet, her first fan.* Becca whispers to Jess from beside that it must have been one of Candi's clones that squealed on them, exposing their confidential secret. Jessica's family and mutual friends in the audience, managed to get the whole crowd to chant, "Put them through, put them through!" It sent the bald spokesperson on edge as he stood frustrated. He then spoke directly into the microphone by saying, "A rule is a rule and they didn't follow it!" Meanwhile, Candi was glowing while holding her golden trophy.

"Excuse me!" Tanya says after walking over and snatching the mic. "We won this fair and square!"

"Sub section 34, numeral II in the handbook, states—" the announcer frustrates after reclaiming the mic from Tanya's hands and pulling out his glasses to look into his handy-dandy handbook, flipping through the pages to find it. "...That any person who performs that is not involved in any particular elective—prior to the performance, should be directed to the district superintendent to conclude if he/she would be deemed allowed to participate!" Jared states when reading the small fine handbook, print from print while walking on stage as Kevin and his father walk up behind.

"That would be me," says Kevin's father, holding out his identification. Jessica and her group held hands in excitement as the announcer began to examine the inscription in the book. "The new revision," his father clarified. "I'll allow this to happen, just this once because you guys did phenomenal," the superintendent concluded to the group.

"Well sir, my apologies."

The announcer cleared his throat as two women hand Silver Streetz the check. The announcer then walks over and reclaims it from Tanya's hands. Then, he snapped his fingers like magic as the women ran back over to overtake the trophy from Candi's possession. "The winners of this challenge, by a shocking total of results, is... GALAXY QUEST!" he exclaimed, throwing the winner's card into the air before he handed the group their renounced trophy and check as the confetti rains down once again. The crew jumps up and down in excitement while the crowd cheers. Jessica ran up to Jared, almost knocking him on his back. "Thank you so much! I don't know how you did it, but thank you!" She smothered her gratitude all over his face. He then ran over to the side of the stage to retrieve the flowers from Jaiden's hands that he's asked him to hold. She was thrilled when he handed her the sweet-scented roses.

"You did amazing," he says, hugging her close.

"Jessica Larson?"

A nicely suited woman approaches her on stage. Jessica returned her attention to this woman after excusing herself to Jared. "Yes?"

"I have reviewed your academic records, and this performance was just beautiful. I was told it was partially student choreographed by you?"

She nodded humbly, "Me and all my teammates contributed to the routine," she mentioned, just tucking a piece of hair behind her ear.

"I am Kayla Polinsky, head of the AIS school board and after examining you up close and hearing marvelous things from your teacher—who just so happens to be a close friend of mine, I wanted to give you a personal invitation, in hopes you would accept the fully paid scholarship to the AIS?"

"Me? Fully paid!" she exclaimed.

This was great because she didn't even need to use the one-hundred-thousand-dollars. The intention originally, was to split the cost between the friends and pay off the rest of the tuition in time when they earned the rest of the money, but this was better than okay, it was great! "Look forward to seeing you this summer, Ms. Larson. Keep up the good work," she says. Jessica sprang over to her group to tell them what just happened.

"You got accepted to the AIS!" Star exclaims.

"So did I!" Jess cheered, hi-fiving each of her teammates. Surprisingly, even Jasmine got accepted.

"But wait, if we all got accepted... what are we going to do with all this money?" Skylar questioned and a couple of ideas popped into their young minds before they all stared at each other with the same wicked reaction.

****

Prom night is the most memorable night in a girl's life, so Jessica Jane was glad she got to share this experience with someone she admirably cared about. Earlier today, the girls and Jess went dress shopping, so that was half of the money being put to good use. They split the cost between the girls and the guys. Now, the men were able to afford a tux too. Hobbs and Jasmine had a thing now thanks to match-maker Jessica and she couldn't be merrier for the two. The friends were all to be color coordinated for the evening of prom so that Jared would match with Jessica's turquoise, Becca and Skylar in wearing a shade of red, Jasmine and Hobbs wearing lavender, and well, Chris was going as well, but he was going to bring a girl no one has heard of before, and as for Star, she was just sure that she would meet a single stud at the party.

"You ready to go?" asked Jared as soon as Jessica stepped down the grand staircase in her mother's house that he awaited her near. His reaction was priceless, the way he gawked at her in this moment was everything for Jessica Jane. She couldn't help but giggle at his adorable, innocent, and nerdish charm that engulfed at the sight of seeing her. He stood tall in the cute little tux that she helped him pick out. "You look incredibly beautiful, like always," he complimented after escorting her the rest of the way down the stairs in her very troublesome heels. He helps her over to the front door, about to leave when Jessica's mother popped back in, to demand a picture on her Polaroid.

"Good?"

"No, one more!" Margret implored.

"Mom, we're going to be late!" Jess groaned on the verge of exiting with Jared, who swung the door closed on their way out. The rented black limo honks at their arrival, with all their friends appearing out all sides of the windows.

"Wait, this wouldn't be official without a customized corsage," Jared says, reclaiming her hand. "I had this customized, I hope you don't mind. I think it's really special," he says taking what would've been Samantha's charm bracelet, out of his coat pocket.

"Jared, you're going to make me cry. This is so beautiful, I wouldn't have it any other way." She blushed as he draped it around her wrist. She cupped his face when he was finished. Her hands then travel around his neck and he planted his hands at her hips so they can continue with their moment.

"Hurry up, Sleeping Beauty! You're going to be late to the ball!" she heard Jaiden's voice descend from above the blasted speakers in the limo, to their dismay. He was certainly not educated about fairytales.

"Is Jaiden here?" she asked after Jared had opened the car for her to step inside.

"Yep, I call this my plan Z," Star shrugged, when folding her arms onto her lap.

"You should be so lucky I even went with you to this stupid thing," Jaiden grumbled, scooting over for Jared and Jess to sit next to him in this bunched up, air-tight limo.

"So Chris, who is this?" Jess asked, off in her own small conversation now.

"This is Grace, my new girl," he introduces, putting an arm around his date.

"Can always count on Mullins to fall for my sloppy seconds, dork," Jaiden snorts when looking out his side window. It wasn't until now that Jessica realized it was in fact the same blonde that was all over Jaiden in the hallways, just the other day during finals week.

"It's okay, we're both just doing this to have a good time, we're just friends, that's all," Chris assures as Grace nods in agreement.

"It's not like I would've went with you anyways, you're a douche if you haven't noticed," the girl sneered to Jaiden.

****

The friends arrived at the prom after picking Jared and Jessica up and Jared never leaves her side, leading her closer inside the party. The music is loud, the party is bumping, and it's everything Jessica has ever imagined it would be. "I'm going to go get us something to drink," Jared says, leaving her on the side of the dance floor for a brief moment. Of course Jessica saw Candi, Courtney, Megan, and the rest of the group of friends twerking on their dates like the trashy bimbos they were known to be. Jared returns with her drink.

"Punch? Such an amateur beverage to be served at prom, don't you think? You know this has to be spiked!" she groaned over the loud music, "Come on, let's dance!" She set her drink aside and parted his drink away from his lips before dragging him out to the dance floor. The DJ soon transitioned the mix into a slower medley after about a minute and a half into the song.

"Care to dance?" Jared asserted, offering a hand out. Jessica placed her hand in his as he gently then placed his second hand on her back to bring their bodies closer. She rested her head on his tender shoulder and his hand trailed up and down her bare back.

****

The prom committee calls for any last-minute prom pictures, and totally forgetting that Jared nor Jess haven't gotten those done, the two of them rushed in line just before they closed off the area as prom was about to end. After they received their photos, they heard the announcement for prom king and queen, so the two of them casually stand in the crowd, next to their friends as they wait for the results. "Our 2016 prom king is… Jaiden Daniels!" the principal announced as the crowd of girls cheer him on. *Surprise, surprise.* It was no surprise to anyone that he would be elected and win. The spotlight finds its way in the audience to seek Jaiden and guide him onstage. "And let's hear it for your 2016 prom queen royalty… Jessica Larson!" Jess stood there frozen in astonishment. Her nomination was a complete surprise.

"Go on beautiful, you deserve it," Jared says and she nods in nervousness. The crowd goes silent except for her few good friends who ravish her in applause. The spotlight shines directly on Jessica now and as she walks towards the stage, she eyes around the room to find Candi, Courtney, and a few others giving her a dirty look.

Everyone was staring her down, as if she had been an accessory to murder. "No way, it's the chick who got knocked up!" one whisper says. "Did you hear? The kid was Jared Daniels, that fruit basket!" a male in the audience said. These comments were snide and made her feel unwelcoming. She heard all of them and wanted to disappear. How could they judge her without knowing her? Jaiden waited for her on stage as they placed a crown over his head. When she finally arrived onstage to receive her tiara, sash over the shoulder, and bouquet of roses, she didn't feel like she was in Kansas anymore. It was overwhelming, she's always wanted to feel like a princess but not in the way she had honestly hoped. Not with all the spiteful eyes wearing her down tonight and certainly not without the right person to share her dance with.

"Time for the king and queen to dance!"

Jessica nervously gulped when turning to gander over at Jaiden, who held out a hand before guiding her to the center of the dance floor. The music started and the two swayed, "This is so awkward," he chuckled, stating the obvious. Her heart was racing, just being the center of attention—with the massive crowd of students surrounding them, including Jared, who looked defeated again but was putting on the bravest face for her anyways.

"I'm sorry, but I can't be your queen," she declined, taking off the tiara. The DJ cut the music after she dropped the tiara in Jaiden's hands while he stood frozen in confusion.

"You don't have to do this," he sighed, dropping his head once again.

"I'm sorry," she apologetically stated before ripping off the sash and handing it off to the principal. She ran past the audience as Jared ran after her. "What are you doing?" he asks, trying to catch up with her in the darkest of nights and coldest of weather. She led him to a table that was set up just outside of this building.

"Why did you just leave?"

"Because!" she hyperventilated. He grabbed her hand and stared into her eyes with worry filling all aspects of them. All she could see was the whites of eyes in this glistening moonlight. "It didn't feel right, there was just so much going on—I felt so attacked in there, I just needed to breathe!" she panics with anxiety, trying to catch her breath.

"Hey, hey… look at me," he whispers, wiping away her tears with his index finger and thumb. He cups her face in an attempt to bring her face closer to his. "You're adorable when you cry, you know that?"

"Now I know you're lying. It's pitch-black dark outside, and for all you know, you could be standing here talking to a serial killer," she sniffled out causing him to chuckle.

"Your eyes tell me otherwise. I know your soul inside and out from just one look…

"—one look into those eyes is all it takes to know that innocence is being overshadowed by darkness and your fear is masked within resilience," he says when brushing a hand over her saddened and puffed cheek. She took his hand in hers as he opened his arms that she fit so perfectly in. He had asked her to dance, "You owe me a dance," he reminds softly as soon as the music starts up again in the distance. They had begun to slow dance under the moonlight to the very distant and faded prom music. All they needed was each other to sway the night away. Her head fell on his chest as they danced to the beat of their hearts.

After they wrapped up their prom that same night, Jared and Jessica took a drive to the lake, disposing of their dresses and suits in his truck. They were left in their undergarments when they took a night swim. Jessica unclasped her bra and threw it further down the lake before clinging onto his body in the depths of the shallow riverbank. Her naked chest brushed up against his ripped body and their lips never broke contact with one another as his bulky arms tied around her back. They touched base with each other, but only ever second base. When they were out of the cold, murky water, they dried off in his trunk. And after exposing more skin to each other, when throwing off the remainder of their wet clothes, there they prepared to camp out under a pine tree for the night. Jared had a comforter prepared in his trunk, no reason being. He folded it out, on top of the two, who were naked from head to toe. They would be making a statement to the world that they could get intimate without going all the way. He admired her body from the glare of the moon that gave them both light and she admired his as they laid side by side. "Put your hands on my body Jare," she requested. He nods, staring into the depths of her eyes before he scoots closer and sits up a bit to examine her body with a hand lifting the blanket. His body stiffened, and his hand nervously hovered at her thigh. "Why are you so nervous baby?" she asked, and his mouth parted open slightly, jaw trembling as his soft eyes find hers.

"I-I don't know, I guess I'm slightly intimidated by you," he admits. "I want to impress you and do right by you, I don't want to screw this up…"

"Jared, you're making me sound high maintenance and I'm not, I swear. In fact, I'm scared too…" she says shifting to her side and wrapping her arms around his neck, "You're different and I want this to be perfect. I know we said we'd wait and we will, it's just easier to take one step at a time."

He nods in agreement and kisses her temple. "I want to touch you, Jess," his breath hitched.

"Then touch me, Jare," she whispers. He scoots closer again before his hand slowly strokes the inside of her thighs as his tongue twirls inside her mouth. Her breath drastically inclined at his rapid hand movements inside her aching body. His lips parted open, awaiting her reaction as she tried to catch her breath, furrowing her eyebrows as his kisses travel now to her wet shoulders. She arched her back as soon as he moved his hand away. His hand then brushed up against her chest to caresses her breast. With the help of her hand, she allowed him to roam and explore the depths of her body, setting his hand around all aspects of her crevasses and features. "This is the body of a woman who's going to carry your baby one day, aren't you scared?" she asked with her hand sliding up and down his toned back muscles.

"And I'm going to be the man that makes that happen for you Jess, I promise you—whether it's twelve months from now or nine years from now," he whispers, and she sees her reflection clearly in his eyes now. "I'm not the same scared little boy I was a few months ago, I let people walk all over me. I've changed, and I want to be the man in your life now. I won't make that same mistake twice. I can't afford to lose you again."

She nodded and cupped his square face. "Maybe you have changed...

"But not all at once, please. I mean, you have to give me some credit, I fell for that scared little boy for a reason," she admitted. He brought their hands together before kissing her cheek. They fell asleep that night, closer than ever—chest-to-chest and skin-to-skin. That morning, they both felt relieved when they woke up knowing, they would abstain until after marriage. Marriage was on the table between the two for a while now, but never as serious of a topic compared to last night.

"Jared?" she asked during the brink of the next morning.

"Yeah?" he cumbersome sat up.

"Move in with me?"

"What?"

"I could get my apartment back anytime I want and we're graduating tomorrow. It's time for us to start living like adults, I think this will be a big step for us... don't you love me?"

"Of course I do," he chuckled. "But, there's something I've been meaning to talk to you about," he sighed, scratching the back of his head. His head rested just a little above hers as he held her in his arms.

"Yeah?"

"I got offered a full ride scholarship to Harvard and I wanna take it. I think it's time I finally start somewhere and make something of myself. For years, I've spent hoping that one day I would become famous and tour the world, but I was living in Jaiden's reality. My dream? Traveling, videos? Doesn't even come close. It's time I grew up. That was a fun start, but right now, my heart lies in law school—it's something I've thought about taking up for a long time now..."

Jessica pulled away, lifting her side of the blanket higher up her chest in the broad daylight. "Twelve years... in Harvard, nearly three thousand miles away, sounds like a really long time to be away..."

So much for saying he wasn't going to leave again. When were these obstacles going to stop?

"I know, which makes it even harder to say goodbye…"

"Goodbye…? Wha-what about yesterday?"

"I meant every word I said but I can't make you wait, I don't want to hold you back—and I don't expect you to wait for me Jessica, I don't expect you to follow me either. Your heart is here, and you've got your dance program to think about. I wouldn't want to take that away from you. I love you and it's a shame that we waited so long, but this is a once in a lifetime opportunity for me to start my life over there and not live in Jaiden's shadow anymore. He's the whole reason I got into this mess. This entire experience from the car wreck, was my wakeup call, that I didn't want to do this anymore."

"What about your family, so y-you're just going to leave them behind?"

"My parents are actually supporting me, they only want me to succeed and my mom even gave me her blessing."

"Guess that makes two of us…"

"Huh?"

"Well, I can't hold you back from doing what you love, it's your dream job and you should take it," she swallowed, fighting back her emotions. Jessica was crushed, if not completely devastated because she cared for Jared so much. She was completely bummed out about this situation, but because she did love him so much, she wanted him to be happy, and his future is far more important than her future with him. *Long distance isn't so bad, right?*

****

Graduation day was today, *done with all the finals, done with school.*

I think we all can agree, this year has been hard on everyone, but we did it, we made it right here. This whole experience was an emotional breakdown for Jessica Jane, looking back at her life here with the twins—and now she won't even get to live her life with the one person who mattered most to her above all. It was about a four-hour ceremony by the time they finished all the speeches and handed the students their individual diplomas of completion, getting through the names of all the high school graduates. The ceremony took place at Fairview High's football field, with all the graduates dressed in their tacky blue cap and gowns. They were sitting in alphabetical order. Both Jared and Jaiden were far from where Jessica was sitting but at least the twins were next to each other, which meant Jessica had a chance to blast them on social

336

media before they do to her. All her family, all of her friends, everyone here to support her final high school moment with her. Jessica would too stand up to cheer, every time a friend walked out onto the field to grab their diploma.

****

Jessica soon stepped off the platform after receiving her diploma. As soon as everyone too received their diploma, they threw their caps in the air in accomplishment. "We are officially done!" Jessica grins, waving her diploma in the air after approaching her boyfriend, who stood by his family. She threw her cap into the air once again before running to his embrace. Everyone began to clear out—friends start saying goodbye for the last time, it was emotional for everyone. Jessica had the opportunity to see most of her friends in the Art Institute of Seattle, but it was still hard to say goodbye without shedding a few tears; after all, it would be a long summer before any of them would see each other again. "I'm going to miss you guys," Jess whines, hugging it out with her dance crew when preparing to say goodbye. Jessica took especially longer than expected to say her goodbyes to Chris and Hobbs, since it was more than likely she will not be seeing them again anytime soon. Chris was going off into med school in Kentucky and Hobbs was going to be enlisting in the military; his cause in joining the military on Lucas' behalf, was brave and she was proud of him, she knew Lucas would be too.

"Jessica, come here," Jared requested, leading her to a quiet area on the field. "So... I turned down that scholarship."

"W-why would you do that?"

"Because... I have waited for you my whole life. I don't want to lose you again..." he sighs, "I'm not sure how this goes, but..."

He descends to one knee and her hand flies directly to her mouth. She pursed her lips together, unable to control the waterworks forming in her eyes while waiting for him to continue. "Call me crazy, but I believe my purpose in life was to fall in love with you and I have. And I've thought about this long and hard for a while now and even tried talking myself out of it—convincing myself I was crazy for doing this here and now, but after the night of prom, I've never been more sure about pursuing anything else in my life. I want this to work, Jessica. I meant everything I said that night and I want to give you my word. I want to grow old with my best friend, I want to spend my youth with you by my side. I hope I don't sound cliché when I say this but you're the Jessie to my Woody, no pun intended..." he giggled causing her to giggle as well. "But I'm certainly at my happiest when I'm with you

337

Jessica, only you. And I hope you can do me the honor of making me the happiest man alive by accepting my proposal. What do you say Jessica Jane, will you marry me?" he asks when grabbing her hand. ..."I had a ring prepared but it's getting engraved as we speak.

"Feel free to say something, any time," he awkwardly suggested, squinting his eyes at the glare from the sun which shone directly at him.

"A-are you sure?" she asks as he traces over her palms.

"I can't risk losing you again. I love you more than some lousy scholarship, Jessie."

"I will say yes... one condition?"

"Anything."

"When are you moving in?"

She bites down on her bottom lip as he grinned, standing up to wrap his arms around her. Although they weren't reunited for very long, she didn't need any more time to know that she truly loved him and wanted to be with him forever. Both their families congratulate the two on their engagement and their graduation before they part ways from the families for Jared to walk her home. "But where will you go to school?" Jess asks on their long walk back to the Larson residence.

"Well, I was thinking... if I go to school here, then I will go with my plan B career... it's not bad, I have quite a passion for it actually..."

"Well?"

"Photography." He stops in his tracks, just a block away from her house now, "And you could be my inspiration... we could rent a studio of our own and it would be amazing!" he explained with great enthusiasm and determination.

"Okay!" She giddily grinned with her tongue between her teeth.

"I can't wait to start my life with you... all over again," he anticipated.

With time, Jessica Jane Larson has learned that not all love was perfect, not all friendships were worth saving, and not all people were to be trusted. But she had also chosen to be part of two different worlds, one called Fallen and another called Faith.